THE CHILD
1557 A.D.
A STORY FOR GIRLS

BY
IAN B. STOUGHTON HOLBORN

DEDICATED
TO
AVIS DOLPHIN

PREFACE

On the analogy of the famous apple,—"there ain't going to be no" preface, "not nohow." Children do not read prefaces, so anything of a prefatory nature that might interest them is put at the beginning of chapter one.

As for the grown-ups the story is not written for grown-ups, and if they want to know why it begins with such a gruesome first chapter, let them ask the children. Children like the horrors first and the end all bright. Many grown-ups like the tragedy at the end. But perhaps the children are right and the grown-ups are standing on their heads. Besides they can skip the first chapter; it is only a prologue.

CHAPTER I
HATE

Sweet children of demurest air,
Pale blossoms woven through your hair,
On shifting rainbows gathering,
Endowed with love's engaging mien
And crowding lips that toward me lean,
Through little hands, outstretched between
In sympathetic wondering.
Children, ye cannot understand,
Floating in that enchanted land,
The pathos of our helplessness;
And yet your winsome faces bear,
Though ye yourselves are unaware,
The antidote of our despair,—
Exorcists of our hopelessness.
Children of Fancy: The Guelder Roses.

THE great ship Lusitania was nearing Queenstown on May 7th, 1915, when a terrible explosion occurred, and in fifteen minutes she had sunk. Among some 1700 adults and 500 children were a lecturer on art and archaeology and a little girl, with whom he had made friends on board. About 700 people escaped and these two were both eventually picked up out of the water. When they reached the land there was no2 one left to look after her; so he first took her across to her relatives in England and then she went to live in the home of the archaeologist, in Scotland, who had three little boys of his own but no little girls.

Archaeologists do not know anything about girls' story books, and he may have been misinformed when he was told that girls' books were too tame and that most girls preferred to read the more exciting books of their brothers. However, this made him decide himself to write a story for the little girl, which should be full of adventures. It was frankly a melodramatic story, a story of love and hate, and he chose the period of the

Reformation, so as to have two parties bitterly opposed to each other; but, except for dramatic purposes, religious problems were as far as possible left out.

One difficulty was as to whether the characters should speak in old English; but, as that might have made it hard to read, only a few old words and phrases were introduced here and there, just, as it were, to give a flavour.

Afterwards the author was asked to publish the story "for precocious girls of thirteen," as it was delightfully phrased; that is to say, for girls of thirteen and upwards and perhaps for grown up people, but hardly for superior young ladies of about seventeen; and this is the story:

Father Laurence, the parish priest of Middleton, was returning home from Holwick on a dark night in the late spring. He had come from the bedside of a dying woman and the scene was unpleasantly impressed on his mind. Sarah Moulton had certainly not been a blessing[3] to her neighbours, but, in spite of that, he felt sorry for the delicate child left behind, as he did not see what was to become of it. He felt very troubled, too, about the poor creature, herself, for was not his task the cure of souls? Not that Sarah Moulton was much of a mother; but perhaps any kind of a mother was better than nothing, and the poor child had loved her; yet, after she had received the viaticum, she had given vent to the most frightful curses on her neighbours. "If I cannot get the better of Janet Arnside in life," she had screamed, "I will get the better of her when I am dead. I will haunt her and drive her down the path to Hell, I will never let her rest, I will...." and with these words on her lips the soul had fled from her body. He sighed a little wearily. He was famished and worn for he had previously been a long tramp nearly to Lunedale. "I do my best," he said, "but I am afraid the task is too difficult for me. I wish there were some one better than myself in Upper Teesdale: poor Sarah!"

Father Laurence' way led through the churchyard, but clear as his conscience was, he had never been able to free himself from a certain fear in passing through it on a dark night. Could it be true that the spirits of the departed could plague the living? Of course it could not; and yet, somehow, he was not able to rid himself of the unwelcome thought. As he passed through the village and drew nearer to the church, he half resolved to go round. No, that was cowardly and absurd. He would not allow idle superstitions to get the better of him.

But when he approached the gate he hesitated and his heart began to beat violently. What was that unearthly screech in the darkness of the night? He crossed himself[4] devoutly, however, and said a Paternoster and stepped through the wicket gate. "'Libera nos a malo,' yes, deliver us from evil, indeed," he said, as, dimly on the sky line he saw a shadowy figure with long gaunt arms stretched to the sky.

He crossed himself again, when a ghoulish laugh rang through the still night air. He turned a little to the left, but the figure came swiftly toward him. He wanted to run, but duty bade him refrain. His heart beat yet more violently as the figure approached and at length he stood still, unable to move.

The figure came closer, and closer still, stretching out its arms, and finally a harsh voice said: "Is that you, Father Laurence? Ha! Ha! I told you Sarah Moulton would die. You need not tell me about it."

It was old Mary, "Moll o' the graves," as the folk used to call her. Father Laurence felt a little reassured, but she was not one whom anybody would wish to meet on a dark night, least of all in a churchyard.

"What is the matter, Mary? Why are you not in your bed," he asked; "disturbing honest folk at this time of night?"

"You let me alone," she replied, "with your saints and your prayers and your Holy Mother. I go where I please and do as I please. I knew Sarah would die. I like folk to die," she said with horrible glee; "and she cursed Janet Arnside, did she? A curse on them all, every one of them. I wish she would die too; ay, and that slip of a girl that Sarah has left behind. What are you shaking for?" she added. "Do you think I do not know what is going on? You have nothing to tell me;[5] I assure you the powers are on our side. There is nothing like the night and the dark."

"You are a wicked woman, Mary," said the old priest sorrowfully, "and God will punish you one day. See you—I am going home; you go home too."

"You may go home if you like," said the old hag as he moved on, "and my curses go with you; but I stay here;" and she stood and looked after him as he faded into the darkness.

"Silly old dotard," she growled; "I saw him at her bedside or ever I came along here. The blessed sacrament indeed; and much may it profit her! I wish now I had waited and seen what he did after she had gone; comforted that child, I expect! Fancy loving a mother like that! Ha! Ha! No, I am glad I came here and scared the pious old fool."

She moved among the tombs and sat down near an open grave that had just been dug. "Pah! I am sick of their nonsense. Why cannot they leave folk in peace? I want to go my own way; why should I not go my own way? All my life they have been at me, ever since I was a little girl. My foolish old mother began it. Why should I not please myself? Well, she's dead anyway! I like people to die. And now Mother Church is at me. Why should I think of other people, why should I always be holding myself in control? No, I let myself go, I please myself."

"I have no patience with any of them," she muttered, "and now there is a new one to plague me," and "Moll o' the graves" saw in her mind's eye a slim, graceful girl of twelve, endowed with an unparalleled refinement[6] of beauty. "What do they mean by bringing that child to Holwick Hall," she continued, "as if things were not bad enough already,—a-running round and waiting on folk, a-tending the sick and all the rest of it? Let them die! I like them to die. Self-sacrifice and self-control forsooth! They say she is clever and well-schooled and mistress of herself and withal sympathetic. What's the good of unselfishness and self-control? No, liberty, liberty—that's the thing for you, Moll. Self-control, indeed!" and again the ghastly laugh rang through the night air. "Yes, liberty, Moll,—liberty. Are you not worth more than all their church-ridden priests and docile unselfish children? What avails unselfishness and affection? Father Laurence and Aline Gillespie, there's a pair of them! No, hate is the thing, hate is better than love. Scandal and spite and jealousy—that's true joy, that's the true woman, Moll," and she rubbed her hands with unholy mirth.

As she talked to herself the moon rose and gradually the churchyard became light. "Love!" she went on, "love! Yes, Oswald, that's where they laid you," she said, as she looked at the next place to the open grave. "Ah, but hate got the better of your love, for all that, fine big man that you were, a head taller than the rest of the parish, and all the girls after you, too!"

She looked at the side of the open grave, where the end of a bone protruded. She pulled it out. It was a femur of unusual size. "Yes, Oswald," she repeated, "and that's yours. You did not think I would be holding your thigh-bone these forty years after!

"Ha! you loved me, did you? I was a pretty lass then. Yes, you loved me, I know you loved me. You7 would have died for me, and I loved you, too. But little Sarah loved you and you loved her. I know you loved me most, but I would not have that. 'I should have controlled myself,' you say; ha! I was jealous and I hated you. Self-control and love;—no, no, liberty and hate, liberty and hate; and when you were ill I came to see you and I saw the love-light in your eyes. They thought you would get well. Of course you would have got well; but there you were, great big, strong man, weak as a child,—a child! I hate children. Was that it? You tried to push my hands off, as I pressed the pillow on your face, you tried; oh, you tried hard, and I laugh to think of it even now. How I longed to bury my fingers in your throat, but I knew they would leave marks."

"Yes, liberty and hate, ha! ha! I would do it again. See, Oswald!" and she took the brittle bone and viciously snapped it across her knee. "Self-control! love! unselfishness! Never! And that child up at the Hall, Oswald, I must send her after you. I have just frightened Sarah down to you. You can have her now, and that child shall come next. Hate is stronger than love. Liberty, self-will and hate must win in the end."

The abandoned old wretch stood up and took her stick—she could not stand quite straight—and hobbled with uncanny swiftness across to a newly made child's grave and began to scrape with her hands; but at that moment she heard the night-watchman coming along the lane; so she rose and walked back to Newbiggin, where she lived.

She opened the door and found the tinder box and struck a light, and then went to a corner where there was8 an old chest. She unlocked it and peered in and lifted out a bag and shook it. It was full of gold. "Yes," she said, "money is a good thing, too. How little they know what 'old Moll o' the graves' has got,—old, indeed, Moll is not old! Ah, could not that money tell some strange tales? Love and learning and self-control! Leave all that to the priests. Hate will do for me,—money and liberty are my gods.

"Aha, Aline Gillespie, you little fool, what do you mean by crossing my path? I was a pretty little girl once and you are not going to win the love of Upper Teesdale folk for nothing, I'll warrant you."

9

CHAPTER II
SECRETS

"I AM so tired of this rain," said Audry, as she rose and crossed the solar[1] and went to the tall bay window with its many mullions and sat down on the window seat. "It is three days since we have been able to get out and no one has seen the top of Mickle Fell for a week. The gale is enough to deafen one," she added, "while the moat is like a stormy sea,—and just look at the mad dancers in the rain-rings on the water!"

[1] The predecessor of the withdrawing room or drawing room.

It was a terrible day, the river was in spate[2] indeed, carrying down great trees and broken fences and even, now and then, some unfortunate beast that had been swept away in the violence of the storm.

2 In torrent.

"The High Force must be a wonderful sight though," she continued, "the two falls must be practically one in all this deluge."

"I do not altogether mind the rain," said her little friend; "there is something wonderful about it and I always rather like the sound of the wind; it has a nice eerie suggestion, and makes me think of delightful stories of fairies and goblins and strange adventures."

"Well, that may be all right for you, Aline, because you can tell magnificent stories yourself; but I cannot,10 and it only makes me feel creepy and the rain annoys me because I cannot go out. I wish that we had adventures ourselves, but of course nothing exciting ever happens to us."

"They probably would not really be nice if they did happen. These things are better to read about than to experience."

"I don't know," said Audry; "anyway, the only exciting thing that ever happened to me was when you came to stay here. I really was excited when mother told me that a distant cousin of my own age was coming from Scotland to live with us; and I made all sorts of pictures of you in my mind. I thought that you would have a freckled face and be very big and strong and fond of climbing trees and jumping and good shouting noisy games and that kind of thing."

"You must be very disappointed then."

"No, not exactly; I never thought that you would be so pretty:—was your mother pretty, Aline?"

"I do not remember my mother," and a momentary cloud seemed to pass over the child's beautiful face, "but her portrait that Master Lindsay painted is very beautiful, and father always said that it did not do her justice. It is very young, not much older than I am; she was still very young when she died."

"How old was she?"

"I do not know exactly," Aline answered, moving over to the window-seat and sitting down by Audry, "but I remember there was once some talk about it. Her name was Margaret and she was named after her grandmother or her great grandmother, who was lady in waiting to Queen Margaret, and who not only had the same name as the Queen but was born on the same day and married on the same day."

"What Queen Margaret," asked Audry, "and how has it anything to do with your mother?"

"Well, that is just what I forget," said Aline with a smile like April sunshine;—"I used to think it was your queen, Margaret of Anjou, who married Henry IV; but she seems to be rather far back, so I have thought it might be Margaret Tudor, who married our James IV.

"I expected their age would settle it," she continued, stretching out her arms and putting her hands on Audry's knees. "I looked it up; but they were almost the same, your queen was fourteen years and one month when she married and ours was thirteen years and nine months. But I know that mother was exactly six months older to a day when she married, and I know that she died before the year was out."

"Then she was not nearly sixteen anyway," said Audry; "how sad to die before one was sixteen!"

"Yes, Audry, it is terrible, but there is worse than that,—think of poor Lady Jane Grey who was barely sixteen when she and her husband were executed. Father used to tell me that I was something like the Lady Jane."

"Had he seen her?"

"No, I do not think so; he was in France with our Queen Mary at the time of the Lady Jane's death and your Queen Mary's accession: for a short time he was a captain in the Scots Guard in France."

"Were you with him and have you seen the Queen? She is about your age, is she not?"

"No, I have not seen her, but she is a little older than I am. She is fourteen and is extraordinarily beautiful. They say her wedding to the Dauphin is to take place very soon. If father had been alive I might have seen it."

"Was your father good looking?" asked Audry.

"Yes, he was said to be the handsomest man in the Lothians."

"That explains it, then," she went on, looking somewhat enviously at her companion; "but I wish you cared more for games and horses and running and a good

6

romp and were not so fond of old books. Fancy a girl of your age being able to read the Latin as well as a priest. Father says that you know far more Latin than he does and that you can even read the Greek."

"But I can run," Aline objected, "and I can swim, too."

"Yes, you can run, though you do not look like it, you wee slender thing, but you do not love it as I do;" and Audry stood up to display her sturdy little form. "Now if we were to wrestle," she said, "where would you be?"

Aline only laughed and said: "Well, there is one good thing in reading books, it gives one something to do in wet weather. Let us go down to the library and see if I cannot find something nice to read to you."

"Come along, then, and read to me from that funny old book by Master Malory, with the pictures."

"You mean the 'Morte d'Arthur,' I suppose, with the stories of King Arthur and the Round Table. That certainly is exciting and I am so fond of it. I often wish that there were knights going about now to fight for us in tourney and to rescue us from tyrants. It would be nice to have anybody care for one so much."

"You silly little one, they would not trouble their heads about you, you are only twelve years old."

"Perhaps not," answered Aline with a half sigh, as she thought of her present condition.

"I do not believe there is anybody in the world that cares for me," she said to herself, "except perhaps Audry, and I have only known her such a little time that she cannot care much. I don't suppose there are many little girls who can be as lonely as I am. I have not even an aunt or uncle. Yes, I do want some one to love me, it is all so very hard; I wish I had a sister or a brother."

In a way, doubtless, Audry's mother did not mean to be altogether cruel; but she had no love for her small visitor and thought that it was unnecessary for Master Mowbray to bring her to Holwick Hall. So she always found plenty of heavy work for the child to do and often made excuses when Audry had some dainty or extra pleasure as to why Aline should not have her share. Aline thought of her father, Captain Angus Gillespie of Logan, and remembered his infinite care for her when she had been the apple of his eye. It had been a sad little life;—first she had been motherless from infancy and then had followed the long financial difficulties that she did not understand; but one thing after another had gone; and just before her father died they had had to leave Logan Tower and go and live in Edinburgh; and the little estate was sold.

Audry in her rough, kindly way, flung her arms round the slim form and kissed her. "Do not think melancholy things; come along to the library and see what we can find." So they left the solar and went down14 through the hall and out into the upper court. They raced across the court, because of the rain, and up the little flight of nine steps, three at a time, till they were on the narrow terrace that ran along the front of the library.

Aline reached the door first, and, as she swung back the heavy oak with its finely carved panels, exclaimed: "There, I told you I could run."

They shut the door and walked down the broad central space. The library had been built in the fifteenth century by Master James Mowbray, Audry's great-great-grandfather, and was supposed to be the finest in the North of England. It was divided on each side into little alcoves, each lit by its own window and most of the books were chained to their places, being attached to a long rod that ran along the top of each shelf. At the end of each alcove was a lock with beautifully wrought iron tracery work that held the rod so that it could not be pulled out. The library was very dusty and was practically never used, as the present lord of Holwick was not a scholar; so for the last four years since he had succeeded to the estate it had been neglected and Aline was almost the only person who ever entered it.

The children walked down the room admiring the delicate iron work of the locks, for which Aline had a great fancy and she had paused at one, which was her particular favourite, and was fingering every part of it affectionately, when she noticed that a small sculptured figure was loose and could be made to slide upwards. This excited her curiosity and she pushed it to and fro to see if it was for any special purpose, till suddenly she discovered that, when the figure was pushed as high15 as it would go, the whole lock could be pulled forward like a little door on a hinge, revealing a small cavity behind. Both children started and peered eagerly into the space disclosed, where they found a very thin little leather book which was dropping to pieces with old age. They took it out and examined it and found that the cover had separated so as to lay open what had been a secret pocket in the cover, which contained a piece of stout parchment the same size as the pages of the book.

The book was written in black letter and was in Latin. "Now you see the use of knowing Latin," said Aline triumphantly, with a twinkle in her dark blue eyes.

"That depends whether it is interesting," Audry replied.

"It seems to be an account of the building of Holwick Hall; but what is the use of this curious piece of parchment with all these holes cut in it?"

"Perhaps you can find out if you read the book," suggested Audry. "It certainly must be of some importance or they would not have taken all that trouble to hide the book and also the parchment in the book. Let us sit down and see what you can make of it."

So they sat down and Aline was soon deeply interested in the account of the building, how the great dining hall was erected first, then the buttery, pantry and kitchen and afterwards the beautiful solar. Audry found her interest flag; although, when it came to the building of her room and the cost of the different items, she brightened up. "Still," she said, "I do not see why all this should be kept so secret; any one might know all that we have read."

There was one thing that seemed to promise interest,16 but apparently it led to nothing. At the beginning of the book was a dedication which could be translated thus: "To my heirs trusting that this may serve them as it has served me." But in what way it was to serve them did not appear, and the evening was closing in and it was getting dark, but the children were as far as ever from discovering the meaning of the phrase or of the parchment with the holes.

"Let us take it to our room," Aline said at last; "it is not chained like the others. We can hide it in the armoire and read with the little lamp when the others have gone to sleep and no one is likely to come in."

So they put the piece of parchment to mark the place, ran to their room and hid the book and went to join the rest of the family.

It was nearly time for rere-supper[3] and Master Richard Mowbray had just come in. He was dripping wet and the water ran down in long streams across the floor. "Gramercy," he exclaimed, "it is not a fit day for a dog let alone a horse or a man. Come and pull off my boots, wench," he went on, catching sight of Aline.

3 A meal taken about 8 o'clock.

He sat down and Aline with her little white hands manfully struggled with the great boots. "You are not much good at it," he said roughly, when at last she succeeded in tugging off the first one. "Ah, well, never mind," he added, when he saw her wince at his words, and stooped and kissed her and called to one of the men to come and take off the other boot. "You cannot always live on a silk cushion, lassie," he went on, not unkindly, "you must work like the rest of us."

17

"It is a strange thing where that man can have got," he continued; "in all this rain it is impossible that he can have gone far."

"Let us hope he is drowned," Mistress Mowbray remarked; "that would save us further trouble, but it is a pity that a man meant for the fire should finish in the water."

"Some of the folk going to Middleton say that they saw a stranger early this morning, playing with a child, but he turned off toward the hills," one of the serving men observed.

"That's he, but it's hard enough to find a man in a bog-hole, particularly on a day like this, yet Silas Morgan and William Nettleship have both taken over a score of men and there must easily be two score of others on the hills; you would think that they would find him. He cannot know the hills as we do," said Master Mowbray.

There was silence for a time and then he spoke again,—"Of course those people might be mistaken; but he could not get over Middleton Bridge after the watch was set, and I do not see how any one could get over the river to-day, it is simply a boiling torrent. Well, they are on the look out on the Appleby side and he must come down somewhere."

"What is he wanted for?" Audry ventured to ask.

"Wanted for?" almost shrieked Mistress Mowbray, "a heretic blaspheming Mother Church, whom the good priest said was a servant of the devil."

"But what is a heretic and how does he blaspheme Mother Church?" Audry persisted.

"I do not know and I do not want to know," said Mistress Mowbray.

18

"Then if you do not know, how can you tell that it is wrong? You must know what he says, Mother, before you can judge him."

"I was brought up a good daughter of the church, and I know when I am right, and look here, you young hussie, what do you mean by talking to your mother like that? It's that good for nothing baggage, that your father has brought from Scotland, that has been putting these notions into your head, with her book learning and nonsense. I assure you that I won't have any more of it, you little skelpie,[4] you are not too old for a good beating yet, and I tell you what;—I will not have the two of you wasting your time in that library, I shall lock it up, and you are not to go in there without permission, and that will not be yet awhile, I can promise you."

4 A girl young enough to be whipped (skelped).

After this outburst the meal was eaten in silence and every one felt very uncomfortable.

When supper was over the sky seemed to show signs of breaking and Master Mowbray ventured to express a hope that the next day would be fine, and that they would be able to find the heretic on the hills. "That man has done more mischief than any of the others," he muttered; but when pressed to explain himself he changed the subject and said he must go and see if the water had done any damage in the lower court.

The children were not sorry to retire to their room when bedtime came. They had undressed and Audry was helping Aline to brush her great masses of long hair. What a picture she looked in her little white night-robe, with her large mysterious dark blue eyes that no one ever saw without being stirred, and her wonderful19 charm of figure! Her colouring was as remarkable as her form. The hair was of a deep dark red, somewhat of the colour beloved by Titian, but with more gloss and glow although a little lower in tone; that colour which one meets perhaps once in a lifetime, a full rich undoubted red, but without a suspicion of the garishness and harshness that belongs to most red hair. The eyes were of the dark ultramarine blue only found among the Keltic peoples and even then but rarely, like the darkest blue of the Mediterranean Sea, when the sapphire hue is touched with a hint of purple.

"What is a heretic?" Audry asked; "I am sure you know."

"I do not know that I do, but I remember father saying something to me about it before he died. He said that they were people who were not satisfied with the way that things were going in the church and that in particular they denied that it was only through the priests of the church that God spoke to his people. They say that the priests are no better than any one else and indeed are sometimes even worse."

"I do not know that they claim to be better than other people," objected Audry.

"Well, dear, I am not defending the heretics. I only say what they think. They do feel, however, that if the priests really were the special channels of God that that fact itself would make them better. So, many of them say that God can and does speak directly to all of us himself, and they all think that it is in the Bible that we can best learn what he desires, and that the Bible should therefore be translated into the language of the people.

"'This has been the cause of great troubles in the20 world for these many years,' father said, 'but, little maid, do not trouble your head about it now; when you are older we can talk about it.'"

"Are the heretics such very wicked people then, do you think, Aline?"

Aline put her little white hand to her chin and looked down. "I do not know what to think about it," she said. "I suppose that they are, but they do not seem to be treated fairly."

"I hate unfairness," said Audry in her impulsive way.

"I do not see why they should not be allowed to speak for themselves, and I do not see how people can condemn them when they do not know what their reasons are for thinking what they do. Of course I am very young and do not know anything about it; but it sounds as though the priests were afraid that the truth can not take care of itself; but surely it cannot be the truth if it is afraid to hear the other side. I remember a motto on the chimney piece at home,—'Magna veritas est et prevalebit,' and it seems to me that it must be so. I wish that father were alive to talk to me. He was so clever and he understood things."

"But you have not said what your motto means," Audry interposed.

Aline laughed through the tears that were beginning to gather,—"Oh, that means, The truth is great and will prevail. If it is the truth it must win; and it can do it no harm to have objections raised against it, as it will only make their error more clear."

"What about the book, Aline?" said Audry, changing the subject; "no one is likely to come up here now, they never do; so I think we could have another look at it."

Aline picked up the book and opened it; she paused for a moment and then gave a little cry,—"I have found out what the parchment is for; come and look here."

Audry came and looked. "I do not see anything," she said.

"Look at the parchment; do you not see one or two letters showing through nearly all the little holes?"

"Yes."

"What are they?"

"b. u. t. o. n. e. m. u. s. t. s. e. e. t. h. a. t. a. l. i. g. h. t. i. s. n. e. v. e. r. c. a. r. r. i. e. d. i. n. f. r. o. n. t. o. f. t. h. e. s. l. i. t. s. i. n. t. h. e.," read Audry, a letter at a time.

"And what does that spell?" said Aline.

"Oh, I see,— It spells, 'but one must see that a light is never carried in front of the slits in the.' How clever of you to find it out!"

"Well, it was more or less accident; the parchment is exactly the size of the paper and as I shut the book I naturally made it all even. So, when I opened it in this room, it was lying even on the page and I could not help seeing the letters and what they spelt."

"I should never have noticed it, Aline; why I did not even notice at once that the letters spelt anything after you had shown me."

"Let us go back to the beginning and then," said Aline, "we shall discover what it is all about."

So she turned to the beginning of the book and placed the parchment over the page and found that it began like this;—"Having regard to the changes and misfortunes of this life and the dangers that we may incur, I have provided for myself and my heirs a place of refuge and a way of escape in the evil day. This book containeth22 a full account of the building of Holwick Hall; so that it will be easily possible to follow that which I now set down. Below the Library on the west side of the house just above the level of the moat, there is a secret chamber, which communicateth with a passage below the moat that hath an exit in the roof of the small cave in the gully that lieth some two hundred paces westward of the Hall of Holwick. The way of entrance thereto is threefold. There is an entrance from the library itself. There is also an entrance from the small Chamber that occupieth the southwest corner of the building on the topmost floor."

"Why, that is our bedroom, the room that we are in now!" Audry exclaimed. "Do let us try and find it."

"Wait a moment; the book will probably tell us all about it," and Aline resumed her reading.

"'There is a third method of approach from the store-chamber or closet on the ground floor in the southeast corner of the lower quadrangle.'"

"That is the treasury, where the silver and the other plate is kept," said Audry; "go on."

"'In the corner of the library that goeth round behind the newel stair there is a great oaken coffer that is fastened to the floor, in the which are the charters and the license to crenellate[5] and sundry other parchments.'"

5 To make battlements or crenellations. A house could not be fortified without a royal license.

"Oh, I have often wondered what was in that kist," said Audry; "how really exciting things have become at last, but I want to find out the way to get down from our room; do go on."

23
THE OLD SWORD-KIST.
"You must not keep interrupting then," said Aline and continued her reading. "'Now the bottom of this kist can be lifted for half its breadth, if the nail head with the largest rosette below the central hinge be drawn forth. After so doing, the outer edge of the plank next the wall in the bottom of the chest can be pushed down slightly, which will cause the inner edge to rise a little. This can then be taken by the hand and lifted. In exactly the same manner the plank of the floor immediately underneath can be raised.'

"I hope you understand it all," Aline remarked.

"I am not quite sure that I do," said Audry. "Yes, I think it is quite clear; it's very like the way the lid works on the old sword-kist."

"But we cannot get into the library and, even if we could," said Audry, "the kist might be locked."

24

"Never mind that now; I expect that our room will come next," said Aline. "Yes, listen to this:—'In the topmost chamber a different device is adopted for greater safety by means of variety. If the ambry[6] nigh unto the door be opened it will be found that the shelf will pull forward an inch and a finger can be inserted behind it on the left hand side, and a small lever can be pushed backward. This enables the third plank near the newel-stair[7] wall to be lifted by pressing down the western end thereof, and a bolt may be found which, being withdrawn, one of the panels will fall somewhat and may be pushed right down by the hand. The newel-stair, though it appeareth not, is double and one may creep down thereby to the chamber itself.'"

6 A small cupboard made in the thickness of the wall.

7 A newel staircase is a spiral staircase circling round the newel, i.e., the centre shaft or post.

The fact was,—that what appeared to be simply the under side of the steps, to any one going up the staircase, was really a second staircase, leaving a space of nearly three feet between the two.

The children did not read further at that time, as they were eager at once to see if they could put their discovery to the test.

Aline put down the book and went to the ambry and opened the door. The single shelf came forward without difficulty. "Have you found anything?" Audry asked eagerly.

"Yes," she replied, "but I cannot move it; it is too stiff."

"Let me have a try," and Audry stepped forward and put her fingers into the space. "My hands are[25] stronger than yours," she said. "Ah, that is it!" she exclaimed, as she felt the lever move to one side, and by working it backwards and forwards she soon made it quite loose.

The Moving Plank and the Way to the Secret Room.
Aline meanwhile had already put her little foot on the third board, at the end just against the wall, and felt it yield. The other end was now sufficiently raised to allow of the fingers being passed underneath. She lifted it up and found that it was simply attached to a bar about six inches from the wall-end. They both peeped into the opening disclosed and felt round it. Aline was the first to find the bolt and pulled it forward. But alas no panel moved. Audry looked ready to weep, but Aline exclaimed, "Oh, it must be all right as we have got so far; let us feel the panels and try and force them down. This is the one above the bolt," and she put her fingers on it to try and make it slide down. She had no sooner spoken than the panel moved an inch and, slipping her hand inside, she pressed it down to the bottom. The panel tended to rise again when she let go,[26] as the bottom rested on the arm of a weighted lever. It looked very gloomy inside but the children were determined to go on. They then found that there was just comfortable room for them to go backwards down the stairs and that there would have been room even for a big man to manage it without much difficulty. There were many cobwebs and once or twice their light threatened to go out; but at last they reached the bottom, crawling on hands and knees the whole way. There they found a long narrow passage, in the thickness of the wall, of immense length. They went along this for a great distance and then began to get frightened.

"Where ever can we have got to?" Audry said at length.

"It is quite clear that we are wrong," said Aline, "as the library, we know, is just at the bottom of the newel-stair and the book said that the secret room was just underneath the library. We must go back."

"What if we go wrong again and lose our way altogether, Aline, and never get out of this horrible place?"

It was a terrible thought; and the damp smell and forbidding looking narrow stone passage had a strange effect on the children's nerves. Then another thought occurred to Aline that made them still more nervous. There were occasional slits along the wall for ventilation and she remembered the words that she had read by chance when she first discovered the use of the parchment. Supposing that their light should be seen; what would happen to them then? and yet they dare not put it out and be left in the dark.

"I wish that we had never come," said Audry as they hurried along the difficult passage. They reached the bottom of the stair and felt a little reassured. They then saw that the passage turned sharply back on itself and led in a step or two to a door. It was of very stout oak and plated with iron. They opened it and found that it had eight great iron bolts that could be shut on that side. Within was a second door equally strong and, on opening that, they found themselves in the secret room itself. It was a long apartment only about eight feet high, and was panelled throughout with oak. There was a large and beautiful stone fireplace, above which was the inscription,—"Let there be no fire herein save that the fires above be lit."

"That must be in case the smoke should show," said Aline; "how careful they have been with every little thing!"

The room was thick with dust and obviously had not been entered for many many years. Even if the present occupants of Holwick knew of the secret room at all, which probably they did not, it was clear that they never made any use of their knowledge. There was a magnificent old oak bed in one corner but some of the bedding was moth-eaten and destroyed. There were also many little conveniences in the room, amongst other things a small book-case containing several books. On the whole it was a distinctly pleasant apartment despite the absence of any visible windows. There were even one or two pictures on the walls. In one corner on the outer wall was a door, which the children opened, and which clearly led to the underground passage below the moat; but they decided not to examine any more that night. So they made their way up the stairs again back to their room.

They were almost too excited to sleep and Aline, as her custom was, when she lay awake, amused herself by building castles in the air. Sometimes she would imagine herself as a great lady, sought after by all the noble knights of the land, but holding herself aloof with reserved dignity until one, by some deed of unusual distinction, should win her favour. As a rule, however, this seemed rather a dull part to play, though there was something naturally queenly in her nature, and she would therefore prefer something more active. She would take the old Scots romance of Burd Helen, or Burd Aline, as her own inspiration, and follow her knight in the disguise of a page over mountain and torrent and through every hardship. This better suited the romantic self-sacrifice of her usual moods and, by its imaginary deeds of heroism, ministered just as much to her sense of exaltation. To-night had opened vistas of new suggestion; and she pictured her knight and herself fleeing before a host of enemies and miraculously disappearing at the critical moment into the secret room. But at last she fell into a sound slumber and did not wake till it was nearly time for the morning meal.

CHAPTER III
HATE AND LOVE

ALINE certainly did not belong to any ordinary type and she would have puzzled the psychologist to classify. She was so many sided as to be in a class by herself. She had plenty of common sense and intelligence for her years and an outlook essentially fair minded and just. But she also had a quiet hauteur, curiously coupled with humility, and at the same time a winning manner that was irresistible; so that the strange thing was that she had only to ask and most people voluntarily submitted to her desires. This unusual power might have been very dangerous to her character and spoiled her, had it not been that what she wanted was almost always just and reasonable and moreover she never used her power for her own benefit. Further, her humble estimate of her own capacity for judgment caused her but rarely to exercise the power at all. In practice it was almost confined to those cases where a sweet minded child's natural instinct for fair play sees further than the sophistries of the adult.

She was practically unaware of this power, which was destined to bring her into conflict with Eleanor Mowbray; nor did she take the least delight, as she might easily have done, in exercising power for power's sake.

Eleanor Mowbray, on the other hand, like so many women, loved power. Masculine force has so largely monopolised the more obvious manifestations of power that it might be said to be almost a feminine instinct to snatch at all opportunities that offer themselves.

Be that as it may, Mistress Mowbray loved to use power for the sake of using it; she loved to make her household realise that she was mistress. She did not exactly mean to be unkind, but they were servants and they must feel that they were servants. Her attitude to them was that of the servant who has risen or the one so commonly exhibited toward servants by small girls, that puzzles and disgusts their small brothers.

She would address them contemptuously, or would impatiently lose her self-control and shout at them. She lacked consideration and would call them from their main duties to perform petty services, which she could perfectly well have done for herself. This was irritating to the servants and there was always a good deal of friction. The servants tended to lose their loyalty and, when once the bond of common interest was broken, what did it matter to Martha, the laundry-maid, that she one day scorched and destroyed the most cherished and valuable piece of lace that Mistress Mowbray possessed; or of what concern was it to Edward, the seneschal, that in cleaning the plate, he broke the lid off her pouncet box and not only did not trouble to tell her, but when charged with it, coolly remarked, after the manner of his kind,—"Oh, it came to pieces in my hands!"

On one occasion, before the discovery of the secret room, when Edward was away, Thomas, a sly unprincipled man, whose duties were with the horses, had taken his place for the day. The four silver goblets, which he had placed on the table, were all of them tarnished; and after the meal was over, Mistress Mowbray said to him sharply,—"Thomas, what do you mean by putting dirty goblets on the high table?"[8]

[8] The table on the raised dais at which the family sat. The retainers sat at the two lower tables. See plan.

"I am sure I did my best, Mistress," said Thomas; "I spent a great amount of pains in laying the table, but we all of us make mistakes sometimes."

"Then go and clean them at once, you scullion, and bring them back to me to look at directly you have finished."

"Please, Mistress, that is not my work," replied Thomas, "and I have a great deal to do in the stables this afternoon." As a matter of fact he had finished his work in the stables and was planning for an easy time.

"Do you dare to talk to me?" she said, her voice rising. "You are here to do as you are told; go and clean them at once, or it will be the worse for you." She knew that this time the man was within his rights; but she was not going to be dictated to by a servant.

Thomas sulkily departed. When he reached the buttery he remembered that he had noticed Edward cleaning some of the goblets the day before. He soon found them, and then drew himself a measure of ale and sat down with a chuckle to enjoy himself over the liquor, while allowing for the time that would have been needed to clean the silver.

Meanwhile Mistress Mowbray began impatiently to walk up and down the hall. The children were generally allowed to go out after dinner and amuse themselves, but it was a wet day and Aline was looking disconsolately out of the window wondering whether she should go into the library or what she should do, when the angry dame thought that the child offered an object for the further exercise of her power. "Why are you idling there?" she said. "They are all short-handed to-day, go you and scour out the sink and then take out the pig-bucket and be quick about it."

Aline gave a little gasp of surprise, but ran off at once. The buttery door was open and she saw Thomas drinking and offering a tankard to one of the other servants, and she heard him laugh loudly as he pointed to a row of goblets, four of them clean and the rest of them dirty, while he said,—"Edward cleaned those, and I am waiting here as long as it would take to clean them." He caught sight of her and scowled, but she passed on.

Aline had soon finished the sink and ran quickly with the pig-bucket, after which she returned to the dining hall to tell Mistress Mowbray she had finished. Thomas had just come in, so she stood and waited.

He held up the four goblets on a tray for Mistress Mowbray to inspect.

"Yes, those are better, Thomas," she said frigidly. Thomas could not conceal a faint smile and the lady became suspicious. "By the way, Thomas, there are a dozen of these goblets, bring me the others."

"Yes, Mistress," said Thomas, triumphantly, "but they were all dirty and I have just cleaned these."

Mistress Mowbray saw that she could not catch him33 that way, but felt that the man was somehow getting the better of her, so she merely replied calmly,—"Then you can clean the whole set, Thomas, and bring me the dozen to look at."

Aline nearly burst into a laugh, but put her hand to her mouth and smothered it without Mistress Mowbray seeing; but Thomas saw and as he departed, crest-fallen, he vowed vengeance in his heart.

"Have you done what I told you, child?" Mistress Mowbray said, turning to Aline. "Marry, but I trust you have done it well. It is too wet for you to go out; you can start carding a bag of wool that I will give you. That will keep you busy."

Aline sighed, as she had hoped to get into the library and she wondered what Audry was doing, who had been shrewd enough to get away, but she said nothing and turned to her task.

At first Eleanor Mowbray's treatment of Aline was merely the joy of ordering some one about, of compelling some one to do things whether they liked to or not, just because they were not in a position of power to say no; but what gave her a secret additional joy was that Aline was a lady and she herself was not. True, Aline's father was only one of the lesser Lairds, but he was a gentleman of coat armour,[9] whereas Eleanor Mowbray was merely the beautiful daughter of the wealthy vintner of York. It caused Eleanor Mowbray great satisfaction to have the power to compel a gentleman's daughter to serve her in what her plebeian mind34 considered degrading occupations. It was for this reason therefore that Aline was set to scour sinks, scrub floors and empty slops, with no deliberate attempt to be unkind, but simply to feed the love of power.

9 A gentleman is a man who has the right conferred by a royal grant to his ancestors or himself of bearing a coat of arms. It is not as high a rank as esquire with which it is often confused.

As a matter of fact, so long as the tasks remained within her physical strength, Aline was too much of a lady to mind and, if need had been, would have cleaned out a stable, a pigsty or a sewer itself, with grace and dignity and even have lent distinction to such occupations.

But these very qualities led to further antagonism on Eleanor Mowbray's part. They were part of that power of the true lady that in Aline was developed to an almost superhuman faculty and which went entirely beyond any power of which Mistress Mowbray even dreamed and yet without the child making any effort to get it. Aline herself indeed was unconscious of her strength as anything exceptional. She had been brought up by her father, practically alone and had not as yet come to realise how different she was from other children.

It was the morning after the discovery of the secret room that Mistress Mowbray had the first indication that Aline had a power that might rival her own. It was a small incident, but it sank deeply and Eleanor Mowbray did not forget it.

She was expecting a number of guests to dinner and it looked as though nothing would be ready in time. She rushed to and fro from the hall to the kitchen upbraiding the servants and talking in a loud and domineering tone. But the servants, who were working as hard as the average of their class, became sullen and went about their labours with less rather than more effort.

Eleanor Mowbray was furious and finding Aline still at her spinning wheel, where she herself had put her, "'Sdeath child," she exclaimed, "this is no time for spinning, what possesses you? I cannot get those varlets to work, everything is in confusion,—knaves!—hussies!—go you to the kitchen and lend a hand and that right speedily."

Aline felt sorry for her hostess, who certainly was like enough to have her entertainment spoilt. She had already noticed that the servants in the hall were very half-hearted, so she said, "I will do what I can, Mistress Mowbray, perhaps I might help to get them to work."

"You, indeed," said the irate lady, "ridiculous child!—but go along and assist to carry the dishes."

Aline rose and passed into the screens and down the central passage to the kitchen. The place was filled with loud grumbling, almost to the verge of mutiny.

As the queenly little figure stood in the doorway, the servants nudged each other and the voices straightway subsided.

"Hush, she will be telling tales," said one of the maids quietly.

"Nonsense," said Elspeth, Audry's old nurse, who was assisting, "surely you know the child better than that."

For a moment or two Aline did not speak and a strange feeling of shame seemed to pervade the place.

"Elspeth," said Aline, while the flicker of a smile betrayed her, "if you run about so, you'll wear out your shoon; you should sit on the table and swing your feet like Joseph there."

"Now, hinnie, why for are you making fun of an old body?"

"I would not make fun of you for anything," said Aline; "but look at his shoon; are they not fine,—and his beautiful lily-white hands?"

"Look as if you never did a day's work, Joe," said Silas, the reeve.

"Oh, no, he works with his brain, he's thinking," said Aline, putting her hand to her brow with mock gravity. "He's reckoning up his fortune. How much is it, Joseph?"

"Methinks his fortune will all be reckonings," said Silas, "for he'll never get any other kind."

"Well, we'll change the subject; there's going to be a funeral here to-night," Aline observed.

"No, really?" exclaimed half a dozen voices.

"Yes, it's a terrible story and it really ought not to be known; but you'll keep it secret I know," she said, lowering her voice to a whisper.

As they crowded round her she went on in mysterious tones, "You know John Darley and Philip Emberlin."

"Yes," said Joe, rousing himself to take in the situation, "they are coming here to-night."

"They've a long way to come and they are not strong," said Aline, "and they will arrive hungry and just have to be buried, because there was nothing to eat. Yes, it's a sad story; I'm not surprised to see the tears in your eyes, Joseph, and, in fact, in a manner of speaking you might say that you will have killed them, you and your accomplices," she added, looking round.

37

A good tempered laugh greeted this last sally.

"Marry, we have much to get through. How can I help? It would be a sorry thing that Holwick should be disgraced before its guests. Give me something to do."

There was nothing in the words, but the tone was one of dignity combined with gentleness and sympathy.

The effect was peculiar;—no one felt reproved, but felt rather as though there was full sympathy with his own point of view; yet at the same time he was conscious that he would lose his own dignity if he became querulous and allowed the honour of the house to suffer.

Aline helped for a short time and then, leaving them for a moment all cheerful and joking but working with a will, she looked into the buttery, where she saw Thomas and Edward, the seneschal, a pompous but good hearted fellow, merely talking and doing nothing.

"You are not setting us a good example," she said laughing; "everybody else is working so hard," and then she added in a tone that combined something of jest, something of command and something of a coaxing quality, "do try to keep things going; Master Richard would be much put about if he failed in his hospitality."

This time there was undoubtedly a very gentle sting in the tone that pricked Edward's vanity; yet his own conscience smote him, so that he bore no ill will.

He said nothing, however, but Thomas remarked;—"Yes, Mistress Aline, the sin of idleness is apt to get hold of us, we must to our work as you say."

Aline raised her eyebrows slightly, the ill-bred vulgarity of the remark was too much for her sensitive nature. Thomas was marked by that lack of refinement38 that cheapens all that is noble and good by ostentatious piety and sentimentality.

Aline gave a little shiver and passed on to do the same with the others. She also took her full share in the work, so that in fifteen minutes everything was moving smoothly. It was done entirely out of kindness, but Eleanor Mowbray felt that it was a triumph at her expense and although Aline had helped her out of a difficulty, she only bore a grudge against her.

Thomas also was nettled. Aline had got the better of him; he suspected her, too, of seeing through his hypocrisy; which, as a matter of fact, she had only partially done, as she was so completely disgusted at his vulgarity that she did not look further.

It was not till the afternoon that the children had any opportunity to pursue their own devices and they decided, as the day was fine and the storm had cleared away, that they would go down to the river near-by and see the waterfall before the water had had time greatly to abate.

They did not go straight across the moor, but went by way of the small hamlet of Holwick. Everything looked bright and green after the rain, varied by the grey stone walls, that ran across the country, separating the little holdings. The distance was brilliantly blue and the wide spaciousness that characterises the great rolling moorland scenery was enhanced by the beauty of the day.

The children turned into the second cottage which was even humbler than its neighbours. It was a long, low, thatched building, roughly built of stone with clay instead of mortar. Within, a portion was divided off39 at one end by a wooden partition. There was no window save one small opening under the low eaves which was less than six feet from the ground. It was about eight inches square and filled with a piece of oiled canvas on a rudely made movable frame instead of glass. In warm weather it often stood open.

The children stumbled as they entered the dark room and crossed the uneven floor of stamped earth. There was no movable furniture save one or two wooden kists or chests, a dilapidated spinning wheel and a couple of small stools. In the very middle of the floor was a fire of peats on a flat slab of stone in the ground and a simple hole in the roof allowed the choking smoke to escape after it had wandered round the whole building.

An old man, bent double with rheumatism, hastened forward as the children came to the door and, holding out both his hands, shook Audry's and Aline's at the same time. "I am right glad to see you," he said, "and may the Mother of God watch over you."

He quickly brought two stools and, carefully dusting them first, bade his young visitors sit down by the fire.

"How is Joan to-day, Peter," asked Aline, "she isn't out again is she?"

"No, Mistress Aline, she has been worse the last few days and is in bed, but maybe the brighter weather will soon see her out and about."

He hobbled over toward a corner of the cottage, where a box-bed stood out from the wall. It was closed in all around like a great cupboard, with sliding shutters in the front. These were drawn back, but the interior was concealed by a curtain. He drew aside this curtain and within lay a little girl about eleven years old[40] with thin wasted cheeks and hollow sunken eyes. She stretched out her small hand as the two children approached and a smile lit up the white drawn face.

Aline stooped and kissed her. "Oh, Joan," she said, "I wish you would get well, but it is always the same, no sooner are you up than you are back in bed again. I have been asking Master Mowbray about you and he has promised that the leech from Barnard Castle shall come and see you as soon as he can get word to him."

"It is good of you to think and plan about me, Mistress Aline, and I believe I am not quite so badly to-day, but I wish that horrid old 'Moll o' the graves' would not come in here and look at me. She does frighten me so. Mother was always so frightened of Moll."

"She is a wretched old thing," said Audry, "but do not let us think about her."

"You mustn't thank us, anybody would do the same," said Aline; "you cannot think how sorry we are to see you like this, and you must just call me Aline the same as I call you Joan. See! Audry and I have brought you a few flowers and some little things from the Hall that old Elspeth has put up for us, and when the leech comes, he will soon make you well again."

"I sometimes wonder whether I shall ever get well any more; each time I have to go back to bed I seem to be worse. All my folk are gone now and I am the only one left. The flowers are right bonnie though and the smell of them does me good," she added, as she lifted the bunch of early carnations that the children had brought.

After she had spoken she let her hand fall and lay[41] quite still gazing at the two as though even the few words had been too great an effort.

The bed looked very uncomfortable and Aline and Audry did their best to smooth it a little, after which Joan closed her eyes and seemed inclined to sleep.

"I wish we could get her up to the Hall," said Aline in a whisper, "the smoke is so terrible and I never saw such a dreadful place as that bed."

"Mother would never hear of it; so it's no use your thinking of such a thing."

They returned to the fire and sat down on the stools for a few moments before leaving.

"Ay, the child is about right," said the old man, "her poor mother brought her here from Kirkoswald when her man died last November. Sarah Moulton was a sort of cousin of my wife who has been lying down in Middleton churchyard this many a long year. She lived in this very house as a girl and seemed to think she would be happier here than in Kirkoswald. Well, it was not the end of March before she had gone too and the lassie is all that is left."

The children bade farewell and went out. As they passed the end of the house they saw the black figure of an old woman creeping round the back as though not wishing to be seen.

"Oh, there's that horrible old woman! 'Moll o' the graves,'" said Audry; "let us run. I wonder what she has been doing listening round the house; I hate her. You know, Aline, they say she does all manner of dreadful things, that it was she who made all old Benjamin Darley's sheep die. Some people say she eats children and if she cannot get hold of them alive she42 digs them up from their graves at night. I do not believe it, but come along."

"No, I want to see what she is doing," said Aline; "I am sure she is up to no good. I believe that she has been spying outside waiting for us to depart, so that she can go in."

"But you cannot prevent her," said Audry.

"We must prevent her," said Aline; "she might frighten Joan to death."

Aline was right and the old woman came round from the other end of the house and approached the cottage door. Aline at once advanced and stood between the old woman and the door, while Audry followed and took up her position beside Aline.

"What do you want, mother?" said Aline.

"What business is that of yours?" said the old dame savagely; "you clear away from that door or I will make it the worse for you."

She raised her stick as she spoke and glared at the children. It was not her physical strength that frightened them, as they were two in number, although she was armed with a stick, but something gruesome and unearthly about her manner. Aline took a step forward so as half to shelter Audry, but her breath came quickly and she was filled with an unspeakable dread.

"You must not go in there," said the child firmly; "there is a little girl within who is sick and she must not be disturbed."

"I shall do as I please and go in if I please," she muttered, advancing to the door and laying her hand on the latch.

Aline at once seized her by the shoulders, saying, "I43 may want your help, Audry," and gently but firmly turned her round and guided her on to the road. Moll made no resistance, as she feared the publicity of the road and moreover the girls were both strong and well built, though of different types. Aline then stepped so as to face her, and keeping one hand on her shoulder, she said, as she looked her full in the eyes,—"go home, Moll, Joan is not well enough to see any one else to-day,—go home."

The old woman's eyes dropped; she was cowed; she felt herself in the presence of something she had never met before, as she caught the fire in those intense blue eyes. "I will never forgive you," she snarled, but she skulked down the road like a beaten dog.

The children stood and watched her, feeling a little shaken after their unpleasant experience.

"What a good thing you were there," said Audry. "I am sure she would have frightened Joan terribly."

"Come, let us forget it," and they raced down to the waterfall.

It was a magnificent sight, one great seething mass of foam, cream-white as it boiled over the cliff; while below, the dark brown peat-coloured water swirled, mysteriously swift and deep, and rainbows danced in the flying spray. They walked down the stream a little way watching the rushing flood, when Aline suddenly cried out, "Audry, what is that on the other side?"

Just under the rock, partly concealed by the over-hanging foliage, could be made out with some difficulty the form of a man. He was lying quite still and although they watched for a long time he never moved at all.

44

"I wonder if he is hiding," said Audry.

"I am sure he is not," said Aline. "It would be a very poor place to hide, particularly when there are so many better ones quite close by. He may be drowned."

"Possibly, but I think he is too high out of the water."

"Then perhaps he is only hurt; I wonder if there is anything that we could do."

"We might go up to the Hall and get help," Audry suggested.

"Yes," said Aline, doubtfully, as the thought crossed her mind that he might be the poor stranger whom the country-side was hunting like a beast of prey and although she could not explain her feelings she felt too much pity to do anything that might help the hunters and therefore it would not be wise to go to the Hall. It was partly the natural gentleness of her nature and partly her instinctive abhorrence of the vindictive way in which Mistress Mowbray had spoken on the previous night.

Then a shudder passed through her as she looked at the foaming torrent. Any help that could be given must be through that. Aline was only a child; but until she came to Holwick Hall she had lived entirely with older people and realised as children rarely do the full horror of death. It was so easy to stay where she was, she was not even absolutely certain that the stranger was in any real danger. It was not her concern. But Aline from long association with her brave father had a measure of masculine physical courage that will even court danger and that overcame her natural girlish timidity, and along with that she had in unusual degree the true feminine courage that can suffer in silence45 looking for no approval, no victory and no reward, the stuff of which martyrs are made. "He is obviously unfortunate," she said to herself,—"Oh, if I could only help him, what does it matter about me, and yet how beautiful the day is, the rainbows, the clear air, the flowers and dear Audry; must I risk them all?"

She was not sure, however, what line her cousin might take and therefore did not like to express her thoughts aloud. On the other hand she could do nothing without Audry, but she thought it best to keep her own counsel and do as much as she could before Audry could possibly hinder her. So she only said;—"But if we went for help to the Hall it might be too late before any one came, if he is injured and still alive."

At this moment both of them distinctly saw the figure move, and Aline at once said, "Oh, we must help him at once. I am sure we should not be in time if we went up to the Hall. We might find no one who could come and there might be all manner of delays."

"But whatever can you do, Aline, he is on the other side?"

"I shall try and swim across," she said, after thinking a moment.

"What, in all this flood! That is impossible."

"I think I could manage it, if I went a little lower down the river where the torrent is not quite so bad."

"Aline, you will be killed; you must not think of it."

But Aline had already started down the bank to the spot that she had in her mind. Audry ran after her, horror struck and yet unable to offer further opposition.

"Well," she said, "you are always astonishing me," as Aline was taking off her shoes; "you seem too timid46 and quiet, and here you are doing what a man would not attempt."

"My father would have attempted it," was all that Aline vouchsafed in reply.

She took off her surcoat, her coat-hardie and her hose, and then turned and kissed Audry. "There is no one to care but you," she said, "if I never come back."

For a few moments the little slim figure stood looking at the black whirling of the treacherous water, her dainty bare feet on the hard rocks. Her white camise lifted and fluttered over her limbs like the draperies of some Greek maiden, the sunlight flushing the delicate texture of her skin, while her beautiful hair flew behind her in the breeze. It was but a passing hesitation and then she plunged in and headed diagonally up the river. She struck out hard and found that she could make some progress from the shore although she was being swiftly carried down the stream. If only she could reach the other side before she was swept down to the rapids below, where she must inevitably be smashed to pieces on the rocks! It was a terrible struggle and Audry sat down on the bank and watched her, overcome by tears. "Oh, Aline, little Aline," she cried, "why did I ever let you go?" At last she could bear to look no longer. Aline had drawn nearer and nearer to the rapids, and although she was now close to the further bank there seemed not the slightest hope of her getting through.

She held on bravely, straining herself to the utmost, but it was no use;—she was in the rapids when only a couple of yards from the shore. Almost at once she struck a great rock, but, as it seemed by a miracle,47 although much bruised, she was carried over the smooth water-worn surface and by a desperate movement that taxed her strength to the uttermost, was able to force herself across it and the small intervening space of broken water and scramble on to the shore.

When Audry at length looked up, Aline was standing wringing the water out of her dripping hair, shaken and bruised and cut in several places, but alive. She took off the garment she had on and wrung it out before putting it on again. She then paused for a moment not knowing what to do. Blood was flowing freely from a deep cut below the right knee and also from a wound on the back of her right shoulder. She hesitated to tear her things for fear of the wrath of Mistress Mowbray, but at the same time was frightened at the loss of blood. Finally she tore off some strips of linen and bandaged herself as well as she could manage and made her way to where the man was lying.

Ian Menstrie had had a hard struggle. He had been working as a carpenter in Paris and had fallen in with some of his exiled countrymen and become for a time a servant to John Knox. It was three weeks since he had left France with the important documents that he was bearing from Knox and others; and only his iron determination had carried him through. Time and again nothing but the utmost daring and resourcefulness had enabled him to slip through his enemies' hands. He had actually been searched twice unsuccessfully before he was finally arrested as a heretic at York. After extreme suffering he had escaped again and the precious papers were still with him. He had reached Aske Hall in Yorkshire, some twenty miles or so, over48 the hills, from Holwick, the home of Elizabeth of Aske, mother of Margaret Bowes, whom Knox had married, a lady with whom the reformer regularly corresponded.

But almost at once he again had to give his pursuers the slip, and he made his way up Teesdale with the precious papers still on him.

Although they were hot on his trail he had managed to get through Middleton in the night unobserved and would probably have reached the hills and got away North, unseen; but he met a little four-year-old boy on the road, who had fallen and hurt himself and was sitting in the rain and crying bitterly. There was nothing serious about it, but the child had a large bruise on his forehead. Ian had hesitated a moment, looking apprehensively behind, but stopped and bathed the bruise at a beck close by, comforted the child and carried him to his home and set him down just outside the little garden.

The delay, however, had cost him dear; the day was now fully up and two or three people noticed the stranger as he left the road to try and make for the steepest ground where pursuit would be less easy. Shortly afterwards he had seen men in the distance, both on foot and on horseback, setting out on his track and, with infinite difficulty, availing himself of every hollow, at the risk of being seen at any moment he had made his way to the river. If only he could get across, he argued, he might consider himself tolerably safe. They would never suspect that he was on that side and it was in any case the best road to the North. He knew little of the country, of course, or that there was a better place to attempt the feat lower down the stream. He leaped[49] in where he found himself and being a strong swimmer he made his way over but was sucked down by an eddy and dashed against the cliff on the opposite side, but on coming to the surface again he had just sufficient strength to get out of the water and crawl along the ledge of rock to where the overhanging leaves afforded at least a partial concealment. Indeed, the place was such an unlikely one that anybody actually searching for him would probably have overlooked it.

He had lain there for hours, the pain in his head being intense. One ankle was badly sprained and much swollen and he felt sure that he had broken his left collar bone. He had had nothing to eat for days and the dizziness and the pain together caused him repeatedly to fall into a fitful doze from which he would wake trembling, with his heart beating violently. It was after one of these dozes that he woke and, on opening his eyes, saw a little figure in white bending over him, whose large dark blue eyes, filled with pity, were looking into his face. Her long hair fell down so as to touch him and her beautiful arms rested on the rock on either side of his head. At first he thought it was a water-sprite with dripping locks, of which many tales were told by the country folk, and then he noticed the blood oozing from below the bandage on the little arm. "Who are you?" he asked at last, as his senses gradually returned.

"My name is Aline and I have come to help you," she said.

"But, sweet child, how can you do that?"

As his brain became clearer he became more able to face the situation. Who could this exquisite fairy-like[50] little damsel possibly be, and how could she ever have heard of him and why should any family that wished to help him do it by the hands of any one so young? Then she was wet and wounded, which made the case still more extraordinary. "Little one," he went on, "why have you come; do you know who I am?"

"No," she said, "but I saw you lying on the rock and so I came across to try and do something for you."

"You do not mean to say that you swam that raging river?"

"It was the only way to reach you."

"And you are really a little girl and not a water fay?" he asked half playfully and half wondering if there really could be such things, as so many people seriously believed. It was almost easier to believe in fairies than to believe that a little girl had actually swum that flood.

"Of course I am; you have hurt your head and are talking nonsense."

It seemed hard to tell her who he was; this charming little maiden would then hate him like the rest. It was not that he thought that she could possibly be of serious assistance to him; but it was a vision of delight and there was a music in the sound of her voice that to the exile reminded him of his own country. Yet he felt it was his duty and indeed the child might be running great risks and get herself into dire trouble even by speaking to him, so intense was the hatred of the heretics.

"Child, you must not help me. I am a heretic."

"I guessed that you were," she said, and the large eyes were full of pity, "but somehow I feel that it is right to aid any one in distress."

"When you are older, little one, you will think differently. It is only your sweet natural child-heart that instinctively sees the right without prejudice or sophistry."

"I am afraid that I do not understand you; but we must not stop talking here, we must get you to a place of safety."

"Will your people help me?" he said, as a possible explanation occurred to him. "Are they of the reformed faith?"

"Are they heretics? you mean; no, indeed." There was just the suspicion of a touch of scorn in her voice; it was true that to her a heretic was a member of a despised class, but there was also a slight, commingling of bitterness that gave the ring to her words, and which he did not detect, when she thought of the unreasoning and uncharitable prejudice that Mistress Mowbray had shown the day before.

"But that does not mean that I would not help you," she went on. "See this is what we must do. Somehow or other we must get back to the other side and first I ought to bandage your head. Have you hurt yourself anywhere else?" She looked him up and down as she spoke. "Oh, your ankle is all swollen and bleeding where you have torn your hose; we must try and do something for that."

"That can wait for the present," he said, glancing apprehensively at his shoes, which mercifully were still uninjured on his feet; "the worst thing is that I think that I have broken my collar bone. But before we do anything I must try and help you bandage your shoulder more satisfactorily for it is bleeding very badly. That will not be very easy," he added, smiling, "as I have only one arm and you yourself cannot reach it."

She let him try and between them they managed it somehow, and he wondered again as he tenderly manipulated the bandage, how such a little fragile thing could be undertaking such a strenuous task.

"I have not time to explain," said Aline, "but there is a secret chamber in the Hall where you could be hidden, but we could not possibly get you there until it is dark. There is, however, a hollow tree on the other side where we sometimes play, in which you can sit with your feet outside and they can be covered up with grass and leaves. It is perhaps a little dangerous but I see no other way if your life is to be saved. Can you bend your arm at all?" she went on. "Has it any strength in it?"

"It is practically useless," he replied.

"Well, somehow or other we have to swim back across that river; and it is lucky that it is enormously easier from this side. The rapids set towards this bank and on the other side there is a sort of backwater opposite to where the rapids begin on this. We can also with very little danger venture to start some twenty yards higher up than I did when I was coming."

"But I do not think I could swim at all in that rush with only one arm, and in any case you will have to go round; you must not dream of attempting to swim that water again."

With all her gentleness there was something very queenly about Aline. She lifted her head and said,—"We must both go and you must somehow hold on to me and there is no more to be said."

He tried to dissuade her, but the little thing was adamant. He despised himself for allowing a child to help him at all, but was almost as under a spell. His will power under normal conditions was one of the most remarkable things about him; but the pain of fatigue and the long nervous strain had deprived him for the moment of his self-mastery. His head was full of strange noises and he seemed as though he were in a dream. At last he yielded, retaining just enough self-consciousness to determine that he would let himself go, and drown, if he were too great a drag on her. It was clear, as she said, that if she had already swum the other way, there was little real risk for her alone. Moreover the water was falling all the time and, even since she had come over, the stream was slightly less.

Before starting Aline looked round everywhere cautiously and then called to Audry, who was watching on the other side, to have a long branch ready to hold out to them. When Audry had obtained the branch they entered the water. Although the pain was almost intolerable he had decided to put his injured arm on her shoulder and it answered beyond their expectations. He was a very strong swimmer and all that it was necessary for Aline to do was to give the slight help necessary to counteract the one-sided tendency and to improve the balance of the forward part of the body, which otherwise would greatly have reduced the speed. So well did they manage it that they even got across with some ten yards to spare, being still further helped by Audry's branch.

They clambered up the bank, a task not easy of accomplishment, and took Ian Menstrie at once to the tree which was close by. Aline put on her clothes, taking the remains of her linen shift for bandages. Luckily she had on several occasions in her father's house helped to nurse the injured and knew how to bind the collar bone and make as good a piece of work of the ankle as the extemporised bandages would allow. Then bidding him good-bye the children hurried back to the Hall. Aline longed to take him food but decided that, sad as it was, it would be better to run no risks whatever. Moreover, she wanted to discover the passage under the moat and there was none too long before the evening meal.

CHAPTER IV
THE PRISONER

AS they walked rapidly back, their tongues moved faster than their feet.

"Well, you've beaten Burd Aline," said Audry, laughing; "you've rescued your knight before you even know his name. But I'm quite sure it's all the wrong way round;—the knight should rescue his lady. Besides, what's the good of a man in homespun; you need some grand person; you do not know how to do these things, my lady. I wonder who he is."

"He's Scots anyway; one can tell that from his accent."

"I suppose you think a Scots peasant better than an English gentleman."

"I will not be denying it," laughed Aline.

"Oh! then yours shall be a peasant-knight, you always choose things different from other people. But I like his face, it looks strong."

"Yes, but I am afraid he has had a terrible time," said Aline; "how sad those deep-set eyes are; but they seem determined."

"Don't you like his mouth and chin? It's a strong chin and I like those well-shaped sensitive lips."

"Yes, but I think the eyes are more striking."

"It's no good, though, having a knight at all, certainly not a peasant-knight," said Audry roguishly, "unless he has nice lips."

Aline smiled. "You're getting frivolous. Now be serious, we have a great deal to do."

They reached the Hall, ran up to their bedroom and before they started on their further explorations Aline took out the book so as to be prepared for emergencies. She read on for some time and discovered several things, one was the way to open the trap door that led into the cave and especially the way that it could be made to open from the outside if the inner bolts were not fastened. Another important discovery was that the door of their room could be locked by an ingenious bolt in the secret stairway, that pushed back from the bolt-hole into the lock itself. This enabled any one to leave the room unlocked when away, so as to excite no suspicion. Yet on returning, after seeing that the room was empty, by peering through a small slit, one could, by locking the door, make sure that one would not be caught by any one entering the room at the same moment. The children again made their way down the stairs to the secret room where they paused a few moments to look at things for which there was not time on the previous occasion. There were several cupboards, one of which had stone shelves and was clearly intended for a larder. There was amongst other things a large iron chest, which did not seem to have any lock and which greatly excited their curiosity. In another chest they found several pistols and swords besides a few foils and some fencing masks. There were also some tools and some rope and a whole wardrobe of clothes of many kinds. Most of the things were very old but a certain 57 number were comparatively recent. At the same time there was nothing to indicate that the room had been used for the last twenty years.

"Come, we must not stay looking at these things, however interesting," said Aline; "we must be getting on. But I am glad there is a nice place to keep food; only we shall have a great difficulty in getting a supply."

She opened a little door as she spoke and once more they found themselves in a narrow passage that led down a flight of steps. It turned abruptly to the right at the bottom of the steps and then went absolutely straight for what seemed to them an interminable length. It was only the thought of the wounded man that prevented them from turning back. There was a little drain at the bottom of the passage and the whole sloped slightly so that the water that percolated freely through the walls was carried off.

At last they reached the end, where the passage terminated in a short flight of stairs. At the bottom of the stairs was a basin hollowed in the rock and this was fed by a spring of delicious water. They went up these and found a curious door made of stone. It was fastened with huge wooden bolts, a precaution, as they afterwards guessed, against rust. They passed through and discovered that the other side of the door was quite irregular and rough and the chamber in which they found themselves, if chamber it could be called, was like a natural cave. In the middle of the rocky floor was a great stone. Even this looked natural although they found that, as the book had said, it was so cunningly shaped and balanced that it would swing into a vertical position without much effort and allow of a man 58 dropping through on one side of it. But the clever part of it was,—that what looked like accidental breaks in the stone were so arranged that certain other blocks could be fitted into them and the surrounding rock so that it could not be moved. If then by any accident any one should make his way into the chamber he would only think that he had come into a natural cave. Audry let herself down through the hole and with the help of Aline dropped to the ground, and found herself in a small fissure or cave, more or less blocked by underwood, where the stream ran through a little hollow or gully. She succeeded in getting back after making several unsuccessful attempts.

"It is an excellent place," said Audry, "but however shall we get him through that passage, it is so very narrow and so terribly long."

"We might even have to leave him in the cave room to-night," Aline replied, "but I think it would be a good idea to count our steps on the way back. It will be interesting to know how long it is, and we shall also be able to tell in future how far we are at any moment from the end."

This they did and found that it was 1100 paces, which they reckoned would be as nearly as possible half a mile. Before they entered their bedroom again they experimented with the secret bolt that fastened the door, which acted perfectly, although, like everything else, they found that it would be the better for a little oil.

It seemed a long evening, but at last it was time to go to bed. The children went upstairs and waited impatiently until they were quite sure that every one was asleep. They had managed to secrete a little food to take with them and also a few pieces of firewood, and put a little more in the secret room as they made their way out. They had already begun to get somewhat used to the stair and found even the long secret passage less alarming. It was a clear night although there was no moon, and they made their way without difficulty to the hollow tree. They found Ian Menstrie stiff with cold and in great pain, but his senses almost preternaturally alert.

"I am so glad you have come," he said. "I thought that something had prevented you and was wondering whether I could live here till the morning."

Ian's nature was a combination of strength and tenderness and was as likely to be exercising its force in protecting or shielding as in attacking. He had resolutely carried on the work that he felt to be his duty in spite of the most terrible risks and, when he had finally been captured and concluded that it was equally his duty to escape, he had carried out his plans with a ruthless determination; but, in the presence of these children, only the extreme tenderness of his character was called into play.

He looked at the two small figures and, in spite of his terrible plight, his heart smote him that they should be wandering about at night instead of getting their rest, and particularly Aline, who had been through so much already.

"It is good of you to come, and oh, I do hope that you will take no harm. How are you feeling, little one?" he asked, addressing Aline.

"Oh, I am all right," she said brightly, for she did not wish him or Audry to know how her arm pained her, and indeed the excitement was in a way keeping her up. "It is you who are to be asked after; we have brought you a little to eat now and there will be something else when we get to the secret room."

It was a painful journey. Ian set his teeth and tried to make the best of it and lean on his small guides as little as possible, but he was at the last gasp and he was a heavy burden. Luckily he had a naturally strong constitution and forced it to do its work by the exceptional strength of his will or he would have succumbed altogether. But he felt that what he had been through in the last two weeks had weakened his mental power and was glad that there was a chance for at least a respite before he would be called upon to face his tormentors again. In his present condition he felt that he could not answer for himself and the thought was too terrible. Supposing that they should put him on the rack once more and that he should deny his faith! Perhaps for the present at least he was to be spared this.

They very slowly made their way along the bed of the stream and eventually reached the cave. Aline helped Audry up through the trap door first, and then the children just succeeded in getting the injured man through, for he was becoming less and less able to help himself. Then began the long weary passage.

It was an exhausting process and Ian Menstrie seemed to be settling into a sort of stupor. They had gone about 700 paces when he fell right down. "I will be going on in a minute," he answered. So they waited a moment or two and then asked him if he was ready. "Oh, I am coming in a minute," he said once more. They waited again for a time but when they roused him, each time it was the same reply. "Oh, yes, certainly, I am coming just in a moment." Finally there was nothing to be done but half carry him and half drag him along.

"I wish we had put him in the cave to-night," exclaimed Audry.

"But we should never have got enough things there to make him comfortable," said Aline. "I think we are really doing what is best and it will not be long now before we are there."

Aline's shoulder was excruciating, and she knew that it was bleeding again. Her other cut had also opened with the strain, and every limb in her little body ached as it had never done in her life. "I must be brave," she said to herself; "what would father have done if he had been here?" The cold sweat stood on her brow but she never uttered a murmur and was anxious that Audry, who was fairly worn out herself, should not know how bad she was feeling. The last 50 yards she accomplished in intense agony and her thankfulness to reach the chamber was inexpressible.

They lit the fire and laid Menstrie on the bed. Then they gave him some water which seemed to revive him a good deal and he was able to thank them and to take food.

When he seemed to have come to himself Aline sat down on a chair. She leaned back and commenced to shiver, her teeth chattered till her whole frame shook. The others were frightened; it was clear that she was suffering from collapse. Luckily there was a fair supply of wood, as there had been several large pieces in the room when the children discovered it, and they had brought a quantity of small stuff. So there was soon a roaring fire and they were able to give Aline something hot to drink. Ian in spite of his own injuries did all that he could. They managed to shift the oak bed a little nearer to the fire and warmed blankets and wrapped Aline in them and laid her on the bed. Gradually the shivering passed away, but she lay there looking very white and shaken, with great black rings round her eyes, as if they had been bruised. Her wounds caused her considerable pain. Audry, who was a sweet hearted child but without the imaginative sympathy and intense self-sacrifice of her little cousin, toiled up the stairs and brought down some fresh linen. They then gently washed the wounds and put clean oil upon them, Ian cursing himself all the while because of his helplessness with his single hand, but able from many fighting experiences to direct Audry in the manipulation of the bandages.

"Is that more comfortable?" he asked when they had finished.

"Yes," she said smiling, "I feel ever so much better and I think that I could go to sleep."

Audry then assisted Ian to bandage his ankle, and under his directions also saw that the broken bone was all right. He then lay down on the bed and Audry curled herself in a great chair and went to sleep.

For Ian sleep was out of the question; and he lay there watching the firelight dancing on the faces of the slumbering children, the one beautiful with a robust health and well cut features and strongly built limbs, finely proportioned throughout; the other beautiful entirely beyond any ordinary beauty, with an extreme[63] delicacy and subtlety in every line of her face as he had already noticed in her figure, yet never even suggesting the least touch of weakness. He had never seen such hair, which seemed to cover the bed. Its rich deep colour glowed with an extraordinary lustre and he noticed that her skin, unlike that of most people with red hair, was absolutely clear and marked by a strange translucent quality that was unique. One small arm was lying out on the coverlet with the sleeve tucked up. He had not realised before that a child's arm could show so much variety of form and modelled surface and yet retain the essential slenderness and daintiness of childhood. She might well have been some fairy princess sleeping among the flowers.

Aline's beauty undoubtedly had about it something supernatural. It was all in keeping with her manner and character. There was an atmosphere of another world about her of which every one who met her sooner or later became aware. It could not be put into words and could not be analysed. In a sense it was unnatural, but so far from repelling any one it had about it a mysterious, almost magical fascination that was irresistible.

Only the basest natures failed to be drawn by it, and even in their cases it was not that they did not feel it, but that they consciously withstood it as a power with which their whole nature was at variance.

Ian was devoutly glad that she was no worse and offered up a prayer of thankfulness that she was at least safe. As he looked at her he recalled her soft, not very pronounced, musical Scots accent, and his thoughts turned to the land of his birth. Her face too!—why[64] had he not noticed it before, how strangely like it was in certain aspects to the face of his dreams, that still followed him wherever he went, although he had not seen it for thirteen years? He had, however, reluctantly to admit that this mere child's face was even more beautiful. After all she too had really been only a child, although rather more than a couple of years older than himself, when he had worshipped her with all the fervour of a boy's adoration and had suddenly lost sight of her when her parents had unexpectedly taken her away to be married. But the face had lived with him day and night, and no other face had ever come between him and his vision. Nor had the discovery long afterward,— that she had died soon after her child was born, ever inclined him to look elsewhere.

Aline moaned slightly and moved her head uneasily as though not quite comfortable. He smoothed the pillow for her and registered a vow that he would do all that he could to serve her, not only in return for what she had done for him, but for the sake of the chance resemblance to that one who had gone and who through all these years had meant so much to him.

And yet who was he to serve or to help any one?—a wanderer with a price upon his head; and he began to turn over the events of the last few years in his mind. All had promised so well with him and yet everything had been adverse. He had early distinguished himself both for his learning and his military skill, which drew down upon him the envy of his brothers, particularly the eldest, when, as a mere boy, he was one of the few who distinguished himself in the unfortunate battle of Pinkey Cleugh and he had looked forward to some recognition65 or advancement, but the jealousy of his brothers had made that impossible. Then he had fallen under the influence of George Wishart[10] and incurred the undying anger of his father, and so great was the enmity of the family that finally he fled the country, first to England and afterwards, at Mary's accession, to France and then to Italy, where he spent some years and followed first the calling of a smith. There he not only learned about the making of arms but acquired a considerable facility in the new art of swordsmanship as practised in Italy. Nor were his fingers idle in other ways; he executed designs first in metalwork and then in wood and other materials and became an accomplished draughtsman besides exhibiting great creative power. He might even have become one of the world's great artists had not circumstances directed his energies into other fields.

10 The great Scottish reformer and martyr.

It was his brothers he knew who were behind his present trouble and it cut him to the quick. He had no enmity to them. It was not his fault that they had not distinguished themselves. For the sake of friendship he would willingly have obliterated his achievements and have given up everything to them; but of course that could not be, yet they would not forget. He had been for the last month in prison and strong as he undoubtedly still was, it was nothing to what he had been. Many a time had his slight wiry frame astonished his comrades by its extraordinary powers of endurance.

He was lightly built and excellently proportioned, with rather broad shoulders that particularly suited the66 costume of the day. He had on more than one occasion sat for artists in Italy, including Paolo Veronese himself, because of the exceptional beauty of his figure.

His escape had been almost a miracle, as he had no friends in the country and he had to think and carry on everything himself; he had been nearly caught again twice and he had shuddered as he thought of the fate of George Wishart whom he had himself seen strangled and burnt at the stake. It was true that for the moment he was safe, but for how long? He looked at the beautiful child and shuddered again. Suppose he should in any way implicate her. The priests would have no more pity upon her than upon himself. No, that he would not do. He would die rather than that. Would it not be best for him to go away at once rather than be a possible cause of injury to anything so gentle and brave and fair?

He rose up as the thought came to him; yes, he would go away; it should never be said that he had brought calamity upon a child. He stumbled across the floor and made his way down to the passage, but he had not realised how weak he was. Hitherto he had been buoyed up by excitement; now that that was over the pain was more than he could stand and he fainted and fell heavily to the ground.

When he again came to, he realised the impossibility of his getting away down the long passage, and he also began to wonder whether after all he might not be of more use if he stayed. He did not as yet know who the child was; it was clear that she was Scots and did not belong to the family of Holwick Hall; perhaps in the workings of Providence he had been sent there to67 be of some use to her. He could at least wait and find out a few things and then see what was best to be done. So he crawled back to the room again and waited for the morning.

To while away the time he took off his shoes to see that they were all right.

They were peculiarly made, with false inner soles of many thicknesses of parchment, covered with oil silk and several layers of paint.

These were the precious documents that had been purposely written in that shape. The false soles were secured by stout canvas and thin leather covers which formed part of the shoes. They could not be taken out without cutting the shoes to pieces.

As far as he could see they seemed to have sustained no damage in spite of the wetting.

There were three minute slits or peepholes in the corners and middle of the room. These were evidently intended as lookout places and were covered with small sliding shutters which he opened. The night seemed almost interminable, but at length the dawn began to break. He waited as long as he dared and then woke Audry.

"Where am I?" she exclaimed; "oh, I remember. How are you and how is Aline?" She rose as she spoke and went towards the sleeping figure. "I suppose we ought to wake her,—Aline, dear, wake up."

Aline opened her eyes and gradually roused herself. She was certainly better than on the previous night, but still obviously very ill. However, there was nothing to be done but to get her upstairs somehow, and then there was no alternative but to leave her in bed.

68

The children looked at each other. "Whatever shall we say?" said Audry.

"We must not say what is not true," answered Aline.

"No, but we cannot tell them everything."

"It is very difficult."

"Could you not say that you fell on a rock, Aline?"

"That is not what I mean is difficult."

"I do not understand."

"I mean it is difficult to know how to speak the truth. Even if we do not say what is untrue we let them think wrongly."

"Well, we cannot help that, Aline."

"I do not know, it seems to me that it comes to the same thing as if we told them a falsehood."

"Oh, bother them; if they ask no questions they will get told no stories."

Aline's mind was not satisfied; but, after all their calamities, fortune now favoured the children. There came a knock at the door and Elspeth, Audry's old nurse, came in. "You are rather late this morning," she said, and then she noticed that Aline was still in bed, "and one of you not up. Marry now, but it is a good thing for you that Mistress Mowbray has other things to think of this morning. She has just received an urgent letter from her sister at Appleby to say that she has been taken sick, and will she come over without delay. The serving man that brought the letter has only just now returned homeward."

"What is the matter with Aunt Ann?" asked Audry.

"Oh, it is nothing to fret yourself about, hinnie," the old woman went on, "but such an upset and turmoil in the house you never saw. Mistress Mowbray is carrying69 he were to be staying there the rest of her life; and Appleby only those few miles away too. Well, I must hurry away; I have more to do than I can manage."

"Oh, nurse, can Aline stay in bed this morning? She is not very well; she hurt herself a little yesterday. I will bring up her breakfast; it is nothing serious."

"All right, dearie,—it's nothing serious?" she repeated as she heard Mistress Mowbray's voice calling angrily from the bottom of the stairs. "I am glad of that, but I must go," and she departed.

Aline had kept her face away so that Elspeth should not see how ill she looked. The children were much relieved when they heard the footsteps die away.

In a way Aline's illness even helped them, as it enabled Audry to take up food without suspicion, and it was thus possible, owing to the general confusion in the house, to lay in a small supply for the other invalid below.

The next morning Aline was considerably better, having the marvellous recuperative power of childhood, but it was clear that she would not be herself for some time.

"You do look a sight, you know," said Audry, throwing her arms round her neck. "Your eyelids and all round the eyes up to the eyebrow are still black. Whatever shall we do now, because nurse will certainly come up to-day?"

"She is a dear old thing and you can always get round her. I shall get up and go down and stand with my back to the light and keep my head low, and hope that no one will notice; then you must get nurse to let us have a holiday and take our dinner with us on to the hills.70 We can stay away till it is dark and then no one will see. I am ever so much better to-day and shall be all right to-morrow. We need only go a little way and it is a beautiful day, and I can lie in the sunshine. I wonder how poor Master Menstrie is," she went on. "I am afraid that he will take a great deal longer to get well than I shall. You will of course look after him."

Aline's plan succeeded beyond expectation. Master Mowbray was in a hurry, as he wanted to ride over to Appleby for a few days and Nurse was busy with preparations. So Aline spent the long summer days on the moors watching the great white clouds roll over the hills and thinking of all that had happened in the last few days and the new responsibilities that had fallen upon her. It was clear that it would be a difficult matter to feed their guest, particularly as she was determined not to take food from the house. Perhaps it was true as Audry said, that people had no right to demand answers to any question that they might choose to ask; but certainly that did not justify one in taking what did not belong to one. She was just at the age when the intelligence begins to arouse itself and face the great problems of life and this was only one of the questions that stirred her young mind. There was also the matter of the heretics and again Audry had in her frank direct way supplied the answer of fair play and common sense.

Aline made up her mind that she would ask Master Menstrie about some of these things; at least, as Audry had said, there could be no harm in hearing both sides and she must judge for herself.

Audry went back after a while to see Master Menstrie; and Aline, when she had been out on the moor for a long71 time, returned to the Hall as the afternoon sun was getting low. Before going in, she sat down by the moat and looked across at the grey pile. The water seemed to be shallow at that point as though the bank had slipped in and yellow irises were growing at the edge.

Although the bulk of the building was little more than a hundred years old, except the early pele tower that had been built into the structure, time had laid its fingers upon it and it looked very mellow in the afternoon sun. The stone shingles of the roof were covered with golden lichen, while, behind the parapet of the little old tower, a piece of ivy had taken root and hung down through one of the crenellations trailing a splash of green over the grey wall. There was a stern beauty about it and the long line of narrow oilettes in the granary added to the somewhat fortress-like appearance.

As she sat there she saw a small figure approaching; it was Joan.

Aline beckoned to her and she came up shyly and Aline drew her down to a seat at her side. "I am so glad to see you out again, Joan; I do hope this is going to be a real lasting improvement," she said, taking a little wasted hand in one of her own and putting the fingers of her other hand round the small wrist. "Why, there's nothing there at all," she went on, blowing at the hand and letting it fall; "see how easily I can blow it away; why, if I blew hard I should blow it off. You must be quick and get stronger."

The little maid shook her head sadly.

"And you mustn't look so doleful either," and Aline kissed her in the corner of each eye which made Joan laugh.

"There, that's better; now you must forget yourself and I will tell you a story."

At that moment Audry appeared on the scene. "Well, you are a pair, you two," she said, with a kindly sparkle in her merry brown eyes; "you could not raise a spot of colour between you; but, Joan, it's good to see you out at all, in spite of your pale cheeks. How are you and what did Master Barlow say?"

"I do not think he knew what was the matter; but he said that I ought to go away and see if other surroundings would help me. He was a kind old man."

"We must see what we can do, Joan, when Master Mowbray comes back from Appleby."

"I do not think it is good for either of you to be out in the evening air," said Audry. "Come along in, Aline."

"What is the matter with her, Mistress Audry?" said Joan.

"Oh, nothing," said Aline; "I shall be all right to-morrow, but I must obey this tyrannous lady; good-bye, Joan."

Audry had had difficulties with her patient. Menstrie so far from improving grew distinctly worse. His head was causing him great pain and the want of sleep made him a wreck. She had no scruples about the food like Aline, maintaining in her blunt way that it was the duty of the house to be kind to the stranger and that, if the other people did not do their duty, then she must do it for them whatever it involved. But she was very glad that Aline had so much improved after a few days as to be able to come and see the invalid with her.

He was obviously in a high fever and was gradually getting delirious. The old nurse took very little notice of them while her mistress was away and they would slip out on to the moors and make their way back to the secret room by the underground passage. As Aline grew strong Ian's illness laid a greater and greater hold upon him. Aline insisted in sitting up with him the greater part of the night. There was not a great deal that she could do; but she prepared a concoction from a little yellow flowered plant that grew upon the moor and that was deemed good for fevers and administered this at regular intervals.

He spoke but rarely, but his eyes would follow her wherever she went. When his head was exceptionally bad he would complain of the burning and she would place wet cloths on his brow, or in fits of shivering she would do all that she could to keep him warm.

At length he seemed to take a distinct turn for the better. One night after a violent perspiration she was trying to change the bedclothes and make him more comfortable when he spoke to her quite clearly and in a voice unlike the almost incoherent ramblings of the last few days,—"What a wonderful little angel you are," he said.

"I could not do less," she replied.

"I see no reason why you should do anything at all; how long have you been tending me like this?"

"Audry has been attending you a great part of the time."

"Then I have been ill for a long while."

"Some little while," she said, "but you are better now; I have been so frightened that you would never get well any more."

74

"But that would not matter to you."

Aline laughed,—"Why then I should have had all my trouble for nothing."

"But it would have been simpler to have taken no trouble at all."

"Simpler, but how dull; do you know this is the most exciting thing that has ever happened to me?"

"A poor kind of excitement," he said; "why, you are looking very ill yourself; do not people notice it?"

"Oh, yes, they say, 'You are a little scarecrow.'"

"Who say?"

"Mistress Mowbray, she has come home again to-day."

"I did not know that she had gone away, but is that all that she says; does she not suggest doing anything?"

"Marry no, she only said, 'Child, you have been eating too many good things while I am away; you must not get ill; I have a great deal of work for you to do. To-morrow you have to work hard after all this time of idleness.' Now you must not talk any more; it is a great thing to hear you talk properly at all, and it would be foolish to let you make yourself ill again."

He wanted her to go on; but again he saw that firm determined look in her manner that he had noticed before and knew that it would be useless to try and move her. "Well, little princess," he said, "if those are your commands I suppose that they must be obeyed."

"Certainly, sirrah, it is time that you went to sleep."

It was fortunate for the children that Menstrie's illness took a turn for the better when it did, for it would have been impossible for them to give him much time after Mistress Mowbray's return. But it was clear that75 it would be a long time before he would be able to get about.

They both came in on the following night and found that while there was no doubt about the improvement, he was miserably weak and ill. Aline tried to prevent him from talking, but he was anxious to hear how things had gone with them. "Well, what have you been doing all day?" he said.

"We have been hemming great holland sheets," said Aline.

"Well, that is not very exciting," he said.

"More exciting perhaps than you think," said Audry. "Mother was very cross, and Aline certainly had an exciting time."

"Hush, Audry," said Aline very softly.

"I shall not hush, Aline. I wish that mother would not act like that to you. Do you know," she went on, "that whenever Aline made the stitches just the least little bit too big or turned down the hem the least bit too much or too little, she hit her. Aline, if I were you I would not stand it; I would tell my father."

Ian half rose in his bed with anger and then fell back again. "There you see what you have done," said Aline, as Ian went as white as the sheet. It was some moments before he was able to speak and the children watched him anxiously.

"What a shame," he went on, in calmer tones.

"Well, we won't talk about that now," said Aline; "let us talk of something nicer. Master Mowbray is going to give me a falcon and I am going to ride like Audry."

76

"I thought that I heard you say that you did not care about riding, little one," he said.

"I do not know that I do particularly, but Master Mowbray wished it for the sake of Audry. I do not think he cared about me one way or the other. I thought that it might help us in several ways in feeding you."

41

"I am afraid I do not quite see that," he said.

"Well, for one thing, the falcon would have to be fed and sometimes there would be things that I could give to you and I could get other things for the falcon instead. I do not like taking things from the house, and that is why I have tried as far as possible to snare you rabbits or catch fish in the river. So far we have done very well, but it is meal or bread that is the chief difficulty."

"And do you think the falcon or the horse is going to get the bread?" he asked playfully.

"If you were not ill," she said, shaking her little hand at him, "I would punish you."

He caught the hand and kissed it. "Well, never mind, but I do not see how either the horse or the falcon is going to help you."

"It is this way. If we go riding it will be a reason for going expeditions, and then we can make it an excuse to buy food. If I were to go and buy food round about here, there would be all manner of questions asked at once."

"But, child, you have not any money, and if you had it would not be right to spend it on me."

"But I have some; I have five pounds Scots that my father gave me long ago that I have been keeping in a77 safe place, and I have six florins that have been given me by other people."

"You never told me that you were so rich," said Audry. "Why, think what you could buy for all that!"

"Can you get down my jerkin, Audry?" asked Ian,—"Thank you! See if you can find in the inner pocket a leathern purse?—That's right, now in that you will find ten gold rose angels. Take out two of them and let me know all that is spent on my account. I would not hear of you spending money on me."

Aline demurred, but Menstrie would brook no opposition. So there was nothing to be done but take the money. After the children had gone Ian began to consider his new responsibilities. He already began to feel that Aline was in some way his special care. He had a peculiar power of seeing both sides of things and realised that there was always something to be said for each. But this never paralysed his action as it does with many. He remembered the Athenian view of the sin of neutrality and that the first duty is to make up one's mind.

In action he was usually able to find a line not neutral, that is to say neither, but one that stood firmly and decisively for something even beyond the best of both and this he would carry through at all costs. He found this all the easier as his personality, his resolution and clear explanations made him a born leader and he generally compelled others to take his higher point of view. But this could not always be the case and then he would take the side that on the whole was the better. He had thrown in his lot with the protestant party, not by any means because he entirely agreed with them,—he often told them they were no better than those they[78] opposed,—but he definitely saw more prospect of progress in that direction. He had an iron will, that is absolute self-control and the determined capacity that no difficulties, no obstacles and no suffering could cause to swerve. He was entirely free from the weakness of obstinacy, or of pleasing himself.

In more personal matters it was the same. At the present there were the claims of his country, the claims of his faith and the claims of this child. He loved children and nothing stirred him so much as to see a child illtreated.

How were these claims to be met? After all, were they so conflicting? The only real problem was that Aline was in England, while his other duties lay in Scotland. Clearly he must get her to Scotland. In whose charge to place her, he could arrange later. That much then was settled.

As he thought this, he distinctly heard a voice say,—"No, it is not." He looked behind, but saw no one. The voice continued,—"She will become a heretic and then...?"

"Who is there?" he cried, sitting up in bed. There was silence and he heard no more, only he fancied he saw Wishart again in the fire and Aline was along with him. "I am overwrought," he muttered; "that is impossible anyway, as poor Wishart died long ago. No, Aline," he went on, "as long as my life can stay it, such shall never be,—never. Where there's a will, there's a way."

He leaned back exhausted and soon fell into a troubled sleep. He remembered nothing when he woke, but found the sheet torn to shreds, as though he had fought some malign enemy.

[79]
CHAPTER V
THE THIEF

NOT many days after, Aline went down to Peter's cottage. Joan had again had a relapse and the physician had paid one or two visits. For the moment she was better and sitting up in bed.

Aline had brought some beautiful roses whose fragrance filled the whole place. Joan's eyes quite sparkled with pleasure.

"Oh, Mistress Aline, how lovely!"

"I said you were to call me Aline, just as I call you Joan," and Aline kissed the little thin hand that seemed almost transparent. "Now you must soon get well and be able to come and play games again; and see what I brought you to wear when you can run about."

Aline's own wardrobe was very scanty, but one day Master Richard had brought back from York a piece of good camlet which he had given to Aline as a special present. "May I do just what I like with it?" she had asked. "Of course," he replied. So Aline had coaxed Elspeth to help her, and, with much excitement, had made Joan an attractive little gown. Aline was rather at a loss for some trimming that she wanted and Audry had found her one day taking some off one of her own garments. She had expostulated but Aline had only said,—"Oh, it looks all right; I have left some on the upper part. I do not mind plain things."

Joan's gratitude was too great for words; she could only gently squeeze Aline's hand.

As Aline sat by the bedside the door opened and a dark bent figure appeared against the light.

"Good-day, Peter," she said, and catching sight of Aline she added, "and good-day to you, Mistress."

Moll had once been a fairly tall woman, but like Peter was now bent, although not to so great an extent and was never seen without her stick. Her face, wrinkled and worn as it was, more from evil living than from actual age, as she was not really very old, still had some trace of its original beauty, but there was a cruelty and cunning in its expression that defied description. All the children were frightened of "Moll o' the graves" and would flee at her approach.

"You have a sick bairn here, Peter," she began, ignoring Aline, "and I have been wondering whether I could not help you."

Peter looked as if the last thing in the world that he desired was old Moll's help.

"You have something laid by under this stone," she went on, tapping the hearth with her stick as she spoke; and Peter's eyes seemed as if they would drop out of his head.

"Ah, you need not think to keep anything from me," said the old crone; and suddenly turning round, she pointed her stick at Aline, "nor you, young Mistress, you have your secret that you wish no one to know," she added vindictively.

It might have been merely a bow drawn at a venture, yet Aline felt absolutely terrified of the old woman and meditated running from the house, but the thought of Joan held her back. "No, and you need not think you can get away either," said Moll, as though reading her thoughts. "You are by yourself this time," and she interposed her gaunt figure between Aline and the door.

"Come, Peter," she said, "what will you be giving me, or shall I lay a murrain on your sheep?"

"I'll give you three silver crowns."

"Ha! ha! ha!—three silver crowns for a child's life," and, dropping her stick and holding out her skinny hands like the claws of some obscene bird, she began slowly to shuffle over the floor toward Peter, who stood rooted to the spot quaking in mortal fear.

Nearer and nearer the old hag drew toward him, scraping her bare shrivelled feet over the floor.

Peter sank on his knees and crossed himself. "God's blood," he said, "I will give you what you ask."

"Then give me twenty crowns," she said, and waving her arms over the fire the flames turned blue and shot up as though to lick her hands.

She then opened a small pouch at her girdle and taking a pinch from it threw it on the fire and a thick cloud of white smoke ascended and filled the room with a pungent odour and then circled round the room in fantastic shapes.

"In the smoke, in the clouds, I see the future writ," she said; "I see three children and their fates are intertwined. Ah, the first passeth, the second passeth, the third remaineth. I see a great treasure. I see trouble. I see joy and a great darkness." Then turning to Peter she said: "Keep your crowns this time; I can do nothing; the child must go," and she laughed a low cruel laugh,—"and your fate," she said, turning to Aline[82] with a diabolic grin, "is like unto hers; but your path is through the fire; yet there is joy and prosperity after strange days for your little friend up at the Hall." She laughed again, a blood curdling fiendish chuckle, and grasping her staff she hobbled to the door and was gone so swiftly that they could hardly believe their eyes.

Poor little Joan had fallen back senseless and it was some time before Aline could bring her round. Was the old harridan deliberately trying to frighten the child to death or could she really in some way foretell the future?

The effect in any case was extraordinary and Aline had to pull herself together before she felt equal to the walk home.

"What does she mean by my path is through the fire?" she asked Audry, when she met her in the courtyard.

"Don't think about it, don't talk about it. Aline, you terrify me."

"I do hope she has not done Joan any serious harm anyway," said Aline. "But come, we must get ready for supper."

Late in the evening as the family was seated in the great hall and the servants had retired, just as the children were going to bed, Richard Mowbray came in from going round the house as his custom was to see if everything was all right. He seemed to be in a very irritable mood and Mistress Mowbray asked him what was the matter.

"Matter, Eleanor," he said, "you know very well I am worrying about that cup. It's the third thing that has disappeared this month and I seem to be no nearer finding out than we were before. I am fairly certain[83] too that money has gone the same way. Beshrew me but I would give a goodly sum to find the knave."

"I think you might keep your discussions for another time," said his wife icily, glancing at Aline as she spoke; "we do not want our affairs discussed by every stranger."

"There are no strangers here, woman," he said. "The child is a Mowbray which is more than you are yourself; her great grandmother was my grandfather's only sister. Old James Mowbray who built this house loved her more than his son and if the old man had had his way, it is likely enough that the lassie would be the Mistress of Holwick. Woman, you are too jealous. The child shall always have a roof to her head as long as I am Master of Holwick."

Master Mowbray was not particularly fond of Aline, although he was beginning to fall under her spell, but he had a sort of rough sense of justice, which was quite inexplicable to his wife; a trait of his character that had descended in a marked degree to his little daughter.

"Anyway it is time for the children to go to bed," said Mistress Mowbray. "Run along, both of you, and, mind you, not a word of what you heard just now."

The children went upstairs and naturally could not help discussing between themselves what Richard Mowbray had been saying. "I should like to help Master Mowbray," said Aline. "It seemed to upset him very much."

"We wanted some excitement, Aline," said Audry, "and now we seem to have more than enough, what with a heretic and a thief. I wonder what Father would do for us if we could find the thief for him."

84

Consequently for the next few days the children were on the alert to see if they could discover anything. When they went down to visit Ian they told him the story and the three discussed it together.

"Anyway it does not matter telling you," said Aline to Ian, "because you are not a real person."

"And why am I not a real person, pray?" said Ian.

"Oh, you do not belong to the world at all; you never see anybody and live down here; you are only a sort of figure in our dream," said Aline playfully.

"That's rather a shadowy kind of existence," he said, "but it's nice to be dreamed into existence by such delightful people."

"Look here, you two," said Audry, "talk a little common sense. What are we going to do about this thief?"

"I think it must be some one in the house," Aline remarked. "I do not think any one could get over the moat."

"People like this lady would think nothing of swimming the moat," said Ian.

"People like this lady would not do anything of the kind," said Aline; "they could not even get out of the water on the inner side at all, as it is a perfectly straight wall all round, and even if they did, they would go drip, drip, drip, wherever they went and we have seen nothing like that."

"They could take off their clothes," objected Audry.

"Yes, and if they were disturbed," Aline continued, "and had to escape in a hurry, I suppose they would not think they looked a little conspicuous and suspicious, eh?"

"Where is the silver kept?" asked Ian.

"Most of it," said Audry, "is kept in the treasury, the little room near the gateway where the secret passage goes. I expect that is partly the reason for the passage; so that if the owner ever had to flee from the house in time of danger, he would come back and get his valuables without risk; but what an opportunity a thief would have who knew of the passage!"

Aline knit her brows and thought for some time. Menstrie, who was very clever with his chalk, was making sketches of her. "What a very thoughtful lady!" he said.

"Oh, is not that beautiful?" exclaimed Audry. "It is as beautiful as you are, Aline dear. Where did you learn about drawing, Master Menstrie?"

It was a charming little head with bold free lines and full of expression, very like an Andrea del Sarto.

"Oh, when I was in Florence and Venice," said Ian; "it was a great time for me and I learned many things that it would have been almost impossible to learn over here. I was lucky enough to get to know both Paolo Veronese and Tintoretto as they called him, but I like the Florentine work better still. I often think I might have been an artist, but I have too many other responsibilities."

Aline looked up at this point. "Yes, that is wonderful. Father was very fond of drawing and had several friends who were artists. There was Master Lindsay, who did a beautiful portrait of mother, but do you know I do not believe he could have drawn as well as that; it is so bold and free and yet sensitive and delicate in its details. His work was much more cramped and over-elaborated. No," she said, holding the drawing at arm's length, "I am sure he could not have done it nearly so well."

"Well, never mind about the drawing," said Menstrie; "what were you thinking about?"

"I was thinking that the theft could not very well have taken place at night. If it had, probably many more things would have gone. But some one may have slipped into the little room for a moment when the old seneschal's back was turned. We might go along and find out when Edward is there, whether we can hear and know what goes on from the secret passage."

"It is just about now that Edward fetches the silver," said Audry.

"Come along then."

So the two children jumped up and ran to the door. "Good-bye," said Aline, waving her hand, "wish us luck."

Ian watched them go and then fell into a reverie. What a strange thing it was that chance should have brought him to Holwick! He looked at the drawing which was still on his knee. "Leonardo would have given something to draw her head," he mused. "But neither he nor Raphael could have done it justice. Yes, she is like her, very like, and yet more beautiful. Who could have believed that any one could be more beautiful? This child's father must have been handsome as she says. I wonder in what way I am to be of service to her. It's a pity that she is of the old faith. Somehow I feel that that is going to be a difficulty. I should find it very hard to get any assistance if it were needed. The other side would not look at me and my side would not look at her. I wonder if they would even help me myself," he pondered. "I do not hold with most of them by any means. I fancy that child's father would have been more to my liking. How narrow and unkind they all are. Think of a Catholic like Sir Thomas More, a very saint of a man, coming to the block. Will nothing ever soften men's hearts? John Knox is all very well, but he's dour. No, John, my friend, Plato was quite right; if you do not understand beauty you will have to serve a little apprenticeship before St. Peter will open the gates. Harmony not strife,—the Beauty of Holiness,—think of it, Master John, think of it! With what humility and yet with what ecstasy we shall worship in that presence.

"Ah, child," he went on, "you are indeed the handiwork of God and, as Plato says, I do pass through you to something more."

As he spoke the vision of the child seemed to shape itself before his eyes. Her little feet were bare as when he saw her first and she was stretching out her beautiful arms toward him. Her face shone with a strange light and then gradually he felt himself lifted up and the vision changed, becoming more ethereal and more beautiful, till his heart stood still. It was no longer a child, it was no longer even human beauty at all. It was altogether transcendent.

He rose slowly and then knelt down. "Now I know," he said, "this is the heart's adoration, this is worship. I never knew before." He bowed down utterly humbled and yet at the same time exalted and a voice seemed to say,—"I am that I am." He felt as one who is purified as in a fire and then gradually a sense of peace stole over him.

He knelt there in a rapture for a long time until at length the vision faded slowly away. But he realised that in some strange fashion new strength had been given to him and that the temptations of life were shrinking into littleness.

Meanwhile Aline and Audry made their way along the passage. It was daylight so they felt that their light would not be seen. When they got to the end they could hear perfectly and even see a little bit through a tiny crack. They saw Edward, the seneschal, come in and take out the great salt and the nef and then he carefully fastened the door. After a while he came back and fetched some of the other things.

When the children returned to Ian, they both exclaimed,—"Oh, you are looking so much better."

For a moment he did not speak; he was watching Aline as she unconsciously glided down the room with a sort of dancing step, humming a tune and slowly waving her arms. She seemed filled with a new sacredness, a new unapproachable otherworldliness; it was an apotheosis of childhood.

"Well, you have come back to me," he said at length. "What did you discover?"

"Not a great deal," Aline answered, "but we can see through a chink and we may some day see the thief himself."

"I am afraid that we shall never catch him," said Audry, "and what is the use of troubling about it? The thing is gone now and what is done is done."

"No, it might come back," protested Aline, "and I shall not give up hope yet awhile. Come along, you have got to finish that piece of tapestry and it's no use[89] saying what is done is done, because what is done is no use, unless you do some more."

Both laughed and ran out.

They worked at the tapestry in the solar. Mistress Mowbray was there engaged in the same occupation. By and by her husband came in. "I suppose you have found out nothing about that cup," she remarked.

"No," said Master Richard, "and meseemeth I am not likely to do so. Edward is confident that it cannot have been taken from the treasury."

"Humph! He may say so. Look you now, Richard, if I were you I should get rid of Edward. Turn him out of doors."

"Do you think that Edward has taken it?" said her husband, looking surprised.

"Why, who else could have taken it? It's as clear as daylight. I cannot see wherefore you hesitate."

Richard Mowbray gazed steadily in front of him for a long time, stroking his pointed beard. "Yes, I think it must be so; I shall do as you suggest. Edward shall leave."

"I am sure Edward did not do it," said Audry impulsively.

"Nonsense, wench," said her father, "what do you know about it?"

"Oh, well, it has nothing to do with me, but it's hard on the old man if he did not do it," Audry replied. "Come along, Aline; I'm tired of this tapestry; we've done enough. I want you to read to me. May we go, mother?"

"Yes, yes, run away, both of you"; and, lest Audry's remark should have had any effect, she added, to her husband;—"It90 will be an excellent plan in many ways. Edward is getting past his work in any case. I shall be very glad to have some one else."

"Certainly, Eleanor, it shall be as you wish."

Audry had run on. Aline had risen and stood irresolutely looking at the Master of Holwick. "But, Cousin Richard, you will wait a bit, won't you?" she said coaxingly.

"Why, child?"

"Because it might not be Edward, and, probable as it seems, you cannot be certain." She rose and put her arm round him and in her most bewitching way added,—"You will think it over, won't you? I know I am only a little girl, but what would you think, Cousin Richard, if afterwards it turned out that you were wrong?"

"Aline," shouted Mistress Mowbray, "I will not have you interfering. Edward shall leave at once. We cannot have a thief in the house."

"It isn't just, Mistress Mowbray. You do not know that he is a thief; you have no proof."

"Wench, I can dismiss my servants when I please, thieves or not thieves."

In addition to the claims of justice Aline felt a definite feeling of antagonism rising in her, a touch of the fighting instinct. "Of course you can do as you please," she said, "but that does not make it fair."

"I tell you Edward shall go; he is getting too old and that is enough reason."

"Richard," she continued, "am I mistress of this house or is that skelpie? The man is only a servant and I can treat him as I like. I am within my rights."

91

Aline could not resist going on, yet she hated the whole thing; she felt that her attitude was unbecoming, if not impertinent; but she could not let Edward go without a struggle, nor could she abandon a fight which she had once begun; that was not human nature. "You may be within your rights," she said, "and he may be only a servant; but that is just it;—if you belonged to the servant class yourself that sort of reason might be enough, but 'noblesse oblige' as father used to tell me. That is so, is it not, Cousin Richard? and we must investigate the case before Edward is sent away."

Eleanor Mowbray flushed crimson; Aline had found the weak spot in her armour. The vintner's daughter was not a lady, but the one thing in life that she desired was to be thought one.

"Yes, child," said Master Richard, for the remark had touched his proper pride. "Yes, keeping within his rights is good enough for common people. But gentle blood demands more than rights. It has higher standards altogether. It is a matter of honour, not of rights. Many things are right but they are not honourable. The churl does not know the meaning of honour. By my troth, lassie, you remind me of my mother's father, the Duke of Morpeth, who used to say that aristocracy was the pride of humility, the pride that could not be demeaned by humbling itself, the pride that could not lower itself by standing on its rights. Our Lord, he used to say, was the noblest knight and the first gentleman of chivalry. Ah, little maid," he went on, "you must forgive me my reminiscences; the serious things of life cannot be left out."

"No, Cousin Richard, I'm listening."

"I remember," he continued, "how he used to quote 'He that sweareth to his own hurt and changeth not shall never be moved,'—'qui facit haec non movebitur in aeternum.' That was his illustration of the principle in practice; the vulgar man sticks to his bargain or his promise; the gentleman goes entirely beyond his promise and does what is expected of him, whether he had given his word or not. The vulgar man tries to wriggle out of an engagement if it does not suit him; the gentleman stands to the most trivial engagement, even if there is no formal promise, though it may cost him much sacrifice. Honour compels him, 'noblesse oblige.' The man of poor blood has no honour; he merely has honesty and he thinks the gentleman is a fool. He has not climbed high enough to see.

"You are right, little one; there would be nothing wrong in dismissing Edward; we have no promise, no contract: we may even act to our own hurt by keeping him, if he really should be the thief, but honour demands it. The matter shall be thoroughly investigated before we do anything with Edward."

Aline having gained her point ran away. She had not intended at first definitely to withstand Mistress Mowbray. However, Master Richard had agreed with her and she dismissed the matter from her mind.

Not so Mistress Mowbray. She was mortified and she was not going to forget it. Besides the child had committed the unpardonable sin of showing that she was a lady and making it equally clear that she, Eleanor Mowbray, belonged to a lower class. Mistress Mowbray was learning her lesson.

Day after day the children used to go at the proper hour and once or twice Edward did leave the door unlocked for a few moments; but they never saw any one come in and finally began to lose heart and feel that they must give it up as hopeless.

CHAPTER VI
BITTERNESS

IAN was alone in the secret room. He had been busy writing and a great pile of papers lay before him. He was tired and felt he could write no more, so he picked up some sketches he had made of the children. They would often come down and sit for him and he had gathered quite a collection. What a wonderful pair they were. Audry was the easier to draw. She was not quite so tantalisingly subtle with her laughing brown eyes and roguish lips. The face was clearly cut, with decided character, from the well defined brows and the strongly marked forms about the eyes down to the firm determined little chin. "Were it not for a certain pair of faces," he said, "that haunt me day and night I should have said that there could not be anything more beautiful." He then turned to the sketches of Aline and put them aside one by one impatiently;—why could he not catch the elusive swing of those graceful poses? It was no use; they were unattainable. He was looking discontentedly at a sketch of her face and wondering whether any one could ever draw the infinite variation in the finely modelled form of Aline's mobile lips, when Audry came in.

He put the drawing down by the papers on the table.

"Writing again," said Audry; "you are always writing. I cannot think what it is all for."

"One must be doing something," he answered.

She hardly seemed to heed his reply. "It is nice to have some one to come to," she said; "everything is all wrong just now."

"What is the matter, dear?" he asked, noticing that the child had been crying.

"Oh, I have such a tale to tell you about Aline. You know that mother thought that the thief was Edward, and father has been spending ever so much time and trouble over it and has practically proved that it could not be Edward; because, though Edward may have taken the cup, there was some money that went one day when Edward was away from Holwick. So mother must needs get it into her head that it was Aline."

"How utterly ridiculous!" said Ian.

"Yes, and at first I do not think she really thought so; it was only because she does not like Aline and is particularly angry with her just now, because it was Aline who was the cause of her being shown up as wrong about Edward; and——and," the child went on sobbing as she spoke,—"it was partly my fault. Mother knows I love Aline and I was rude to her the other day and she knows it punishes me more than anything else for her to be unkind to Aline"; and here Audry quite broke down.

"Do not cry, dear child," said Ian, stroking her thick brown locks. "Come, tell me all about it and we'll make a nice plan to put things right for Aline."

Audry and her mother never got on very well together. Both were headstrong and impulsive, but whereas Audry's nature was generous and kind, the lady of Holwick was a hard selfish woman. She loved her daughter[96] in her selfish way, but power was her one desire, and she wanted entirely to dictate the course of her life for her; and even in the things of little importance was apt to be tyrannical. Aline had become a cause of much contention between them, and Eleanor Mowbray had now added to her natural dislike of Aline a desire to spite her daughter by ill-treating her little friend.

"Well, you know that Aline is in the habit of taking things to the sick people round about," Audry went on, when her grief had a little subsided, "and old Elspeth generally acts as almoner. Mother, however, has interfered lately, and has said that she will not allow it without her permission and that, she will hardly ever give,—never, for the people that Aline most cares about. So Aline has been buying things with her own money and you know she has not much."

"No, poor child, it must be very sad for her."

"Indeed it is, Master Menstrie, but what has happened is sadder still. I met her coming back from the Arnsides yesterday, and some one must have told mother that she had been there; for mother said I was to tell Aline to go and speak to her directly she came back. I warned her how angry mother was and Aline asked me what it was all about. I said that I was not absolutely certain, but that I thought it was because she imagined that Aline had been taking things from the Hall. I went with her to see mother," Audry went on, "and I never saw mother so furious, and you know how angry she can be."

"I cannot say that I do," said Ian, "I have never even seen her."

[97]

"Well, anyway, she was purple with wrath and would not allow Aline to say a word,—'What do you mean, you dirty little thief,' she said, 'taking things that do not belong to you and giving them to your good-for-nothing friends, you little beggar-brat, you? Here you are living on charity and you must needs steal things from under our very noses.'

"When she paused to take breath, Aline told her that she had bought the things with her own money. But that only made mother more angry than ever. 'What, you dare to lie to me, money indeed, what money have you, you miserable child of a penniless wastrel? Your father was never more than a petty laird at the best and he had not even the sense to keep the little he had. If you have any money we all know where you got it. No wonder you were so certain that Edward had not taken it,' she said with a sneer.

"Aline drew herself up in that stately way that she has. She took no notice of what mother said about her being a thief, but answered;—'My father was a gentleman, your father did not bear arms. You may call me what you like, but I will not have my father spoken of like that.'"

"Dear little princess," said Ian.

"Mother nearly choked with rage and almost screamed; 'You insolent hussie, he was a wretched good for nothing ne'er do weel, or he would not have left you unprovided for.'

"Then for the first time in my life I saw Aline lose her temper. It was not like mother at all, but a sort of unnatural calm. She turned as white as chalk and said very slowly and softly, almost hissing the words;-'Woman,98 you are not fit to have cleaned father's shoon. Leave the dead alone.'

"Mother rushed at her, calling her thief and liar, and I tried to stop her, but she hit me and sent me down full length upon the floor. She snatched up a heavy riding strop and beat Aline furiously with it. I implored her to stop but she only hit out at me. I think she was out of her mind with passion.

"Oh, I am so unhappy. I try to love mother and it is so difficult. I wish that I had never been born."

Ian did his best to comfort the child and after a time she calmed down and said that she would go and find Aline.

When she had gone Ian paced rapidly up and down the room, going over the miserable story in his mind. Certainly there was one good thing in his not escaping the first night as he had intended; he was at least here to try and make plans with her to help her, but how was it to be done? The more he thought the more hopeless he became. Delighted, as he knew his mother would be to look after the child, he knew that as long as his father lived it was impossible; he would find out who had sent her and turn her out of the house or worse than ever—and Ian felt his flesh creep—his father might think that she was a heretic too and then.... Again the vision of Aline burning in the flames rose vividly and distinctly before him, as though it were an actual sight. Ian groaned in agony. "O Lord," he cried, "not that, not that!" He was nearly beside himself; but as the vision passed away he grew calmer. He still walked rapidly to and fro, however, and clenched and unclenched his hands till the nails dug into the flesh. Here was this99 sweet child, the sweetest thing that he had ever seen in his life, for whom he was ready to do anything,—he was perfectly willing to suffer all things for her, he was willing to die for her if need be, not only to save her life, but even to make her happy, if he could make sure of it,—and yet, here he was, absolutely unable to do anything at all, not even to save her from one jealous woman. It was pitiable, it was almost ludicrous; he who had escaped the forces of the inquisition and the united endeavours of the whole countryside, to be foiled in this way by one woman.

Then he clenched his teeth. No. There must be a way and he must find it: "And if there is not one," he said, bringing his fist down on the top of a chair with a crash, "I will make one." The chair broke under the blow. "Exactly so," he said; "if they will not yield they shall break."

After a time Audry returned with Aline. The child did her best to be cheerful, but it was obviously impossible; so Ian thought that it would be best for her to relieve her feelings by talking about it, if she could not put the subject away from her mind altogether.

"Everything sad seems to have happened all at once," she said. "Mistress Mowbray said such dreadful things about father and now she has been telling every one that I am a thief and poor little Joan does not seem able to get over the effects of Moll's visit."

"You mustn't pay too much attention to what mother says," Audry said softly. "She loses her temper just as I do and I do not think that she really meant anything that she said about Captain Gillespie. It was only that she was so angry."

100

"Well, that is what I minded most, at least at the time. After all, poor father has gone and it does not really matter to him now what she says, and it does matter to me when people think that I am a thief. Every one seemed to be staring at me as I passed to-day."

"I think that must be mainly your imagination, little one," said Ian, toying with a tress of the wonderful hair. "No one who really knew you could believe it for a moment, and the other people do not really matter, do they?"

Aline was a little bit consoled, but she said rather pitifully,—"All the same I wish we could find out the thief." Then a fresh cloud seemed to gather and she went on; "Do you think that 'Moll o' the graves' really can tell the future? She said that little Joan and I were going to die,—and what did she mean when she said that my path was through the fire?"

Ian shivered and caught his breath as he thought of his vision, but he spoke as calmly as he could. "Oh, one cannot say; I am afraid that the awful old witch is trying to frighten the child to death."

"Yes," said Audry, "they say that she and Joan's mother, Sarah Moulton, had a terrible quarrel about something and many people think that it was old Moll who terrified her into her grave and that she wants for some reason to do the same with the child."

"The best thing," said Ian, "is to take no notice of her. We must not give way to superstition. It is only by allowing her to frighten us that she can really do anything. What were you going to tell us about Joan, Aline?"

"Well, she just seems to get weaker and weaker. I101 met Master Barlow to-day, who had come over again from Barnard Castle to see her and I said, 'Of a truth, what is the matter with Joan?' and he replied, 'I do not know what is wrong with her, little maid; but I fear she has no chance in that abode.'

"So I feared greatly and asked him what might be done and I told him what Master Richard had said about sending her to Barnard Castle. That, he said, was good, but he would suggest better. He knew a very learned physician in Durham and also a good woman who would house the child if Master Mowbray would be at the expense of sending her, it being a far cry, nigh upon forty mile. Yet he did not hold out much hope even then."

"Oh, I am sure father will do that," said Audry, "and then you will see little Joan coming back well and strong. Come, what you want is a run in the fresh air."

"I want to go down to Janet Arnside's again, so I will go now."

The children left the room and climbed the secret stair. On their way out they turned along beside the moat, which always had a certain fascination for Aline. There were now king-cups and bog myrtle growing on the outer bank, where the part of the wall had broken away, and sheltered from the wind on the south side, water lilies were floating in the dark water. It was a still, lovely day and the beautiful walls and windows of the old Hall were perfectly reflected in the wide expanse of the black mirror, where also could be seen the clear blue of the sky and the great cumulus-clouds.

"I love this old moat," said Aline.

"I cannot say that I do; yet I am unable to say why, but I always think it looks cruel and I feel that something terrible might happen in that deep water, some unsolved mystery, I do not know what it is."

"Yes, I see what you mean, but at the same time it looks kindly and protecting as it goes round the house; it might be cruel, but somehow I feel too that it might be kind."

"Well, I must go and darn my hose," said Audry, "and you said you wanted to go down and see Janet Arnside and her boy."

Audry picked up a large stone as she went, and threw it into the water; it fell with a heavy sullen splash and the sound echoed back from the walls. Aline stood a moment and watched the widening rings till they gradually died away, and then turned down toward the hamlet.

THE HALL FROM N. W. SHOWING PELE-TOWER GRANARY AND LEDGE

CHAPTER VII
DEATH

JANET ARNSIDE was a widow and lived in a small cottage not far from the Hall. She had a son who had been very ill; and Aline had been in the habit of coaxing Elspeth to get her small delicacies to take round to them as they were very poor, or she would buy things with her own money.

When she reached the cottage the old woman came forward and seized her by both hands. "Bless your bonnie face," she said, "I am glad to see you."

"How is John getting on?" said Aline.

"Oh, he's quite a new creature, thanks to all you have done for us, my dear. When I see him swinging along with great strides I say to myself,—now if it had not been for our little St. Aline where would my boy have been?"

"Oh, you must not thank me, Janet, and I really do not like you to call me that, you must thank Elspeth and Master Mowbray."

"Ay, true, hinnie, the Master has been very good and has always said that we were welcome to a few things, but, there now, when I asked Mistress Mowbray, she said that she had something else to think of than attend to any gaberlunzie body that came round the doors. And where should I have been with my laddie105 if it had not been for you with your sweet face and your kind heart?"

Even Janet Arnside realised that Aline's was no ordinary beauty as she watched the lightfooted graceful child moving round her room and setting things straight, or helping her to cook for her sick boy, or sitting, as she was then, with the sunshine coming through the open door and throwing up the outline of her beautiful form against the dark shadows within the cottage.

"Ah, but Mistress Mowbray is very busy, Janet, she has a great deal to manage in that huge place. It is Elspeth, dear old Elspeth, who looks after all the sick folk and you should try and go up and thank her, now that your son is better and you are able to leave him."

"Ay, Mistress Aline, that should she," said a voice from the door as John entered, "but it is our little mistress here that should be getting most of the thanks, I trow." The boy pushed back the little window shutter as he spoke that he might the better see the child. She was for him his conception of the heavenly angels and during his long illness he used in his delirium to confuse her with the messengers from above who were to take him to the other land. He had been ill for a weary while and had had more than one relapse but she had been a constant visitor when opportunity allowed, and had often soothed him to sleep when even his mother could do nothing. He worshipped Aline in a curious half-fatherly way, although he was only some four years her senior, and the dream of his life at that time was to be of assistance to her some day.

Aline was just on the point of going when they heard rough angry voices passing along the road, so she shrank106 back into the shadowy recesses of the cottage;—"I tell you what it is," one of the voices was saying, "if you do not help me I'll see that you never forget it."

"Now, there you are again," the other voice replied, "you never can keep a civil tongue in your head."

"Why that is Andrew Woolridge and Thomas Carluke," Aline exclaimed. "What are they doing down here?"

Andrew and Thomas were two of the men from the Hall and Aline knew that at this time of day they ought to be at work.

"They are up to no good I'll be bound," said Janet.

"Andrew Woolridge seems to be doing a good thing for himself somehow, mother," said John. "I wonder where he got all that meal he has been bringing home from the mill lately; I saw him with a boll early this morn and he brought two bolls yesterday and two the day before."

"Ay, John, and I saw him the day before that with a boll."

"He must have enough for the winter and some to sell too, if he has been going on at that rate, mother."

"Ay, that must be, but I should not like to be the one to ask him where he got the oats he has been so busy carrying to the mill."

"It is time I was going," said Aline, and bidding them good-bye, she turned homeward, pondering on her way what she had heard.

"I fancy that the oats will come from Holwick," she thought to herself. "I wonder if he is still taking them," and she resolved that she would herself keep an eye on Andrew and Thomas.

107

She had not long to wait. That very evening she managed to slip out near the granary at dusk when the outside servants went home. Thomas slept in the hall, but she saw him going to the gate and talking to Andrew very quietly.

The moat ran round the east side of the Hall, but there was a narrow ledge of stone at the foot of the wall on that side, some eight feet above the water, which went from the northeast corner where the granary was, as far as the drawbridge. It was possible to climb on to it from the drawbridge and walk along it with some difficulty. What purpose it was intended to serve was not clear. The drawbridge was never drawn up till the last of the servants had departed. Andrew went outside, but dark as it was, Aline without coming near, saw that apparently he did not cross the bridge. Thomas ran back and made his way to the granary. Aline followed, her heart beating violently, and saw him produce a key and unlock the granary door. She waited a moment wondering which would be the best thing to do and then decided to go back to the drawbridge. She turned round and was just in time to see the dark figure of Andrew emerge from the left and cross the bridge with a heavy bundle on his shoulder and vanish into the night. It was all very quietly managed, he had evidently crept along the high ledge, and as Aline passed through the archway to the upper quadrangle she heard Thomas behind her breathing heavily, but she did not look round.

At first she thought that she would go and tell Master Mowbray at once, but then she hesitated. In those days it might be a hanging matter for Andrew and she also108 had some scruples about playing the part of an eavesdropper. She finally decided that she would speak to Andrew herself, but was very nervous about it; as Andrew was a great big man and from what she knew of him and from the way she had heard him speak to Thomas on the previous night, she guessed that he would stop at nothing.

She watched for him the next day, but no opportunity presented itself. He was always with the other servants. But late in the evening she saw him in the quadrangle evidently waiting for Thomas. She was shaking with excitement and the darkness added to her nervousness, but she approached him and said in as steady a voice as she could muster, "Andrew, I want to speak to you. It is something very serious; there has been grain taken from the granary."

"What of that?" he replied, determined to brazen it out.

Aline had hoped that her point blank assertion would have made him confess at once and the way would have been easier for her; it was very difficult to go on with this great burly bullying ruffian scowling at her. However, her mind was made up and she had to go through with it. "I know who has taken it," she said firmly, "and I want you to promise me that you will not take any more and that also you will replace as much as you have taken away."

"Oh, do you, my fine young lady? You are not the mistress of this Hall, not by a long way, I reckon. Who are you indeed? A penniless Scot that no one would listen to. I should like to see you go with your tales to Mistress Mowbray. She'd soon turn you upside down109 and spoil that pretty skin of yours," he growled coarsely.

"But I shall find it my duty to tell Master Mowbray," said Aline.

"Oh, that is the way the land lies, you miserable tell-tale, is it?"

Aline felt herself blush, as the retort stung, but she knew she was right, and she only said, "But I should not tell any one if you would give back the grain."

"Would you not?" he said fiercely; "well, I'll see you never get the chance, you little she-devil." As he spoke he stepped forward and placed his great hand over her mouth and lifting her up as though she were a mere nothing, he ran with her to the gate and on to the middle of the drawbridge. "No one will miss you in this house, you blethering babe, and they will just think that you have somehow fallen in, playing round in the dark. Mistress Mowbray would give me a month's pay, if I dared ask for it, you wretched brat."

She was absolutely powerless in his strong arms and he raised her above his head and flung her into the moat. She struck the side of the bridge as she fell and then dropped into the dark water. Andrew did not wait, but ran some way into the gloom of the night and then stood to listen whether any hue and cry was raised. Not a sound was to be heard and after about a quarter of an hour he dimly could distinguish his fellow servants walking home. Obviously they were unconscious that anything unusual had happened and he was able to breathe freely as he muttered to himself, "That was well done, she will tell no tales now." He crept back to the moat and peered in. All was still and black and the110 moat gave no sign of the horrible deed that had just taken place in its waters. Hardened wretch that he was, he could not help a shudder as he thought of what lay under that inky surface.

CHAPTER VIII
REMORSE

ANDREW argued with himself as he walked homeward. No one could suspect him. No one? Wait! There was one. What about Thomas? Thomas was not a man to be trusted. At any moment he might find it to his own interests to tell what he knew. Andrew began to be afraid. "I was a fool," he said, "after all. I must escape, escape at once; I will not go home."

He was not very clear in what direction to go. His original home was near Carlisle, but for that reason he avoided it. He would go south, he would make his way over the hills to Brough and Kirkby Stephen and then strike for Lancaster.

He had plenty of money and was able to secure horses at Brough so that he actually got as far as Lancaster the next night. Here he thought he might escape notice and right thankful was he to get to his bed.

But he could not sleep. He was overtired and turned restlessly from side to side, now drawing up his feet, now stretching them out. As he lay there the thought of the black, glistening, silent moat returned to him. "Meddlesome brat," he muttered to himself, "you got what you deserved." The thought, however, would not depart but kept returning to him, and his imagination would dwell upon something dark floating on the surface of the water. "The fiends of hell get hold of thee," he uttered aloud in a hoarse whisper, sitting up in bed.

As he sat up he heard a noise as of some one at his door. "Could any one be listening?" He rose softly and listened himself on the inner side. No, there was surely nothing. He cautiously opened the door and peered out into the shadowy passage. As he did so the door was drawn sharply from his hand and closed. For a moment he dared not move, but stood trembling, waiting, expectant. He heard a distant horse on the cobble stones, then absolute silence save the low wailing whistle of a gust of wind. It seemed to bring back Aline's little white terrified face as she tried to cry out when he held her in his grip with his hand over her mouth. The cold sweat broke out on his forehead and then suddenly the tension relaxed,—"The wind, the wind; it was the wind that had blown the door out of his hand."

He shivered and got back into bed. Again he heard horses' hoofs; this time they came nearer and nearer, they were surely coming to the inn. Yes, they had stood still at the door. He leaped up and frantically slipped on his clothes, while they were knocking for admission. Should he try and escape down the stairs or through the window, down into the yard of the hostel? He went to the other window and peeped out. It was a man and a woman,—probably an eloping couple! He laughed a thin mirthless laugh and once more got back into bed.

This time he slept and dreamed that he was looking out of the window into the hostel yard. Gradually it filled with dark water nearly level with the sill. Then he saw something on the other side, floating on the surface. It seemed to be coming his way.

Slowly it113 rose;—it was Aline, her arms hanging limply from the shoulders and the head falling over to one side, with the mouth open and a great gash above the forehead. It came nearer still. He tried to get away from the window, but something held him. He strove and struggled in vain. "Oh, that terrible mouth, that blood in the long wet hair." Then the figure lifted a hand and pointed at him. In another moment she would touch him. "Maria! God!" he shrieked, but slowly it came closer and closer. He shut his eyes; there was a great shock and he woke. He was lying on the floor with his heart beating violently and a pain in the back of his head.

He did not dare to go back to bed this time; to sleep was worse than to be awake. He sat down on the bed and held his throbbing brow between his hands while his elbows rested on his knees; but gradually fatigue overcame him and he fell asleep again. This time he found himself standing among a crowd of other persons with lanthorns by the side of the moat at Holwick. A little figure was being drawn up from the water. He saw it carried in over the drawbridge, where the old arms of the Mowbrays looked down,—argent, a cross engrailed azure;[11] but he dared not follow. He seemed to stand there waiting for days and days. "Would no one ever come out?" Then the funeral cortège appeared from under the same gateway. He followed with the crowd, no one seemed to see him, and there, in the ancient churchyard of Middleton, he saw the little coffin lowered into the ground.

11 I.e., the field of the shield silver or white, the cross blue with an irregular border.

When every one had gone he still stood by the grave, dazed and wondering. He was just about to leave, when114 a child's figure in the crowd turned back. It was Audry. She came slowly up to him and looked from him to the grave and from the grave to him. Her face was filled with unutterable reproach. "You," she said, and lifted her finger at him and was gone.

He tried to run after her, but it was like running in heavy clay; his feet were as lead and he seemed to slip back a pace for every step he took forward. Finally he abandoned the attempt and, putting his hands over his face, he wept bitterly.

He was still weeping when he woke. "Holy Mother," he cried, "why did I do it?" The thought of the frail child bravely withstanding him in the courtyard of Holwick came back to him,—"little St. Aline," as the villagers called her. Oh! how could he have done such a deed? "I am lost, damned, and nothing I may do can ever bring her back. Cain! Cain! unclean, branded and accurst!"

It was morning now, should he go back and give himself up? Give himself up and be hanged! Surely it were better to slay himself with his own hands than do that! But the love of life is strong. Though he were dead, she would not come to life again; the only thing that seemed to offer any interest or hope was that some day he might be able to serve little Mistress Audry, Aline's playmate, Aline's friend, all that was left to represent the sweet child.

So he rose and ate a few mouthfuls, by way of breakfast, and mounted his horse, intending to make his way to London. But the agony of his remorse would hardly allow him to sit his steed and, as he looked at the bright sunshine, he shuddered and cursed it in his heart.

CHAPTER IX
THE JUDGMENT

WHILE Andrew was starting over the hills in the darkness, the family had gathered in the hall. Master Mowbray had seen that the drawbridge was raised and that everything was safe for the night. Audry soon wondered what had become of Aline and after a time made an excuse to get away and went up to their room and down to the secret chamber. "Is not Aline here?" she queried.

"No," said Ian, "she has not been down for a long time."

Ian came towards Audry as she spoke. "Why? cannot you find her?" he said.

"No, she is not in the hall and not in our room."

"Perhaps old Elspeth knows."

"I had forgotten her for the moment," and Audry's face brightened up. "I will run and find her." This she did at once but Aline had not been seen.

At length Audry felt that she must tell the others. So she came back to the great hall and told Master Mowbray that Aline had disappeared.

"'Sdeath," he exclaimed, "what has happened to her; call the men at once, run, Audry."

"Oddsfish man," said Mistress Mowbray, "one would think the child was an infant that could not take care of itself,—making such a fuss as that! And I do not see that it would be so very great a matter if she were lost. Why, you make as much a to-do about her as though she were your own daughter. The hussie is up to mischief and she will see that she does herself no harm."

Master Mowbray did not wait for all this, but left his wife talking to the empty air. The first thing was to rouse all the servants and every room inside was speedily examined, but with no result. "She must have gone out before the gate was shut," suggested Audry, "but that is a very unusual thing. She might have gone to speak with one of the servants and crossed the bridge just before it was closed. But even if she had walked a little way and not heard them close the gate, she would have rung the great bell. Surely she would not be too frightened."

To be out after the drawbridge was raised was a very serious fault as every one in the Hall knew full well, and many a servant had rather run the risk of staying out all night than incur the wrath and penalties that would follow such an offence.

"I hope the child has not come back and walked into the moat," said Master Mowbray. "It is a terribly dark night. Come this way," he added in a husky voice. In his rough way he was fonder of her than he would have admitted even to himself, and her spell was increasing its hold upon him.

They went to the gate and the drawbridge was instantly lowered. They then crossed the bridge and divided into two parties, taking their lanthorns to the right and left.

Audry accompanied her father to the left and they had not gone ten paces before they came upon Aline's little form lying in a broken piece of the moat-wall, half in and half out of the water. It was easy to get down to the water in many places on the outer side although impossible on the inner side. Master Mowbray stepped down and picked up the slight figure and carried it into the hall.

She had apparently been dead for some time, and Audry broke into uncontrollable weeping; her whole frame shook violently and it almost seemed that she would choke herself. Every one stood aghast. Even Mistress Mowbray felt something of the atmosphere of grief; she was the only one sufficiently unmoved to speak at all, but she said, "Poor little lassie, that was a hard ending. But, Audry dear, you must try and control yourself, you will make yourself seriously ill."

"I do not mind if I do," the child sobbed in reply. "Oh, Aline, darling Aline, do not leave me, I cannot bear it," and she flung herself on to the small still form on the old oak settle and they feared her heart would break.

By this time every one was weeping, even the men-servants and Mistress Mowbray herself.

But as Audry passionately pressed the cold wet features to her face, she suddenly cried out, "She is not dead. I am sure she is not dead, I am sure that she still breathes."

There was a fire in the hall, as the summer was getting on and the evenings were chilly up in the moorland district. In less time than it takes to say, a bed had been made up by the fire and warmed with a warming pan, and old Elspeth had tenderly undressed the child and put her in the bed, while some one else had brought some warm milk. Elspeth was bending over her and lightly rubbing the damp hair, half crooning to herself, "My bairnie, my bonnie bairnie, wake up, my sweetest, wake up once more." Suddenly Aline opened her eyes and looked round for a moment, and then closed them again. She gave no more sign that night and it was an anxious time; but hope was strong. Hardly any one went to bed but Mistress Mowbray. Even the servants for the most part wandered about, coming every now and then to ask if there was any news. The child was a favourite with nearly all of them, as much on account of her gentle thoughtful ways as on account of her extreme almost supernatural beauty. Then there was that strange mysterious power that seemed to hold practically every one with whom she came into contact. There were, of course, one or two who felt her very presence was a sort of standing reproach and who disliked her accordingly, but such was the extraordinary sweetness of her disposition that some, even in this class, found themselves coaxed to a certain extent out of their worse into their better selves against their will.

In the morning it was apparent that immediate danger was passed, which caused Mistress Mowbray to exclaim,—"Drat the bairn for frightening us all like that without any reason. How stupid of her to fall into the moat."

As soon as Aline was able to talk she had to explain how it happened. They had gently moved her to another room and Audry and Master Mowbray were seated at the bedside. She had told them of what she had seen119 and how Andrew had thrown her into the water. "As I fell," she went on, "I felt my head strike violently against something. I luckily did not become unconscious at once, but was able to scramble through the water to the bank. I remember trying to get into a sort of hole in the wall, and then I remember no more till this morning."

"But can you swim?" said Master Mowbray in blank astonishment, as it was not considered a little girl's accomplishment.

"A little bit," said Aline, not too anxious to draw attention to her powers in this direction; as after the River Tees incident she felt it might be better if they did not know what she was capable of doing.

"I am afraid, sire, that the man is likely to be the same that took your silver cup and other things," she said, "but I am glad that I have not had my wetting for nothing, and that you will be able to stop any more corn being taken."

Master Mowbray stooped and kissed her. He did not often kiss the children, not even Audry, as his was not a demonstrative nature. "Poor sweet soul," he said, "how can I repay you for what you have done?"

"Let us go into the library again," said Aline at once.

"Of course, of course," he said hastily; "however, we must do something better than that; but for the present I must see about those scoundrels, Andrew Woolridge and Thomas Carluke."

When Thomas heard what had happened on his arrival in the morning he cursed the fates, saying to himself, "Why was Andrew such a fool as not to go and get a long rod and feel all around that moat-side. She120 could never have got out on the inner side. But who would have known that the skelpie could swim?" and he bit his lips in indignation. "I wonder if they will suspect me? No, Andrew is gone. I shall be safe; but curse her, curse her a thousand times."

Andrew had not even dared to go to his own house but had slipped away over the hills at once; consequently, when they sent down there, nothing was known of him. News, however, soon leaked out of what had happened and soon the whole country-side was on his track, with the consequence that, before three days were spent, he was safely lodged in what was known as the lower tower-room, in the old pele-tower on the west side of the Hall.

Master Mowbray was determined to send him to York to stand his trial as soon as possible, but to his great surprise he met with opposition from a very unexpected quarter. He went and told Aline the next morning after the successful capture and added that his intention was to send Andrew to York on the following day but one, expecting that the news would give her satisfaction.

Aline did not seem particularly pleased; but Audry, who was there, said, "Oh, I am glad they have caught him; I hope he will soon be hanged."

Aline looked up rather puzzled. "Isn't that rather blood-thirsty?"

"Oh, no! Aline, dear Aline, if he had succeeded! Oh!" and Audry nearly wept at the bare thought.

"I don't know. I am not sure that people should be hanged."

"Of course they should be hanged," said Master Richard.

Aline felt a certain spirit of opposition arising.[121] "Certainly," she thought, "hanging does not seem to be a particularly helpful road to repentance." Her head ached and she could not think very clearly; but of a surety if once she let the man be hanged it would be too late to do anything.

The others watched her silently for a few moments and then to Master Mowbray's amazement Aline begged with tears in her eyes that he would let Andrew off if he would confess all that he had taken and restore it as far as possible, and promise to make all the amends that lay in his power. Master Mowbray at first absolutely refused; but, at last, to humour the child, promised that he would reconsider the question on the following day if she were better.

Aline was stronger and brighter the next day and when Richard Mowbray came in to see her she renewed her request,—"You said, sire, yesterday," she began, "that you would like to do something better for me than just let Audry and me use the library again, so I want, please, to make this my request,—that you will not punish Andrew and Thomas if they show that they are really sorry."

"Of course, if you put it that way, child, I shall have to do what you ask, as far as is possible." He sat for a few moments without speaking, and then added,—"I have examined into the matter and find that Thomas did not actually steal anything himself, nor did he get anything out of it; but he seems to be a poor cowardly sort of fellow whom Andrew used as a tool. I might let him stay on in the house if you greatly wish it, but I really cannot, even if we pardon Andrew, have him any longer at the Hall. I think that the man is too violent to be[122] trusted. He does not really belong to this neighbourhood at all and it might be possible to send him back to Carlisle whence he came. That is about all that I can suggest. There is a cousin of mine near there who might keep an eye on him, and if he gives sign of trouble this could still be kept hanging over him. But do you really wish it? Do you understand, child, what you are doing?"

"Yes, I really would like it," she said.

"Then I shall go and speak to the men," said Mowbray, and departed.

After half an hour he came back again. "Would you mind seeing them?" he said. "I think it would be good for them. I have told them what you asked and at first they hardly seemed to believe it. Andrew scarcely said anything, though Thomas was profuse in his gratitude."

"I will see them if you wish it, but it is not easy."

He looked at the sad little figure and his heart smote him and yet somehow he felt that it was the right thing to do, so he went down again and brought up the men.

Aline was propped up on pillows; she looked very weak, but the wonderful pearly, almost translucent, complexion that distinguished her had for the moment recovered its usual brilliancy. Andrew was led in with his hands tied behind his back; he looked sullen and sheepish, whereas Aline had seldom looked more queenly in spite of her condition. Thomas was not bound and looked singularly at ease.

"You have both of you behaved most disgracefully," Master Mowbray said in a judicial tone; "you have meanly taken advantage of the house that had provided123 you with your livelihood and one of you has committed a crime so vile that it is not for me to find words in which to express my abhorrence. If I were doing what my real judgment tells me I should do, you, Thomas, for your part, would spend a long time in York Gaol, and as for you," he continued, turning to Andrew, "the world would soon be rid of you altogether. However, Mistress Aline has asked me to give you both another chance, as you know; but I wanted you first to see the result of your sin and to give you an opportunity of thanking her for what you do not deserve; so I have brought you here. Aline, child, tell them what you want them to do."

It was a very difficult task for the small invalid, and Master Mowbray did not at all realise what he was demanding from the sensitive highly strung little maiden. But she nerved herself for the task and tried to forget herself and everything but the men before her.

"Oh, please, Andrew," she said, "I only want to tell you that I am feeling much better. I shall be all right in a day or two, and Master Mowbray says that you are to go to Carlisle, where you used to live. My father once took me to Carlisle when I was a very little girl and it is a fine town, much bigger than Appleby. You should easily find work there and you will not forget, will you, to send Master Mowbray something every month to replace the things that have gone? Master Mowbray's cousin will let us know how you are getting on, and please, sire," she continued, turning to Richard Mowbray himself and then looking at Andrew's bonds but not mentioning them, "I want to shake hands with Andrew and hope that he will be happy."

124

The Master of Holwick looked at her rather amazed and then untied the rope. "You will promise to repay what you have stolen," he said.

"Yes," mumbled Andrew sulkily.

"Now say how grateful you are to her and how sorry you are for what you have done."

"Thank you, I'm sorry."

Aline held out her beautiful little hand and smiled sweetly at him. Andrew stiffly responded and then let his arm fall to his side. This was all entirely beyond his comprehension; why she did not wish him hanged he utterly failed to grasp. What was the use of having one's enemy in one's hands if one did not crush him? "Certainly," he thought, "there were some foolish people who were generally called good, who did not behave in that way, and who preached to one about one's sins, but this child said nothing about his sins and was simply beyond calculation altogether."

She turned to Thomas with the same frank smile to take his hand, "So you are going to stay with us, Thomas; I wonder whether you would be kind enough to help Mistress Audry to look after my falcon while I am ill."

"Oh, yes, indeed, Mistress Aline," he replied, "I shall never forget your kindness to me. May the Mother of God bless you for what you have done. We are all of us sinners and may God have mercy upon me." He kneeled as he spoke and pressed her hand to his lips and added, "You may be sure that I shall always be ready to serve you to my dying day. It will be my lasting honour to carry out your least wish."

Thomas congratulated himself on having escaped so easily, and as they were dismissed and were crossing the courtyard he said to Andrew,—"She is a soft one and no mistake." Andrew did not reply; he had not recovered his senses. She must be a fool, he thought, and yet she made him look a pretty fool, too; he was not sure for the moment that he did not hate her more than ever. But, as he came to think it over in after years, the scene would rise before his eyes, and he would see that fascinating delicate face with pain written all over it, and hear the musical voice pleading,—"You will not forget, will you?"

CHAPTER X
THE PACKMAN'S VISIT

WHEN the men had gone Aline lay thinking, dreaming, building castles in the air. What a narrow escape she had had! Life seemed full of troubles and dangers. Here was she whose life had been a series of misfortunes and now she had only just escaped death, and there was Ian, whose escape had been as close as her own and who was still in uncertainty and peril. He not only had misfortunes but was in danger all the time. "It must be terrible to live in perpetual anxiety," she thought. "What a pity Ian is a heretic," she mused; "it means that he is never safe anywhere and it hinders his chances. He is obviously very clever in spite of his humble station. Only think,—if he had not been a heretic he might have become a prince of the church; after all the great Cardinal Wolsey was only the son of a butcher and Ian is better than that. I think his people had a little bit of land. Why, some of these yeomen round here are almost like gentlemen. Ah! but if he had been on the road to a cardinal, I should never have seen him and so I should not be interested in him at all.

"Now I wonder,—but I suppose he could hardly be as clever as all that; but why should he not become a[127] great doctor in a university?" and Aline drew herself a vivid picture of Ian as a sort of Abelard gathering thousands of students round him wherever he went. But the picture was spoiled when again she remembered that his heresy would stand in the way. "How cruel they were to Abelard," she said, "but marry, they are worse now, and that was cruel enough."

Then her thoughts turned from Abelard to the heart-rending picture of Heloise and her love for him. "She was clever, too," she thought, "I should like to be clever like that. Why should not a girl be clever? The Lady Jane was clever, as father was always reminding me and then they chopped off her head, alas! So is the Lady Elizabeth's Grace. I dare say the Queen's Grace will have her sister's head cut off, too. I believe the best people always have a sad time. Poor, poor Heloise!"

"I wonder," she reflected, "if I ever could love like that, with absolute entire wholehearted devotion, giving up everything for my love,—my friends, my honour, and even the consolations of religion. And yet I believe that's the right kind of love, not the kind that just lets other people love you. Well, if one can't be clever or love or do anything that is best without suffering, then I think I would choose the suffering. But, oh dear! it is very hard, I wonder if things get easier as one gets older. I am afraid not. Yet fancy having the praise of one's love sung by all the world hundreds of years after one was dead! That must have been a love indeed. Ah, Heloise, I should like to love like you when I grow older. Yes, I would rather be Heloise with all her sorrow than the grand ladies who marry[128] for wealth or position or passing affection and do not know really what love is at all.

"Yes, and I think I should prefer to marry some one very clever, some one who really in himself was superior to other men, a man with something that couldn't be taken away like riches or titles or outer trappings of any kind. Yes, my knight must be clever as well as brave. I should like some one like father. But I think I should like him to be great and wealthy, too, although these other things are best. It would be rather nice to be allowed to wear cloth of silver and gold chains,[12] but I suppose that is very silly. I wish father were alive now to help me. I should like to be clever myself, too, and there is no one here who can give me aid. Master Richard does not care about these things; I wonder if Ian would be any good. It's marvellous what he has picked up. I wonder if he knows Latin. But that isn't likely. I shall ask him next time I see him, but I suppose I really ought to try and sleep now."

12 The sumptuary laws very strictly regulated what people were allowed to wear according to their rank.

So she fell asleep and dreamed; and dreamed that she was dressed in velvet and cloth of silver and a gold chain; and a knight in shining armour was kneeling at her feet and calling her his most learned lady.

Aline did not get well very quickly. It was not many days before she was able to get up, but she was much shaken and easily tired, so that she was hardly able to do more than walk a little bit about the house. She was quite unequal to going upstairs and although at her particular request she had gone back to her own room, Richard Mowbray himself used to carry her up when it came to bed time. Sometimes he would even carry her out on to the moors, and altogether he paid her more attention than he had been wont to do. This made his wife more jealous than ever and, although at the time it prevented her from ill-treating the child, it only made matters worse afterwards.

One afternoon when she had somewhat gained strength, he carried her out across the court and up the nine steps on to the library terrace. "I am going to take you into the library," he said as he set her down, while he opened the door. Aline was pleased, as it was now some weeks since she had entered the room.

He seated her in the glorious oriel window at the end, with its beautiful tracery and fine glass, and put her feet up on the window seat. The lower part of the window was open and revealed a wonderful view of the rolling purple moors, while in the foreground was the glassy moat, blue as the heaven above, bright and beautiful, as though nothing untoward had ever happened there.

"It is a nice, quiet retreat this," he said, "but it was more suited to your great-great-grandfather who built it than to me. My father used to spend a great deal of time here as a young man, but latterly he was almost entirely at his other place in Devon as it suited his health. Of course that has gone now; we are living in hard times, although we still hold the old Middleton property, which is our principal estate; Holwick is only a very small place. But he always took an interest in this library and right up to the last he used to send books up here to add to the collection, but his own visits here must have been very rare."

"What was my great-grandmother like, did you ever see her, sire?" said Aline.

"Yes, Aline Gillespie was a very beautiful woman, and exceedingly clever. She was also very gentle and a universal favourite. My great-grandfather, James Mowbray, was almost heartbroken when she married, although he was warmly attached to your great-grandfather, Angus, but it meant that she had to go and live in Scotland. My grandfather was fond of her, too, although he was always a little bit jealous."

"Do you remember her, sire?"

"I saw her now and then and remember that she used to give me presents, one was this well-wrought Italian buckle, which I still wear on my belt. She was very fond of books too, and there was some talk of my great-grandfather having intended to leave her half the books in this library; but he died rather suddenly and I imagine, therefore, that he had not time to carry out his intention."

"I suppose then that she would often sit where I am sitting now. How interesting it is to picture it all."

"Oh, yes, she had a special ambry in the wall, that old James Mowbray had made for her. It is there behind that panel, with the small ornamental lock. I think that the key of it will be about somewhere. The library keys used to be kept in the little drawer in this table at the end."

"I did not know that there was a drawer," said Aline.

"I fancy it is made the way it is on purpose, so as not to be very conspicuous. You cannot call it a secret drawer though. I doubt if that kind of thing was in the old man's line, although he had some strange fancies.131 Yes, here they are," he said, pulling out the drawer. "See, this is the ambry," he went on, opening the cupboard as he spoke. "Would you like it for your own treasures?"

"Very much indeed."

"Then you can have it."

Aline's face lit up with pleasure. "Oh, thank you so much, that is delightful."

"I am not certain what these other keys are for," said Master Mowbray. "This is, I think, the key of that old kist which used to have some papers that were at one time of importance relating to the house. If you like to rummage over old things you may enjoy having a look at them. I think that you are a good girl and that I may trust you, but you must remember always to lock it and put everything back. One of the other keys is, of course, the key of the rods that hold the books and the remaining key I have forgotten. You had better take your own key off the bunch, but keep them all in the drawer as before."

He put the keys in the drawer and came back and sat on the seat opposite her. "I have never heard you read," he said, "and Audry tells me that you are a fine reader. I have almost forgotten how to read myself, so little do I practise it nowadays. Are you tired, child? Would you read me something?"

"Yes, sire, if it would please you," she said.

"You can call me Cousin Richard," he replied. "I remember how my aunt, your great-grandmother, whom you slightly resemble, once read to me in this very room, when I was a boy."

"Oh, what did she read?"

132

"There was one story, a poem about a father who had lost his little daughter, and saw a vision of her in heaven."

"Oh, 'Pearl,' a lovely musical thing with all the words beginning with the same letters. I do not mean all the words; I do not know how to explain it; you know what I mean."

"Then there was another one about a green girdle and a lady that kissed a knight."

"Yes, 'Sir Gawain and the Green Knight'; it is a pretty tale."

"But I think what I liked best of all was Sir Thomas Malory."

"That is what Audry likes best," said Aline; "she thinks that some of the books that I read are too dry, because they are not stories, but I am not sure that I too do not like 'The Morte d'Arthur' best of all."

"Read me something out of that."

She turned to the well known scene of the passing of Arthur. Master Mowbray leaned back against the window-jamb and looked across at her in the opposite corner. The late afternoon sun was warm and golden. She was wearing a little white dress, which took on a rich glow in the mellow light. Over her hair and shoulder played the colours from the glass in the upper part of the window. She knew the story practically by heart and her big eyes looking across at him seemed to grow larger and rounder with wonder and mystery as she told the tale.

Under the spell of the soft witching music of her voice he was transported to that enchanted land, and there he saw the dying king and Sir Bedivere failing to throw the sword into the water:—"But go again lightly, for thy long tarrying putteth me in great jeopardy of my life, for I have taken cold ... for thou wouldest for my rich sword see me dead!" Then followed the passage where Sir Bedivere throws in the sword and the mystic barge comes with the three Queens, and as Richard Mowbray looked over at the little face before him he saw in the one face the beauty of them all. So on the wings of a perfect tale perfectly told he forgot the perplexities and anxieties that encompassed him, and himself floated to the Land of Avilion while he gazed and, like Ian Menstrie, was lured by the same charm and began to wonder whether she were not indeed herself from the land of faëry. "'For I will go to the vale of Avilion,'" he repeated to himself, "'to heal me of my grievous wound.'"

"Yes, this is a healing of the wounds of life," he added. "I never realised before that beauty had such power. Come, child, it is time we went," he said aloud and gently lifted her in his arms; "we must see what the others are doing." So he carried her out on to the terrace that ran in front of the library and down the steps and across the quadrangle to the great Hall. There they found considerable excitement; a packman with five horses had arrived from the south and every one was making purchases who had any money laid by.

"Now that is a fine carpet," he was saying as he unrolled a piece of Flemish work. "It was made at Ispahan for the Shah of Persia and is the best bit of Persian carpet you will ever see. That would look well in my lady's boudoir. I would let you have that for five florins."

He did not seem very pleased at the master's entrance at that moment; Richard Mowbray glanced at it and remarked, "But that is Flemish weaving."

"Did I not say Flemish?" he said. "Oh, it is Flemish right enough; it was made for the Duke of Flanders."

"And if I had said it was Tuscan I suppose it would have been made for the Duke of Tuscany."

"Ah, master, you make mock of me; see, here, I have some buckles of chaste design that might take your fancy or these daggers of Spanish make, or what say you to a ring or a necklace for one of the ladies?"

"We have no moneys for gauds and vanities."

"But beauty will not bide, and when you have the money it may be too late; you would not let it go ungraced. Prithee try these garnets on the Lady of Holwick. They would become her well, or this simple silver chain for the young mistress," looking at Aline for the first time. "By my troth she is a beautiful child," he exclaimed involuntarily.

"Ah well then, my friend, good wine needs no bush."

"Nay, sweets to the sweet, and for fair maids fair things."

"Truly you are a courtier."

"Ay, and have been at court, and those of most courtesy have bought most of my wares."

"Enough, enough, what have you of good household stuff, things that a good housewife must buy though the times be hard. Come, show my lady such things as good linen and good cloth."

"You bring him to the point," said Mistress Mowbray; "yes, sirrah, what have you in the way of linen?"

135

"I have linen of France and linen of Flanders; I have linen fine and linen coarse."

He unrolled several samples as he spoke, and Mistress Mowbray selected some linen of Rennes of fine texture, which she said would do to make garments for Audry and herself. "And your supply of clothes that you brought from Scotland is in need of some plenishing," she said, glancing at Aline. "There will be work for idle hands. Here, this stout dowlas[13] will stand wear well, and be warmer too."

13 A very coarse sort of canvas used for underclothes by the poorest classes in the sixteenth century.

Aline felt the blood rush to her face, but she said nothing. It was not that she thought much about her clothes; indeed she had the natural simple taste of the high born that eschews finery, yet a certain daintiness and delicacy she did desire and had always had, and it was a bitter disappointment, a disappointment made more cruel by the public shame of it.

Walter Margrove, the packman, looked at her; he had not travelled amongst all sorts and conditions for nothing and he took the situation in at a glance.

"Yes, Mistress Mowbray," Aline said at length, "I shall have a great deal to do."

Richard Mowbray had left the hall, but old Elspeth who was standing by said, "I will help you, childie."

Mistress Mowbray scowled at her, and muttered,—"Well, I hope, Aline, that you will work hard," then turning to Margrove she asked to look at other wares. Such opportunities did not often occur in a remote place like Holwick and it was very difficult to do one's purchasing at a distance; so although she only bought things136 of real necessity she laid in a large supply from the packman's stock.

On these occasions the surrounding tenants were allowed to come up to the hall and Walter Margrove, when Mistress Mowbray had departed, started to put his things together to take them into the courtyard. The children stayed behind to watch him for a few moments and as he was leaving the Hall he pressed a small packet into Aline's hand and said in a whisper, "Do not say anything; it is a pleasure, just a small remembrance."

The packet contained the small silver necklace that he had been showing before. It was not of great intrinsic value, but was of singularly chaste design and though exceedingly simple was of much beauty.

Aline was immensely surprised at the unexpected joy, and for the time it quite made up to her for her previous disappointment.

As the packman went into the courtyard a great crowd gathered round him, both chaffering and gossiping. "Who is the beautiful young mistress that has come to Holwick?" he asked.

"Oh, she is a distant cousin of Master Mowbray," said one, "but you have no idea of the things that have been going on since you were last at Holwick."

"What things?"

"Why, the child has been nearly killed," said old Elspeth who had followed the packman out. "Poor wee soul, it makes my old heart bleed to think of it even now."

Elspeth then recounted the tale of all that had taken place.

137

"Then why is Mistress Holwick not more grateful? She seems to have saved her and her good man a pretty penny indeed."

"The woman is crazed with jealousy or envy or what not," said another.

"But the child seems a lovable one to my thinking," said Margrove.

"There has never been a better lassie in Holwick is my way of looking at it." It was Janet Arnside who was speaking; she had come up to see Elspeth, and take the opportunity of buying a few trifles at the same time. "My boy just owes his life to her; she has been down to us times without number, and I have never seen anything like the way that she gets hold of one's heart. I cried the whole day long when I heard of her being hurt like that, and it just makes me rage to hear the things that they tell of Mistress Holwick and the child. It would have been the worst thing that ever happened to Holwick if anything really serious had befallen her that night."

"Ay, ay," said several voices in chorus.

"And why should not the bairn have fine linen, I should like to know?" she went on.

"It is a downright shame," said a man's voice.

"Well, neighbour," said Janet, "I am not the one to interfere in other folk's business, but I am not the only one that the child has blessed, not the only one by a long way."

"No, that you are not, mistress,"—"No, indeed, think of my wife's sickness,"—"Think of my little lass,"—"Ay, and mine,"—"And my old father,"—said one voice after another.

"Can we not do something, neighbours?" said Janet. "Why not speak to Master Richard himself?"

"It is an ill thing to meddle between husband and wife," said Margrove. "By my halidame I have a half mind to speak to the jade myself. She cannot hurt me."

"No, but she can hurt the child more, when you have gone," rejoined Elspeth. "Look here, it is not much, but it is something; let us get the linen ourselves, and it will help Master Margrove, honest man, at the same time. I shall be seeing to the making of the clothes and I can make a tale for the child and prevent her speaking to Mistress Mowbray. The Mistress does not pay that much attention to the little lady's belongings I can tell you. She leaves it all to me, and bless you if she sees any linen garments I shall tell her that they are of those that came from Scotland."

"Ay, ay, agreed, agreed," they all shouted. "Give us the very best linen you have, master, and some of your finest lace and we will clothe her like a princess under her kirtle."

"I' faith, you are the right sort, but it is no profit I will be making on this business; no, you shall have the things at the price I paid for them and not a groat more, no, not even for carriage and I will give her some pieces of lace myself. See here are some fine pieces of Italian work. This is a beautiful little piece of punto in aria and this is a fine piece of merletti a piombini: But stay; she shall have too a finer piece still, something like the second one; it is Flemish, dentelles au fuseau, from Malines"; he drew it forth as he spoke and fingered it lovingly amid marked expressions of admiration from Elspeth and the other woman.

"It's nothing to some beans that I shall give her," interposed[139] Silas, the irrepressible farm-reeve. "They are French, you know, from Paris," imitating Walter's manner.

"Be quiet"; "stop your nonsense," they all shouted.

"I am not quite sure," he went on dreamily and quite unperturbed, "whether I shall thread them on a string to wear on her bosom, or cook them for her to wear inside; but certainly she shall have them for nothing; not a groat will I take. I should scorn to ask the price they cost me."

Jock, the stableman, stepped forward and struck out playfully at Silas. "He always carries on like that," he said; but Silas dodged aside and put out his leg so that Jock stumbled and collapsed in confusion into Walter's arms.

"A judgment on the stableman for insulting the reeve," said Silas, marching off with mock solemnity.

As he reached the gate he turned back. "No offence, Walter; put me down for ten florins for our bonnie little mistress. I'll bring it anon."

The others gasped at the largeness of the sum as the good-natured face of the reeve disappeared through the archway.

Soon after, the crowd thinned away and Walter was packing up his things, when Aline happened to come to the hall door. He saw her and went quickly to her and before she could thank him for his present of the necklace he said, "If at any time there is anything that you would like me to do out in the wide world, a message for instance, remember that I am always ready to help you."

"I do not think that there is anything just now," she said.

"Then God be with you,"—and he was gone.

[140]
CHAPTER XI
SWORDS AND QUESTIONINGS

ALINE had rather overtaxed her strength and had a slight set-back, so that it was some time before she was strong enough to climb down the stairs and visit Ian again. He was feeling very dejected that day. His collar bone and his ankle had healed; but although in some ways better, he was beginning to feel the want of fresh air and it told not only upon his health but his spirits. He was also desperately anxious to get on to Carlisle where it was arranged that he should hand over the papers to Johnne Erskyne of Doun, but he was by no means fit to travel on his dangerous errand. The worrying, however, made him worse and what he felt he required was some gentle exercise to get up his strength.

Altogether it was with keener pleasure even than usual that he saw Aline come. "Oh, I am so glad to see you," he said; "Audry has been telling me the dreadful things that have happened, but I want you to tell me something yourself. Sit down and make yourself as comfortable as you can."

"But I am not an invalid now," said Aline, "and do not need special comfort. How are you; are you not tired of being shut up here?"

"Yes, indeed, and you too will be wanting some fresh141 air to put you to rights again. Audry says that you did not suffer much pain; is that so? But it must have been a terrible shock; you may well take some time to recover."

"I am getting on marvellously well," said Aline, "and I have been thinking that you might be getting out a little bit. You could sit out near the mouth of the cave if one of us kept watch, and after dark it would even be safe to walk a little."

"Yes, I have been thinking that myself," he replied. "I have been looking round this room to while away the time and have found some interesting things. I wonder, by the way, what is in that old iron chest there. It does not seem to have any lock, which is most strange."

"Yes, we must find that out," said Aline, "but really so many things have happened and there has been so much to do that we have not had time to think about it."

"Well, amongst other things I have found some rapiers," he said, "and have been practising thrusts and parries, by way of getting a little exercise, but one cannot do much by oneself. Two men imprisoned in this place might keep themselves in fair condition, although it is rather short of air for such activity; however, that cannot be."

"Oh, let me see the rapiers," said Aline. "Ah, here they are,—and helmets and leather jerkins and gloves. I am going to dress up," she added, laughing.

"There now, what do I look like? You must dress up too; I want to see how they suit you."

Ian put on a helmet and the other things while Aline executed a graceful little dance round the room. When he had finished she said roguishly, "Do you know anything142 about fencing? I have seen people fence. They stand something like this," putting her right foot rather too far forward and turning it outward and not bending the knee sufficiently. "Shall I teach you?"

"No, but I might teach you," said Ian, quite innocently.

"Well, but do you know anything about it?" and Aline smiled mischievously.

"I ought to do; when I was a wanderer in Italy I learned a great deal that is entirely unknown here."

"Stand on guard then, and show me something." As he moved, she appeared to copy his attitude. "Engage," and mechanically from long use he brought down his sword. In a flash she disengaged and cut over. He parried; she made a remise, and was in upon him with a hit over the heart.

Aline burst out laughing while Ian was thunder-struck. She took off her helmet saying, "We must not have any more to-day as I am not well enough, but we shall have some fine times later on. It was rather a shame though, but I could not help it, it was such fun. I was a little afraid that you would be too taken aback to parry at all, and that would have been very dull. I hope you are a good fencer really; there was said to be no one in Scotland who could come anywhere near my father."

"Oh, that is how you come to know so much about it," said Ian, sitting down. Even the slight effort had been too much.

"Yes, my father taught me and told me that I was getting on very well, but I have had no practice since I came to Holwick some eight months ago. Things are much harder than they used to be. Father used to give me much of his time. You see he had no boys and so he always said that he would like me to know the things that boys know. And yet I do not know that I am altogether fond of them. But I have always loved swimming, and fencing is delightful. Somehow I never cared particularly about riding, but I have come to like it in the last week or two, since I have started again. It takes me away from the Hall and that is a great thing."

"I always loved riding," said Ian. "There is nothing like a good horse at a canter and the wind rushing over one's face."

"Yes, I do not know why it was. Of course we never had good horses after I was eight years old."

"Why do you want to get away from the Hall?"

Aline did not speak at first; then she said, "Well, you see it makes a change."

"Is it Mistress Mowbray that is the real cause? Come, little one, tell me truthfully, doesn't she treat you well?"

"There is always a great deal to do, cleaning and mending and, when there is nothing else, there is always spinning and carding."

"Well, I suppose that we must all of us do our share of work."

Aline could not keep back the tears, which welled into her eyes and made them glisten. "Yes, it is not really the work, I should not mind the work. Indeed I am used to very hard work indeed; because, before the end, I used to have to do almost everything at home."

"What does she do to you, child? Has she been losing her temper again? Come, tell me."

"I do not like to say, but she does all kinds of things."

"Well, never mind if you do not want to tell me."

"No, I do not mind telling you; it is that I am not sure how far I should say anything to any one at all. But you will never see her and it does relieve one's feelings to be able to speak to any one."

"Then come and sit by me and tell me all about it."

Aline came and sat by him on the old settee. "You see it is not exactly because she hits me that I mind, although I have never been hit by any one before; but she is always doing little petty things that in some ways are harder to bear than being knocked about;—for instance, when we sit down to breakfast there are always two pitchers of milk, which we have with our porridge. They are neither of them quite full, and she takes one of them and pours out some for herself and Cousin Richard, then she looks into it to see what is left and generally pours most of it into the other pitcher. After that she hands the full one to Audry and the one with only a little drop in the bottom to me."

"Does Audry know?"

"Of course not,—dear Audry,—I am sure if it would benefit Audry I would go without milk altogether. I would not have her know for worlds; she would quarrel with her mother over it."

"What else does she do?" Ian asked.

Aline then told the story of the packman. She did not yet know what had been done by Elspeth and the others about the linen, but she pulled up the necklace which she was wearing under her dress and shewed it to Ian. "Now is that not pretty? I have always wanted a necklace and father had promised only a little while before he died that as soon as he could afford it he would get me one; so I try to think of it as if it was father's present."

The tears again gathered in the beautiful eyes and this time one rolled over on to her cheek. She brushed it away hastily; but Ian drew her gently towards him and kissed her for the first time. "Sweet little maiden," he said, "I hope that God will be good to you after what you have been through in your young life."

"I do not like the priest here," she continued; "of course I like Father Laurence, but Middleton is too far away and when I went to confession the other day I said something to Father Ambrose about father, but he was not a bit kind and sympathetic like our dear old priest at home. I always keep a candle burning for father; that is what I mainly spend my money on, and I wanted him to tell me how long he thought it would be before my father's soul would get to heaven; do you think it will be very long, and will my candles help him? Somehow I do not see why God should make any difference because of our candles; suppose my father had had no little girl to burn candles; or suppose that I had had no money, that would have been worse still."

"These things are very difficult, sweet child, but I am sure that the love of your little heart that happens to show itself in buying the candles must meet with its own reward, whether candles themselves are necessary or not. But I am afraid that I cannot be of much use to you, little one, because I am no longer of the old faith."

"Tell me something about that then. Father said that he would tell me when I got older."

"I do not want to unsettle you," Ian said; "but of one146 thing I feel sure,—that God would never deal harshly with a child that believed what it had been taught. When we get older it is different, just as it is in the other responsibilities of life. That is largely why we are put here in this world,—to learn to think for ourselves and take up responsibilities: things are not made too easy for us, or we should not have the high honour that God has given us of largely building our own characters,—of making ourselves."

Aline sat quiet and thoughtful for some time. "Master Menstrie," she said at length, "I am not so very young now and I think that I should like to begin to know something about these things."

"You have not read the Bible, I suppose," said Ian.

"No, it is wicked to read the Bible."

"Why?"

"The priests say so."

"But how do you know that they are right? After all, what is the Bible? It is the word of God, and although even the Bible was written by human beings, it is largely the words of our Lord himself and the writings of people who actually knew him or lived in that very time."

Ian talked to her for some time, and then Aline said that she would like to read the Bible.

"There is no reason why you should not," he said, "but you must remember that you are undertaking a great responsibility, and that though it may bring great joy and comfort, it will be the beginning of sorrow too, and you are very young," he added, looking at her wistfully. "I have a little English translation of the New Testament," he went on after a pause, "which I can[147] lend you, but Audry was telling me the other day that you could read Greek."

"Oh, only easy Greek," said Aline. "I have read some of Aesop and that is quite easy, but father and I used to read Homer together and that was delightful although more difficult."

"Did you read much? What did you like best?"

"Oh, yes, I read a great deal; at least it was really father reading, at any rate at first. I did not do much more than follow, but I got so used to it at last that I could read it without great difficulty. There was so much that I liked that I could not say what I liked best, but there was little that was more delightful than the story of Nausikaa. I shall never forget her parting with Odysseus.

"Father told me that the Lady Jane Grey read and enjoyed Plato and Demosthenes, when she was about the age I am now, besides knowing French and Italian thoroughly. I have read a little Plato and have tried Demosthenes, but I did not care about him so much."

"I love Plato," said Ian. "After the Bible there is nothing so helpful in the world. You seem to have done very well, little maid; but can you read Latin?"

"That is amusing," she said, "because I was going to ask you if you could read Latin. Now I shall want to know if you can read Greek or if you read in Latin translations. Oh, yes," she went on, "I can read Latin quite easily. I dare say there is some Latin that I cannot read, but anything at all ordinary I can manage. Yet I do not like Latin as well as Greek, and the things that are written in Latin are not half as interesting."

"I quite agree with you. I learned Latin as a boy,[148] but when I was in Venice working on some great iron hinges, my employer, who was a great scholar, took an interest in me and he enabled me to get a fair knowledge of Greek. I have steadily practised it since and can now read anything, except some of the choruses and things like that, without difficulty. However, if you can read Latin, there is no need for you to read an English translation at all, and it is much safer; as the priests do not mind any one, who can read Latin, reading the Bible nearly so much as those who cannot. I expect that there will be a copy of the Vulgate in the library; although it is very unlikely that there will be anything in the original Greek; though there might be the Septuagint."

"What is the Vulgate then?"

"Oh, a translation of the Bible into Latin. It is really a revised edition of the 'Old Latin' translation, made in the time of Pope Damasus and after, largely by St. Jerome in the fourth century."

"I shall go and have a look as soon as I can."

Ian sat and looked at her without speaking. She certainly was a most unusual child, but he was by no means anxious to trouble her mind with disturbing perplexities. There is a good deal to be said even for the priests, he reflected; responsibility may be too crushing altogether.

"Well, I have to go and do some spinning and Mistress Mowbray will be wondering where I am; but you will give me lessons in Greek, will you not?"

"Certainly, we will start next time you come to see me. See if you can find some Greek books in the library. Good-bye."

Aline departed and sat at the wheel till supper and then went up with Audry to their room.

149

What was her surprise as she looked at her bed to see it covered with neatly folded little piles of beautiful linen.

Child as she was she knew at once that both the linen and lace upon it were of exceptional quality.

"O Audry dear! what is all this?" she exclaimed.

"Well, you will never guess, will she, Elspeth?" said Audry, turning to the old nurse who had stolen in to see how the gift would be received.

"Nobody could bear that you should wear dowlas, hinnie," said the old dame, "and so practically every one in the neighbourhood has had a hand in what you see there. Janet Arnside made this camise, and Martha, the laundry-maid, made that nightrobe. Joseph, the stableman, and Silas bought the bit of lace on this. Edward bought this larger piece of punto in aria here. I made these with the tela tirata work with my own hands and I do hope you will like them."

"Indeed I do," said Aline, bewildered as much by the demonstration of widespread affection as by the altogether unexpected acquisition. "Elspeth, you are a dear, and, oh, it is good of them, but what will Mistress Mowbray say?"

"Mistress Mowbray is not to know, that's what they all said; if she did, marry, she would say that we were all doited, and you would not let her think that, would you, dearie?" said the old woman slyly. "You will be careful not to get us into trouble, for we meant it kindly."

Aline was quite overcome and they went through every piece and learnt its history.

"I cannot help liking nice things," said Aline.

150

"And why should you not?" exclaimed the old woman; "it is only vulgar when you put dress before other things or think about it every day. Old Mistress Mowbray,—your grandmother, my dear," turning to Audry, "used often to say that it was the mark of a lady to dress well but simply and not to think much about it."

"I should much prefer simple clothes except for great occasions," said Aline, "if only for the sake of making the great occasion more special; but even then I like the rich broad effects that father used to talk about with long lines and big masses and full drapery rather than elaborate things. Some of these newer styles I do not like at all."

"Yes, I agree with you," Audry chimed in, "but I should like to wear velvet other than black, and I have always longed to have some ermine."

"Well, unless they alter the laws of the land for your benefit, childie, you will have to marry a baron; but you should be thankful for what you have got. I should soon be tried in the court[14] if I started wearing black velvet," said Elspeth.

14 The sumptuary laws regulated what each rank was allowed to wear.

"Does your ambition soar to diamonds and pearls, Audry?" asked Aline, laughing.

"No, I will leave them to the princesses and duchesses. But look here, Aline," said Audry, with an air of triumph, picking up a particularly beautiful smock, "I bought all the material with my own money and made it every bit myself, and Elspeth says I have done it very well."

151

"You darling," said Aline, and kissed her cousin again and again. "Oh, I do feel so happy."

"But you have not finished," said Audry, "and here's a parcel you have not undone."

Aline picked it up and turned it over. On it was written:—"From Mistress Mowbray."

"A parcel from Mistress Mowbray; how strange!" and the little smooth white brow became slightly wrinkled.

Inside she found a note and a second wrapping. The note ran as follows,—

To Aline Gillespie,

Finding that others are concerned about your garments I have made it my duty to let you have something really appropriate to your condition at Holwick and that will express the feelings with which I shall always regard you. I trust you will think of me when you wear the necklace, although the contents of the pendant are another's gift.
Eleanor Mowbray.
X Her mark.

"How does she regard me and what is appropriate to my condition?" queried Aline as she undid the second wrapper.

To her astonishment and amusement it contained an old potato-sack made into the shape of a camise. After what Mistress Mowbray had said about the coarse dowlas, Aline was half inclined to believe the gift was genuine. But, as she smiled, there fell out a red necklace made of small pieces of carrot with an enormous potato as a pendant.

"Now, whoever has done this?" she cried, breaking into a merry peal and looking at Audry and Elspeth.

They both shook their heads.

She examined the potato and found that it had been scooped out and held a packet very tightly rolled up, within which was a piece of Walter's choicest lace. On the packet was written, "To Somebody from Somebody's enemy."

"From whose enemy?"—said Aline,—"Mine?"

"'Who chased whom round the walls of what?'" Audry observed. "I expect the two somebodies are not the same."

"Well, but whom is it from?"

At this moment Aline caught sight of the upper part of a head trying to peep round the door. It vanished instantly.

She paused for a moment and then gave chase down the newel-stairs. Round and round and round lightly flashed the little feet and she could hear great heavy footsteps at much longer intervals going down, apparently three steps at a time, some way below her.

She reached the bottom just in time to see the figure of Silas dash into the screens; but he vanished altogether before she had time to catch him and thank him for what was obviously his gift.

The next day after dinner Aline ran out gaily across the quadrangle, lightly reached the eighth step in two bounds, covering the remaining step and the terrace in two more, and was in the library ready to prosecute her search. She had a long hunt for the Latin Bible in which after much diligence she was successful.

She then thought that she would try the key of the old chest and on opening it found it half full of ancient parchments concerning the estate. She discovered that they were quite interesting, but she did not linger looking at them just then. The chest was divided one-third of the way from the front longitudinally up to about half its height and it was possible to put all the parchments into the front half.

83

Aline moved all the papers and then got into the back part of the chest to see what it felt like, before she did anything else. Just as she did so, she heard the library door open and her blood ran cold. In a flash she wondered whether it would be better to get out of the chest or to shut the lid. She decided on the latter, and was just able to shut down the lid quietly when she heard the footsteps that had first gone into the other part of the library turn back in her direction. She had luckily taken the key in her hand with which the chest could be locked on the inside and succeeded in fastening it with hardly any noise.

The steps approached the chest and then a voice said, "I thought Aline was in here;—and what was that noise?"

It was Audry's voice so Aline ventured to laugh.

"Good gracious, what is that?" exclaimed Audry, and after a click the lid of the chest, to her still greater astonishment, lifted itself up. She sprang back and then in her turn broke into laughter, as Aline's head emerged from the chest.

"What a fright you gave me!" said each of the children simultaneously, and then they both laughed again.

"You dear thing, Aline," and Audry flung her arms round her cousin. "Oh, I am glad that it is you, but you must be very careful about that kist; I do not think that we had better use it unless one of us is on guard. How did you find the key?"

"Cousin Richard gave it me; I forgot to tell you, but he does not know anything about the secret room as, oddly enough, he happened to say, when speaking of secret drawers, that he did not think that old James Mowbray had any fancies of that kind."

"He would have found that he had rather elaborate fancies of that kind if he knew what we know, would he not, you little wonder-girl;—what adventures you do have;—whatever will you drag me into next?"

"Anyhow I never had adventures till I met you, so perhaps it is due to you."

"Oh, no, you, not I, are the wonder-girl right enough; you have great adventures by yourself."

"Let us come down and see Ian," said Aline.

"All right; you go down this way," Audry replied. "I want to know how it acts; I'll wait to see you safe down and then I will go round the other way."

"No, you would like to try the new way; I will go round."

"Thank you, very well."

A few minutes later the children met again in the secret room, and Audry explained how simple and convenient the new way was.

Aline then produced the Bible and after a little talk she read several chapters, translating as she went.

It was a new world to the children and Ian watched their faces eagerly as she read.

Audry, in her impulsive way, was taken with the simplicity of the story. Aline, who was an unusually thoughtful child, was surprised, but reserved her opinion.

It was the beginning of many such readings. At first Ian said nothing; but, when they had finished reading two of the gospels and began to ask questions, he talked with them and explained many difficulties. What amazed Aline was the entire absence of any allusion to any of the ceremonial that had seemed to her young mind to form so large a part of religion. Also the simplicity of the appeal, to come directly to the divine without any intermediary, attracted her greatly in a way that perhaps it would not have done when the old parish priest of her earlier days was a really beloved friend.

Ian was disturbed in mind; he saw that the children were gradually but surely being influenced and that the old faith would never be the same again. But it must mean trouble and affliction; the district where they were was staunchly Catholic, and the measures that Mary's advisers were taking were stern and cruel. That little face with its associations of bygone years, and its own magical attractive power that seemed to hold all but a few of every one with whom Aline came into contact! How could he bring lines of pain there? And yet how could he withhold what meant so much to himself, this which seemed to be a new and living light? Then that awful vision of George Wishart rose up again before him and with a vivid intensity he thought he saw the form of little Aline standing by him in the heart of the flames. There was too that awful prophecy of the horrible old woman about Aline's path being through the fire. Surely there could be nothing in it? The perspiration stood on Ian's brow: he caught his breath. Slowly the vision cleared away and there were the children seated before him. What if things, however, should come to this! His very soul was in agony torn this way and that.

CHAPTER XII
"MOLL O' THE GRAVES"

HOLWICK generally pursued the even tenour of its way from year's end to year's end, with nothing more eventful than a birth, a death or a marriage. Aline's adventure therefore, was likely to remain a staple topic of conversation for many years. But now there was a strange feeling in the air as though something further were going to happen. An atmosphere of uneasiness enveloped the place, an atmosphere oppressive like a day before a thunderstorm. It was nothing definite, nothing explicable, but every one seemed conscious of it; it pervaded Holwick, it pervaded Newbiggin on the other side of the river. Ian and the children were particularly aware of it. The placid life of the Tees Valley was to be stirred by things at least as striking as Andrew's villainy.

It might have been old Moll's ravings, it might have been the stirrings of religious troubles that had started the apprehension; but there it was, something not immediate but delayed, a presentiment too vague even to be discussed.

One day Thomas Woolridge was walking down from the Hall through the rocky ravine under Holwick Crags. It was a dull grey day with a strong wind, and the rocks seemed to tower up with an oppressive austerity out of all proportion to their size. He was157 in a gloomy frame of mind and kicked at the stones in his path, sullenly watching them leap and bound down the hill.

"Steadily there, neighbour," said a voice from below, "do you want to kill some one?" and the head of Silas Morgan, the farm-reeve, appeared above the rocks beneath.

"Methinks I should not mind an I did," answered Thomas, "provided it were one of the right sort. I am tired of slaving away under other folks' orders. Who are they that they should have a better time than I have, I should like to know?"

"They all have their orders too, man; who do you think you are that you should have it all your own way? There is Master Mowbray, now, who has just set forth to York, because the Sheriff bade him."

"And a fine cursing and swearing there was too, I'll warrant ye," said Thomas. "Master Mowbray doth not mince matters when he starts a-going."

"No, but he doth not pull a face as long as a base-viol. Thomas, if so be that I had a face like yours, I would put my hat on it and walk backwards. Be of good cheer, you rascal, no one doth as he pleaseth from the Queen's grace downwards."

"That may be so, neighbour, but you'll not deny that some have an unfair share of this world's gear."

"No, by my troth, that is so; but I do not see how you are going to set it right. Besides, oddsfish, man! you would never even get as large a share as you do, you lazy varlet, if you got what was meet. I have never seen you do a stroke of work that you could avoid"; and Silas gave Thomas a dig in the ribs.

158

"Here now, sirrah, you let me alone," Thomas said gruffly. "Why should we not all fare alike?"

"All fare alike, old sulky face! Not for me, I thank you. I would not work for a discontented windbag like you. What's your particular grumble just now?"

"I'm not grumbling."

"Not at all, you are saying what a happy life it is, and how glad you are to see your fellow creatures enjoying themselves."

Thomas lifted a stone and threw it, but Silas jumped aside and it flew down the rocks.

"I'm not grumbling so much at the Mowbrays, but at that Gillespie-wench. There have always been Mowbrays up there; but that wench, she has nothing of her own, why should she not addle her bread the same as you or I. One day she had the impertinence to start ordering me about and made old Edward and myself look a pair of fools. The old ass did not mind, but I did and I am not going to forget. I am sick of these craven villagers louting[15] and curtseying at the minx and she no better than any of us. She gets on my nerves, pardy! with her pretty angel face."

15 The earlier form of curtsey.

"Well, I am glad you admit you are grumbling at something, but you have less cause to grumble at Mistress Aline than any one in Holwick, you graceless loon. So here's something else to grumble at"; and Silas gave Thomas a sudden push which made him roll over, and then he ran off laughing.

"You unneighbourly ruffian. I'll pay you out," said Thomas, as he ruefully picked himself up and started down the steep.

He went on to the hamlet and, on his way back, he met Aline, who was going down to see Joan Moulton. Beyond all expectations, by getting Audry to sue for her, Aline had arranged that Joan should be moved to Durham and she was going to pay her last visit.

"It's a fine day, Mistress Aline," observed Thomas as he reached her. "I hope you are keeping well. The falcon is doing splendidly, I notice. I shall never forget your kindness to me. By the way, I found some white heather the other day, and I meant to tell you I took up the root and transplanted it in your garden."

"Oh, was that you, Thomas? You are good; I noticed it at once, but somehow I thought it was Mistress Audry's doings. I love white heather."

"I am fain it pleaseth you; well, good day, Mistress Aline, there is no time to waste and some of us have to work very hard betimes."

On the way up to the Hall, just before he reached the crags of the ravine he saw some one else. It was old "Moll o' the graves."

"How now, neighbour," he said, "I have not seen you for a long time, but what's the good of your hocus pocus? Where's that fine hank of wool I gave you, and those two cheeses and the boll of meal? That Gillespie bitch is still running round; and you said that before a year was away she would be gone. But Andrew's little play didn't work, damn the fellow. She's alive yet, I tell you," and he put his hand on the old woman's shoulder as though to shake her.

"Hands off, you coward," said the old hag. "Why do you not do your own dirty work? Andrew was worth half a dozen of you. Pah, you devil's spawn!160 If you touch me I'll burn your entrails with fire, day and night, and send you shrieking and praying for your own death. But I tell you, that skelpie may not have to die by water. There are other ways of dying than being drowned. I cannot read all the future, but you mark my word, and I have never been wrong yet, she will be gone by the time I named. Little Joan will go as I said; and if we are safely rid of one you need not fear for the other. The stars in their courses fight on our side," and she laughed an evil laugh. "There is no room in this world for your weak-minded gentle creatures, bah! cowards, worms, with their snivelling pity. Does nature feel pity when the field mouse is killed by the hawk? Does nature feel pity when a mother dies of the plague? Does God feel pity when we starve a child or beat it to death? Let him show his pity for the victims of disease, for the beings he has brought into the world, humpbacked, blind, halt, imbecile, ha! ha! ha! No, the forces on our side are the stronger, and the innocent, the gentle and loving must go. I hate innocence, I hate love; and hate will triumph in the end.

"Do you think I love you, you coward?" and she advanced slowly as though to clutch his throat with her skinny hand, laughing her demoniacal laugh. "You are on our side, but you are a worm;—Thomas, I spit at you, begone."

Thomas looked at her in terror and slunk away till the old woman's mocking laughter grew fainter. "Faugh! she was mad—mad—what did it matter? And yet, suppose she took it into her head to put a spell on him, the same as she had done on little Joan!161 What then? But he would be even with Aline yet; Andrew was a clumsy bungler, he would see if he could not secure a more efficient agent."

Thomas had allowed his imagination to dwell round his grievance against Aline until it had grown to colossal dimensions. She could not even smile on any one without him reckoning it up against her as an offence. The thing was becoming an obsession with him.

But what did the old crone mean? Something certainly was going to happen; did it involve Thomas, or was he himself to be unaffected by the play of forces? The feeling was unpleasant and he could not shake it off.

After meeting Thomas, Aline had gone on to Peter's cottage. She found that the dying child was weaker than ever, but she still seemed to cling tenaciously to life. She raised herself a little when Aline came in and her eyes shone with an unnatural brightness.

"I shall never see you any more, Aline," she said. "And I have several things that I want to say to you. They are going to take me away. I know they mean to be kind, yet I would rather have died quietly here. But listen, it is not about that that I want to talk," the child went on excitedly.

"Hush, dear," said Aline, taking the small frail hand in her own and stroking it, "you will tire yourself out."

"Can you put your hand under my pillow, Aline? You will find there a little packet."

Aline did as she was asked.

"Now undo it."

She opened the small parcel and found in it half a groat that had been broken in two, a child's spinning top and a short lock of dark curly brown hair.

162

"He was my playmate," said Joan, "and he used to help me every day to carry the water from the spring up to the house, and he said that when he was a big man he would marry me. I know I am going to die soon and no one loves me but you, so I want to give you my secret."

"O Joan, darling, you must not talk like that," and Aline stooped and kissed the sad little face on the pillow, while her tears, in spite of herself, would keep welling up and rolling down her cheeks.

A faint little smile spread over Joan's face as her thoughts wandered away back to the old times in Kirkoswald and talking half to herself and half to Aline she said: "His name was Wilfred Johnstone. Oh! Wilfred, Wilfred, if only I could kiss you good-bye! but I shall leave your top and the half groat and your dear hair with my beautiful little lady, and some day she may see you and give them back and say good-bye for me."

"O Aline," she went on, trying to raise herself as she put her arms round her neck—"give him this kiss for me and say that if I had grown up I would have been his little wife as I promised"; then, pressing a kiss on Aline's lips, she fell back exhausted on the bed.

"I will do everything you ask," said Aline, and sat by her for a long time, but the child did not speak again.

At last the evening began to get dark and Aline knew she must be getting home. "Good-bye, sweet Joan," she said and for the last time printed a kiss on the child's forehead. "I wish you could have said good-bye," and she turned to the door.

As she turned Joan's eyes half opened. "Good-bye,"163 she murmured, and Aline went sadly from the house.

"They are going to take her away from me and I believe I love her even more than Audry, but it is all meant for the best. Oh, I hope and I hope that that horrid old witch was not telling the truth."

Aline lay awake for a long time that night thinking of Joan and old Moll and wondering how she would find Wilfred Johnstone; and when she slept she still dreamed of her little friend.

The next morning they carried Joan away on a litter. The journey was to be made in three stages of a day each. Aline would have liked to see her off, but unfortunately Master Richard had specially arranged to take the children with him on a long expedition and make an early start, and he did not wish any interference with his plans.

He had been so very kind in making the elaborate arrangements about Joan's journey and future welfare that Aline did not like to say anything, though it cost her a pang.

They mounted from the old "louping on stone" in the lower courtyard and were not long reaching Middleton. Master Richard had some business in Middleton, and afterward they turned up the left bank of the Tees.

It was another grey day, but the water looked wonderfully beautiful down below them, and Holwick crags rose majestically away to the left. The bleakness of the surrounding country enhanced the richness of the river valley; but the wild spirit of the hills seemed to dominate the whole.

On the way they passed through the village of Newbiggin. It consisted almost wholly of rude stone cottages and byres. "We have a great deal of trouble here," remarked Richard Mowbray. "They are a curiously lawless lot; it is not only their poaching but there is much thieving of other kinds. Their beasts too are a nuisance, straying, as they pretend, on our Middleton property. A murrain on them! My tenant there, Master Milnes, is very indignant about it and is sure that it is not accidental. He also makes great complaint about continual damage to the dykes. Mistress Mowbray is determined to have the whole nest of them cleared out."

"But the village does not belong to you, does it, Cousin Richard?"

"No, there are three properties besides mine that meet there, the Duke of Alston's, Lord Middleton's and Master Gower's."

"Then how are you going to do anything?"

"Oh, Mistress Mowbray saw Lord Middleton, and he has arranged that his reeve and the Duke's shall come over to Holwick and meet Master Gower and ourselves. I do not expect there will be any difficulty."

Aline thought it was rather a high handed proceeding, but she said nothing. She looked at the little cottages and then her thoughts flew over to the cottage on the other side of the river that Joan had just left. She wondered rather pathetically whether nearly all life was sad like her own and Joan's and Ian's. Did every one of these cottages mean a sad story? It would certainly be a sad story to be turned out of one's home. Here was a new trouble for her. "Was it true," she thought, "that all these people were as bad as Cousin Richard supposed?"

Suddenly Audry exclaimed, "Look—there goes old Moll."

As they overtook her she stopped and shook her staff after them, crying,— "Maidens that ride high horses to-day eat bitter bread upon the morrow."

Master Mowbray did not catch what she said, but Aline heard and again felt that peculiar shudder that she could not explain.

A week or two later the words came back to her with bitter meaning indeed. Joan safely reached her destination and the first news that came from Durham was hopeful; but shortly afterwards the news was worse and then suddenly came word that she was dead.

Aline put the little packet carefully away in the ambry. She did not tell any one, not even Audry, but some day she hoped to carry out the child's request. There was too much misery in the world, she must see what she could do. Perhaps she might begin by doing something for the people of Newbiggin. At least she could find out what was the real truth of the case.

CHAPTER XIII
COMING EVENTS CAST SHADOWS

IT was a fine moonlight night and Ian was pacing up and down by the side of the stream. He walked very fast, partly because the season was getting cold and partly to calm his mind. He was agitated concerning the future and troubled not only about himself but about Aline. He was now distinctly better in health and felt that he would soon be well enough to leave Holwick Hall. There were many difficulties. First there was the immediate danger of getting away unseen. Then when he had performed his mission in Carlisle there was the problem of the future. He would be safer in Scotland, but he did not want to be too far away from Aline. She might need his help.

Again he felt that sense of apprehension, almost of terror; something was going to happen, but what? Which way was he to meet it? This threatening, uncertain atmosphere, what did it portend?

Aline seemed touched by it. He had not spoken to her about it, but he had noticed it in her manner; indeed they seemed mutually aware of it as he looked into her eyes.

In any case he could not go to his father's house. Should he go to Scotland at all? The country he knew was in great confusion, torn between her fear of France and the Regent, Mary of Guise, on the one hand and her hatred of England on the other.

He was strongly tempted to go and fight, if fighting were to be done, and the very documents that he carried might be the things that would bring matters to a head. On the other hand if there were no fighting he felt drawn to do something more for the faith. He had no home duties and he hated inactivity. At last he settled the matter. Of course the papers were to be safely delivered first, but neither the fighting in Scotland nor Aline's need for his help could be reckoned on as a certainty. He would stay in Carlisle and be in reach of both. As for the reformed faith he had for some time come to the conclusion that the calling of a packman offered the best opportunities for spreading the word. This, however, would require money which at present he had not got. He would therefore try and find work as a smith or a carpenter in Carlisle until he had saved the money.

That matter was settled then; and his health was now such that his departure must not be long delayed. He stood still and looked up at the clear sky. The roar of the waterfall not half a mile away filled the silence of the night. It was very peaceful and the hills were bathed in a sad mysterious beauty. But through all the calm lurked a suggestion of dread.

Dare he leave the child behind at all? Yet if he took her he would be putting her to greater risks every moment than the worst she could suffer from Mistress Mowbray. Besides how could the expenses be met; for the scheme would be impossible without horses; as,168 although he himself could escape alone on foot, immediately Aline disappeared a hue and cry would be raised? His mind grew tired with thinking and finally he began to build wild castles in the air, in which he took the child with him on foot and fought pursuer after pursuer, until he was slain himself, not however before he had managed to put Aline into a sure place of safety and happiness.

He had wandered rather further than usual down the stream and decided that he had better turn back; moreover it was late and it would soon be daylight. He retraced his steps until he came within a few paces of the opening that led to the cave and was intending to enter, when he caught sight of a dark figure seated under a small birch tree that had found a sheltering place in this hollow on the bleak moor.

It was a woman and she was watching him. The shock was so sudden that he had the greatest difficulty in preserving his presence of mind. He decided to continue in the direction he was going as though bound on some definite journey.

"You like the night-air, stranger, for your travels," she said in a shrill voice. She evidently did not mean to let him pass her.

"Ay, mother," he said, "a night like this is as good for travel as the day."

He gathered at once who it was from Aline's description. It was "Moll o' the graves," and she seemed to rivet him to the spot with the gaze of her unholy, but still beautiful eyes. She was holding a bone in her claw-like hands and was gnawing the flesh off it. He could not help noticing that she yet had excellent teeth.169 Could she by any chance know who he was? In any case she had seen him now, so he might stand and see if he could draw her out. However, she went on,—"I've heard physicians recommend the night air for travellers with a sick conscience."

"Then if that be the case," he answered, "it might apply to you as well as to me."

"Perhaps it may," she said, "but I enjoy the fresh night air for its own sake:—

O Moon that watches from the sky,
We see strange things, the moon and I."
crooned the old woman, beating time with her staff.

"Do you know this part of the world?" she said suddenly.

"I cannot say that I do," he answered.

"Then you miss things that are worth knowing. There are all manners of folk about here from the Master of Holwick to miser Simson, from bullying Eleanor Mowbray to gentle Janet Arnside, and from tough, withered, bloodless old Elspeth to fresh tender morsels like Aline that dropped in the moat," she said as she grinned, shewing her teeth, "and I know the fortunes of them all."

The old woman was eyeing him keenly, but he managed to betray no particular interest.

He thought, however, that he had better move away lest she should ask him such questions that he would lose more than anything he would gain from talking to her. He was thankful she had not seen him go into the cave.

"I think I must be moving on," he said.

"Will you not wait and hear your future told?"

"No, I thank you; that can bide."

"It's not good anyhow," said old Moll with a vindictive light in her eyes, "it begins with heartache and goes on to worse."

"Good night to you," said Ian and started up the gully.

"Are you not coming back to your hiding place in there?" the old woman called maliciously. "I saw you come out and I shall be sitting here till you come back."

"Horrible old villain," he said to himself, but he called out, "No, it's all right for a temporary shelter, but no one could stay there."

Things indeed looked serious, how was he to get back? But he could not bear the thought of not saying good-bye to the children. Besides they absolutely must know that part of their secret had been discovered.

He decided that unless the old hag roused his pursuers he was fairly safe; he could keep out of sight in bog-holes or the like during the day. If some one came very near, he must chance it and move on. True there was some risk, but Aline must know.

The old woman was in the hollow where she could not see him; so he crept round and hid himself where he could watch without being observed.

When daylight came he saw her rise and go into the outer cave; but he could not see what further she did.

She then came back and sat down. Hours passed on, but she did not move. About mid-day she produced a small sack from under her kirtle and took something out and gnawed at it as before. She did the same again towards evening.

171

Ian felt faint and hungry, but determined not to give in, even if he had to wait another night, though as he would have to go some twenty miles before he dared ask for food, his plight was becoming desperate.

He crept quite close to her on the bare chance of her going to sleep in such a way that he could be quite sure of it and be able to slip past.

However, toward sunset he heard her mutter to herself,—"Well, I cannot wait any more, it will be too cold." She rose and hobbled over to the cave, where she broke down a light switch and bent it across the entrance, as though it had accidentally been done by the wind or some animal.

She started a step or two down the little gully and then came back to her resting place and looked about. She picked up three bones. "They might tell tales," she murmured, and, hiding them under her mantle, she walked down toward the river. When she reached the river she threw the bones into the dark water and watched them sink. But this Ian did not see.

When Moll had gone, Ian went back to the secret room. He was overwrought. This was a new peril for Aline and it made him grasp what he had not realised before,—that if the children were caught harbouring a heretic the consequences would be terrible indeed. He must get away forthwith.

He went to bed, but he could not sleep. How far had he really been wise after all, to say anything to Aline about the new faith? She certainly was a most unusual child, but perplexities and responsibilities might even be too much for an adult.

Was not my first instinct right, he argued, children172 are too delicate, too frail, too beautiful to be flung into the anxieties of life? There is a good deal to be said even for the priests, he reflected, responsibility may become too crushing altogether.

Then too, his own mind was not at ease about the course that things were taking, either in Scotland or England. On the whole he felt that the Protestants were nearer the truth, but there was a beauty and a spirituality of holiness not unconnected with the beauty of holiness itself, which he saw in the old faith and which he was not willing to abandon.

"I would not have a faith without beauty," he said; "it would be a travesty of faith, an unlovely thing and no faith at all. If we do not consider the lilies which we have seen, we shall certainly never be able to understand the King in his beauty whom we have not seen; and, of a surety, this child flower hath lifted me higher than any other experience of my life."

But methinks it is meet that both sides should be presented, and some day we may grow broad-minded enough to learn each from the other.

He lay awake most of the night so that when the children came down in the evening he was looking tired and worn.

They came in slowly, very downcast and sad. Suppose that Ian had disappeared for good and that they would never see him again! He was seated where they could not see him at once, but when they caught sight of him they both rushed forward.

"Oh, you are here safe and sound; what has happened? I am so glad," said both in a breath. Each child flung her arms round him and kissed him.

173

"You will pull my head off if you are not careful," he said, laughing.

"Oh, you did give us a terrible fright," exclaimed Aline.

"Yes, we came and found the room empty," said Audry, "and we hunted all down the passage to the cave room; and I wanted to go through, but Aline said, 'No, there is evidently something wrong and it might not be safe, we had better come round outside.'"

"I am glad you were cautious," Ian interposed.

"But first we went down the other passage and found nothing, and then we set out. Aline said we must be very careful in coming near the cave, so we crept round very slowly; and suddenly, what do you think we saw?"

"Well, what did you see?"

"We saw 'Moll o' the graves,'" said Aline, "and we stooped down at once and then ran away. She did not see us, as the back of her head was turned our way."

"I'm thankful for that," said Ian, and then recounted his experiences. He omitted the bone incident, but concluded by saying,—"We must be careful about that birch twig. She evidently set it as a trap."

"Do you suppose that she discovered the inner cave, the cave room itself?" asked Audry apprehensively.

"Not at all likely," said Ian. "She cannot stand up straight even; besides she was not there long enough; of that I am certain."

Audry gave a sigh of relief.

"But she may tell other people," said Ian. "You must keep your ears open very carefully."

It was an awe inspiring prospect, the future certainly was not reassuring.

174

In order to give a new turn to the conversation Aline said:—"Do you know, the day before yesterday I went over to Newbiggin and talked to several of the people? I did not ask any questions, but they told me a great deal of themselves. There evidently are some pretty fair scoundrels in the village, even on their own showing."

"What are you going to do?" said Ian.

"I do not know yet," she said, "I must find out some more, but I am tolerably sure that the villains are in the minority."

"I do not suppose there is much to choose," said Audry. "I should let them all go. Why trouble yourself?"

"But, Audry," Aline objected, "you yourself hate unfairness; and I cannot bear to think of Mistress Mowbray having her own way with those who are innocent."

"I think, also, my princess enjoys some other kinds of fighting than with foils," Ian interposed.

"Well, perhaps there's a little bit in that too; my father was a fighter."

"Somehow, little one," said Ian, "I cannot help wishing you would leave it alone. I feel you would be better to have nothing to do with Newbiggin. It sounds very silly, but old Moll lives in Newbiggin, and I have a strange dread of it that I cannot explain."

"That is very curious," said Audry, "so have I. There has been something weighing on me like a bad dream for many days. I cannot explain it. Aline, dear, you let it alone."

"I wish you two would not talk like that," said Aline, "because I have had exactly the same feeling175 and it is most uncanny; but I cannot give up the Newbiggin people because of my feelings."

"Come, let us have some fun," she continued; "we look as if we had not a backbone among us."

She went to the sword-chest as she spoke and took out a pair of foils. "Now, this will do my stiffness good, and Audry can act as umpire."

They had a good deal of practice since the first encounter. Ian was really a brilliant master of the art and was much amused at the way that Aline had completely hoaxed him. Aline made rapid progress and Ian used to tell her that, child as she was, she would probably be able to account for a fairly average swordsman, so little was the art then understood in Scotland or England.

After a bout or two, they sat down to rest.

"You know," said Ian, "I think I ought to be leaving you soon. I am ever so much better than I was and it would be well for me to be away."

"Why," said Audry, "are you not comfortable here?"

"Of course I am comfortable," he said, "but I cannot stay here forever, it would not be fair to you. Besides it is time that I was doing my work in the world."

"But it would be terribly risky," said Audry, "and after the narrow escape you had, I think you might consider you had done your share."

"No, because I feel that I have something so valuable for people, that it is worth any risk."

"But look how you have suffered and you will bring the same suffering to others; in fact you hesitated about telling us."

"But that was because you are children, and somehow[176] I do not feel that a child is called upon to undertake such great responsibilities."

"I do not see why a child should not judge," said Aline; "it is all so simple and beautiful. If it is worth dying for, people should be glad to have it, whatever the suffering. I think I feel ready to die like poor George Wishart. So if your going helps other people, even if it makes us very sad you must go. When do you think you ought to start?"

"I have a definite errand to undertake. I have never told you about it, but I am acting as a special messenger with some important papers, and I have been thinking it over and have come to the conclusion that I should be leaving here in a week at most, but less if possible."

"What, so soon?" exclaimed both the children at once.

A deeper gloom than ever seemed to fall over the party as this was said, and although they tried to feel cheerful, they knew it was a poor attempt. No one spoke for a long time. Ian sat with his head between his hands and Aline gazed into the empty fireplace at the dead ashes of the fire that had been lit when Ian came.

These days with Ian had made the Holwick life far more bearable for her. There were her Greek lessons and the fencing lessons, but bad as it would be to lose them it would be worse to lose her friend. He was generally very reserved with her; but if she was in trouble he always opened out. She glanced up. Ian had lifted his head and their eyes met. What would she do without him?

Audry held one of the foils and drew with it on the floor. The silence was oppressive.

At length Aline spoke. "Where shall you go, when[177] you leave us? You cannot think how sadly we shall miss you."

"I shall probably miss you more than you will miss me, sweet child," and Menstrie looked at her with a strange longing pain in his heart. It was thirteen years since any one person had filled his life as this child had done, and now he was to lose her. "Surely," he said to himself, "life is compact of most mysterious bitterness"; but he tried to be cheerful for the child's sake and said, "Never mind, Aline, I shall come and see you again. I think I shall try and become a packman like your friend who gave you your necklace, if I can get some money somehow to begin, and then I can pay many visits to Holwick. I believe I could disguise myself well enough, as I do not think that any one here really knows me,—the few that saw me will have forgotten me. We can meet in this room and I shall be able to bring you news and some interesting things from far away."

"Yes, do bring me a chatelaine," said Audry. "I have always wanted one and Father has either forgotten or been unable to get it."

"Is there anything you would like, birdeen?" said Ian, addressing Aline.

Aline thought for a moment; why should he bring her things, he was obviously poor and never likely to be anything else? What was the younger son of a yeoman who had been a wanderer, a smith and a soldier of fortune ever likely to have in the way of money? Even her own father who had been a small Laird had never been able to purchase her the necklace that he had so desired to do. "I do not want you to bring me anything," she answered finally, "if only you can keep yourself178 safe," and then she added hesitatingly, "Would a Greek Testament be expensive?"

"No, not at all," said Ian. "Would you like one, little angel?"

"Yes, very much indeed; but oh, I am afraid it will be a long time between one visit and the next, and we shall not know what has become of you," and Aline sighed.

"I think I could write to you sometimes," he said. "We might get hold of Walter Margrove, who suggested something of the sort to you, and for greater security we could make duplicates of the parchment with the holes that you found in the book. I could write the letter so that it looked like an announcement of my wares."

They discussed the matter for some time and the next day set about making the parchment slips, and for the following few evenings they were busy with several preparations. Ian's clothes all had to be mended and put in good order and they took some of the clothes that they had found in the secret room and by slight alterations were able to make him a second outfit.

They also found a leathern wallet that with a little patching made a sound serviceable article.

Ian further made a suggestion to Aline in case they should have reason to suspect that the key to their correspondence was known. "Let us take your name and mine," he said, "to make the foundation of a series of letters and we will write the names downward like this—

A
L
I
N
E"

179 "Yes, and what next?" said Aline.

"Well, after each letter, we will write in order the letters in the alphabet that follow it. After A we will write B C D E F G, and after L we will write M N O P Q R, and whenever we get to Z we start the alphabet again. So if we write our whole names it will look like this—

180

A.	B	C	D	E	F	G
L.	M	N	O	P	Q	R
I.	J	K	L	M	N	O
N.	O	P	Q	R	S	T
E.	F	G	H	I	J	K
G.	H	I	J	K	L	M
I.	J	K	L	M	N	O
L.	M	N	O	P	Q	R
L.	M	N	O	P	Q	R
E.	F	G	H	I	J	K
S.	T	U	V	W	X	Y
P.	Q	R	S	T	U	V
I.	J	K	L	M	N	O
E.	F	G	H	I	J	K
I.	J	K	L	M	N	O
A.	B	C	D	E	F	G
N.	O	P	Q	R	S	T
M.	N	O	P	Q	R	S
E.	F	G	H	I	J	K
N.	O	P	Q	R	S	T
S.	T	U	V	W	X	Y
T.	U	V	W	X	Y	Z
R.	S	T	U	V	W	X
I.	J	K	L	M	N	O
E.	F	G	H	I	J	K

Now there are 25 letters in each column, and if we just put a number at the top of our communication, we shall know where we are to begin to use the sequence."

"I see," said Aline, "if the number is 51 we shall begin at the top of the third column; if it is 56 we shall begin 6 letters down the third column."

"And if it was 176," said Ian, "what should we do?"

"Well, we should have to make another column the same way and we should begin at the top of it."

99

"Now suppose the number is 1, we shall then begin at the very beginning, and the way we should use the letters would be like this. Suppose this is the message,—

"Arthur Melland wishes to notifie the good people in the Lothians of the lasting excellence of his wares. His pack is regularly filled with all the newest materials and, too, all is most marvellously finished in design.

Our first letter was A, and the first A we find is the A of 'Arthur.' Our second letter was L, and the next L that we find is in 'Melland.' Our third letter was I and the next I that we find is in 'wishes.' Our fourth letter was N and the next N that we find is in 'notifie.'"

"Oh, that's quite easy," said Aline, "and so you mark them all like this—

"Arthur Melland wishes to notifie the good people in the Lothians of the lasting excellence of his wares. His pack is regularly filled with all the newest materials and, too, all is most marvellously finished in design.

and then cut them out."

"Yes," said Ian, "and the only other thing necessary is that the paper should first be neatly ruled with quarter181 inch squares, and each of the key letters carefully written in a square. It does not matter about the others. But then when the receiver gets the letter he knows that the squares to be cut must be exactly an even number of quarter inches from the edge of the paper."

"I hope I shall remember it if needful," Aline said.

"I don't," said Audry.

"Why not?" exclaimed the others in astonishment.

"Because I hope it won't be needed and that would certainly be simpler."

182
CHAPTER XIV
GOOD-BYE

THE days slipped by all too quickly and the children spent every available moment in the secret room. But it was not very safe for them to disappear from sight too often and moreover, other obligations had to be fulfilled. Sometimes they were able to arrange that one should remain with Ian while the other was occupied elsewhere.

On one of these occasions, while Audry was in the secret room, Aline went down to the Arnsides. On the way she met Father Laurence coming up from Middleton. It was an unusual thing for him to come to Holwick and Aline was surprised. "Good day, Father," she said, as she dropped a curtsey.

"Bless you, my child," said the old man, looking at her keenly, "talium enim est regnum dei,"[16] he whispered softly to himself. "How profound Our Lord's sayings were. Yes, it does one good even to look at a child," and then he noticed that Aline seemed sad and troubled and lacked her usual buoyant vivacity. "Are you not happy, little maiden?" he said gently.

16 For of such is the kingdom of God.

Aline looked at him with an expression of wonder; "No, not exactly," she said.

"What is it, my child?"

"Oh, many things, Father; the world is difficult."

They had drawn near to the side of the road and Aline was leaning against the wall; she plucked the top of a tall ragwort and began pulling off its yellow petals one by one.

The priest put his elbow on the wall and looked down at her. He was very tall indeed, with a rather thin face and deep sad eyes. He at once saw that she did not want to tell him her troubles and he had too much instinctive delicacy to press the child. He laid his disengaged hand kindly on her head, and she looked up at him.

"Strange," he thought, "I might have had such a child of mine own; but no, it was not to be. Yes, I know what sorrow is: I have indeed made my sacrifice.

"All things work together for good, Aline," he said aloud, "the forces of good must win in the end, but the powers of darkness are strong and the victory may be long delayed; yet it will come."

"But the world is cruel, Father," said Aline.

"Yes, my child, I know, and the world often seems to be victorious; but it is only victorious in the things of the world. The principle of love and the principle of beauty will outlast the world," and he smiled a sweet smile.

Aline gazed into his face and he seemed to be looking into the things beyond.

"Be of good courage, little maiden, fear not them that have power to hurt the body. The Lord be with you, and may the Mother of God watch over you; farewell."

He turned as he spoke and Aline saw him cross over to the cottage of Benjamin Darley. She went on to the Arnsides and found both mother and son at home.

"Ah, Honey," said the old woman, "it is good to see your bonnie face, it's a sight for sair een."

"Mistress Aline is not looking very well, mother," said John.

"Nonsense, John," said Aline, and added brightly,—"I have come to ask you all you can tell me about Newbiggin. I know I can trust you."

"Dear heart," said Janet, "you do us honour." She skilfully lifted the peats with the long tongs and rearranged them on a different part of the hearth and soon there was a bright fire.

"That's a merry blaze," said Aline; "it seems to cheer one's heart."

For an hour they sat and talked about Newbiggin; and the child, with what she already knew, was able to make a shrewd estimate of the true state of affairs.

After a while the subject not unnaturally turned to "Moll o' the graves" and Aline was dismayed when she heard that Moll had been talking about seeing a man on the moors, and saying that it would be the beginning of troubles.

"What did she mean by that?" asked Aline.

"She would not explain," said Janet; "she refused to tell any one anything more. 'The time is not yet, the time is not yet,' she kept repeating; 'when all is ready and I have discovered the workings of the fates, I will tell you more than you wish to know.'"

"People have gossiped about it a great deal," Janet went on, "but Moll will say nothing further."

"I trust that her evil desires may be foiled," said Aline, "but I must not tarry."

185

As she went up the street she again met Father Laurence coming out of Peter's cottage and he seemed more sorrowful than ever.

"Peace be with you, Aline," he said. "I have a right melancholic thing here," holding out a letter. "But it cannot grieve thee beyond what thou already knowest. It is a letter from Durham, long delayed in transit, concerning the death of little Joan. Will you read it or shall I?"

Aline's eyes filled with tears, "I should like you to read it," she said.

Father Laurence then read—

"To Peter Simson in Holwick

"It beseemeth me to send thee word, although my heart is right heavy within me, of the passing of the small damsel y-cleped[17] Joan, who came from Upper Teesdale. Of this you will have already heard: but my sister was herself sick of an ague at the time and Sir Robert Miller, her confessor, saith that her mind wandered. He writeth this for me.

She herself lingered not many days,—God rest her soul,—and, when I came from Skipton, where I dwelled, she was buried.

"I only know from a neighbour that the damsel had gained health until latterly and that the end was on a sudden. She spake much of the young lady at the Hall, who had given her great bounty; and in especial would she have the shoon and the belt returned, which were new. But these same I cannot find, and methinks they must have gone to Newcastle with the other orphans who were in my sister's house, and whom the good dame who came thence to nurse my sister, took home in her charge, and may our Lady requite her kindness.

"An thou wouldst speak to the Mistress Alice or Ellen,—the name escapeth me,—I would give thee much thanks.

"Elizabeth Parry."

17 Named.

"But I never gave her any shoes or belt," said Aline. "Poor little Joan, her mind must have failed her at186 the last, or Mistress Parry must have been as much in error as she was about my name. She was a dear child," she continued, "and it is bitter dole[18] to me. I have burned a few candles for her soul, but I have not much means."

18 Grief.

"Trouble not thy gentle heart," said the old priest, "I will myself say mass for the child, and no one shall be at any charge. God keep thee, Aline, as he may."

When she reached the Hall she went to Ian and Audry and told them what she had learned, and they were much disquieted at the evil speaking of old Moll; but there was nothing that they might do and they could only hope against hope.

Ever since hearing the letter that Father Laurence had read, the sad figure of little Joan had floated before Aline's eyes, and that night she went to the library and opened the ambry and took out the little packet and gazed at the pathetic contents. "I wonder whether I shall ever be able to find the boy, Wilfred Johnstone," she said. "But I expect he will have forgotten already, boys never remember long," and then she recalled a remark of her father's,—"A boy remembers longer and is more constant than a girl, unless he has won her; but after she is won she is the more faithful." "I should like to know if that be true," she thought.

At length the evening came when Ian had to start. It was a fine bright night as the three made their way down the secret passage for the last time.

"How strange it has all been," said Aline, "since we first discovered the secret room and this passage. What a different thing life means to me from what it did187 then!" She was leading the way carrying the wallet containing the food, while Audry carried a staff and a big heavy cloak.

"It has been a wonderful time for me," said Ian, "and I can never realise to the full the marvellousness of my escape or your great kindness to me. I feel that God must have arranged it all, just because it is so strange. I seem to have every little incident written in undying characters in my mind, and I could recall almost every word of your conversations with me. Even if we never meet again, you will live with me always."

"Oh, but you will come back and we shall meet again," Audry interrupted, "you must not talk like that."

"I hope that I shall," he said, but the tone of his voice was so sad that no one spoke again till they came to the cave-room.

They lifted the stone and Ian climbed down first and then lifted the two through the opening. As he held Aline in his arms a great wave of feeling nearly overcame him altogether. For the moment he felt as though he could not put her down; it was like voluntarily parting with all that made life precious. He clasped her tightly to him for a moment and then he set her very gently on her feet. It was not too dark to see her face, and as he looked at it he realised that he had never seen it more sad and yet it had never looked more beautiful. The light was not bright enough to see the colour, but he could just discern something of its richness in the gleam of her thick long wavy hair, reaching far down below her waist. They all found it very difficult to speak and the children wished him a safe journey and a happy issue with very trembling voices.

188

"Think of me sometimes," he said, "when I am gone, and pray for me. May God be with you and do more than I can ever ask in my feeble prayers."

He kissed both the children, and holding Aline's little face in both his hands he said,—"Oh, if I could only do something for you, little one, I could be happy, no matter what it cost. Somehow I feel that we shall never meet again in spite of what Audry says; still that does not make it impossible for me to do something for you. Remember that I shall always be living in the hope that some such chance may come and that the greatest pleasure you can give me is to let me use myself in your service. But now I must go." He kissed her once again and then took the cloak, staff and wallet and strode into the darkness; which soon closed round him and hid him from their sight.

After he had gone a hundred yards or so across the moor, he paused; it was almost more than he could bear; so he knelt down and prayed that all good things might come to Aline and, if it were not selfish to ask it, that it might be given to him to suffer on her behalf,—some pain, some sacrifice, some physical or mental anguish, that might directly or indirectly add to her joy or lessen her sorrow. After this he felt strengthened and even elated at the thought of the suffering that he hoped would come. It was not enough to give her happiness, the more it would cost him, the more he would welcome it.

He walked as fast as the light and the nature of the ground would permit, and when the morning dawned he had passed the wild cataract of Caldron Snout and was on the spurs of Knock Fell.

CHAPTER XV
THE TERROR OF THE MIST

IT was a raw, damp morning and the day struggled up with difficulty. Ian was very tired as it was long since he had made any continuous physical effort and, anxious as he was to make progress, he felt that he must rest. He sat down by a stream and opened his wallet and broke his fast, while he thought out what would be the best road for him to take. So far he had been sure of the way from Audry's description, but he was a little more doubtful about his ability to find the route further on and yet, if possible, he did not wish to ask questions of any one he met. He was just able to distinguish the sun rising through the mist and hoped that the day would brighten. From this he calculated that the wind which was very steady was from the northwest.

He knew that, when they were hunting him before, a description of him had been sent as far as Alston and Kirkoswald; so he determined to try and reach Carlisle without going through these places. In Carlisle people had more things to think about; and the incident of his escape, even if news of it had travelled so far, would by this time be forgotten. Moreover a stranger in the great border town would not arouse any curiosity.

He therefore decided that he would keep along by the highest ground following the ridge of summits. This he knew would ultimately bring him to Cold Fell, where the drop on every side is very marked and whence, if he had not seen Carlisle itself before, he could drop down by Naworth or Brampton.

After a long rest he turned up the steep. Unfortunately the mist, instead of lifting, grew thicker until he had nothing to guide him but the wind and the general lie of the ground. Used as he was to the hills, he always felt the eeriness of the mist seething and curling and scurrying over the heather. It was bitterly cold as the wind was strong and the mist grew so thick that he could only see the ground for a few paces. He was afraid of coming suddenly upon the precipice of some corrie or cross-gully. He had heard too of the terrible "pot" holes in the limestone district, and pictured himself falling down into one of those black bottomless chimneys, where even his body would never be seen again.

He decided to strike straight up for the top, even though it was more fatiguing, and he followed the steepest line of the ground, scrambling over the rocks where necessary. He started violently as he suddenly heard the scream of an eagle somewhere near him in the mist, and later on he was surprised actually to come upon one tearing the body of a grouse. The great bird rose and hit him, whether intentionally or not he was not sure, but he shrank involuntarily and the sight of the small mangled victim stirred his heart. "Why was the world of birds and men so essentially cruel?" "Poor little Aline," he thought, as he looked at the little bird.

When at last he reached the height he was met by an icy wind of tremendous force from the weather side of the hill and it was only with extreme difficulty that he could keep his footing. Using the wind as his guide he decided on a place where the gradient was less and the direction right as far as he could judge and trusted that this would be the col between the summits.

It was anxious work and at last he began to feel that he had descended too far. He had missed the col. He was lost. Although better in health his nerves were still shaken. For a moment he half broke down. "Oh, if I could only see you once again, Aline," he cried, "and you will never know that months afterwards the shepherds found the remains of an unknown man upon the hills." He peered into the mist as though by strength of will he would force its secret. It was vain, the mist was blankly impenetrable. Under ordinary circumstances he was too good a hillsman to mind and would simply, worse come to the worst, have followed down stream till he came to the haunts of men, but it was a matter of life and death to him now not to come down the wrong valley. Moreover, there were the precious papers, for which he had already risked so much.

Gradually he recovered, but what was he to do? Which side had he gone wrong? He stood and reflected for a moment. The direction of the wind seemed all right, but it was very much less in force. Surely then he was to the east of the col. Oh, if only the mist would lift, but it still raced past, with its white swirling, cruel fingers. The wind sighed sadly in the rank, red tinted grass, and away below he heard the falling of many waters and the endless bleating of sheep. Every now and then some gigantic menacing forms192 would seem to shape themselves out of the mist;—they danced round him, they pointed at him, they mocked him. They were trolls, they were the spirits of death, the lost souls of the sons of men. A brooding horror seemed to sweep over the desolate hillside, chilling him with a nameless dread. He turned a little further into the wind and the ground grew more wet and mossy. This must surely be somewhere below the middle of the col, he argued, and he struck still more to the left.

Suddenly he came upon a sight that froze his marrow. It was the skeleton of a child,—some poor little wanderer who, like himself, had been lost and who never had returned home. The wind whistled through the small slender bones. They were quite clean, save for a little hair clinging to the skull, from which Ian guessed that it was a boy. He might have been ten or twelve years old. How had he come there? What had brought him to his fate? The clothes had entirely gone save one little shoe. Ian picked it up, looked at it and shivered. Oh, the horror of it! Then the mood changed and he found himself filled with unutterable pity. "Poor child, poor child," he said; "another victim of a heartless world." He knelt down and laid his hand on the small skull and his emotion overcame him. Then he gathered the bones together and carried them to a small hollow under a great rock. As he was doing this, his fingers came across something in the grass. It was a small wallet or purse. When he had taken all the bones he managed with some difficulty to cover them with earth and then he built up a little cairn of stones. The small shoe he put with the bones, but the wallet he took with him.

193

With very mingled feelings he struggled up the slope and at last to his great relief he felt the icy blast of the northwest wind, with the ground sloping upward in the right direction. He decided to make for the very summit, the better to check his position, and at last he reached the point and then cautiously made his way in the same manner to what he believed was Cross Fell.

It was very slow work and the ground was very wet and heavy; he was footsore and stiff from lack of practice and when the evening began to close in he had made absurdly little headway.

At last he felt he could go no further and must spend the night upon the hills. He climbed over the ridge to the leeward side and dropped until he came to the heather line, where he found a dry hollow between some rocks. Tearing up a quantity of heather he made himself a bed to lie on and sat down on the soft extemporised couch. Then he opened the little wallet or pouch that he had found by the skeleton. It contained some knuckle bones and a piece of cord; but with them was a wonderful bracelet of peculiar workmanship. Ian judged it to be Keltic of a very remote date as it somewhat resembled work that a friend had found in the Culbin sands. An inscription and other alterations had been made at a later date.

The design was in bold curving shapes that expressed the very spirit of metal. Most remarkable were three large bosses of a strange stone of marvellous hue; they were a deep sky-blue, brilliantly clear and transparent, but with a slight yet most mysterious opalescence in the colour. He had never heard of such a stone and there was something almost uncanny about the way they shone194 in the dim light. Whether they were original or substitutes for enamel or amber he could not tell.

The inscription ran:—
WOE TO WHO STEALETH ME
PEACE TO WHO FINDETH ME
BUT WEAL WHERE I COME AS A GIFT OF LOVE.

It was a marvellously beautiful thing and Ian could not help speculating how the boy had come by it. "If these charms and amulets really had any power, he might well have stolen it," he thought, shuddering at what he had seen. "But that is a thing we shall never know. However, it would be a pleasing gift for Aline, and some day I will clasp it myself on that little white wrist."

He pictured Aline to himself wearing the bracelet and then rolling his cloak about him went to sleep.

For a few hours he slept well and then he woke with the cold. He was very tired and sleepy but unable to sleep again for the pains which shot through him. The miserable night seemed endless, he tossed and dozed and tossed again, but at last the dawn broke. It was still misty but he was anxious to get on. He opened his wallet and found it was getting low; there was enough for two fair meals, but he divided it into three portions and took one.

The wind had dropped but he had taken the precaution of marking its direction on the ground before he slept. However, that would not avail him long. He wondered what Aline was doing. He was sure that somehow Providence had intended him to help her. Suppose he had done wrongly and should meet his death and deprive her of his aid! Why was life so continually perplexing?

195

When he started to move, his swollen blistered feet made every step painful, but gradually he became more used to it and struggled on mechanically.

He was going very slowly, although it was down hill, and it was with joy that in rather less than four hours he came across a mountain track running according to his guess east and west. "This must surely be the road from Alston to Kirkoswald," he said, and feeling more or less reassured he sat down. But he was so worn out from fatigue and lack of sleep that he almost at once fell into a deep slumber.

When he awoke he found a shepherd-boy looking at him. "You sleep soundly, Master," he said; "whither are you bound?"

"I am going to Carlisle," he answered.

"I have been in Carlisle once," said the boy. "It's a fine town, with bonnie sights; but that was not yesterday. I spend all my time with the sheep and it is rarely that I get a chance for such things. No, it's not much pleasure that they let come my way," he added dolefully.

Ian looked at the boy, who had a fine face and was well proportioned in length of limbs and figure, but thin and ill nourished, with hollow cheeks and angular shoulders. "I am afraid they do not feed you over well," he remarked.

"Not they," said the lad,—"I get my brose in the morning and none too much of that and then generally I get some more brose in the evening."

"Do you get nothing all day?" said Ian.

"Why, no," he replied.

"Would you like something to eat now?"

196

The boy's eyes lit up as Ian undid his wallet. "Surely," he said.

Ian gave him all that the wallet contained and smiled with pleasure as he watched the boy ravenously devour every morsel. It was the first glow of satisfaction that Ian had had since he left Holwick.

As the boy munched away Ian thought he might get what information he could; at least he would know how much more road there was before him, which was advisable now that he had nothing whatever left to eat.

"Do you know the names of the hills?" he asked casually, as though hunting for a topic of conversation.

"Why, of course," said the boy. "Black Fell is up that way and Cross Fell is over there. If it was a clear day you could see the hills in the west too, Skiddaw and Blencathara and Helvellyn, and all the rest of them.

"I wish I was going with you to Carlisle," he added somewhat wistfully; "a city is better than the hills; not that I do not love the hills," he continued, "but an apprentice gets more to fill his stomach than a shepherd lad, leastways than one who has no father and mother and who works for Farmer Harrington."

Ian's heart always went out to children and this gaunt but rather handsome boy interested him not a little. "How old are you," he asked, "and what is your name?"

"My name is Wilfred Johnstone and I shall be twelve come Martinmas."

"Would you like to be apprenticed in the city and do you know anything about it?"

"That should I," he answered; "I should like to be[197] a carpenter like Johnnie o' the Biggins, whom they sent to Thirsk last year. Some day he will be a master carpenter and be building roofs and houses and sic like bonnie things."

"But, Wilfred, what would Farmer Harrington say if you left him?"

"Well, I cannot tell but he would not have cause to say much, for the way that he treats the men and the lads that work for him. I very nearly left him and tramped into Carlisle last week; but it's hard to become an apprentice if you cannot pay your footing."

Ian had two or three gold pieces left, so he took out one and gave it to the boy. "That will enable you to get to Carlisle, and back again if need be, and stay a while anyway to see if you can find a place. I might be able to help you if you can find me. See the sheep are all right to-night and then come along. I shall be about the market cross most days at noon, and if you do not find me the money will take you back."

The boy's eyes grew round with astonishment. He took the money and tried incoherently to express his thanks, and then after a pause he asked, "What's your name?"

"Oh, call me James Mitchell; but look you," Ian added, "do not tell a soul about meeting me or ask for me by name in Carlisle. I cannot help you if you do. Promise me."

The boy looked Ian squarely in the face and held out his hand. "I promise," he said.

Ian grasped the hand and felt the magnetism of a mutual understanding, the boy was clearly honest and true and would keep to his word. "Well, good-bye and God[198] be wi' ye," said Ian, and turned away northward.

After they parted Ian kept along in the same manner as before and to his great gladness the mist towards evening began to lift. But he was faint and famished and felt weak from want of food. The sleep had done him some good, but he had slept too long and lost most of the day. He felt a little less melancholy after he had seen the boy, but he was still very depressed. His mind ran on old Moll and her talk about the spirits of darkness. Consequently it was a distinct shock when he caught sight of a gigantic figure looming through the mist and striding along a little below him as though seeking a place so as to come up on his level. It was many times larger than himself and in the dim curlings of the mist had a most terrifying aspect.

Ian began to run but the figure started running also. At last he stood still and the figure stopped and turned towards him. For a moment his brain, dizzy with hunger, contemplated a fight with this supernatural being. He mechanically grasped his staff and raised it, and the figure did the same.

Then the tension relaxed and Ian laughed. It was the brocken, the strange spectre of the hills formed by the distorted shadow of his own figure on the mist! In all his hill-travelling this was the first time he had ever seen it; and, although he laughed, the little incident had not helped to steady his nerves. "It has, however, one advantage," he said; "I now know my direction from the position of the sun."

Then suddenly the mist broke and there before him was revealed a glorious view. The sun was setting in a crimson glory and the hills of Cumberland, still cloud199 capped, were flushed with delicate colours. He was below Blacklaw Hill, and Cold Fell blocked the view to the north. Immediately in front was the great plain of Carlisle and beyond that the waters of the Solway. Far on the left a silver glitter showed the position of Ulleswater. It was radiantly beautiful and the more so, because of the contrast with the cold and darkness of the mist.

He decided that on the whole he had better keep to the hills, but it grew dark and he had to spend another cheerless night on the high ground, which was made worse by the gnawing hunger; but somehow his spirit seemed brighter, and in spite of the cold and pain he did not feel so unhappy.

When the morning broke, he set off with a light heart to Brampton, where he secured food without being asked any question and in the evening he found himself in Carlisle.

200
CHAPTER XVI
A DESPERATE TASK

WHEN Ian reached Carlisle he secured himself a room at the old hostelry near the Cathedral, sent a message into Scotland that he had arrived, and then spent some days in general enquiries as to the possibility of getting work. In this he was not very successful, but was more so in the case of Wilfred Johnstone, whom on the fourth day of his arrival he met at the Market Cross.

Ian was sitting watching the people, when the boy came up. He had a stick over his shoulder with a small bundle containing his belongings.

"How long have you been in Carlisle?" asked Ian.

"I have only just arrived," said the boy.

"Come along then; we must see what we can do for you. I suppose there is no likelihood of Farmer Harrington coming to look for you."

"I do not know," said the boy, "and I do not know whether he could compel me to come back, but he might. I am an orphan and all my folk are dead. I lived with my Aunt Louisa Johnstone until she died this winter; she had no children of her own."

"Then she was really only your Uncle's wife."

"No, she was my mother's sister. My name is not really Johnstone, but I was always called that because I lived with her."

"What was your father's name then?"

"It was Ackroyd."

"So your real name is Wilfred Ackroyd?"

"Yes."

"Then we can call you Will Ackroyd or Willie Ackroyd, and if Farmer Harrington comes asking for Wilfred Johnstone, he won't find him."

"You are right, Master."

"Come along then, Will. I have found a carpenter called Matthew Musgrave who is actually in need of a lad, so I think we can settle that difficulty."

Matthew Musgrave was a good hearted fellow, who took kindly to the boy and the arrangement was concluded. The result was that he also began to take an interest in the stranger who had introduced him, with the final issue that James Mitchell, as we must now call Ian, who was remarkably clever with his hands, used to go round to help Matthew when he was extra busy; and gradually Matthew found him so useful that he gave him more or less regular employment.

He had decided to keep to the name of James Mitchell, which was the name he had used on the Continent when he fled from England not long after Mary's accession. Even his friends in France did not know his real name. If ever he should return to his own country he would resume it; meanwhile James Mitchell did well enough. Moreover his recent captors knew him by his real name and it might be some slight safeguard. He smiled as he remembered how he had instinctively given the children his own name. It had seemed the natural thing to do.

After about a week Erskyne arrived and he was accompanied by Mortoun himself, who hoped to obtain further personal information by word of mouth, beyond that contained in the documents.

"I hear you have had some sore delays, James Mitchell," he said.

"Yes, my Lord, I was imprisoned for some time in York and wounded and sick and in hiding for over two months."

"You are a Scot I understand."

"I am, my Lord."

"And of the reformed faith?"

"That is so."

"We shall need the services of all good Scots if there is any fighting to be done. Can we rely upon you?"

"By my troth, you may, my Lord; I shall be found here."

Ian then put the shoes on the table and they ripped them open. The contents were practically uninjured and they talked till late into the night.

As they retired to rest, Erskyne remarked;—"Master Knox has found a good servant in you, James Mitchell. I am glad to have met an honest man with an honest heart, ay and an honest face," he added. "Good night."

The next morning they left early and Ian felt that an epoch in his life had closed. He also, not unnaturally thought that, having reached Carlisle in safety and found employment, his adventures were for the time at an end, but instead of that they were only just beginning.

Although Wilfred had obtained his wish, he was obviously restless and unhappy. On several occasions Ian203 had tried to get at the reason, but the boy was uncommunicative. At last he admitted that it was because he had left something behind at Master Harrington's near Kirkoswald.

"I think I shall go over and get it," he said.

"But that would hardly be safe," Ian objected; "Master Harrington might not let you have it or let you go again."

"It is not in a house," said Wilfred; "it is hidden in a tree. I could find it easily in the dark."

"How did you come to forget it?" asked Ian.

"I did not exactly forget it; but I had to slip away in a hurry and did not dare to go back; besides I thought I might have to return to Kirkoswald in any case and perhaps it was as safe there as anywhere. I knew it would be possible to go and fetch it and I must go now."

"I cannot but think you are very unwise, Will."

"But you do not know what it means to me," said the boy.

Ian respected the child's secret and asked no further. "Well, I shall be very anxious until you come back; you cannot do it in a day. Where will you sleep? It is getting late in the year."

"Oh! I shall manage somehow," said the boy. "I shall start to-morrow forenoon, Wednesday, and shall be back on Thursday soon after noon."

"Then if you are not back, I shall be very nervous about you and shall come after you."

"No, do not do that, Master; I shall be all right."

Ian was not satisfied, but he let the boy set off early the following morning.

Wilfred trudged away along the road without mishap, resting now and then and taking it easily, as he did not want to arrive before dusk. A little after sunset he arrived at the outskirts of the farm and made his way cautiously to the hollow tree. He looked round carefully, but no one was about. He then crept into the tree and felt in the corner for a pile of stones. In this was concealed a small wooden box. He took out the box and drew from it a packet wrapped in oiled canvas; within this was another with the open edges thickly smeared with tallow.

He took that off also and within was another piece of oiled canvas, but the packet was now small enough to go into his pouch, where he put it without opening it. "It would be too dark to see it," he said to himself.

"I think I shall sleep here, it is as good as anywhere." He waited until he was certain that no one was about and came out from the tree to gather leaves with which to make a bed and then he lay down.

Excitement and cold, however, kept him awake for hours and it was not till far on in the night that he fell asleep. When he awoke it was broad day, although still early. "I have slept too long," he thought; "it was a pity I did not fall asleep earlier." He peeped out and there was nobody in sight, so he softly stole away toward the road.

But he had not gone fifty yards, before the thundering voice of the reeve, his particular enemy, called out,—"Hulloo there, I see you sneaking round, you young thief. But you will not hide from us again, I'll warrant."

The reeve started running and Wilfred took to his heels. The reeve was a powerful athletic fellow, but Wilfred was light and nimble. He dodged under a fence that the reeve had some difficulty in surmounting, and in that way gained a little at the start.

For a time the distance between them did not alter, both were holding themselves in reserve; then it occurred to Wilfred to turn up hill; he might not be so strong, but his wind would be better. The reeve puffed and panted after the boy, who steadily increased his lead. When Wilfred reached the top of the slope he glanced round, the reeve was far behind; then he plunged down the hill where there was a burn at the bottom, and splashed through it with some difficulty, as the water was up to his waist and the bank on the other side was steep.

The reeve gained during the process and, being taller, made light work of the burn and was close behind. Terror lent wings to the boy's feet but the reeve slowly overhauled him and could almost reach him with his arm. Wilfred could hear his loud breathing just behind him, when the reeve, tripping over a root, not only fell headlong but rolled into a ditch.

Wilfred laughed and fled like the wind; there was a thick wood not a hundred yards away and he would be safe.

His adversary picked himself up and was just in time to see Wilfred approaching the wood. He would easily have escaped, but another man appeared coming out of the wood at the same moment. "Catch him, Joseph," yelled the reeve, and the exhausted boy fell an easy prey to the newcomer.

206

The reeve was considerably hurt by his fall and it greatly increased his anger. "Where have you been, you young rascal," he roared, "and what have you done with the sheep you stole?"

"I never stole a sheep," said Wilfred indignantly, "and it is no business of yours where I have been."

"Oh, isn't it; we'll soon see about that. Do you know what happens to boys who steal sheep?" said the reeve vindictively.

Wilfred was silent.

"Come now, what happens to boys who steal sheep?" he went on with malicious glee.

Wilfred was still silent.

"You need not be so proud; come answer my question," and taking the boy's arm he twisted it round till the tears stood in his eyes, but he restrained himself from crying out. "What happens to boys who steal sheep?"

"They are hanged," said Wilfred at last; "but I have not stolen sheep or anything," he said doggedly.

"You can say what you like, but the sheep disappeared and you disappeared, and here you are sneaking round in the early morning. The case is as good as proved," and the bullying ruffian kicked the boy brutally.

The two men led him along to the old grange and locked him up in a small room, high up near the roof.

Wilfred knew that the reeve had spoken truly. Young lads with no friends were not of much account, and nothing but a miracle could save him.

He sat there for hours, as it were dazed and stunned, and then toward evening he opened his pouch and took out the little packet and unfastened it. It contained half a groat and a long lock of hair. "Oh, Joan," he said, "I wonder what will become of you when I am gone. I wonder if any one will ever tell you what happened to me. Master Mitchell was quite right. I should not have come back. No, even for your sake it was better not to come. For now I have lost everything, everything. And there was I going to become a carpenter and lay by a plenty of money and come and marry you when I was big. They say a boy can't love," he said bitterly; "they know nothing about it;—I do not suppose they know what love is. If only I were dying for you, Joan, I should be quite happy, but to die for what I have not done...!"

He threw himself on the floor and sobbed and sobbed until from the sheer physical exhaustion of the paroxysms of grief he fell asleep.

Meanwhile Ian was anxiously awaiting his return. The strange feeling that had possessed him ever since the day that Aline had talked about it in the secret room and that lately had been somewhat less intense, came back stronger than ever. He could not explain it, he could not reason about it, he only knew that something terrible was in the air and that it did not only affect Wilfred or himself. So strong was the feeling that he did not wait till the next morning. He merely lay down for a few hours and set off soon after midnight, so as to reach Kirkoswald at dawn. It was one of the last places where he wished to be seen, but he seemed to be drawn by fate.

He had grown a beard while at Holwick and he further disguised himself before starting by pulling out half his eyebrows, which were thick and bushy, and likewise the hair above his forehead for the space of half an inch.

"No one would be able to recognise me, who did not actually know me," he said. "I certainly do not answer to any description of myself that can have been sent around."

He went to the different hostels and gossiped with every one. He could not ask questions at all direct, as that would have raised suspicion. He began to despair, but at last his patience was rewarded. By good luck his informant was a young farm hand who had been friendly with Wilfred and whose sympathies were strongly on his side. Like every one else, so he told Ian, he was certain that Wilfred had committed the theft and equally

115

certain that he would be hanged; but in a guarded way he let it be seen that he strongly disapproved of such extremities.

"Yes," he said, "they will never take him out of that little top-room except to his trial and death." Ian longed to ask where the top-room was but felt it would be too risky. When the young fellow rose to leave the hostel, Ian strolled out. "I may as well stretch my legs," he said.

He had turned the conversation to other subjects, but, as he had hoped, they passed the grange and he looked up and remarked casually, "I suppose that's where the boy is of whom you spoke."

"Yes," said his companion, "in the second window."

"From the left or the right?" he managed to say unconcernedly; "it's strange what scenes may be going on behind a wall and no one know."

209

"From the left," said his companion, "the one with the dripstone half off."

"Poor boy!" Ian said; "how foolish to risk one's life, though, for a sheep; but other people's doings are always inexplicable. Where did you say you lived yourself?" he went on.

"A quarter of a mile down the path."

"Where the oaks are? Those are good trees; there must be some timber worth having."

Ian did not return to the subject of Wilfred and he parted from the youth as they neared his cottage. He strolled back to the grange. It seemed a fairly hopeless case, ladders would be impossible without an accomplice; moreover there was a moat that ran around two sides of the house and the window was over the moat. Could he try and save the boy by his own evidence? No, that was useless. It might be of little avail in any case, and, as he himself was a suspected fugitive it would more probably destroy any slender chance that there might be.

He did not dare to linger, but he cautiously inspected the situation and saw a desperate chance. Away on the far side was a tall elm tree whose branches came very near the battlement; the tree itself was unclimbable but another tree whose branches actually touched the first one seemed to offer an opportunity. It was that or nothing.

A very long rope was clearly necessary and how to get that without exciting suspicion was indeed a problem. Ian secured a room in the principal hostel and looked round the stable yard, gossiping with the ostlers. When no one was there he found a short length of stout210 rope, but it was not enough. At last he bethought him of his bed and, on examining it, he found that the rope carried across and across under the mattrass was nearly new. This would mean that he would have to come back to the hostel, but as he had purposely obtained a room on the ground floor so as to be able to slip out easily, that presented little difficulty.

It was a dark night and rain was falling slightly; he undid the rope from the bed which was in two lengths and spliced them and the other rope together. As he set out his heart smote him. The risk was immense. If he were caught it was more than likely he would be hanged; if he escaped that, there was a very considerable chance of being recognised as the escaped heretic and then he would be burnt. But, even without being caught, the operation itself was so dangerous that it was as like as not that he would break his neck. Was he justified in risking his life when Aline's necessities might require him? There certainly seemed no other chance for the boy; he had thought of all the obvious possibilities of saving him, but every case was barred by an insuperable objection less obvious, perhaps, but fatal nevertheless. "Why am I made so that I always see both sides so clearly?" he said. "Other people have no such difficulties in making up their minds."

It did not occur to Ian that even the difficulty would probably have presented itself to another man in a different way. Ian's problem was merely when and for whom to risk his life; some of us might hesitate before risking our lives at all. However, after pondering for a while it suddenly occurred to him that Aline would wish it. That settled it; the two problems disappeared;211 there was only one problem and that was to act as carefully as possible. Aline would undoubtedly counsel that much.

He crept along very quietly; it was almost too dark; every twig that cracked, every slight stumble that he made caused his heart to beat violently.

Once he started a dog barking and had to remain motionless for a long time, but the most trying experience was that when he had cautiously stolen very near to the grange, a figure on horseback rode up and passed within a yard of him. He stepped behind a tree and saw the door opened. A flood of light streamed out and before he could get on the further side of the tree again he felt he must be seen.

Once more he waited a long time till all was dark and quiet. He climbed the first tree with less difficulty than he expected, but the branches of the two trees were further apart than he had thought. Finally he had to go up higher and lay the rope over a branch and lower himself, holding the two ends and then, after reaching the other tree, pull the rope over the branch by one end.

The rain and the darkness made discovery less likely; but everything was slippery and the difficulties were greatly increased. Having climbed up higher he started along one branch but after he had reached the furthest safe point he found that he was still a long way from the wall.

Again he tried a second branch, but, although a little nearer, it was an awful gulf in the black night.

A third time he crept slowly along another slippery branch that swayed and bent under his weight. "Suppose212 the whole thing should break, elm trees are notoriously treacherous," he thought.

The branch was worse than the second and he had to go back to that one. This time he managed to wriggle out a couple of feet further, where the branch gave a sudden turn upward and to the left, parallel to the face of the wall. He could dimly discern the top of the parapet on a slightly lower level, perhaps six feet distant. He tied a heavy knot in the rope and swung it out to hit the stonework, so as to measure the distance. It was perhaps rather under than over seven feet. But a seven foot jump from a wet swaying branch, with a forty foot drop in the pitch darkness was a fearsome task. The thought made him feel quite sick and the nausea made his brain reel. A slight squall of wind blew up and the branch rocked and creaked ominously. He had to hold on with all his strength or he would have fallen.

When he had recovered himself a little, a thought struck him; he would double the rope and loop it round the branch and then tie the ends firmly about him under the arm-pits. The rope was not very strong; but surely, if doubled, there was just a chance of its standing a sudden jerk.

After he had done this, he nerved himself for the last effort, but before standing up, he prayed for Aline passionately, fervently, as though the intensity of his prayer should insure its answer. He then rose and, balancing himself with difficulty, leaped across. He reached the parapet; but it was wet, while the lichens on it made it like glass and he slipped down, down, down, into the void.

213

He heard a laugh as of a fiend and saw Aline's face blanched with pity; there was an awful wrench under his arms and a snap above; one of the thicknesses of rope had broken;—but he was still alive. He climbed hand over hand feverishly, without pausing an instant, up the slimy rope and then held on to the branch, while wave after wave of uncontrollable terror swept over him. His excitement was so violent that he feared he would lose his reason. He used all his will power to bring it under control; but he could not do it. Must he abandon the attempt, could he ever force himself, there, in the horrible yawning blackness to go through with it again? His teeth chattered and, do what he would, his hands shook till he nearly fell again. Then he thought of Aline and saw her swimming the river, while he rested his wounded arm upon her shoulder. "Coward," he hissed through his teeth, "coward. But oh, Aline, if only it were for you!"

"It is for her, though you do not see how," said a voice within.

Gradually he grew calmer, so that by a supreme effort he forced himself to tie the broken rope and again stand up. He stooped over to the left, where the branch turned, and holding on with both hands he kicked the branch till he broke the bark a little and roughened it. Then he raised himself upright and putting every ounce of strength and will into the leap, he cleared the space and landed in a crenellation. He fell and hurt himself considerably, but what did that matter?

Untying the rope from himself, he slipped it from the tree and cautiously made his way round the parapet. He had to climb three gables and there were other difficulties,214 but at last he was over Wilfred's window. He slipped the rope round a merlon[19] and climbed down and knocked at the window.

118

19 The merlons are the projecting upright portions of a battlement.

The boy, who was sleeping a light nervous sleep, woke at once and luckily had the good sense to make no noise. Clearly any one at the window was a friend; enemies came to the door.

He rose and went to the window and opened it. "Gramercy, Master Mitchell, is that you?"

"Hush, yes," said Ian, and stepped into the room. He pulled down the rope by one end and, before doing anything else, properly spliced the broken piece lest it should catch.

They then set the bed a trifle nearer to the window and looped the rope round the bed post.

"Can you swim, Willie?" said Ian.

"No, Master."

"That is very serious," he said, "as this rope will not stand both of us, and it is so dark that I cannot first lower you till you just reach the water."

"But I can climb well," said the boy.

"That is all right then, but remember the rope is very wet."

Ian tied the two ends together and lowered them slowly, till the rope hung looped at its middle point round the bed post.

"Now, as you cannot swim I must go first. I only hope the rope is long enough. It cannot be more than a few feet short anyway, and worse come to the worst you must take a long breath and drop into the water.215 But before letting go, when your legs are dangling, grip one end of the rope and hold it, cut the rope above and the other end will fly up and we can pull it through. I want to leave no evidence."

Ian gave him a knife and then climbed out and gently let himself noiselessly down the rope. He found that the ends hung about two and a half feet above the water, just beyond a swimmer's reach.

Wilfred then followed, full of apprehension. When near the bottom Ian whispered,—"Hold on, but let your feet down into the water." As the boy's feet reached the moat, Ian trod water and put his arms up to him. This reassured him; as the child, who could not swim, naturally shrank from the plunge into the black deeps in the specially trying surroundings.

"Cut the rope, hold the knotted end tight and let go," said Ian. As the boy dropped, he caught him and by going under himself prevented the boy from being completely submerged.

119

"Give me the rope," and Ian pulled down a long length so as to swim over. "Hold on to me," and he swam across.

Just as they reached the bank the short end ran up suddenly, and the whole rope fell with a loud splash.

The two fugitives waited fearfully lest it should raise the alarm, but nothing further broke the silence of the night.

As they walked, dripping, to the hostel, Ian said,—"I wish you were not wet, but who would have thought of this? What shall we do?" They climbed through the window and Wilfred shivered violently, partly with cold and partly with excitement.

"I shall leave the bed on the floor," Ian said. "Come, let us get off your clothes." He stripped the boy, rubbed him down with a dry towel and put him into bed. The friction started a warm glow and he was soon all right. Wilfred asked for his precious packet and while Ian was busy wringing out their clothes he opened it and dried the contents and put it under his pillow.

At four o'clock Ian woke him. "I am so sorry about the wet things, but you must make for Carlisle at once as best you may."

"Never mind, I am warm again now, and used often to be wet through all day, when I was with the sheep."

After Wilfred had gone, Ian replaced both ropes and put the bed right. He stayed in Kirkoswald till nearly evening so as not to attract attention, and for the same reason went on to Penrith and returned by the other road to Carlisle the following day.

He overheard a little of the gossip about the boy's escape. The most popular belief was that he had flown out of the window with the devil. Those who prided themselves on their superior intellects said that some one had obviously opened the door and hidden him in their house, just as they had clearly done at his first disappearance. An orphan boy, however, was not of much value one way or the other, and the thing as a practical question was a nine days' wonder; although a favourite topic of gossip, relating to things mysterious, for many a long day.

CHAPTER XVII
CARLISLE

LUCKILY Matthew Musgrave, who had given Wilfred permission to go, asked no questions beyond inquiring whether he had settled things to his satisfaction.

"I had some difficulties," said Wilfred, "but everything is all right now."

Wilfred lodged with Musgrave, but they would often both come round to the hostelry where Ian was. On one of these occasions a number of men were seated round the fire with tankards of ale, when a big burly fellow came in and asked mine host to draw him a tankard. Catching sight of Matthew, he went up to him and clapping him on the back, he asked how things were going.

"Well enough, thank you, Andrew, and how is all with you, now that you have settled down near the old place again?"

"Oh, not so badly; it is harder work than at Holwick, but it's good being near one's own folk."

Ian started slightly at the name of Holwick, but no one noticed and he guessed that this must be Andrew Woolridge. He waited a moment and then cautiously entered the conversation. "Where is Holwick?" he questioned.

218

"It's not very far south from here," said Andrew, "on the Tees a few miles from Middleton."

"What were you doing there?" asked Ian.

"Oh, I was working at Holwick Hall, Master Richard Mowbray's place."

"What sort of a place was that?"

"A fine big place, but they had not the money that the family used to have."

"What were they like?" inquired Ian.

"Yes, tell us something about them," said Matthew; "you have never told us much."

"Oh, they were all right. Master Mowbray was excellent and so were the young mistresses, but Mistress Mowbray herself was a tartar."

"Was that why you left?" asked little Wilfred.

"Well, no, not exactly," said Andrew. "I had a bit of a quarrel with them. These things will happen, you know"; and he laughed. "In fact, now that I think over it, I believe they were in the right. They were decent people, but queer in some ways, and so I thought I had better shift over here."

"What was the quarrel about?" asked Matthew.

"Oh, that is too long a story; but I thought they should supply me with enough corn for the winter and they were not willing. Maybe I wanted too much; anyhow I came away, but I am sorry sometimes too."

121

"Why?" said Ian.

"Well, if you must know I was sorry for the little mistress, Aline Gillespie, who lived with them. She and I did not get on very well; but Mistress Mowbray treated her like a dog. Mistress Aline, though, did me a good turn once, when I got into trouble, and somehow[219] I would have liked to do her a good turn too, by way of paying back. I do not like being in any one's debt. But there, I make mistakes like most of the rest of us. What do I owe you?" he said, turning to the innkeeper. "It's time I was going."

Andrew settled his score and was just leaving when another man entered.

"Hullo, Andrew," said the newcomer, "whither away in such haste? Come back, man," and then he added something in a low voice in which Ian distinctly caught the word "Holwick."

This was a strange coincidence, Ian thought, to meet two people within a few minutes who both knew Holwick and he wondered who the newcomer might be. He had not long to wait.

The stranger turned to the innkeeper and said, "Timothy, man, I'm back again; you've got a place for my pack-horses for the night, I hope."

"There's always room for old friends," said the innkeeper.

"Is there anything you'll be buying yourself?" asked the stranger. "Faith, man, but I've some fine things, but you're getting that set up in Carlisle that a man who only brings goods from Flanders and Italy and Persia and India, to say nothing of the latest novelties from London, is hardly likely to please you. But I've got some rugs now that would just stir your heart. You never saw the like. I have just refused 300 florins for one of them, but I'll let an old friend have it for that price."

"Oh, stop your gammon, Walter," said the innkeeper. "You need not tell me your tales. If there's[220] anything good and cheap, I may take it, but I do not want any of your flowery word fancies."

"Odds bodikins! mine host is very plain spoken," rejoined Walter, "but come along, sirs, what do you want?" addressing the little group, and he unrolled a bundle as he spoke.

Although Walter made the most of them, his wares really were thoroughly good stuff, and he had a happy taste in making his selections; consequently he always did good business wherever he went, and it was rumoured that he had a pretty pile laid by for a rainy day.

He sold a few things to those present and was rolling up the bundle, when Ian caught sight of a singularly beautiful silver buckle of admirable design and workmanship. It was of a superior class to most of the trinkets that the packman had with him. He said nothing at the time but waited for a more favourable opportunity, as the packman was staying for the night.

In the evening Ian and the packman were seated alone at the fire. Ian looked around carefully, the door was shut, so he decided that he might broach the subject of Holwick.

"I suppose you travel far," he said.

"Yes, Master Mitchell, I cover the length of the country once every year, but I work mainly in the north between here and York."

"Are you going to York now?"

"Well, I expect to do—after a time; but I am going to Hexham and Newcastle and Durham and shall then work my way up the Wear and down the Tees and probably up Wensley dale."

"Do you know Upper Teesdale?"

"Why, yes, but it's an out of the way place. Yet, do you know,—many of these out of the way places are my best customers. When I was last there I sold a large quantity to Master Richard Mowbray of Holwick Hall."

"You know them then?"

"In a business way, yes," said Walter.

"There's a little girl that is living there, that I know slightly," said Ian.

"What, Mistress Aline Gillespie! the bonniest child I ever saw in my life. I shall never forget that child, although I have only seen her once. 'Sdeath, man, she has the face of an angel and the soul of one too, beshrew me if she has not."

"Well, she comes from my country, although I cannot say that I have any extended acquaintance with her any more than you have."

"I am sorry for that bairn," said Walter, lowering his voice and looking round; "she has none too happy a time with the Mowbrays. But there, it may be gossip," he continued, as the thought occurred to him that he was not sure of his listener. "One hears such funny tales as one goes about the country; one does not know what to believe."

"You are going that way again then?" said Ian.

"Yes, yes, and perchance if you know the child, you would like me to tell her that I had seen you."

"May be so; and I might send her one of your trinkets. I saw a little buckle that might take her fancy."

Walter got up and fetched the bundle and produced the buckle. "Honestly, man," he said, "that is a more expensive class of thing than most of my stuff; but I will let you have it cheap. Yes, really cheap; I know you think I always talk like that, but I swear I am speaking true."

There was an earnestness in the man's tone and manner that was quite unlike his usual jaunty way of talking and Ian felt he might venture to say more.

"I believe you," he said. "Well, I will buy it and send a letter with it, but promise me that no one else shall see you give it to her."

"You know the old cat too, then, do you?" said Margrove, a little off his guard.

"Mistress Mowbray, you mean," said Ian. "Well, I know about her; and in these days least said is soonest mended."

"Yes, we dwell in strange times," the packman responded, "the land has passed through sad experiences," and then, fearing he might have said too much, he added, "Maybe it is all right, but I have no fancy to see human flesh fry."

"Nor I either," said Ian. "I saw them burn George Wishart, and I shall not forget that on this side of my grave."

"It's my belief," said Walter, "that the church does itself more harm than good by the burnings; it does not have the effect that they expect."

"I believe your sympathy is with those who are burned," said Ian, looking at him keenly.

"Maybe it is and maybe it isn't; but anyway I say that Mother Church does not always see where her own interests lie. But my business is chaffering and I do not meddle in these matters, see you there."

"Tut, tut, man, you need not mind me, say what you like. I care for the burning no more than you do and no finger of mine would ever be stirred to get a man into trouble."

"Well, neighbour," said Margrove, "you speak fair, neither would I. If George Wishart had come to me I should not have told them where to find him."

"Then keep my secret," said Ian, "and give Mistress Aline the buckle without a soul knowing it. While I am about it," he added, "I will take this chatelaine, and that will do for the other little mistress."

"Then it was not only in Scotland that you knew Mistress Aline," remarked Walter, looking at him shrewdly.

Ian was half sorry that he had said so much, he might have enclosed the chatelaine for Audry without telling Walter Margrove; but he said off-handedly;—"The Gillespies

124

lived in Scotland, but were cousins of Richard Mowbray. I have never seen him, but I know he has a daughter."

"Ay, he has a daughter, and she would be worth going some way to see too; only she is outshone by her cousin. But Mistress Audry is a bonnie lassockie and will make a fine woman. Yet it's a pity the Mowbrays have no boy. It's a sad thing for the family to die out."

Both men were silent for a time and then Margrove spoke. He looked at Ian questioningly,—"I believe I have seen your face before," he said; "your name's not James Mitchell." He gave the fire a stir, and as the flame shot up he said, "Were you ever at Northampton?"

"I was," said Ian.

"Then you are the man to whom I owe everything.224 Why did I not recognise you before? I have heard they had seized you and I heard afterwards that you had escaped to France,—see this," he went on, drawing a small copy of the New Testament from his doublet. "I have not the courage to go about as you do; but I too have done a little, and, if need be, I hope I shall have strength not to deny the faith."

There was silence again, this time Ian spoke. "I wonder if you know where a Greek Testament could be obtained, you travel much and see many things."

"It is strange that you should say that. I have two concealed in an inner pouch in my pack, that have come over from Amsterdam and I was taking them to Master Shipley near York, who had asked me to obtain one for him."

"Then will you let me have the better one and take it along with the buckle?"

"Is that it, then?" said Margrove. "Poor child, poor child!"

"No," said Ian, "you are wrong, they do not know at Holwick that the child has any thoughts that way; you must act with all the caution you can command."

Walter brought the testaments and Ian chose the smaller one, which was most beautifully bound with little silver clasps. Walter wanted not to charge for it, but Ian pointed out that that would deprive him of the pleasure of being the donor.

"Before we retire," said Ian, "I should like to ask you how you came to meet Andrew Woolridge. Do you know his story? You can be quite open with me, as I know why he left Holwick."

"Then for heaven's sake don't tell the people here,"225 said Walter. "The man is consumed by remorse, though he tries to pass it off lightly. He is honestly trying to do everything that he can. You are not the only one who has sent a present to Mistress Aline. I can tell you that much, and if Andrew knew who you were, he would not mind. He is a changed man since he left Holwick. He told me that the vision of the child haunted him day and night.

"He does not like to talk about the child, but really, if I believed in spells, I should think the child had magic in her. I never saw a man so completely spell bound and I must confess that although I only saw her once, she holds me almost as though I were enchanted."

"It is the same here," said Ian.

"It is a most marvellous thing," Walter continued, "because she seems quite unconscious of it; not in all my experience have I ever met or heard of anything like it before. That's three of us, in fact the only people that we know anything about, and it may be the same with every one she meets."

They talked a little longer and Ian discussed his plans for taking up the packman's life when he had gathered sufficient money, as a means of spreading his message through the land. Then as the hour was getting late they went to their rooms.

226
CHAPTER XVIII
A DIPLOMATIC VICTORY

IAN had started a letter to Aline some time before, using the parchment with the holes. This he finished and carefully wrapped it up with the buckle, the testament and the chatelaine.

In the morning he found Walter and drew him aside. "She may have a letter to send back," he said, "so try and give her an opportunity. Keep your eyes and ears open too, and find out and tell me everything that you can."

Walter Margrove put the packet inside his doublet, and, after settling the girths of his horses, shook hands warmly with Ian, mounted and rode away down English Street to the South Gate, leaving Ian looking after him, as he gradually drew away.

He had a long journey before him and his thoughts were full of the man he had left behind. He had heard Ian Menstrie speak at an open air meeting in Northampton, and at first had been struck by the fiery eloquence of the young Scot and had then been arrested by his message. He had always longed to meet him again; and here he was, actually able to do him a small service. Then his thoughts turned to Holwick and the beautiful irresistible child that had so strangely fascinated him, in spite of himself, in the few minutes that he had seen227 her. He had not liked to question Master Menstrie, but he wondered what could be the connection between the two; what could the child, obviously a lady, have to do with Menstrie, a common carpenter? Truly it was a remarkable world.

He reached Haltwhistle that evening and did a little business there on the following day and called at a number of outlying houses on the way to Hexham. Business was good and it was nearly three weeks before he found himself turning his horses' heads over Middleton bridge to reach the hamlet that has a way in but no way out. "No wonder they say, 'do as they do in Holwick,'" he muttered,—the local proverb for "doing without," as his horse stumbled in the thick muddy track.

Somehow he felt full of forebodings as he approached the Hall.

Fortune favoured him in one respect, however, as he met Aline herself a few hundred yards from the gate. She smiled brightly when she saw him, and held up her hand. He took the little hand and then dismounted and led the horse. "I am so glad to have you come," she said; "I have been looking for you for a long time. You look tired. I wonder if Elspeth could get you something nice before you have to undo your pack. I'll run on and ask her."

Before he could stop her she had run on, and he had to mount his horse and trot after her and call;—"Not so fast, Mistress Aline, I have something to say to you and we may not get another opportunity. Here is a small packet from Master Menstrie. Hide it in your dress." Aline's eyes shone with sudden pleasure; but as Walter looked at her he thought she was not looking well.

"How did you find him? Do you know him? Where is he? How is he? What is he doing?" said Aline, all in a breath.

"Softly, softly, fair and softly; one question at a time," said Walter. "I found him in Carlisle, and by accident I mentioned Holwick and he sent this to you."

"But how is he and what is he doing?" asked Aline.

"He seems fairly well and is working as a carpenter."

Aline looked surprised. "I did not know he was a carpenter," she said. Ian had not spoken much about his past life. She remembered him saying something about working on hinges, but she had thought of him in that connexion as a master artist, and so humble an occupation to one of her birth and surroundings was a little bit of a shock; but she checked it instantaneously and added, "But I expect he is a very good carpenter."

Walter Margrove was puzzled. Aline then apparently did not know a great deal about Ian Menstrie and he did not know how much to say and how much to leave unsaid.

"I am afraid I do not know very much about him," Walter deemed the safest reply; "but he seemed to be getting on all right."

Aline too felt something of the same sort, while Walter thought it best to change the subject, and added,—"But I have something else for you, Mistress Aline." He produced another small packet, which he undid, and took out a beautiful carved ivory comb. "This," he said, "is from Andrew Woolridge. You can let the others see it if you like, but perhaps it would be wiser not." Walter was thinking that it would be best not to call the attention of people to the fact that he was in any way a means of communication between Aline and others. "Andrew cannot write, like Master Menstrie, but he bade me tell you that he wished you well and that he hoped some day to show himself worthy of your forgiveness, but that meantime he would say nothing more."

Aline was quite overcome for a moment. "I am afraid I judged him too harshly, and he has already sent something to Master Mowbray."

"Yes," said Walter, "I think the man has turned over a new leaf. But we are near the house and I want also to give you a little thing from myself; it is only a length of fine linen, but it may be as useful as trinkets. I have it here in my holster. If you do not care to be seen with it, I daresay old Elspeth will manage it for us."

"But you must not give me things," said Aline. "Why should you?"

"Well, Mistress Aline, I know of something in Master Menstrie's package, as he bought it from me, and I fear me that you will meet with trouble. Pray God the way may be smooth to you; but it is not so for many who have dared to read the Scriptures for themselves. I am of the reformed faith myself and He has dealt mercifully with me; for I know I am a weak vessel. But remember you have only to call on Walter Margrove and if ever he can help you he will do it."

"Good day to you, Walter," said the voice of Master Mowbray. They were approaching the drawbridge and there was no opportunity for further conversation.

Master Mowbray was coming out, but he turned back230 when he saw them approaching. "So you have fetched the packman and all his fine wares," he said to Aline. "Are you trying to buy up the best things before we get a chance, lassie?"

The thud of the hoofs on the drawbridge and their clatter on the stones within, had already drawn forth heads from the windows and in a moment a crowd of persons was gathering round Walter and asking him a hundred questions.

Walter answered the questions as well as he could and made his way to the great hall, where Mistress Mowbray had the first chance of inspecting his stock.

She was in a more affable mood than usual and laid in a good supply of materials, amongst others some very fine kersey, which she said should be used to make a cote-hardie for each of the children, and a piece of applied embroidery for orphreys.[20] Audry was standing with her arm round Aline, next to Walter, and, as Mistress Mowbray turned aside to examine some silk nearer the light, he slipped the parcel of linen into her hand and whispered that it was for Aline.

20 Broad bands of applied embroidery.

It was somewhat late in the day when Walter arrived, so that he decided that it was necessary to stay the night. His horses were stabled at the Hall and he himself lodged at the house of Janet Arnside.

Walter knew that she had recently come over to the new faith and he sought an opportunity for a meeting with two or three others in her house. They came very quietly, but their coming was not likely to arouse suspicion, as the packman was considered good company wherever he went.

After they had all gone Walter began to talk about Aline, her strange power of fascination and her unique, almost unearthly beauty. "I wonder if the child can be happy up there," he said.

"I doubt if she is," said Janet; "she comes in here often and John and I have many times noticed a far-away wistful look in those deep blue eyes of hers, bright and cheerful as she always is."

"I wish, Mother, she could hold our faith," said John. "I am sure it would make her happier. Life has been a great deal more to me since these things first came my way."

Walter sat and said nothing; he thought that on the whole it was far safer for little Aline if no one knew. "Poor little soul," he said to himself, "it is a different matter for these people who can confide in each other, with no one else in the house; but for her, sweet innocent, it is indeed a case of the dove in the eagle's nest."

John watched Walter's thoughtful face and then said, "Is there anything we could do for her?"

"Not that I can see," said Walter; "but look you, there might be; the child, as we know, is not exactly among friends and none can say what a day may bring forth. She has had a narrow escape already. You keep a careful look-out, my lad, and if ever you can get a chance you can let Walter Margrove know all that goes on. By my halidame, I would not have any harm come to the bairn. I do not know why she has got such a hold on me, but so it is."

"That will I do," said John, "she has the same hold on all of us. There can hardly be a man or woman in the parish that would not die for that child. They just worship her. Those of the old faith are sure she is a saint. I should not be surprised but that they say prayers to her, and she is sweetly unconscious of it all. You know old Benjamin Darley? Well, I was passing his house the other day, and Mistress Aline was seated near the door with her feet on a little wooden stool. She rose up when she saw me and said good-bye, as she wanted to come and see my mother; but ran across into Peter's cottage to fetch something. Old Benjamin did not see me, as I stood there waiting, but I saw him pick up the stool and kiss it reverently and put it away on the shelf, while the tears stood in his eyes."

"I guess, lad, you have done the same," said Walter.

"And what about yourself, Walter?" said John, evading the question.

"Maybe I do not get such opportunities; are you coming up to the Hall with me to-morrow to see me off?"

"No, I must be off to work, but good luck to you."

So the next day Walter said good-bye to Janet and went up to the Hall. He met Elspeth in the courtyard. "Good morning, neighbour, how is all with you and how is your bonnie little mistress?"

"I am doing as well as can be expected, and Mistress Audry is not ailing."

"I meant Mistress Aline, not that Mistress Audry is not as bonnie a child as one would meet in a nine days' march."

"Ay and a good hearted one too, neighbour," said Elspeth. "It's not every child who would take kindly to ranking second after they had always been reckoned the bonniest in the whole countryside. But there, Mistress Aline might give herself airs, and yet one really233 could not tell that she knew she was pretty; so I do not think it has ever occurred to Mistress Audry to mind and she just enjoys looking at her. They are fine bairns both of them."

"Ay, they are that," said Walter.

"I just pray," continued Elspeth, "that I may live to see them well settled. My mother served in the Hall and my grandmother and her father and his father again, and so it is. As long as there is a Mowbray I hope there will be some of our blood to serve them and Mistress Gillespie is a Mowbray, mind you that, and some say," she went on in a whisper, "that she should be the Mistress of Holwick. It was a new place when the old man built it, the old Mowbray property is down Middleton way and is now let. Maybe, if there's anything in it, that's partly why Mistress Mowbray does not love the child. But there, it is all gossip, and I must be moving."

Walter settled his packs and took as long over it as he could in the hope of catching sight of Aline. In this he was successful, for a few minutes afterwards he saw the children, who were really looking for him. Aline handed him a letter for Ian and asked how soon he expected to be able to deliver it.

"I wish we could see him," said Audry involuntarily.

Aline looked at her and Audry subsided.

But Walter, who spent his life studying human nature, saw the glance and began to puzzle it out. "So Ian Menstrie does know both the children then and it was not a mere matter of courtesy to send the chatelaine for Audry. But this is very curious," he reasoned. "Janet Arnside has not mentioned him nor have any234 others of the reformed faith. Strange how he could be in Holwick and not see them. And I mind too, that he said he had never seen Richard Mowbray. Truly it is mystifying."

Another thing that perplexed him was Janet and John's desire that Mistress Aline should hear of the faith. Obviously, she knew of it and yet they were unaware of the fact. He began to see daylight;—somehow the children must have found Menstrie in some hiding place. Walter was too cautious a man to mention anything that he discovered in his journeys that might conceivably bring mischief, and too honourable a man to try and discover a secret that clearly did not concern him.

The children seemed to cling to Walter as though loth to let him go and even after he had mounted his horse they accompanied him a long way down the road; then, fearing, if they went too far, it might give rise to questionings they bade good-bye and after waiting to wave a last farewell as he reached the next bend they turned reluctantly back.

"You should not have said that just now," observed Aline.

"Said what, dear?"

"Said that you wanted to see Ian. Of course Margrove may really know Ian and his affairs but he may be doing this as a kindness to a stranger and probably he did not know that Ian had ever been here, he might simply have met my family in Scotland."

"Well, all this suspicion and concealment is not like you, Aline," said Audry.

"Oh, dear," Aline answered, "yes, I do not like it; life is really too hard."

235

The children had reached the Hall and went up to their own room to undo the package. Aline opened it and within were the smaller packets marked respectively,—"For Audry" and "For Aline."

Both uttered a cry of delight as they beheld their treasure.

"I am afraid you will hardly be able to wear the chatelaine," said Aline, as she bent affectionately over her cousin. "I am so sorry."

"Not just now perhaps, and you will not be able to wear the buckle, but isn't it beautiful and was it not good of him to remember that that was what I asked for; and after New Year's Day, when I have had other presents, I do not think it would be noticed. I have always wanted a chatelaine so badly."

Aline's long hair had fallen forward as she stooped; she tossed it over her shoulder with the back of her hand and rose and held out the buckle to catch the light. It was far the finest thing she had ever possessed. Fortune was not so unkind after all. Here was a treasure indeed!

"Now we must see how the chatelaine looks," she said, dropping to her knees and sitting back on her heels, while she attached the chatelaine to Audry's belt. Then a thought struck her. "Let us also see the effect of the buckle," she went on with a laugh, and the sensitive fingers deftly adjusted the buckle to seem as if it were fastened to the belt.

"Oh, they do go well together! Audry, they look charming!" Would Ian mind, she wondered to herself; no, he would like her to be generous. So, stifling a touch of regret, she said aloud, "They look so nice that you236 must keep the buckle"; and she pulled Audry down to the floor and smothered her objections with kisses.

Then she sat up somewhat dishevelled and reached over for the Testament. "You wanted a chatelaine and I wanted a Greek Testament. Isn't it a lovely book?" and she fastened and unfastened the chastely designed clasps. "With the help of the Latin I shall soon be able to read it. I am so glad I can read Latin easily. I must keep it in the secret room, I suppose. It would have been safe in the library; but Ian has written my name in it."

"Master Menstrie is not as cautious as he might be," observed Audry, "but I must not stay here, Mother and Elspeth want me, to go over my clothes. Then there are those people coming to-morrow about that Newbiggin matter and she may want me to have some special gown. Good-bye."

Aline was left alone. So to-morrow was actually the day they were coming! She had gathered her information, but she had not laid her plans. Somehow or other those people at Newbiggin must not be unjustly treated. Mistress Mowbray must not have her own way in the matter if she could prevent it.

She found herself, therefore, definitely setting out to fight Mistress Mowbray. She had never before quite realised that it was an actual contest of wills; but, when she came to think about it, Mistress Mowbray had been making so aggressive a display of her power lately that Aline did not altogether shrink from a trial of strength, as though she had been challenged; in fact she rather enjoyed it. The problem was, how was it to be carried through?

237

It was certainly not likely that she would be invited to the discussion. If she came in, as it were by accident, she would undoubtedly be turned out. She must get Master Gower on her side beforehand anyway. After that there were several possible plans of campaign. They were certain to have a meal first and one plan would be to raise the subject herself and get it discussed at the table, another would be privily to interview every guest, if opportunity offered.

She decided that she would go and see Master Gower alone and set out on foot to Middleton. She crossed the bridge and turned up to the left bank of the river till she came to Pawlaw Tower. It was a small pele with a barmkin.[21]

21 A small tower with a little enclosure or courtyard.

After being admitted at the gate, she asked to see the master, and was conducted up a narrow wooden stairway to the hall, which was on the first floor.

"What would you have with me, little maid?" said Hugh Gower, as the child came in.

Aline had been very nervous, but his kindly manner reassured her. "I want to talk about the people of Newbiggin," she said.

"The people of Newbiggin! and a sorry set of loons, too!" and his face clouded a little. "What have you to say about them, fair child!"

"I want to speak to you that they be not all dispossessed."

"By all accounts," he replied, "the sooner there standeth not stone upon stone, nor one stick by another of all that place, the better will it be for the country-side."

238

"Not so," she said, looking fearlessly at him, "it would be a right sore thing that the innocent should suffer." Aline was no sentimentalist and was quite willing that the wicked should suffer their deserts according to the stern measures of the day; but this proposal of indiscriminate chastisement had roused the mettle of the high spirited child.

"How now, Mistress Aline Gillespie; but you are too young to understand these things. Children's hearts are too soft and if we hearkened to what they said, there would be an end to all order."

"Marry, no," she answered boldly, drawing herself up, "it is order I want to see and not disorder. Punish the guilty and spare the innocent. Wanton destruction is not order, and that indeed liketh me not."

"It is a nest of scoundrels, little maid, and all your pretty haughtiness cannot save them."

"Some of them are scoundrels, I know, harry them as ye may, but some are god-fearing folk that never did harm to you or other. I know one carline there, whose like would be hard to find by all Tees-side."

Her mien was irresistible. "Come sit and talk," he said. So Aline pleaded for the better folk, while she spared no condemnation of the worse.

She not only gained her point, but she gained a staunch ally as well. Master Hugh fell under her witchery and nothing would content him, but that he should find her a horse and ride back with her to Holwick.

"It's a fine old place, this home of yours," he said, as he looked up at the gateway-tower, with the arms of the Mowbrays over the entrance archway;—"a meet abode for so fair a princess," he added gallantly;239 then helping her to alight and bowing low over her hand, like a courtier, with a gravity half playful, half serious, he kissed it, mounted his horse and rode away.

Aline had tried also to get hold of Lord Middleton's reeve, but was unsuccessful; her plans, however, were favoured next day by the representative of the Duke of Alston arriving an hour too soon.

Mistress Mowbray was busy in preparations and, little knowing what she was doing, caught sight of Aline and called,—"Hither, wench, come you and take Master Latour into the pleasaunce and entertain him as ye may."

Ralph Latour was a tall stern man and Aline's first thought was that she would fail, but she soon found that, though hard and in a measure unsympathetic, he had a strict and judicial mind, and was quite ready to accept her standpoint, although entirely without warmth or show of feeling.

The child, however, fascinated him also, like the rest. Yet it was in a somewhat different way from her hold on other people. He was a man of considerable learning and taste, who had travelled widely, and in his cold critical way was absorbed in the subtlety of her beauty. Aline thought she had never met any one so awe-inspiring as he made her walk in front of him or sat her down opposite to him, in order that he might look at her.

They discussed the subject thoroughly and he concluded by saying,—"Mistress Gillespie,—you are Mistress Gillespie, I understand?"

"Mistress Aline," she corrected.

"I am told that you have neither brothers nor uncles and that the line ends in you, does it not?"

240

"True," she said.

"Mistress Gillespie, then, I repeat, you have shown considerable acumen and you may take it that there is a coincidence of view between us. Yes," he added, absent-mindedly speaking aloud, as he looked at her little foot, "the external malleolus has exactly the right emphasis, neither too much nor too little, and I observe the same at the wrist in the styloid process of the ulna. I crave pardon," he added hastily, "it is time that we joined the others."

They found that Master Bowman, Lord Middleton's reeve, had just arrived with his lady, and the company proceeded to the hall.

Aline had thought best not to mention the matter to Cousin Richard, as he might discuss it with his wife and her plans be frustrated. She felt sure, however, that he would take her part if any were on her side at all.

"These be troublesome days, madam," said David Bowman, addressing Mistress Mowbray. "It looks as though all authority were to go by the board and every man go his own way. Mother Church is like to have her house overturned by these pestilent heretics."

"Ay, and a man will not be master in his own house soon either, methinks, neighbour," said Richard Mowbray.

"How now, Mistress Mowbray, what think you?" Bowman resumed. "Shall we not at least keep our kail better in future, when we have cleared the rabbit-warren?"

"What rabbit-warren?" said Audry innocently.

"The rabbit-warren of Newbiggin, child," replied Bowman; "only these rabbits are fonder of sheep and chickens and folks' corn and money than of kail, but we'll have them all stewed shortly."

"In the pot, with the lid on," chimed in Eleanor Mowbray, "and it shall be hot broth too."

"I hardly think your broth would be very tasty," observed Master Richard.

"Tasty," echoed his wife; "it would be the tastiest dish served to the Master of Holwick this many a long day."

"Master Richard's imagination is too literal," said Bowman; "he's thinking of the old leather hide of William Lonsdale, and tough bony morsels like Jane Mallet; but we could peel them and take out the pips."

"Your humour is a trifle broad, neighbour," remarked Master Gower; "the little ladies might appreciate something finer."

"Finer indeed—what, and get as thin as your humour, Master Gower, that we must needs go looking for it with a candle. But humour or no humour, what are we to do with these knaves? How counsel you, Mistress Mowbray?"

"Turn them out and burn their houses," she answered, "and let them shift for themselves."

"I think we should give them something to help them to get elsewhere," said Master Richard.

"Ay, their corpses might be an unpleasant sight, lying round here," dryly put in Ralph Latour.

"But why turn them out at all?" asked Aline at last. "It's only one or two that have done any harm, why be so hard on the others?"

"Nonsense, child, where there's a plague spot, the whole body is sick," cried Mistress Mowbray. "The plague spot will always spread, and they are all involved already, I'll warrant; away with them all I say. And what do you mean, child, advising your betters and thrusting yourself into wise folks' counsels?"

"It liketh me to hear a child's views, if the bairn be not too forward," said Latour gravely. "There is a freshness and simplicity about them that we are apt to miss after our long travailing in the world."

"'Simplicity,' indeed," rejoined Mistress Mowbray, "simpleton is the kind of word you want. In my young days we were taught our place; 'freshness,' forsooth! We want no fresh raw wenches to open their mouths in this place, anyway."

Latour took no notice of his hostess' rudeness, but turned to Aline saying,—"But do you not think, child, that a severe example would be a terror to evil-doers far and wide, and Mistress Mowbray is doubtless right, they will all be infected, even if the evil in every case does not show itself. All through the world's story the innocent have suffered with the guilty; moreover, it will quicken in them a responsibility for their associates. Besides, if, as Master Mowbray suggests, we help them on their way there will be no hardship done, it is only a change of abode. Come now, Aline, is that not so?"

Mistress Mowbray watched exultantly. She was not sure that these calm measured phrases were not more crushing than her own invective. "Now, child, you see how little you understand things," she observed patronisingly.

Master Latour, however, was not acting as a partisan; he was merely putting the case, partly to show all sides243 and partly because it interested him to test Aline's powers.

"Master Latour is a just man," said Aline with some hesitation, "and I think he will understand when I say that I really know that these people are not all bad,—that the disease, as you call it, has not spread so far but that it may be checked." She paused for a moment from nervousness, and looked a little confused.

"Take your time;—festina lente,[22]—develop your argument at your convenience," said Latour not unkindly.

22 Make haste slowly.

"With regard then to the question of example," Aline went on, recovering herself and catching something of Latour's manner of speaking, "with regard to the question of example, you all know that this 'change of abode' will only stir up bitterness and that that will spread tenfold and may wreck us altogether. A punishment that the others feel to be just is a lesson; a punishment that is felt to be unjust is a flame for kindling a revolutionary fire.

"You say I am a child and I do not know; but, please, I do know more about these people than any of you. I have spoken to every one of them. I know them all; and about some of them I know a great deal. I do not suppose there is any one here, except myself, who even knows their names, beyond those of his own tenants. Marry, now, is that not so?"

Aline having flung down her challenge looked around with flashing eyes.

Latour had been watching her with his cold aesthetic appreciation, admiring her instinctively beautiful gestures,244 but this time, he too felt a real touch of the child's magic as she glanced scornfully round.

"I do not pretend to be old enough to know what is the right thing to do," Aline went on, "but surely, surely," she said in earnest pleading tones, "people who want to be just should carefully find out everything first. Is that not so?" she asked, turning round quickly to Mistress Mowbray;—"Do you not think so yourself?"

Eleanor Mowbray was so astonished at the child daring to cross-examine her like that, that she was struck dumb with astonishment.

"Yes, of course you think so," Aline said, giving her no time to recover herself. "Mistress Mowbray entirely agrees," she went on, "as every just person would agree. That is so, is it not, Master Gower?" Master Gower bowed assent. "And there is no need to ask you, Cousin Richard."

"Yes, dear, you are right," he said.

Aline had swept swiftly round in the order in which she was most sure of adherents, so as to carry away the rest.

"Master Latour," she continued, "I am sure you will not disagree with them and will say that a proper examination must be held first, and that everything must be done that will stop bitterness and revolt while keeping honesty and order."

"That is entirely my view," said Latour, captivated by the child's skill and the gentle modesty which, in spite of her earnestness, marked every tone and gesture. "Who would have thought," he said to himself, "that anything so gentle and modest and yet so princess-like withal could be in one combination at the same time?"

245

Aline was least sure of Bowman, but while looking at him she concluded;—"Then I take it that you all think the same, Master Bowman."

She had not exactly asked him his own view, and he was sure that if left to himself he would have taken a different line. He was by no means certain that he was not literally spell-bound as he answered;—"Surely, Mistress Aline, we are all of one mind, including my wife, I think I may say." The lady smiled her complete acquiescence.

"Oh, I am so glad," Aline said, and slipping from her seat she went up to Master Richard and, in her most irresistible way, put her arm around him, saying:—"And you will let me help you to find out things, won't you, even though I am only a little girl?"

"Yes, if it is any gratification to you, sweet child," he answered, kissing her.

"That is all settled then," she said, "and when the ladies retire, you can examine me as the first witness."

"A very good idea; you seem to know every one's tenants," said Master Latour, much amused at Aline's triumph and adroitness, and determined that she should secure the fruits of her victory. As he was the strongest man there, both in himself and as representing the largest and most powerful owner, the others at once concurred. Part of the secret of Aline's extraordinary power was her entire selflessness. In her most queenly moods there was never the least suggestion of self, it was the royalty of love. Aline might use the very words that in other children's mouths would have been conceited and opinionated; yet from her they were more like a passionate appeal. This, associated with a quiet dignity of manner, generally produced a feeling of "noblesse oblige" in the hearer. The basest men will hesitate to use foul language and discuss foul things before a child. In Aline's presence the same occurred in an infinitely greater degree. It was for most people, men or women, impossible to be anything but their best selves before her; to do anything less would mean to be utterly ashamed.

Aline's conquest was complete and Mistress Mowbray saw that she would only expose herself to further defeat if she attempted now to open the question again. It was made the more galling as Aline's last thrust had practically shut her out of the council altogether. Why did that fool Bowman bring his wife with him? It would be too undignified for her to insist on coming after they had accepted Aline's proposition, unless she forbade Aline to be there; and that Aline had made impossible. So there was nothing left but to accept the situation with the best grace that she could and bide her time.

CHAPTER XIX
THE LOSS

MISTRESS MOWBRAY had not long to wait. The day after the matter of Newbiggin was settled Father Laurence was crossing Middleton Bridge, when he met "Moll o' the graves" coming in the opposite direction. He instinctively crossed himself at her approach. She saw his action, and stopping on the side of the bridge in one of the refuges, she pointed her finger at him and laughed a shrill discordant laugh. "Ha, ha, Sir Priest, you think you will triumph in my despite. I dreamed a dream last night and all the devils in hell got hold of thee."

"Peace, woman, peace, brawl not upon the Queen's highway."

"Nay, it is not peace," she said; "who talketh to me of peace?"

"Mary, you had better go home," said the priest kindly. "I was glad to hear that little Mistress Aline Gillespie put in a word for you and your folk at Newbiggin yesterday, so that there is the more reason for your peaceful homecoming."

"Mistress Aline Gillespie," said the old woman calming down and looking mysteriously about her. "Mistress Aline Gillespie, nay, she is not on our side. I see the hosts gathering for battle and she and thou are with the legions of the lost. Nay, Sir Priest, mock me not and mock not the forces that are over against you."

"Woman," said Father Laurence, "you speak that you know not, the powers of darkness shall flee before the powers of light."

"No, never, nothing groweth out of the ground but it withereth, nothing is built that doth not fall to ruin, nothing made that doth not grow old and perish, nothing born that doth not die. Destruction and death alone triumph. Shew me one single thing of all the things that I have seen perish before my eyes and that liveth again. No, you cannot, Sir Priest."

"The things that are seen are temporal, the things that are unseen are eternal," he answered.

"And who, thinkest thou, knoweth the unseen, thou or I? I tell thee that all alike shall pass save the darkness and the void into which all, both seen and unseen shall be swallowed up. Yes, in this very valley where we now stand, you shall see iniquity triumph and all your feeble prayers be brought to naught. Avaunt, avaunt, nor may I tarry here longer."

She brushed past him as she spoke, and the old priest looked sadly after her. "Poor thing," he said, "she is indeed in the hands of Satan."

He passed up the road on the way to Holwick and, as he entered Benjamin's cottage, he met Aline coming forth. The wind blew her hair out somewhat as she stepped into the open, and the sun's rays caught it, while she herself was still a little in shadow and it shone like a flaming fire. "It is a halo of glory," said the old man to himself as he looked into the beautiful innocent face. "Child, you did well yesterday," he said.

249

"Oh, but I am afraid, Father."

"Afraid of what, my child?"

"Afraid that Mistress Mowbray was not pleased."

"Fear not, Mistress Mowbray is an honest woman, she will approve of what thou hast said."

Aline did not like to say more; she wondered whether she had misjudged the lady of Holwick, or whether the old man's estimate was too charitable.

"God bless you, Aline," he said, as she turned to go up the hill, and before entering the door he stood and watched her out of sight.

She went straight up to the Hall and found Audry. "I wonder what Ian is doing in Carlisle now," said Aline. "Let us go down to the secret room. I have just met Sir Laurence Mortham. I think he looked sadder than ever, but he is a right gentle master. Do you remember that talk we had with Ian about our forebodings? I thought that it must have meant Ian's departure, but it is something more than that. I felt it again strangely to-day when I met Father Laurence, and somehow it seemed to me as though there was some terrible conflict going on somewhere, and Father Laurence was trying to stop it, but that he could not do so."

"Oh, do not talk like that, Aline, you do not know how creepy you make me feel. Come."

"The room looks very melancholy now," Audry said when they had descended. "I always associate this room with Master Menstrie. It seems very curious that we should discover him and the room at the same time."

"It is very cold down here," said Audry, "let us light a fire. That will do something to make the place more cheerful."

250

"Are there any fires lit upstairs?" asked Aline, pointing to the inscription over the fireplace.

"Oh, yes," said Audry, "several, it is getting nearly winter."

So the children lit a fire and occupied themselves in giving the room a thorough cleaning.

"I wish we could open this chest," Audry exclaimed, as she was dusting the great iron coffer. "It is very strange that it has no lock." Aline came and bent over it too. But although they pressed here and pushed there and peered everywhere, they only succeeded in getting their hair caught on a rivet, so that both children were fastened to each other and to the chest at the same time. So with much laughter they abandoned the attempt for that day.

"You know it's my belief," said Audry, "that that old iron coffer is the most important thing in this room; people don't put great heavy iron coffers into secret rooms unless they have secrets inside."

"But the secrets might have been taken away," said Aline, "although I admit that it does not look likely. The room seems to have been unused for so very long. But do you remember, Audry, we never finished reading that book after all. Why should it not tell us about the chest?"

"I expect it would; where is the book?"

"It is in this room, I think, in one of the bookcases." Aline rose to fetch it, but the book was not to be found. The children hunted all round the room, but they could not find it. They then went upstairs to their own room, but still it was nowhere to be seen. They looked at each other aghast.

251

"Oh, whatever shall we do?" said Aline. "Suppose that they find it, then our secret room will be no longer safe."

"But they may not be able to read it," Audry suggested.

"Oh, they are sure to find out, for they will have the parchment."

"The parchment," echoed Audry, "the parchment; then you will not be able to write any more letters to Master Menstrie. Why, you must have had it last night when you read his letter."

"So I must," said Aline. "Well, that proves it cannot be out of the house, for I have not been out except to see Walter Margrove go, and I am certain I did not take it with me then. So it must be somewhere here in our room."

They turned everything off the bed, they looked in the ambry, they lifted the movable plank and looked under the sliding panel, but the book had absolutely disappeared.

"It is very mysterious; do you suppose any one has been in and taken it, Aline; it is very small and thin, it is true, but it could not actually vanish."

Aline sat down on the bed and could not keep back the tears. "There is only one comfort," she said, "and that is that Master Menstrie told us how to make another parchment; besides I read his letter three times over last night and I think I could make a new one from that, for I believe I could remember it. But, oh, dear, I am certain some one has taken the book and it will be found out, and then they will see that the secret room has been used and will guess that that was how Master Menstrie escaped and that we helped him. It may even lead to their finding out where he is."

Audry knelt down on the floor and put her head in her cousin's lap, and her arms round her waist. The late Autumn sunshine flooded the room, but it brought no joy to the sorrowing children.

"Who can have been in the room?" Audry said at last.

"Elspeth, I suppose," said Aline. "I think we must run the risk of asking her. She cannot read, but even if she has not seen it, she might tell some one that we had lost it. However, we must take our chance."

So they went and found Elspeth and began to talk to her about the packman's visit. Just as they were going Audry managed to say quite casually, "Oh, by the way, Aline, I suppose Elspeth cannot have seen your little book."

"What book, hinnie?" said the old dame. "I cannot read and all books are alike to me."

"Oh, it was a very thin little book; I must have mislaid it in our room. You may possibly have noticed it lying round somewhere if you have been in there this morning."

"I have seen no such book, dearie, and I would not have touched it if I had."

CHAPTER XX
PERSECUTION

THE children went about with terror in their hearts expecting every moment that they would be discovered. On coming in to dinner they fancied that Mistress Mowbray looked at them with unusual severity, but she said nothing, yet perhaps it was only because Master Eustace Cleveland of Lunedale was there.

The guest looked at Audry, who came in first. "Is that your daughter?" he said to Richard Mowbray. "By my troth, sir, but you have cause to be proud of her."

Master Mowbray presented the child and she louted[23] low and went to her place. Meanwhile, Mistress Mowbray had signed to Aline to be seated. When Master Cleveland looked across again he saw Aline and started visibly. He did not as a rule take the least interest in children, but this was a revelation. "I did not know that you had two daughters," he said, and was going to say something further, when Mistress Mowbray, who had noticed his pleased surprise, cut him short by saying: "She is Master Mowbray's cousin, a Gillespie, her great grandmother married one of those Scots; the family of course came to grief and Richard seems to think it is his business to see after her. But you would254 not believe the trouble she is, to look at her. It's amazing how sly and dishonest some girls can be. I have something to say to you later, Aline, about what I found in your room this morning."

23 The "lout" was the predecessor of the curtsey.

Aline shook and looked terrified, to Mistress Mowbray's joy, who was delighted at confusing her before the stranger.

Master Cleveland felt his heart fill with enmity toward Mistress Mowbray. "I am sure that woman is a liar," he said to himself, and he could hardly take his eyes off Aline all through the meal, except for an occasional glance at Audry, who also fascinated him not a little.

"Well, I shall never think children uninteresting again," he thought, "if ever they can look like that. 'Sdeath, I should like to see those two when they grow up, they will be fine women. That Gillespie girl is quite uncanny,—simply to look at her makes one feel a low born brute. Widow Pelham shall have a new cottage, by my halidame she shall; and Jock Mostyn shall have a pension. God in heaven, what a face, and what hands! I did not know there were such hands."

After dinner Mistress Mowbray went with her guest and Master Richard through the Hall and the gardens, and the children escaped.

Cleveland saw Aline again for a moment. He was coming back from the garden and she nearly ran into him. "I cry you mercy, Master," she said.

"Then give me some Michaelmas daisies as a token of repentance," he said laughing.

There was a magnificent show of huge blooms along one of the quaint old paths, so she ran and gathered255 them and held them out. He took them from her hand with a ceremonious bow and put them in his bonnet. "My favour!" he said, "it is a pity there is no tourney, little lady. Mother of God," he added to himself, "it's time I turned over a new leaf."

At supper Mistress Mowbray said nothing to Aline, because her husband was present. He for his part saw that the child was looking unhappy, but had forgotten the remark at dinner, as Mistress Mowbray was always saying sharp things; so he tried to enliven her.

"Thou hast never read to me again, little one, to-morrow thou must read something from one of those old books that thou hast found in the library."

Aline trembled; then Cousin Richard knew too, she thought. What should she do with herself?

"Methinks I would as lief have some more Malory," he went on, "and Audry would like that too, or mayhap ye would like to ride over to Stanhope with me, what think ye, the two of you?"

Aline breathed again. Then perhaps he did not know after all. "I would fain go to Stanhope," she said.

"So would I," said Audry, as both the children saw that it might put off the evil day with Mistress Mowbray. "It will be our last chance of a good ride before the winter, it may come any time now."

The next morning therefore, the three rode over the moors to Stanhope. It was a glorious day and Aline for a time forgot her troubles.

The day following they had to go in to Middleton Market, so it was not till after rere-supper that Eleanor Mowbray took Aline apart and said,—"Come with me, I want to speak with you."

256

Aline's heart sank.

"I want to know," Mistress Mowbray began, "what you mean by taking such liberties in my house? I have told you what you may have and what you may not have, and you dare to take things to which you have no right."

Aline hung her head.

"You may well look ashamed, you young hussie, but I tell you there is going to be an end to this kind of thing. I cannot think why Master Mowbray interfered with my arrangements about the library, when I had forbidden you to go in, but he will not interfere this time I'll warrant you.

"I went up into your room yesterday and found there a length of fine new linen. What business have you to be buying fine linen withal, when I say that any coarse dowlas is good enough for you? When you are in this house you will crave my leave before you do such things; you will do as I say and dress as I say or, certes, I will know wherefore."

Aline felt relieved. After all it was only the linen and Mistress Mowbray even thought she had bought it; but the angry dame went on;—"The more I see of you the more I mislike your conduct and I do not care for such baggage to associate with my daughter. It would be my will to turn you from the house, but Master Mowbray sheweth a foolish kindness toward you, so I have compacted with my sister Anne that Audry shall go over to Appleby right speedily and pay her a long visit. She hath ever wanted to have the child there and it will be an opportunity for Audry to come to know her respectable cousins, and meanwhile I can keep you more under my eye."

257

Poor little Aline. At the moment this seemed more terrible even than anything that could have happened if the book had been discovered.

"Moreover," said Mistress Mowbray, "you are getting too much of the fine lady altogether, you seem to forget that you are not a member of this family and that your position should in sooth be that of a menial."

Eleanor Mowbray calculated that, with Audry out of the way, it would be more possible for her to wreak her spite on the child without it being known. Why should this pauper dependent, this mere skelpie, dare to thwart her will? Master Gower and Master Latour indeed! should she not be mistress in her own house? And by way of further justification, was not Aline depriving Audry of her birthright, since, attracted as all undoubtedly were by Audry, they were attracted by Aline still more?

She then sent for Audry and Aline escaped to her room and flung herself on her bed. She was too heartbroken even to cry and could only moan piteously,—"Oh, Father dear, why did you go away and leave your little girl all alone in the world?" She then took out the miniatures of her father and mother and gazed at them. "Mother dear, when Father was alive, your little motherless girl could be happy; but now it is so very hard; but she will try to be brave." She then knelt down and prayed, and after that the unnatural tension passed and the tears flowed freely, so that when Audry came up to their room she was calmer.

"I call it a downright shame," said Audry. "If I am to go to Aunt Anne, why should not you come too? Aline, dear, I cannot bear to go away without you. I258 think I love you more than any one else in the world. Of course I shall have my cousins, but, oh! I shall miss you; and you will be so lonely."

"Yes, but grieve not, Audry, darling, you will come back again, and in sooth you should have a good time and Master Mowbray anyway will be kind to me and so will Elspeth."

144

"But that is not the same thing at all; there will be no one even to brush your hair, so this will be almost the last time."

The children were by now half undressed and Audry with the assistance of the new comb went through the somewhat lengthy process of brushing and combing the wonderful hair that reached nearly to Aline's knees.

When Aline had done the same to her, they put on their bed-gowns and Audry said, "You must sleep with me to-night." So Aline got into her bed and although they both cried a little, they were soon asleep locked in each other's arms. The moon peeped in and lit up the picture with a streak of light, which fell where one of Aline's beautiful hands with its delicate fingers and perfect skin lay out on the coverlet. No one but the moon saw the picture, but she perhaps understood neither its beauty nor its pathos.

CHAPTER XXI
TORTURE

THE few days before Audry's departure ran swiftly by and Aline found herself alone. Mistress Mowbray was determined to make the most of her opportunity and devised all manner of new tasks "to curb her proud spirit," as she phrased it. What did this child mean by coming to disturb their household, and why should she be so beautiful, a wretched pauper Scot? Of course she must think herself better than other people! "I have no doubt," said Mistress Mowbray to herself, "that the minx spends half her time when she gets the chance, looking at her reflection in the mirror. Yes, she's pretty, no doubt, with her saintly hypocritical face, the Devil is handsome, they say; and I am sure she is a bad one." It was no use for people to argue with Mistress Mowbray that Aline cared not the least about her looks, and indeed, strange as it seemed, was apparently unaware of her beauty. Mistress Mowbray only retorted that that was all part of her hypocrisy. "Why should the child have such hands?" she angrily asked herself one day, just after Audry had departed, "as if it wasn't enough that she should have a face fairer than any one else without having hands that no one could see without comment."

So one of Eleanor Mowbray's devices was to set Aline to clean down some old furniture with lye. Naturally this greatly injured the skin, and as the cold weather set in, she contrived that the child should always be washing something, till in a very short time the little hands were chapped and cut and in a shocking condition round the nails. When they were in this state she was set to clean brass and iron, until it was a continual torture, and yet Aline did not complain.

How she longed for Audry when she went lonely to her bed at night. If only there had been some one in whom to confide it would not have been so terrible; but day after day it was the same thing.

At last the hands became so sore that one morning in handling a pitcher, she let it fall and it was broken to atoms. This was the kind of opportunity for which Mistress Mowbray had been looking, but Aline was such a careful, thoughtful child that the chance had been long in coming. She told Aline that her punishment was that she should be confined to the house for a fortnight and in this way she knew that she would deprive her of her principal pleasure, which was to visit the people in the hamlet, particularly those who were sick.

It was no use, when Aline offered to pay for the pitcher. Mistress Mowbray would not hear of it. So the little girl would sit by the window when she was not actually being made to work and watch the oncoming winter, with the first snow on the high ground and the brown withered grasses blown by the wind. All the purple of the heather had long since gone and the moor looked sere and joyless. "But, oh, for a breath of the fresh hill-airs." Aline gradually began to long wildly and pine for a run in the open breeze.

The longing grew to an uncontrollable desire and at last Aline, the law-abiding innocent child, could bear the injustice no longer. After all, Mistress Mowbray was not her mother and there was no absolute reason why she should obey her. Master Mowbray, she knew, would disapprove of her being kept in, and so at length she decided one afternoon to make her way into the open along the secret passage.

No sooner thought than the thought became a deed, and she found herself swinging the stone and letting herself down into the cool open fresh air of heaven. It seemed at once to make her better; she filled her lungs, she laughed and stepped quickly down the stream, and then broke into a run. Oh, the joy of it after being cooped up for so long. It was so delightful that she was tempted to make her way down to the river and look at the waterfall.

She stood watching it and her mind turned to what she had been doing. Was she right? After all Mistress Mowbray was her guardian and responsible for her, no matter how cruel she might be. Aline was filled with doubt.

"I am afraid I have done wrong," she said to herself; "the world would all go to confusion if every irresponsible person and child behaved as it pleased toward those who have the management of things. Of course they do not always manage properly, and they make mistakes and do wrong, and so should I if I were in the same place. But somebody has to manage things. Oh, dear, it is very difficult, but I suppose until I am old enough and wise enough to manage things better, I must submit to be managed and be learning how not to do things when my time comes. I am afraid I have been very naughty."

Aline had a developed power of reasoning far beyond the average child of her age but a capacity, however, by no means altogether uncommon, particularly at her time of life.

What was her consternation on turning round to see Thomas Carluke standing on the bank a little lower down and watching her.

He came up and spoke, saying,—"It's a fine day, Mistress Aline; we do not often get so good a day so late in the year. You will be enjoying the fresh air. I noticed you have not been out much lately."

Aline winced, as she was feeling a little ashamed of herself,—but she only said, "No, but a day like this is irresistible."

"Well, I am glad you are enjoying it," said Thomas, with an evil look in his eye, and turned back in the direction of Holwick.

Aline wondered what to do. She felt a strong temptation to go back as fast as possible by way of the secret passage and be in before Thomas could get there. He would, of course, be astonished at seeing her and would probably say something; she could then draw herself up stiffly and say;—"Thomas, you are dreaming, I hope you have not been taking too much liquor," a thing of which Thomas was notoriously fond. "How can you talk of such obvious impossibilities." If he were inclined to persist she could suggest that it was her263 wraith;[24] and that would frighten Thomas terribly, as they were all very superstitious.

24 The ghost of a living person.

But she felt it would not be right, however unjust Thomas and Mistress Mowbray were, and however justified she felt in refusing to obey her.

Meanwhile Thomas went on gloating over his discovery, and he found Mistress Mowbray at once.

She took him into the hall and bade him be seated.

So there they sat for a moment looking at each other, the sly undersized man, with his low ill-developed forehead, and the keen looking, cruel, but dignified woman. "What is it, Thomas?" she said.

"I have but newly seen Mistress Aline out by the High Force," he replied, "and I know that you bade her not to go without doors."

"Yes," said Mistress Mowbray. "Is that all?"

"That is all about Mistress Aline," he answered, always greatly in awe of the lady, "but, an it please you, may I have a little of the new meal?" he added with sudden boldness.

Eleanor Mowbray looked at him. This came of listening to servants' tales. She paused an instant; it was very undignified to be bargaining with menials, but the man might be useful to her; she bit her lip and then said, "Yes, Thomas, you can have a boll."

Thomas did not attempt to conceal his delight. He had obtained something that he wanted and he had gratified his spite against Aline, whom he hated as something petty and mean and base will often hate what is lofty and pure and noble.

Mistress Mowbray was glad that she had now a genuine264 case against Aline and was determined that she would act with exceptional severity.

Aline was sick at heart, there was no one in whom she could confide and she was utterly lonely and miserable. She thought of telling Cousin Richard, but she was rather afraid even of him; and then too, although Mistress Mowbray was unjust, she felt that she had no right to take the law into her own hands.

She lay on her bed in a paroxysm of grief,—"Oh, I wish and I wish that I had not done it," she exclaimed again and again, and it was long before she felt equal to facing Mistress Mowbray once more.

When she came down to rere-supper, Mistress Mowbray was waiting. Master Richard had not arrived. "What do you mean, you dishonest child, by going out? I hate a child I cannot trust," she said in freezing tones.

"I have not been dishonourable, Mistress Mowbray. I never said that I would not go out. I was disobedient and I am sorry, but if Father was alive, he would not have liked me to be kept in doors; and I do not think Cousin Richard would approve," she added with some boldness, as she knew it was really unjust and had no one to defend her.

At that moment Master Mowbray entered. "What is this, about 'Cousin Richard'?" he exclaimed.

Aline was silent and Mistress Mowbray looked confused. After a pause, as he was obviously waiting for an explanation, Aline said,—"An it please you, Cousin Richard, Mistress Mowbray and I do not agree, that is all, it is nothing."

"I insist on knowing," said Master Mowbray.

265

"I forbade Aline to go out," said his wife, "and she not only flatly disobeyed me, but she questioneth my authority."

"Is that so, Aline?" he asked, looking very surprised.

"Yes, cousin, I did disobey and I am sorry." Aline knew, if she said more that he would take her side, and although she could not pretend that she had any great love for Mistress Mowbray, yet she did not want to get her into trouble with her husband.

Richard Mowbray was silent for some time and then he said, "You have not explained everything." He glanced at the sad little face opposite to him and noticed that it was looking thinner and a little drawn; the child was not only unhappy, but unwell. Surely, he thought, she has something more to say on her side. His wife looked triumphant.

"You have not explained everything," he repeated, "have you, little one?" he added tenderly.

It was said so kindly that it was almost more than Aline could bear, but she managed to say, "That is all that I want to say, Cousin Richard."

Richard Mowbray saw pretty well how the land really lay and said somewhat sternly to his wife, "Eleanor, I heard my name mentioned as I came in, I should like to know why it was used."

Mistress Mowbray had thought her triumph complete and was so taken aback that there was not time to think of anything to say, so she could only blurt out the truth.

Richard Mowbray stood up, as his manner was when roused, and walked up and down the hall with a heavy measured tread; he was a huge, powerful man, and although266 kind hearted, was very strict and most people, including his wife, were afraid of him.

"The child is right," he said, "I do not approve. I cannot think what is the matter with you and why you do not treat her more justly. Aline," he said, "I do not think you ought to have gone out without my permission, but you can go out when you like. In future, however, always ask me before you disobey Mistress Mowbray."

"Yes, Cousin Richard," said Aline, "it was wrong of me."

Mistress Mowbray breathed a sigh of satisfaction. Richard Mowbray's last few words undid all that he had done before. She knew that Aline was far too proud ever to appeal to her husband and, in a qualified way, he had even supported her authority.

So things grew worse for Aline instead of better. Mistress Mowbray had even descended to telling Thomas to keep an eye on the child and he followed her about whenever he could, and made her life hateful.

She was occasionally able to get up to her room and down the secret passage into the open, away from Thomas, but gradually even this grew dangerous, as Mistress Mowbray would keep her at work all the time, and, if she slipped away upstairs, would send some one after her to fetch her down. Twice the messenger had gone up very soon after Aline and had found the room empty; and Aline's explanation that she had gone out of doors was received with incredulity. Aline was also frightened of meeting old Moll at the other end and always peered round nervously as she emerged from the cave-room.

267

If they should follow her closely and suspect the secret passage then she would lose her one retreat which somehow she felt might be of help in an emergency. The secret room too was her one solace, the only thing of interest left to her.

Although she knew she was watched, she did not know to what extent and would carry her Greek Testament about with her and pull it out and read it when she had an opportunity. After all, neither Mistress Mowbray nor Thomas could read, so she did not think there was much danger.

Thomas, however, had noticed her take the book out of her dress and had observed its silver clasps.

His own intelligence would probably not have been sufficient to enable him to hurt the child, but he was a friend of the priest who served the chantry in Holwick. He was a low born fellow given to loose living and very fond of liquor, which Thomas would occasionally manage to steal for him from the Hall. He was one of the very few who did not like Aline. He felt her purity and charm was a reproach to him, and once, when she had met him in a condition somewhat the worse for drink, she had very gently spoken to him in a reproving tone, though she did not actually presume to reprove him. But he never forgot it. He liked enjoining heavy penances for the gentle sweet-natured child; while Aline, for her part, tended to avoid the confessional, when she could, not for the penances, but because she disliked the man and felt little or no spiritual value from communication with him.

He had once or twice had slight suspicions about her orthodoxy, although he had paid no attention to it; but268 one day, when he and Thomas were talking over a measure of stolen ale, the conversation turned upon Aline.

"I hate her pious face," he said.

"So do I," assented Thomas. "It was a pity that Andrew did not finish his job."

"These wretched folk think more of her than they do of me," said the priest. "When they are sick, it is always little St. Aline they want and not the good Father,—'Little St. Aline,' ha, ha, ha!" he laughed viciously. "The devil take her."

"Ay, that may he; it angereth me to see them blessing her and carrying on as they do; what right has she to act so grandly with her herbs and comforts from the Hall and her good talk? Who is she, I should like to know? Mistress Mowbray saith she is but a dependent."

"Good talk, indeed," said the priest. "It's just blasphemy. What is she to be talking about,—a girl too,—a wretched female."

"Yes, a lot of evil bringers all of them, eh, Father, from Mother Eve onwards?" and Thomas' wicked face gave an ugly leer. "Ah, they are a deceitful lot, and there she is breaking Mistress Mowbray's crockery and running out when she is forbidden and you will see her sitting with her book as if she did not know what wrong was."

"What book?" said the priest. "Can she read?"

"A fine confessor you must be," said Thomas, "if you have not found out that the skelpie can read. They say she can read like the Lady Jane Grey."

"The Lady Jane Grey, a pestilent heretic! Mother Church is well quit of her; a pestilent heretic, I say!269 Ay, and Mother Church would be well quit of this brat with her sanctimonious ways."

"I should not wonder if she be a heretic, too," said Thomas. "What will Mother Church give me, if I catch her a heretic?" he asked greedily.

"Oh, I cannot say," said the priest, "but I think I could do the catching myself; but it is not in the least likely that she is a heretic. Where could she come by it?"

"You catch her forsooth! The skelpie is no fool, and she won't blab to the priest, but she might tell her tales to me. Indeed even if she is not a heretic, why not make her one and get rid of her?"

The priest rubbed his hands and the two heads bent close together.

Thomas agreed to swear that he had heard Aline say all manner of heretical things and this, with the testimony of Father Ambrose himself, they reckoned would be sufficient.

They were nearer the truth than they knew, but truth or no truth that did not trouble them.

Father Ambrose walked down to Middleton to discuss it with his superior, Sir Laurence Mortham,[25] but although he painted the heretic and her villainy in glowing colours and added that he was quite sure that she was a witch too and had sold her soul to the devil in exchange for beauty, he met with no response, even in a superstitious and bigoted age.

25 Those in priests' orders had the title, "Sir," in the 16th century.

"I am probably as zealous for Mother Church as you are and far more earnest against heresy," said the old priest, "but I do not agree with your point of view or approve of your spirit. Mother Church must be gentle and kindly and persuasive. There may now and then be a few obdurate cases where, for the benefit of the faithful and perhaps for the heretic himself, a warning example is necessary. It may, if he be obdurate, be well that he should purge his sin; but it must be but rarely and, personally, I am doubtful of its efficacy. God will punish, and, as for the example, it will work both ways. I will go and see the girl myself, an it please you."

Father Ambrose was afraid that this might defeat his plans; so he pretended to fall in with the old man's point of view and said, "Well, perhaps, Father, you are right and it is not necessary to take further measures just at present, so I will not trouble you."

But he had no difficulty in finding others who were more ready to assist him, and finally he got the matter carried to Bishop Bonner himself.

Unhappy as Aline was, she was, of course, quite unconscious of what was in store for her, although something unusual in Thomas' manner made her suspicious. He was aggressively obsequious and tried to induce her to talk to him, but she would say little.

One day, however, there arrived a tall priest with instructions to make a preliminary enquiry. Master Mowbray happened to be out, so he was taken to the lady of Holwick.

Mistress Mowbray opened her eyes in astonishment when she heard that Aline was accused of heresy. "I knew the jade was of little worth," she said, "but to think of that!"

Aline was sent for and the priest plied her with questions. He was very wily and spoke in a kindly way and tried to lead her on. It was soon very clear that she knew a good deal about the Bible that most people did not know. It was equally clear that, comparatively speaking, she attached little importance to the dogmas and authority of the church. But though unorthodox and heretically inclined, it was difficult to make a case against her from anything she said.

The child was so transparently honest that it was impossible to reconcile her position with Thomas' fabrications. However, this was Father Martin's first case and he was naturally anxious to prove his zeal for the cause, to his superiors, so he made of it what he could.

Not until he had secured every piece of evidence likely to help him, did he broach the subject of the book, which he thought was probably another of Thomas' fictions.

"By the way," said he, "you have a book that you carry about with you. Show it me."

Aline hesitated.

"Shew it me at once," he said sternly.

"I will make her shew it," said Mistress Mowbray, seizing the child roughly.

"You can let her alone, madam," said the priest. "Child, hand me the book."

Aline drew it forth and he looked at it. He could not read a word of Greek, and at first looked visibly chagrined; but he turned to the title-page, which was in Latin.

"Can you read this?" he said. Aline bowed assent.

"It is a most pernicious book. How much have you read?"

"All the first part and most of the rest."

He wished it had been an English translation, as his case would have been easier. "Have you an English translation?" he asked.

"No," said Aline, and he could see that she spoke the truth.

"Who gave it you, or how did you get it?" he asked next.

Aline was silent.

"Come," he said, "did you find it, or was it given you?"

Aline still held her peace.

"I must know this," he said impatiently, but Aline vouchsafed no reply.

"I cannot wait for you," he went on, his voice rising. "Answer my question this instant."

"I cannot do it," she said.

"By the authority of Mother Church, I command you to speak," he cried angrily.

Aline looked up at him fearlessly, as she sat there opposite to him on the other side of the long narrow table, her beautiful arms stretched over toward him and the delicate fingers moving nervously. The great masses of rich glowing hair flowed in waves over the board, and the perfect oval face with the chin slightly lifted showed the exquisite ivory skin of her throat, subtly changing into the more pearly tones of her face. The sensitive lovely lips with their clear cut form, trembled a little, but she said bravely,—"It would not be right, Father Martin. I am ready to suffer for anything I273 have done myself, but I cannot reveal what is not my secret."

Father Martin looked at her. "Mother of God and St. Anthony!" he exclaimed. He had never seen anything so beautiful as the sight before him in the fine old hall and he feared he might relent. He cast his eyes down, he would not look at her. Indeed she was a witch, a witch and yet so young! "Do you dare to deny the authority of Mother Church?" he hissed. "You are a heretic and guilty of contumacy. You blaspheme." Then turning to Mistress Mowbray he continued, "See that she is confined to her room and fed on bread and water till she comes to her senses. Failing that, the rack!"

He rose to his full height and gave her one contemptuous glance, curling his thin lips and drawing down his brows, while the nostrils of his aquiline nose were lifted in scorn. "Good day to you, Mistress Mowbray," he said, "see to my instructions," and he departed.

Aline went up to her room as bidden. Eleanor Mowbray followed. She did not lock the door, as, in her heart of hearts, even she trusted Aline as she would trust the laws of nature, much as she hated her. Aline might disobey, but she would never break her word. "Do not pass through that door again, until you are told. Promise me."

"I would rather you locked it," said Aline. "The house might catch fire and I could not stay and be burned, even to obey you."

"Little fool," said Mistress Mowbray, "if the door were locked you would be burned anyhow."

274

"That would be your doing, though. I should not have to do it myself. I want to keep my own liberty of action."

Mistress Mowbray slammed the door and went down-stairs. But she did not lock it.

Aline was merely thinking in a vague general way that it would be risky to make any such promise and did not realise how nearly her words might have applied to the actual facts.

She sat down on the edge of her bed, dazed. Surely she had been singled out for misfortune; blow after blow had fallen upon her, and she was only twelve and a half years old. First she had been left motherless, then her father's small estate had been ruined. Next she was made an orphan. Then she had lost her only friends Ian and Audry and was left to the cruelties of Mistress Mowbray. And now there was this. The little heart almost grew bitter and she was tempted to say;—"I do not mind if they do kill me, everything is so terrible and sad and, O Father dear, your little girl is so very very lonely and unhappy she would like to die and come to you."

But the thought of her father made her think of life again and some of life's happy days and of Audry and Ian, and she gave a great sob and a lump came into her throat; but she checked it before the tears came and stood up and drew herself together. "Father would have me brave; Ian would have me brave. Come, this is no time for crying, I must think hard."

"I might get out on to the moor at night, but I should certainly be caught. Besides I have nowhere to go.

275

"I could disappear into the secret room, but I should soon starve—for all the food I could get.

"I might get over to Audry at Appleby, but that would be no use in the end; what should I do next? Still if I could have her back here, she could feed me in the secret room.

"Then again Ian might be able to help—I must get a letter to Audry and a letter to Ian."

So she sat down and wrote; and it was not until she began to write to others that she fully realised the desperateness of her situation and that, if help did not come, she would certainly be imprisoned and tortured on the rack and probably burnt alive. Aline knew that they thought nothing of hanging children, often for quite trivial offences and had heard of plenty of instances of executions of children under twelve.

When she had finished writing the day was nearly done and she crept very forlornly into bed. Her head ached and her heart ached still more and she fell a-thinking how the letters were to be sent. Even if Walter Margrove should come she would not see him, though it was getting time for his return. She was getting desperate. She pressed her little hands against her forehead and at last the stifled tears broke forth. They were some relief and bye and bye she fell asleep.

The next morning old Elspeth came to her room to bring her bread and water. She was shocked when she saw the condition of the child. The sleep had been broken and feverish and Aline looked wretchedly ill.

"O hinnie," she said, "my hinnie, what have they been doing to you now? Prithee do what they want,276 dearest. I cannot bear to see you shut up here. See, I have brought you a pasty with chicken in it. Old Elspeth will not see you starve, dear heart; and Walter Margrove came yesternight after they put you up here and he hath sent you this little packet. He said if I gave you the linen I could be trusted to give you this. 'Trusted,' indeed! I trow so; what aileth the man?"

Aline sat up in bed and stretched out her hand eagerly and as she took the packet she wondered whether she dare send her letters by Elspeth. On the whole she felt it was rather risky to send Ian's, but Audry's would not rouse the old dame's suspicion. Should she chance them both? "Is he downstairs now?" she said.

"No, hinnie," said Elspeth, "he had to leave very suddenly this morning."

Aline fell back on the bed but managed to turn her face away and say in a half joking tone;—"Oh, dear, how unlucky! Margrove always makes a pleasant change and I have been so stupid as to miss him."

"I am so sorry, dearie," said Elspeth; "I am sure he would have been right fain to see you, he hath a great fancy for you, I know."

"Well, an they keep me up here till he cometh again, you tell me, Elspeth, there's a dear, when he is here; and I will write a little note to him. He hath been very kind to me."

"All right, hinnie," and Elspeth went down-stairs.

Aline ate the bread and the pasty. She was not hungry but she knew that she was getting ill and she thought that it would help her to keep up her strength, if she ate all that she could. As she ate, she turned the parcel over and over with her left hand. It was a bitter blow277 that Margrove had gone; but here was Ian's letter and it might mark the turning of the tide. When she had finished she still looked at the packet for a few moments, wondering, hoping, dreaming.

The figure of Ian rose to her mind, sitting as he often did, leaning back with his hands clasped round one knee and the foot raised from the ground.

She had found her knight; would he be able to rescue her? True, he was only a carpenter, but in his many travels and experiences he had acquired so many accomplishments that no one would know that he was not of gentle blood. "Oh! I do wish he were here," she said; "yes, even if he could not help me I wish I could see him again;—well, this is from him." So she opened the packet.

The first thing that she saw was a beautiful pair of silk hose of a very rich deep blue. Fastened to these was a label, saying:—"These are from Walter Margrove and myself, mainly from Walter."

155

They were an absolutely new thing in Britain, although they had been in use for a short time in Italy, and were so much lovelier than anything she had ever seen before that she could not resist the temptation of trying them on at once. She threw off the bedclothes and stretched out one small rosy foot, straight as a die on the inner side, and altogether perfect with its clearly articulated toes and exquisitely formed nails. Aline was blissfully unaware that there was not another to compare with it in the whole world except its own fellow delicately poised on the firmly built but slender ankle, which she drew up and slipped into the delightful soft silk hose. It fitted to perfection.

278

She then put on the other and stood up, holding her little nightrobe high while she looked down to admire them. Aline had not the slightest touch of vanity, but new clothes are new clothes all the world over. She then stepped across to Audry's cherished and rare possession, a long mirror which had come from Italy. "They really are a glorious blue," she thought, as the light fell on the soft lustrous material.

She had pleated the middle of the nightrobe into a sort of band round her waist; the front below the neck was unfastened, so that the effect was that of a short tunic. "Why, I look like a boy!" she said to herself; "if it were not for my hair."

In spite of her slimness there was a muscular development, very refined and beautiful in line, that was distinctly boyish. Her slender hips and exceptionally well modelled forearms, which were bare, completed the illusion.

"Yes, I look like the pages I used to see in Edinburgh"; and then a bright thought struck her;—"If ever I have to try and escape I shall dress up as a boy." She pinned the nightdress with the broad belt as it was, with the lower hem reaching to the thigh. It fell down at the back somewhat, but that did not show in the mirror. She then hurried down the secret stair and came back with a man's bonnet that she had there noticed among the things. She had such an immense quantity of hair that it was only by twisting it very tightly indeed that she was able to get it into the bonnet; but she succeeded at last. She was rather tall for her age, although her form was still absolutely that of a child, and an admirable boy she made.

279

Aline laughed aloud; it was the first time that she had laughed for a weary while.

"Now let me read the letter," she said. She took off the stockings and folded them neatly up, put them away and opened the letter.

"To my dear little Aline,

"Walter Margrove hath kindly promised to bear this letter. It is with deep regret that I will tell thee how that my plans have not prospered. As thou knowest, I have been working with one, Matthew Musgrave, a carpenter, hoping to lay by money that eventually I might betake me to the road like our friend Walter. But Matthew hath been sick of an ague these many weeks past and I find that he hath little or nothing saved. I have done what I might but my small means are exhausted, and we are even in debt for the purchase of wood. The boy, Will Ackroyd, hath also been somewhat of an anxiety to me, so that I am much cast down in spirit and indeed as Matthew will tell thee am somewhat ailing in body. This I regret the more as thy face liveth ever before me and I have thought that it might at any moment be needful for me to come unto thine assistance, whereas I even fear that I am not in any wise able. I trust that Mistress Mowbray is not treating thee ill and that thou and that dear child, thy cousin, are enjoying all happiness.

"My hard times will doubtless pass and better will come. I think of thee day and night and pray for thee without ceasing; and sweet child, remember that whatever the difficulties, I would fight through everything to come to thine aid if need should arise.

"To-morrow I hope to be able to send thee some small token from Walter's pack. Meanwhile I say,—May the peace of the Lord Jesus be with thee and all the love of this poor mortal heart is thine; as Homer saith; 'for that thou, lady, hast given me my life.'

"My blessing and love be also to thy cousin Audry, for right kindly did she minister to me.

"Farewell, bright angel of my dreams.
"Ian Menstrie.

"An so be that thou writest, it is better to put upon the cover the name of James Mitchell whereby I am known here."

Ian had been very seriously ill himself from trying280 to undertake more than was possible. His unceasing care and tender watchfulness had saved Musgrave's life, but it was nearly at the cost of his own and he was but a shadow of his former self.

Aline's sympathetic little heart read more between the lines than Ian had intended her to see and the letter seemed the last drop in her cup of sorrow.

It was too much and this time she fainted right away. When she came to, she found that she was lying on the floor and old Elspeth was bending over her and sprinkling water on her face. The old woman was nearly beside herself with grief. "O my bonnie bonnie child, what shall poor Elspeth do? They will kill you, heart of mine, if they go on in this way. See you are cold as a stone and nothing on you but this thin rag and that unfastened too." She lifted the child back into bed and rushed down-stairs to the kitchen, where she found some hot broth ready for the table and came back with a bowl of it.

On the way she met Mistress Mowbray.

"What are you doing, Elspeth?" the lady almost shrieked.

"Mistress Aline was in a dead faint on the floor of her room and stone cold and like enough to die. Such goings on as there have been in this house lately I have never seen in all my days. First the child is nearly murdered by that ne'er do weel Andrew and now the whole house seems bent on doing the same. In my young days old Mistress Mowbray would not have countenanced such doings and the priests, gramercy, knew better than to meddle in other folk's houses."

Elspeth who had known three generations of Mowbrays[281] was a privileged person, but this was more than even she had ever before ventured to say.

"How dare you speak like that?" said Mistress Mowbray.

"Marry, you would not have the child's death at your door, would you, whatever the priest may bid? That at least was not of his ordering."

Mistress Mowbray glared at her, but said, "Well, take the broth; how was I to know the child had fainted? Yet i' faith she shall not have all of that," and she took the bowl and carried it down and poured half of it back. When Elspeth reached the child she was so overcome that she could only sit on the bed and moan. Aline put her arm out and took the old woman's hand and stroked it and said,—"Elspeth, do not take it so to heart. I am all right and, look you, the broth is excellent. See, I shall be quite well again in a moment. A little faint is nothing. Tell me how deep the snow is on the road to Middleton and how the sheep are getting on in this cold and whether there be any news from Appleby."

So she gradually coaxed Elspeth away from the subject of her own troubles and even made her smile by telling her about the blue hose and how she had tried them on, and how pleased with them she was; but she kept the little plan of dressing up like a boy to herself.

282
CHAPTER XXII
TO THE RESCUE

THAT evening Elspeth went down to the Arnsides. She was really very much concerned at the line that things were taking and, staunch Catholic as she was, she had no mind to have her little mistress ill used. She of course knew nothing about her neighbour's faith and simply went to them because of their interest in Aline; and she told them the whole story from the time of the coming of Father Martin.

"We helped her with the linen," she said, "but I fear this is a more difficult matter; but it makes my heart bleed for the poor innocent and she only twelve years old. We can manage to feed her, but the child will pine away shut up there. I cannot think what to do."

"The thing would be to get Mistress Audry back," said Janet. "That would be something."

"Ay, that would it," Elspeth assented.

They talked it over for some time and Elspeth decided that she would try and say something in an indirect way to Master Mowbray, which might result in his sending for his daughter.

When she was gone John turned to his mother,—"Mother, somehow I believe Walter Margrove is the man to help us, and he told us to let him hear how things283 went and they have gone a deal worse than any of us could have dreamed. He knows the world and he knows, too, what the real risk is. Even if Mistress Audry comes back, methinks that will not alter the true danger."

"Ay," said his mother, "but Master Walter was here but yesterday, how are we to get him?"

John thought for a time and then said,—"I have no regular work here and Silas, who sees to my hours, is one of our faith. I would even risk telling him something; although I need not say it is for Mistress Aline that I want to see Walter."

"But how would you find Walter even if you did consult Silas?" said his mother.

"That should not be difficult," said John. "He always calls at Carlisle on his rounds and I think I heard him say that he expected to be there this time within a sennight. In any case, however, he gets there long enough before he gets here. He generally stays with one, Timothy Fenwick, at the sign of the Golden Keys."

"How will you go," said his mother, "round by Middleton?"

"No, it is such a long way round; I shall keep this side the river."

"What, with all this snow!"

"Yes, if I can get off to-day; the sky is clear and the weather set and the snow hard."

"Well, good-bye, my boy. God bless you and I trust the Lord will grant you success."

John Arnside obtained the permission with no trouble at all, made himself up a bundle, put it on a stick over his shoulder, kissed his mother and set off.

284

Fortune favoured him and on the third day he was in Carlisle without mishap.

He enquired for the Golden Keys and easily found the house, but Walter was not there. He found, however, a man seated by the fire; he was of medium height, lightly built and well proportioned. He looked very ill and was holding one knee with his hands as he leaned back, and was gazing into the fire with his deep set eyes.

"Come and sit by the fire, lad, the day is cold."

John came as invited. "I heard you asking for Walter Margrove," said the stranger, "he will not be here for some time. I hope your business is not of importance."

"Well," said the boy, "I must just wait, unless you could tell me where he is to be found."

"That could not I," replied the other. "I know he was going to Newcastle and then up Tyne and down Tees; after that I think he was going to Skipton and West to Clitheroe and then North. He should be somewhere on the Tees now, I reckon, perhaps down as far as Rokeby."

"Do you know the Tees?" said John.

The man lifted his grey deep set eyes; they had a far away look in them, as though he did not see the boy before him. They were watching the Tees come over the High Force and the rainbow that hung in the quivering spray.

"Yes, I know the Tees," he said at length. "I know the Tees.

"Do you know the Tees?" he went on; and it seemed to John that the hollow eyes in the sick man's face285 looked at him hungrily. "Maybe you come from those parts yourself."

"I do," said John; "I was born and bred in Upper Teesdale."

"What is your name?"

"John Arnside."

The man looked at him and then the sad eyes seemed to brighten a little. "John Arnside, son of Janet Arnside?" he asked.

"Yes," said John, wondering what was coming next.

The man got up and closed the door softly, he then came back and held out his hand to the boy. "I am so glad to see you, John; I know about you. I heard you asking for Walter Margrove, and oh," he continued, apprehensively, "I do hope it is nothing about Mistress Aline that brings you here. Yes, I know quite well who you are and you may trust me."

John's was a simple nature and not easily suspicious; he just hesitated a moment and then reflected that if he merely said what was known to every one he could not do any harm. Walter Margrove's part in the matter, he could keep for the present as a second string to his bow.

"They say that Mistress Aline is a heretic," he said, "and they are going to burn her."

The man clutched at the table to try and prevent himself from falling; the shock was so terrible in his weak condition; but he slipped back and was only saved by the boy catching him as he fell.

"O God," he exclaimed, "not so, not so."

He then made a tremendous effort and pulled himself together, but it was enough for John, there was no286 doubt that this stranger was in some way as interested in Aline's welfare as himself.

"We must save her then," said the stranger in a steady voice, while within him his thoughts and feelings tossed as in a storm.

"Marry though, what are we to do?"

"Let us sit down and think— Now look you here; it is not easy to think quickly, but we must act quickly. Can you get speech of Mistress Aline?"

"No," answered John; "she is confined to her room, but old Elspeth sees her."

"Can you write, John?"

"Gramercy no, Master, you would hardly expect the likes of me to be able to do that."

"Well, you must get her my letter, somehow, and, furthermore, tell me what you yourself are willing to do for Mistress Aline."

"I would give my life for her," said John simply.

"Then," said the other, looking him straight in the face, "you must hie you home at once and I will follow as soon as I can be ready. Keep a sharp look-out for the inquisitors and, if I do not come before them, you must get speech of her by hook or by crook and tell her that I, James Mitchell, told you that she must reveal to you our secret and that you must feed her. She will know what that means and you must do as she bids you. Indeed, if you get there before me, you had better do this in any case."

"Surely I will; how could I other?"

"Marry then, hasten; for, even now we know not what an hour may bring forth. We must not wait for Walter, though he would have been our best aid. God speed thy287 feet, John; my heart goes with thee and I myself shall follow hard after thee."

Without more ado John took his small bundle and started off at once.

Ian was nearly beside himself, the shock had brought on the pains in his head and he put his hands to his throbbing brows and strove to think. His money had all gone; how was he to act? Certainly the first thing was to get the child away somewhere, but how even was that to be done without horses? If only Margrove and his horses had been to hand! But that was a vain wish. Of course she could be concealed in the secret room, but he felt this was too perilous. There was risk enough in feeding him when Aline and Audry had been in the house. Suspicion would be roused tenfold if Aline were simply to disappear. John would certainly be seen, sooner or later, carrying food to the gully. Mortifying as the discovery of old Moll had been, it was a mercy to be forewarned. No, it might do as a very temporary expedient, but no more.

Of course it might be just within the bounds of possibility to get horses from Holwick Hall itself; but failure would mean absolute and irretrievable disaster. No again, nothing must be left to chance. Suddenly a thought struck him, there were horses on the estate where Andrew Woolridge worked. Possibly Andrew might help him and, if not, the risk was comparatively small.

This then decided him. He would set out immediately; but there was one more thing to consider. Should he say anything to the boy, Wilfred? It was true, he argued, that the more people that knew, the greater the chance of discovery. But on the other hand, if anything should happen to him, how was Aline to be saved? After all there was still Walter Margrove, who would surely attempt to do something. Finally he went and found Wilfred.

"Wilfred," he said, "I want to ask a favour of thee."

"That mayest thou well ask, Master Mitchell."

"Well, I shall not tell thee more than that it concerns a matter of life and death, so that if any enquire of thee, there will be little that thou canst say, however they question thee. But when Walter Margrove cometh, tell him that Mistress Aline is in great jeopardy and let him do that which seemeth him best and may the Lord quicken his steps."

"What, the little lady of whom they were talking one night not long syne?"

"Yes, that same; now be faithful to us, Wilfred."

"But, Master Mitchell, thou art not going to leave us," said the boy piteously. "After all that thou hast done for us that cannot be. See, prithee let me come with thee an thou must go."

Ian considered for a moment as to whether the boy might be a help or a hindrance and decided that it would rather complicate matters than otherwise to take him.

"No, Wilfred, it cannot be," he said; "but thou mightest, so far as thou art able, go out on the road to Brampton when thou art not at work and keep a look-out for me coming from Alston or Kirkoswald between the third and the seventh day from now.

"Indeed thou mightest do better. I will show thee more. Keep thine eyes and ears open for all the gossip of the city. I know thee well enough to know that thou wouldst not see any one burned alive and I go to save one from the burning. If thou hearest aught of inquisitors come as far south along the road as thou mayest."

Wilfred bade good-bye and promised by all that was holy that he would do everything that he could.

Ian had decided to take nothing but one small wallet, as less likely to rouse suspicion, and started off. What was his horror, before he had gone ten paces from the door, to see a group of black robed figures on horseback approaching the hostelry, and his horror increased to terror when he recognised one of the figures as Father Austin, who had superintended, when he himself had been tortured in York.

The keen shrewd face shewed instant recognition in spite of Ian's altered appearance. "Whither away, Ian Menstrie? Come return to the hostelry with us and have a talk with an old friend." An evil smile of triumph spread over his face and he added quietly but firmly to his attendants,—"That is the man we have sought these many months, our Lady hath delivered him into our hands."

Ian said nothing, but Wilfred, who was still standing at the door, said,—"That is not Ian Menstrie, that is Master James Mitchell."

"I am pleased to make your acquaintance, Master Mitchell," said Father Austin sarcastically, bowing from his horse.

"My name is Ian Menstrie," said Ian.

"You have varying names then, like a gaol-bird," replied the inquisitor with a sneer.

"We shall have two for our burning, perdy!" he290 continued to his companion. "It will make a right merrie blaze. What think you, Father Martin?"

"Burning's too good for them; I would give them a taste of something first. As for that young witch up in Holwick, the Devil will be sorry to see her in Hell before her time. If she had lived to grow up, she would have charmed men's souls to Satan more surely than any siren ever charmed a mariner."

"If we burn the body shall we not save the soul?" said Father Austin.

"That doctrine liketh me not; no, Father, methinks in these cases we do but hasten the final judgment."

"Have a care, friend, lest these be heresies also."

"I a heretic! That is a mirthful jest." Then looking toward Ian he went on,—"As for this fellow, he seems a sickly creature; I reckon by the looks of him that he has not long to live. But it is good for the souls of the faithful that he should blaze to the glory of God rather than die in his bed. Marry, methinks he is like enough to faint even now."

Nothing but Ian Menstrie's iron will indeed prevented it. The pains shot through his head like knives and his back and joints ached as though red hot with fire, but it was nothing to the anguish of his heart; yet he felt that his only chance was to keep up somehow.

He would have died on the rack some five months ago had it not been for his sheer strength of will. He had done it before, he would do it again; he would defy them yet.

Great cold beads of perspiration stood on his forehead, but he held himself erect. "Is it Timothy Fenwick's hostelry you seek, gentlemen?"

There was a touch of defiance, even of scorn, in the lordly ring of his voice. Father Austin knew only too well that, clever as he was himself, he was no match for this man, who had beaten him once; "But he shall not escape me this time," he said to himself, and having already alighted, he followed into the hostelry. "The day is past its prime," he remarked, "and we have caught our main game. We have come far and there is no haste. We will bide here and rest till Wednesday; the little bird at Holwick will not flutter far, I warrant ye."

It amused Father Austin to have Ian with them at meals to taunt him and to gloat over his own triumph. Ian realised that he would have little chance unless he were well nourished, so he fell in with their scheme and humoured them. At first he would talk brightly to the others and then, as he was an excellent raconteur and had a pretty wit, he made himself such good company that they could ill spare him. He played with Father Austin, assuming an attitude of deference and fear with an anxious desire to please; but if he wanted to retire to rest, he would lead him into an argument and when the father was worsted he would order the guards to take Ian to his room.

Again, by extraordinary will power, he would achieve the almost impossible feat of forcing himself to sleep. It was Aline's only chance, he argued; and in that way he almost miraculously overcame the raging torments of his mind.

By the Wednesday he had even recovered slightly and felt rather like one going into battle than like a beaten man. He had thought out several plans; but the best one was to try and contrive to cross the ford of the Eden when it was getting dark. For this some delay was necessary, and he even managed to whisper to Wilfred unobserved, while he set the company off into boisterous and uncontrollable laughter, that he should loosen one of the horse's shoes. He reckoned further to be able to do something more in the way of delay by his powers of conversation.

Another part of his scheme was to put his captors off the scent, if he should succeed in making his escape, and therefore he took occasion to remark; "Well, Father, and when we set out on our travels, whither are we bound? Is it south we shall be going?"

"Forsooth, man, you do not think we should go north, do you?"

"No, may be not; but I should like to see Scotland again."

"Trouble not yourself, you will never see Scotland more; and when next I visit Scotland the Regent Mary will be glad to hear that her daughter has one heretic the less among her subjects."

"But what if I should reach Scotland first," said Ian jocularly. "That might spoil the pleasure of your visit."

164

"There is no fear of that," replied the other.

"Bishop Bonner may think differently from yourself," Ian rejoined; "it is not every heretic that even Bonner burns. There's many a slip twixt cup and lip; and Bonner might send me to Scotland if I promised to stay there. I warrant if once I were on that side again, there would be little temptation to come over."

"Come, this is no time for talking, we must be off," said Father Austin.

All fell out as Ian had planned; the shoe was quite loose and before they had reached the city gate, Ian said to Father Martin, "Methinks, Father, your mare will shortly cast her shoe."

So they returned to the hostelry where there was a smithy. Ian then succeeded in getting them all interested in a thrilling narrative just as the mare was ready, and put off the time until it seemed best to stay and have dinner before starting. More stories lengthened the meal, so that it was not till well on in the afternoon of the short winter day that they actually set out.

Ian was placed in the middle, surrounded by the guards, with loaded pistols, and his hands were tied, but not very tightly, as they allowed him to hold the reins. Try as he would he could not help the violent beating of his heart. Could he, one man, unarmed and bound, outwit all these knaves? The vision of little Aline rose before him. "I must fight the very fates," he said to himself, "verily, I must win." His thoughts travelled back to those days, long ago, when as a mere child he had given his heart-worship to the beautiful girl who had gone from him, but whom he had loved with a passionate devotion ever since. He had said practically nothing to Aline, but he was sure that he knew whence the strange likeness came; and for the double claim that she had upon him, fate, that had so cruelly treated him long ago, should be made to yield. He felt the strength of his own will like a white fire and then he trembled for a moment lest he should be fighting against God. "O Lord," he prayed, "Thou hast brought me on this road and Thou hast made this lovely child; let her not perish by the machinations of evil men. Take my life, O God, give me all torture and the terrible burning, but grant her happiness."

He felt a sudden influx of power and prayed again a prayer of thankfulness. "Yes," he said, "I will bend fate to my will and God will smile on my struggle and then I will yield myself to Him and He shall toss me into the void or do unto me in my despite whatsoever seemeth Him good."

It was a long road and the spirits of the party flagged. It was, moreover, bitterly cold, but Ian had not dared to put on more clothing for fear that it should defeat his plans. There had been a thaw and he watched anxiously for the river. He had succeeded during the long ride, in very considerably loosening the cord that tied his wrists, and although it was still quite tight round one wrist and he could not be certain of freeing the other, he was sure that he could slip it sufficiently to get twenty to thirty inches of free play between his hands. He had managed, too, greatly to fray the portion that would be the connecting piece.

It was getting dusk when they reached the river, and, owing to the recent heavy weather and thaws, the ford was so high that the water was more than up to the horses' girths. Ian's heart beat more violently than ever; it seemed almost as though it could be heard. "Aline, Aline, had she no more reliable deliverer than himself?"

As they crossed, the horses had to pick their way and they spread out a good deal so that they were almost in a line, with Ian in the middle, who managed also to coax his horse a little bit down the stream. He then nerved himself for the supreme effort and, first jerking295 his horse back almost on to its haunches, so as to give in the gloom the appearance of the animal having stumbled, he flung himself from its back shrieking,— "Help, help," as he went. As soon as the water closed over him he struck out and swam under water as far as he possibly could. Unfortunately the cord did not break as he hoped and the swimming was exceedingly difficult, but there was sufficient play of cord to make the feat quite possible, and the swift current helped him not a little.

It was perhaps fortunate that nearly all the pistols were discharged at once, before he came to the surface, as they were fired at random into the confused water round the horse, which had some difficulty in regaining its footing.

When he rose he immediately took a breath and went under again. Only one man was looking in that direction and he did not seriously think that the dark spot in the turbid river was really anything; where occasionally a half hidden boulder would appear above the water. But he took aim, more or less mechanically or from intuition, and fired, and the bullet actually grazed Ian's shoulder.

Before he had appeared again the little company had turned to the riderless horse and those who had lances were prodding into the deeps of the river. Again he swam under water; it was still very shallow and he bruised himself several times more or less severely on the boulders in the river bed. He did this twice more and the water grew deeper; and then he ventured to glance back. They were already but dimly visible and he knew that he himself was out of sight, so he slowly296 made for the bank with some difficulty across the current. When he reached the bank they were no longer to be seen, and he was glad to get out of the icy water. But the air was miserably cold, even more trying, as is often the case, than during the frost itself.

He was only two miles from Andrew's cottage, which he had once visited, and he wondered whether it would be safe for him to go there at once. After all, the risk was about as great one way as another. Besides, he hoped that they would think he was drowned and, even if they did not, that they would think he would endeavour to make his way north to Scotland. In any case it would not take him long to perish from exposure. Of course, he would have to cross his enemies' tracks and he decided to keep near the water's edge as at least affording some chance of escape. He soon managed to get rid of the cord that tied his hands and crept along by the wooded banks looking and listening intently.

After a few minutes he heard voices and they grew louder; he lay down on the brink and waited a moment. In the still evening they could be heard quite distinctly.

"Oh, the fellow is drowned right enough," said one of the voices.

"Yes, curse the knave," said the other voice, which was that of Father Austin. "It grieveth me sore. Mother Church hath missed an opportunity for a great lesson. I would even that we had his corpse, it would be something to show; and at the least I should get the credit for the bringing of the loon to his death. I am greatly afeared lest he may have gotten away to Scotland. Did he not say something to me himself about Scotland and the slip twixt cup and lip? He is a deep one as I know to my cost. I would that this had happened earlier in the day. It will be quite dark in about half an hour. Beshrew me, how came it that the rogue was not tied?"

"His wrists were tied, Father," said the other voice. "I noticed that just before we came to the river."

"Oh, I meant tied to the horse, but who would have thought of such a thing! However, if the wrists were tied, belike it may have been an accident and the knave must be dead. I trow it was but a dog's chance. Besides, one of those bullets must have hit him. The body must have been swept down stream."

The surmise about the bullet was true enough, as Ian knew to his cost, and the wound was an added pain. "It is wonderful what the human frame can stand," he said to himself. "I cannot think how I am alive at all. I must win this game somehow and the next move is mine."

He slowly lowered himself into the water. The men had stood still, a little higher up the stream, not twenty yards from where he was. It was a trying test to his nerves, but he hoped he was concealed by the brushwood on the flooded bank.

He waited awhile and heard them discuss how a few of the party would try and make search in the direction of Scotland and the remainder go south. Apparently they were waiting for some of the others to join them and the conversation turned to other subjects.

Ian was standing on the bottom, but had to work his arms all the time to prevent himself from being carried down by the current. His teeth chattered and his fingers were numb with the pain of the cold. "If I stay here any longer," he thought, "the cold will finish me." So he struck out and by the aid of the brushwood swam within a foot or two of where they were standing. It was an anxious moment and although the stream was slacker near the bank it was slow work. But he passed them unobserved, although he experienced a tumultuous wave of feeling when the conversation stopped short for an instant and he feared that they were listening.

But at last he judged that it might be safe to creep out, and at first he crawled and then walked quietly, but finally broke into a run, as much for the cold as for any other reason; and, in twenty minutes from the time he started running, he found himself at Andrew's cottage.

It was in a secluded spot, quite near the river, and about a third of a mile from the Hall where Andrew was employed. He crept softly to the window and peeped in. Andrew was there alone. So he knocked at the door.

Andrew's astonishment was immense as he opened the door and still more so when he saw that his visitor was dripping wet.

"Can you let me have some dry clothes, Andrew, and help me to get warm, and provide me with something for the inner man?"

"That I can, Master Mitchell," and Andrew bestirred himself, brought the clothes and made up a roaring fire and prepared a simple but appetising supper.

When Ian had finished he stretched out his feet to the cheerful blaze. It was tempting to stay and rest299 after all his sufferings. The wound in his shoulder was very painful, although Andrew had bandaged it, and the sundry cuts and bruises made him feel very stiff. But there was much to be done and no time to be lost.

He talked things over with Andrew, very cautiously, as he was not sure what line he would take. It so happened that the Hall was nearly empty; the family and their immediate entourage were South during the winter and the reeve was away on business with two of the other men; so Andrew's help in getting the horses was not needed after all. Ian led him into all kinds of general gossip about the place and discovered how many horses were kept and where the stables were, without exciting any suspicion. Andrew offered to come with him to Holwick, but Ian doubted whether it would not make matters more and not less difficult and Andrew's disappearance would itself give a clue.

Luck favoured him, he found that the man who had charge of the horses, while the reeve was away, was a drunken fellow, whose cottage was not far from Andrew's on the way to the Hall. Owing to the absence of the reeve he was having a more dissipated time even than usual. It was his custom to see to the horses the last thing at night, and Ian determined on an attempt to get the better of him.

Without explaining his movements to Andrew he said it was time for him to be going, and he set out into the darkness. There was just enough starlight to find his way and he soon reached Jock's cottage. The man had not returned, so Ian crouched down behind a tree to wait for him.

300

He was trembling with excitement and apprehension and was disturbed in spirit about the part of the venture in which he was engaged. He was deliberately setting out to steal the horses and he felt that it was a sin. He did not try to justify himself, although he had determined that he would make all possible reparation so that the owner of the horses would not suffer. He had written a note to his mother which he had given to Andrew, just saying that if his adventure should miscarry and Andrew did not hear from him shortly, he was to take it to Stirling and ask for some relatives of his of the name of Menstrie, as he had no relatives named Mitchell still alive. In the letter he had said that she was to clear his honour as far as was possible by replacing the horses if death should overtake him.

Yet he did not feel that this in the least altered the crime; but he argued to himself, that if the crime did not hurt any one that it was only his own soul that would suffer. For that he was absolutely ready. He would gladly give his life for Aline, would he not also gladly give his soul? It was a great shock to his naturally upright nature and when he had lied to Andrew and told him that he was going to make his way south on foot, and while his blood boiled with shame within him, he yet welcomed the sacrifice. "She shall have my honour and my good name, she shall have my soul indeed as well as my life. Fate may crush me in eternal torment at the last or annihilate me altogether; but Aline must escape these fiends; she must live to be happy. Sweet little child-heart, who never did any wrong to any one and whose short life has been so sad301 and who yet has only been sunshine in the lives of others, why should she be cheated out of her due?"

As he wrestled with himself Jock came stumbling from side to side down the path, babbling incoherently. Ian braced himself for the struggle and, as the man opened the door and entered the cottage, Ian stole in after him. He was utterly unprepared and, as Ian leaped upon him from behind, he gave one wild shriek and collapsed. Ian tied his hands and feet with his own cord that he had saved, put the man on the bed and secured the key of the stable.

He had comparatively little difficulty in getting out the two best horses, taking the precaution of tying some sacking over their hoofs so as to lessen the noise. Fortunately the wind was rising and a storm of rain was clearly on its way.

Before leaving he fastened a note at the stall-head:

"I require these horses but will replace them when I reach Scotland. Necessity knows no law.
One in great need."

He took the horses first in a northerly direction as though making for Scotland, so that their tracks might throw pursuers off the scent. Then when he reached the harder road, he followed it only a little way and turned back south. Finally he struck over the high ground to the west, hoping to get into another district altogether, where any travellers that he might meet would not carry any description to the neighbourhood of Kirkoswald.

It meant a considerable detour and the inquisitors had a long start as well; but he felt so certain that they302 would rest somewhere for the night, that he felt very little alarm. Shortly afterwards the rain came down heavily and he trusted that this would at least help to obliterate the tracks.303

304
THE UPPER COURT SHOWING TERRACE AND TURRET-STAIR TO ALINE'S ROOM
305
CHAPTER XXIII

A DUEL TO THE DEATH

MEANWHILE Aline had been having a very unhappy time. She was practically confined to her room the whole day long, but she did come down for the mid-day meal. Master Mowbray, strong as his Catholic sympathies were, not only resented the interference of the priests in his house, but was concerned at seeing the child look so starved and ill, and therefore he had insisted on this much.

It did enable Aline to get some nourishment, although she only had bread and water for the rest of the time, and it did make a slight break in the day, for she dared not use the secret stair except when every one was in bed, for fear of any one coming to her room and finding that she was not there.

But the meals were anything but a pleasure. Master Mowbray would look at her sorrowfully, but he scarcely ever said anything, and Mistress Mowbray would make cruel biting remarks and watch the child wince under them.

Her poor little soul grew very sad and night after night she would cry herself to sleep; "If only Ian would come—If only Ian would come."

She was some time before she actually grasped that the inquisitors would take away her life; but one day306 when Father Ambrose was at dinner he had tauntingly asked her whether she had repented of her folly; and then, with a leer, had rubbed his hands and said:—"You obstinate minx, they are coming for you right soon and ah, how glad I shall be to see your long hair shrivel up and your pretty face swell and burst in the fire."

Aline suddenly realised that he was in earnest and for the moment was petrified with terror. Then she remembered that many children younger than she had been martyrs in the old Roman days, and for the moment there was a revulsion of feeling and she smiled to think that she was worthy to suffer death in the Master's cause.

Richard Mowbray had not realised it before either, and was shocked beyond measure. He said nothing to his wife, but decided to set off at once for York to see the Archbishop, whom he knew personally, and discover what could be done.

He was on the point of forbidding Father Ambrose entry to the house; but he restrained himself, as that would excite suspicion. He was accustomed to going away suddenly for a few days at a time, so that his departure that very afternoon surprised no one. He reckoned that it would take him at least a week and told his wife not to expect him before that time.

When Aline reached her room, her feelings swung the other way again. "Why should she die; what had she done? She was sure that God would not wish her to die." She waited till night and crept down to the secret room. She did not often do this even at night, as although there was a good store of candles she saw307 no prospect whatever of replenishing it and was afraid of using it up.

She sat down on the oak settle and tried to face the situation. If the inquisitors came she must try somehow to escape and the incident of the blue hose had suggested that she should do so in the garb of a boy. She rummaged over the clothes that she found and set to work to put them in order and adapt them for her own use. She chose the strongest things that she could find and during the next few nights she managed with a little alteration to fit herself out with a boy's doublet, cote-hardie, surcoat and a pair of trunks. She found an admirable mantle of russet cloth that only required shortening and she herself possessed a pair of strong sad coloured hose.

She reckoned that it would not be possible to cut her hair before her escape; so she prepared three hats, one that was very large into which her hair could be put in a hurry, a medium one into which it could be put if very tightly twisted, and a smaller one, that she could wear with her hair cut short to the ears.

She also began to lay in a store of provisions, saving all that she could from her slender allowance, as she judged that it would be safest to spend a week if possible, in the secret room until the first hue and cry had subsided, if she should have to make the desperate attempt to escape alone; but, poor child, her plan was frustrated.

It was very cold in her little chamber, so she had been wearing some extra clothing; she decided therefore that the wisest course would be to dress exactly like a boy and wear what was necessary of her own clothes308 on the top. So she put on a boy's shirt and trunks and stitched points to her hose and tied them to those on the trunks. Over this she put a cote-hardie and then a belt with a dagger. Above this again she wore a girl's longer cote-hardie and above that again a short surcoat. The medium sized hat was made of silk and the finest kersey and was therefore easily concealed under her clothes. It had a full silk crown and a brim turned up all round nearly to the crown itself, with slits every three inches, giving it a sort of battlemented appearance with the crown just appearing above the top. Old fashions still lingered in the North and Ian had had one like it, which he said resembled one worn by Prince Arthur of Wales. She was helped by a little drawing which Ian had made for her when they were talking about the well known portrait. When she had done she felt very proud of her handiwork and the long mirror was a welcome joy at the end of the doleful days. She looked out a sword for herself and practised making passes.

All was ready four days after Richard Mowbray's departure and, three days later, when he had not yet returned, there was a sudden stir and noise in the outer courtyard while they were having the mid-day meal.

"That will be Walter Margrove, I'm thinking," said Mistress Mowbray. "They always seem to make that man's arrival an excuse for neglecting their work, idle hussies and varlets all of them!" She rose as she spoke and went out into the screens. Aline followed her.

A tall priest had already crossed the threshold. "May I speak with Master Mowbray?" he said.

"Master Mowbray is away, you must ask what you309 want of me. Come this way," she said, and stepped out of the door at the other end of the screens, so as to be away from the servants and Aline.

"We have come," said Father Austin, for it was he, "with a warrant for the arrest of a heretic, a certain Aline Gillespie; see, here are the seals thereon of Queen Mary and Bishop Bonner himself. It is well that one be careful in these matters," he said smiling grimly. "Some would be content with lesser signatures and seals, but then their work might be overset."

They had been strolling toward the further end of the quadrangle and were nearing the entrance to the stair that led to Aline's room. It had only taken an instant for it to flash through Aline's mind that the hour had come and it was now or never. She followed quietly behind them and hoped to be able to slip up the stair before they could catch her, and was ready to make a dash as they turned.

They turned just before reaching the door and Aline made a rush.

"Not so fast, my child," said the priest, stretching out a long interposing arm. "Whither away? I may want speech of thee shortly." He turned with a look of sanctimonious triumph to Mistress Mowbray. "Mother Church will clean your house of its vermin for you, madam," he said.

Aline gave one little gasp of mortal terror and then stood dumb for a second like a small bird caught by a beast of prey. She gave one appealing look toward Mistress Mowbray and then swung round facing the dining hall and paused a moment, with Father Austin's hand still on her shoulder.

310

"I prefer to clear my own house," Mistress Mowbray said icily. She disliked the man, she disliked his interference. He could not have said anything more foolish. Aline's interference had been outrageous, but it was nothing to this; at least the child was one of themselves. Mistress Mowbray's wrath raged at the insolence of this outsider. She looked again at Aline, delicate, fragile, ethereal, and the thought of the appealing look of the beautiful child at last thawed her hard heart. "What if ever Audry should be in a like plight?" she mused.

All this was in a flash, as she turned to Aline and looking her full in the face, said,— "Audry, dear, run and tell Silas that there's a ratcatcher or something, who thinks that we have vermin in the house and would like a job. You can also find Aline and tell her that he seems to like catching little girls."

Father Austin dropped his arm at the name of Audry; and Aline, though puzzled, ran off swiftly. As Mistress Mowbray finished her sentence, he bit his lip; he saw that he had made a mistake.

"Who is Audry, madam?"

"Audry is my daughter," answered Mistress Mowbray with her chin very much in the air.

"I thought that child there was Aline Gillespie," said the priest.

"So it was," said the lady, calmly.

"But you called her Audry, madam," he replied, "and told her to speak to Aline."

"Did I?" she said with well feigned surprise. "You confused me so with your peculiar language."

Meanwhile Aline ran back to the screens, intending311 to go through and cross the lower court and slip out over the drawbridge. She might reach the stream and make her way up to the cave before any one clearly grasped what was happening.

But when she came to the further door she was met by a large crowd that had followed the inquisitors and it was useless to try and make headway against it; besides she saw Father Martin's head appearing above the rest away in the background.

She turned back again with the head of the crowd and half mechanically picked up a staff that was standing in the corner by the door, as she passed into the court. She pushed her way past two men who were armed with swords and were just stepping through the doorway. She might still be able to get into the library and, desperate as the chance was, she hoped to throw them off the scent by breaking a window before going down through the kist to the secret room.

Father Austin was still standing near the bottom of the stair to her chamber. That way was closed; so she ran toward the small flight of steps leading to the little terrace in front of the library.

"Seize her, Hubert," shouted the priest.

The big burly man, addressed, rushed after her. Aline swung round suddenly and hit him unexpectedly with her staff on the side of his head and darted on.

The man gave a great yell and the crowd roared with laughter, which doubled his rage and, drawing his sword, he dashed again in pursuit. Aline was fleet and reached the library door before he was half way across the quadrangle.

She feverishly grasped the handle.

312

Alas, it was locked.

As she turned back, Hubert nearly reached the bottom of the steps. Four more paces and his sword would be through her.

The heavy man took a great stride half-way up the stair. The hunted child stood at bay.

How frail and slight she seemed; only a delicate flower ineffectively beautiful. The crowd stood motionless and held their breath, while some closed their eyes.

Hubert laughed at the absurd sight of the child barring his way. She could no longer hit him unawares; he was armed and ready, he expected nothing; when Aline, quick as lightning, by a dexterous turn of her staff, twisted the sword out of his hand, and lunging forward, caught him under the chin with her full force so that the big man overbalanced and fell backward down the steps, stunned.

Aline stooped and picked up the sword. Hubert's fellow, however, was close behind.

"Kill her!" shouted Father Martin.

"Slay the witch, Gilbert," echoed Father Austin.

As she picked up Hubert's sword she had to draw back in rising and Gilbert was already up the steps. He was a more active man than the other, but he had taken in the situation and was no fool; so, child as she was, he advanced more cautiously.

Poor little Aline had to think and fight at the same time. What was she to do? Even if she overcame this man, there were others; obviously she could not fight them all. But she thought of a faintly possible chance and, before Gilbert closed with her, gave a glance across the moat. Could she cross it? As she glanced she saw313 a sight for which she had been longing all these weary weeks,—it was a single horseman with two horses, evidently making his way toward the gully. He was turning to look back at the Hall. She saw no more, and straightway began a very pretty bit of sword play.

Gilbert proceeded warily and foyne, parry and counterparry followed with monotonous precision. Aline kept very cool and at first attempted little; but after a short time she tried a feint or so in order to test him. She soon found that he was no mean swordsman; but she had learned much from Ian, which he had brought from Italy and France; so Gilbert in his turn discovered that she was not an opponent to be despised.

He reckoned however that his greater strength must tell in the end and took things somewhat easily. For a time therefore nothing happened, but a little later, after a riposte on Aline's part, Gilbert made a counter-riposte and just touched her on the arm. He began to feel his superiority and pressed in harder, while she gradually drew back a little and a little along the terrace.

Gilbert thought that he was slowly mastering her; but Aline was playing for her own ends as her one slender hope was to let him wear himself out.

The crowd by this time were spell-bound and even the two priests were overcome by the fascination of the scene,—the beautiful agile child and the dexterous but far slower swordsman. The silence was intense, broken only by the clash of the swords.

Gradually they neared the end of the terrace. It was an awful moment for Aline. The man was obviously getting tired, but she shrank from trying to inflict a severe wound and he was far too skilful for her to disarm314 him. There was nothing for it, however; and, when almost at the little low wall at the terrace end, the instinctive struggle for life began to tell and the fighting on both sides became more serious.

Aline received a slight scratch on her left shoulder and this settled the matter and nerved her to a supreme effort.

As he lunged again she parried, made a riposte with a reprise following like a lightning flash and swift as thought her sword was through his heart and he fell dead on the pavement.

The crowd gasped. Aline stayed not an instant, but leaped upon the low terrace wall. Standing still for a moment she tore her outer garments from her and stood there like a lovely boy, save for the great flood of hair that had come entirely loose and that was caught on the windy battlement and blown like a cloud high behind her.

Then she paused and turning to the quadrangle thronged with people she said: "How dare you play the cowards' part, setting two armed men to attack one small girl? God will punish you, Father Martin, and you, too," she said, pointing to Father Austin, "and the blood of the slain man will cling to you and remorse shall tear your hearts. I am only a child and it is little that I know, but I do know that there is no love for a hard heart from God or from men.

"And you, Elspeth, Janet and those I love; it is hard to say good-bye, but I must go."

"Shoot her, shoot her!" shrieked the priests, "she blasphemes, she takes the name of God in vain." But the angry crowd surged round the guard and would not315 let them move. One, however, broke loose and raised his pistol; but as he did so, Aline, to the utter astonishment of all, still holding the sword, dived into the moat.

"Our Lady shield thee, St. Aline," cried a voice from the crowd; and as the wall was too high to see over, except from the terrace itself, they swept up in a mass, the priests, the people, the guards and all.

A few strokes took her over the water; Ian stooped and seized her under the arms, drew her out of the water, lifted her on to the one horse, vaulted himself on to the other and they fled like the wind.

Shot after shot then rang out and the bullets whistled only too alarmingly near them, but they were soon out of reach.

"Mount and pursue," shouted Father Austin, as he stumbled over the body of the dead man, "and take this clumsy loon and bury him."

"The horses are tired, we need fresh steeds for that," said one of the guard.

"Gramercy, take them from the Hall," he roared.

But no one would find the keys of the stable and Mistress Mowbray, coming up a moment later, said in acid tones, "Take your own horses, Sir Priest, warrant or no warrant you cannot steal, and if you touch my horses I will have you hanged as a common horse-thief."

She looked at him triumphantly, the exercise of power delighted her and she even felt a glow of reflected glory from Aline's achievement. "We know how to manage these interlopers," she thought; "I am mistress of this situation. Aline, you have done very well."

Father Austin looked cowed, and the sullen people[316] stood in the way and blocked the road. One managed to secure a stirrup, another broke a girth, while a third removed a halter altogether.

"You shall suffer for this," said the priests, when they at length reached the horses; but the attitude of the crowd was so menacing that they became afraid for their very lives and finally had to fall back upon entreaty before they were allowed to go away at all.

The result was that the fugitives had two full hours start on good horses, before Father Austin could get his little troop under way.

"Had God sent a deliverer from the skies?" mused Mistress Mowbray, as she sat and pondered the strange events of the day.

317
CHAPTER XXIV
A RIDE IN VAIN

AS Aline and Ian rode over the rough ground they kept turning back; but nothing was to be seen. They wondered what had delayed the pursuit, but felt sure it would come.

The snow had more or less melted and the day was clear, so that they could see far behind them. When, therefore, they reached a place where they could clearly see two miles and no one following, they slackened pace, so as to give their horses every chance.

Ian's plan was to swim or ford the swollen river at the Weal, the long pool-like stretch, of the Tees,—and then take the track to Garrigill. His present anxiety was to keep Aline warm. He had brought away two big heavy riding cloaks from Andrew, saying that he needed to be warm sleeping on the hills. One of these he had put round Aline, but she was at first very cold. The exercise, however, warmed her a little and they did not dare to stop until they had put the river between them and their pursuers. It was fortunate for them that there was no wind and that the day, although cold, was bright and sunny. The hills looked hard and colourless, but the sunshine seemed to conquer the austerity.

They reached the river and negotiated it safely, Ian taking off his boots and lower garments to keep them[318] dry. When they reached the other side Aline undressed and put on all of Ian's clothes that he could take off and they wrung out hers and hung them where they would best dry with the motion through the air.

176

Ian had obtained a sword and two pistols from Andrew, while Aline had the sword with which she swam the moat.

They passed through Garrigill without mishap. Ian was particularly nervous of their being caught just as they reached a village, lest a hue and cry should be raised that would stop them. He looked anxiously back when they neared Alston, but no one was in view. It seemed best to make no attempt to keep out of sight by detours, but simply to press on.

Their foes, he guessed, would probably get fresh horses in Alston. Oh, if only they had money to do the same! It was impossible to reach Scotland that night, so the best plan seemed to Ian to be to rest their horses at the loneliest part of the road beyond Alston, where they could be concealed themselves and at the same time get a distant view of the road. After a rest they might make a good run for it, as the day was already getting on, particularly if their pursuers cantered their horses from Alston and came up with them at all blown. Then in the dark the best thing would probably be to abandon the horses and escape on foot.

They did as he had planned, and after they had rested an hour and a half, during which time the horses had some oats, Ian saw their adversaries about a mile behind. There were six of them and they had been badly delayed getting fresh horses in Alston. They were galloping rather wildly down the hill.

319

Ian held his hand for Aline to mount and then vaulted into his seat and they set off at a trot. The others saw them and put spurs to their horses, yelling as they rode.

"Keep cool, not too fast," said Ian, "wait till they come much nearer."

Slowly their pursuers gained upon them, but Aline and Ian reserved their strength.

A mile they rode and the interval was lessened by a quarter; their hearts were too full to speak; another mile and the distance was again less by a quarter. Aline looked back: "Oh, Ian! We shall never get away, and they will catch you, too. I wish you had not come to rescue me. Do you think 'Moll o' the graves' really does know anything about what is going to happen?"

"No, little heart, but do not be afraid, we have been helped so far. I think we shall get away."

Another mile's ride and they were only separated from their pursuers by a quarter mile.

Ian waited,—three hundred yards,—two hundred,—one hundred,—fifty. "Now," he said, "let them go," and both riders lashed their horses and the distance began to lengthen out again till it reached three or four hundred yards. Three of their pursuers fell behind altogether, the mounts they had obtained in Alston were not equal to the strain. One was Father Martin, and it would have made Aline's ears tingle if she had heard the curses heaped upon her and Ian.

The other three kept together for a time and then they also began to spread out a little. At length there were forty paces between the first and second, and a couple of hundred yards to the third.

It soon became clear, however, that, though they need not fear the third horse, both the other two would ultimately be a match for them, nor would it get dark soon enough for them to escape. Ian kept absolutely cool, but it was a terrible moment. If he were killed, even if Aline did escape, who in the wide world would look after her?

When the nearest horse was only about sixty yards behind he said to Aline, "Ride on, I think I can deal with these fellows, but I wish we had more pistols,—two shots will not see us far. Get to Carlisle and find Matthew Musgrave. I doubt not he will smuggle you away over the border; and, if I come not, when Walter Margrove arrives he will somehow provide for you."

"But I won't leave you," said Aline. She looked at him so beseechingly, that he knew it was useless to say anything.

"Then you must do as I tell you. I am going to stop; you go on thirty or forty paces beyond and then stop also. Be ready to dismount if necessary. You are a good swordswoman, but you know nothing about shooting."

Ian then reined in, turned and pointed his pistol at the leading horse. The man was taken aback by the sudden move, but fired wildly as he rode and the bullet whizzed past Ian's head. It was only a matter of seconds, but Ian waited to make quite sure and then fired at the horse, which fell and brought its rider with a horrible crash to the ground.

The second horse was treated in like manner; but its rider saw what was coming just in time to slacken his pace and leap to the ground as the horse fell. He then fired twice, missing the first time, but grazing Ian's left side with the second shot.

He was a big powerful man and before Ian had time to step back and mount, he was in upon him with his sword. Ian had time to draw, but found that the man was no fool with his weapon. Time was precious, too, for the third horseman, who had drawn rein for a moment, was now advancing and would be upon them immediately.

Aline, who had seen this, dismounted and shouted: "Leave him to me and load your pistols"; but before she could reach them, Ian's sword was through the man's neck.

Luckily the horses stood; but he had only time to load one of the pistols, while Aline mounted again, before the third man arrived. He slowed up as he approached and attempted to fire from his horse, but the pistol only flashed in the pan and missed fire. Again Ian brought the horse to the ground, and as the man, who was not seriously hurt, picked himself up, Ian said; "Well, good-bye, my friend, I am sorry that urgent business prevents our waiting," and springing to his saddle he galloped off.

Before the man could fire they were some distance away and the bullet went hopelessly wide.

"That's twice I've been shot in three days, little one," said Ian. "It's a mercy these fellows cannot shoot better."

"Oh, you never told me about the other," said Aline, "and you must wait now and let me attend to this; the blood is all over your arm and down nearly to your knee."

"Indeed, I must not, sweet child, we shall soon have the rest of the gang after us. In fact, I do not know what to do, the horses are completely done and yet it is not safe to put up anywhere. Whatever happens we must not be caught in a town. I believe it would have been safer to have waited and killed them all."

Aline shuddered. "Oh, how awful."

Ian tore a piece off his shirt sleeve and stopped the bleeding of his wound as well as he could, and they rode on in silence for a time, till they came to the place where the road divided for Haltwhistle and Brampton. The trees grew thickly by the stream and it was getting dark. "Let us hide here," Ian said. "They are unlikely to see us and we can then go whichever way they do not. They cannot be here for some time, so the horses can again get a feed and a rest."

They piled up some dead leaves where two fallen trunks made a sort of shelter, did what they could for Ian's wound and huddled together and waited.

At last, after about two hours, they dimly saw three horses. There was only one rider, but the fugitives guessed that the others carried the dead and the injured man. Four men walked beside them.

"I can hardly move another step," they heard one of them say.

"I do not suppose you are as tired as I am," said a second voice, "besides I bruised myself pretty badly when that devil brought my horse down. I shall be too stiff to move to-morrow."

"Well," said a third voice, which both recognised as that of Father Martin,—"This kind of game is not in my line anyway. Ride, ride, it is nothing but ride. I shall be too sore to sit down for a week; when on earth are you going to bring me to a place for a night's rest? S'death. I almost feel as though I did not care what happened to the villains, I am so worn out. That's three of my men dead; for I reckon Philip there will never speak again. Fancy that little she-cat killing Gilbert."

"That's you, Pussie," softly whispered Ian in her ear.

"Well, this is the way to Haltwhistle; that's six miles nearer than Brampton," said one of the other voices, "and they are more likely to have gone there to put us off the track. Anyway, we can get men over to Brampton soon after daylight."

"Thanks for the information," again whispered Ian.

Gradually the voices died away in the still evening air, and finally the sound of the horses' hoofs also.

"Thou art a naughty boy to whisper like that," said Aline.

"Marry, it was safe enough for such a noise as they were making."

They waited a little longer and then Aline put on her own clothes which were now quite dry. She was also going to cut off her hair, but Ian dissuaded her; so she braided it very tightly and concealed it with the bonnet.

They walked by their horses for an hour and then mounted and reached Brampton at ten o'clock at night. They approached the small hostelry and dismounted. "Can you give my page and myself supper and a night's lodging?" Ian enquired. "The horses will want a good rub down, too; they are tired."

324

"Whence have you come and whither bound?" said mine host.

"We've come from Alston to-day and we're bound for Scotland to-morrow. But show us a seat and a fire, this is no time for talk."

"Come in, then; but you should not be travelling to Scotland now; there's trouble on the border again and you may fall in with more than you desired; but it's none of my business."

At first the place looked empty; but there was a boy curled up on a settle and fast asleep.

Ian looked at him and to his surprise it was Wilfred. He hesitated a moment before waking the lad; it seemed unkind, he looked so comfortable; but it might assist toward Aline's safety. So he lightly touched him on the shoulder. Wilfred looked up and rubbed his eyes. When he saw who it was a look of pleased surprise spread over his face.

"What are you doing here, Will?" said Ian.

"You said you wanted me to keep a look out for you near Brampton, Master Menstrie; so Matthew and I, finding there was work to be done at Naworth Castle, have come over here. Matthew is lodging at a house near the castle, but as Master Forster, here, is a friend of Matthew's, I am staying with him. I was to go and help Matthew as soon as we had news of you; but I have spent all my time on the road for some days. He will be so glad to hear you have got back again. We heard in Carlisle that you had been drowned, but I knew you were a great swimmer and felt it could not be true and that you would go on to Holwick as you said. Did you get there?" asked the boy.

325

"Yes, I got there all right."

"And what did you do about the little lady?"

"The little lady is safe so far," said Ian, "and Angus, one of the pages from the Hall, is coming with me to see if we can make arrangements for her in Scotland."

"I am glad to hear she is safe."

"The boy, Angus, and I are leaving early to-morrow for Longtown. If those rascals follow us up and you get a chance to delay them, do so. A loose shoe proved very useful before."

William Forster, the innkeeper, brought supper, and Wilfred, who was now thoroughly awake, boylike, was not averse to sharing their meal.

"There's a room prepared for you upstairs," said Forster. "I suppose your page will be all right on the other settle?"

"Yes, that will do," answered Ian. "You do not mind, little one," he whispered softly after the man had gone. "I think it is best."

"Of course not," she answered.

After the meal they sat by the fire for a few minutes, and Ian looked across at the two boys, as they seemed. Wilfred was immensely better in health and had entirely lost the half starved look. "He's certainly a beautiful lad," Ian mused. "They make as fine a pair of boys as Aline and Audry were girls. I must paint those two, just like that, if ever we get safely through. I wish I could sketch them now."

When Ian had retired, Wilfred, who was fascinated by his companion, tried to draw her into conversation; but she was very reticent and pleaded that she wanted to go to sleep, which was indeed true.

326

"You have a fine master now," said Wilfred, "even though he is only a carpenter. He doesn't look like a man to have a page in those rough home-spuns of his. But you are lucky, going round and serving him. I wish I had the chance. I would die for that man."

"So would I," said Aline quietly.

"Then I'll love you, too," said the boy; "but you are right, we must go to sleep."

181

In the morning Wilfred woke early, while it was still quite dark and roused Angus, as Ian named Aline. "Go you and wake your master," he said.

Aline found Ian and after a meal they took lanthorns out to the stable and prepared to start.

Wilfred helped them and chattered away to Aline, trying in every way to lighten her share of the labours.

While Ian was settling the score Wilfred took Aline aside: "Remember, Angus," he said, "that we are both willing to die for him; and if ever I am wanted I am ready. He risked his life for me and I can never repay him."

"Risked his life for you! When? I never heard of it."

Wilfred looked at her. "Do you mean to say he never told you?"

"No, he is not the kind that would. Oh, I should like to stay and hear all about it! But I must not wait, Master Menstrie will be wanting me."

"I wish I could tell you everything; but I am so glad that you love him. I am sure that you and I would be great friends,—very great friends; oh, if only I could go with you! But we must say good-bye," and then Wilfred hesitated, "I am sure I do not know how327 it is," he said shyly, "I sometimes used to kiss my best friend, Hugh, when there was no one else near; but boys don't kiss much. However, we two shall never meet again and somehow I want to kiss you."

He approached her a little awkwardly, there were tears in his eyes, and Aline let him kiss her.

"Good-bye again, Angus, I shall not forget you," he said.

At that moment Ian returned and they mounted their horses and bade farewell and rode off.

The boy stood in the grey dawn, gazing regretfully after them down the road. Then a thought struck him. He felt puzzled. "Why, I do not believe that was a boy at all,—No, I am sure it was not. It must have been the little lady herself. What a fool I was not to think of it before. But fancy her taking a kiss from the likes of me!"

They had hardly disappeared from sight, when he heard the clatter of hoofs behind him and a body of armed men rode down the street.

"Good morrow, my lad," said their leader, "you are up betimes."

Wilfred had decided that it would be best to appear very communicative and then perhaps they would not trouble to ask any one else.

"Yes," he said, "there have been some silly loons here, who did not know what a good thing bed is on a cold winter morning, routing me up to look after their horses," and Wilfred half turned on his heel as though he would go back to the house.

"Not so fast, my lad," said the leader, "who were they, and what were they like?"

"Oh, there were two of them, a man in homespun and his page, though why he should have a page perplexed me not a little. Do you know who he was, good sirs, I should like to know the meaning of it?"

"That is not your concern, lad; come, can you tell me any more? Was he a big man?"

"No, he was about middle size; but very well built, with deep set grey eyes and a fine face."

"Humph," grunted the horseman, "deep set grey eyes, yes; to the devil with the fine face! And what about the other?" he added.

"Oh, he was a pretty slip of a boy."

"Were they armed?"

"They both had swords and the man had pistols."

"That's they, right enough; but one more question—Where did they come from and where are they going?"

"They came from Alston and arrived very tired last night."

"That settles it, and which way did you say they had gone now?"

"Oh, they set off along the Carlisle road, long before it was light. You don't want to find them, do you? You'll never do it if you stand talking here; marry, you've got your work cut out for you if you want to catch them."

"Come along, men," said their leader.

"They must be pretty well in Carlisle by now," shouted Wilfred, as they started off. "You will hardly do it."

"To hell fire with them; but we'll get them yet"; and the horses thundered down the road.

CHAPTER XXV
AMAZING DISCOVERIES

WILFRED stood and rubbed his hands. "I would give a week's pay to see them in Carlisle," he chuckled.

Meanwhile Ian and Aline gently made their way along the road to Longtown without mishap. They saw a small body of troopers once; but the troopers took no notice of them. In the desultory border warfare people went about their business practically unconcerned. Life had to go on and, if they waited till there was no fighting, to all intents and purposes they might, in those districts, wait for ever.

"What are we going to do when we reach Scotland?" Aline asked, when at the last it appeared that immediate danger was passing. "Old Moll does not seem to have been right this time," she added.

"We cannot say yet, birdeen, there are many perils and difficulties ahead, perhaps greater than we have yet passed. I wish I could shake off the feeling of that woman. It is not that I believe any of her prophecies. Of course they are all nonsense, but she is the very incarnation of the spirit of evil, a continual oppressive reminder of its presence in the world. There is no doubt, too, that she has a snakelike inexplicable influence over people and puts evil suggestion into their minds, just as some other people have exactly the opposite power. To talk with Moll rouses one's worst nature; to talk with some rouses one's best." He looked at Aline and thought how wonderful her power was. What was this power, mysteriously possessed by some natures, that almost by their very presence they could change men's lives;—Aline and Moll might themselves be the warring spirits of good and evil.

"My only object for the moment," he said aloud, "was to rescue you from your desperate danger. I thought that then we might have time to think out something. There are difficulties indeed; the country is in a very unsettled condition, partly the troubles with England, partly the religious troubles and the difficulty with the regent, Mary of Guise, and France. But our first trouble is,—that I have no money and people with no money always find it hard to live," and he smiled a rueful smile.

"Neither have I," said Aline, "at least not to live on. I have two gold pieces with me."

"Well, you are richer than I am," he said playfully. "It will help us somewhat, while I find something to set us going. I left a note, too, with Wilfred for Walter Margrove, in case he should come within the next few days, asking him to send Wilfred to Canonbie with a little money at once for our present needs."

"Wilfred," said Aline, "is that Will Ackroyd?"

"Yes," said Ian, "I have a story to tell you about how I met him, but we must leave it for the present. I am very perplexed about this matter of making a livelihood." He paused a moment and then continued;—

"I might find work as a carpenter, or perhaps there will be more call for a smith in these turbulent times. But I cannot think what to do with you. Even if I found some people with whom you could live and worked to keep you, there would be all kinds of questions as to where you came from and all about you?"

"Then why not let me work with you as carpenter's boy, like Will does for Matthew Musgrave?"

"What! and spoil your beautiful hands. By the way, though," he added, "what have you been doing to get them in such a shocking condition? I have noticed it all along but my mind has been so full of schemes and plans for our escape, that I have not been able to talk about it."

Aline told him the story and continued;—"Anyway, carpentry could not be as bad as that."

Ian was shocked and looked at her thankfully. "I trust we have broken the evil spell," he said. "But, princess, you are a lady and such very hard work is beyond that to which you have been used."

"Yes, I hope I am a lady and just because I am a lady it does not matter what I am used to do. I can turn my hand to anything; I do not mind. It is only common people who are afraid of demeaning themselves. I have often noticed"—and then she suddenly stopped:—was not Ian himself one of these "common people," and was it not unmannerly anyway for a real lady to talk like that?

"Noticed what?" asked Ian.

"Oh, just noticed that it is so," and by way of changing the subject she went on,—"but there is one thing I should mind;—I should mind having to cut my hair short."

332

Ian sighed: "Yes, you must not do that, little one, we must think of some other plan."

"But I have quite made up my mind and I am going to cut it," she said in her most queenly manner. She said it so firmly and cheerfully that even Ian did not realise the struggle that was going on in the little heart.

"Well, princess, if it must be so, it must; but you need not cut it above the shoulders. Many pages wear it down to the shoulders."

"Pages, yes, but not carpenters' boys." At the same time Ian's words gave her a gleam of comfort. That was not quite so terrible. It would have a good start as soon as she could let it grow again. "Do you think a carpenter's boy could wear it down to his shoulders?" she asked wistfully.

"Certainly," said Ian; "it might be a little peculiar, but if we could afford to dress you a little more like a page though you were a carpenter's boy, I doubt even if any one would notice."

They had reached Longtown by this time, but Ian decided not to stop if they could get safely over the border. They rode on, therefore, until they met a small patrol near Canonbie but were allowed after a few explanations to pass.

At the little inn they made enquiry as to the news of the day. This was surprising, but to Ian by no means altogether unexpected. The Protestant feeling had been growing and some of the Protestant leaders had met at the house of James Sym in Edinburgh and signed the first covenant, called the "Godlie Band." They were the Earl of Ergyl; Glencarn,—the good Earl;333 Mortoun; Archibald, Lord of Lorne and John Erskyne of Doun.[26]

26 The spelling of the names is taken from a surviving copy of the covenant.

But what was of immediate interest and importance to Ian was that the Earl of Hawick[27] was at that moment raising forces in the border shires, nominally to fight on the border, but in reality to be ready to support the Protestant cause against Mary of Guise.

27 This is a fictitious title and likewise the border incident, although there were several such affrays in this year.

His headquarters were but a few miles away and Ian wondered whether it was not his duty to throw in his lot with them. His own feelings on the whole were friendly to England and he hated the policy that the regent was pursuing of making Scotland an appendage of France, but if English marauders invaded the border he was quite ready as a true Scot to fight against them, although it was the religious cause that he had more deeply at heart.

"Methinks I ought to join them," he said. "I have seen a good deal of fighting in my day and I might be useful to the cause."

"I will go with you," said Aline.

"Nonsense, child, girls do not fight."

"Joan of Arc fought and why should not I?" she replied.

"Joan of Arc was older than you and could stand a strain that would be quite beyond you, little one, hardy as you are."

"But I should go as your page or attendant. Would334 you fight as a trooper or on foot, because that, of course, would make some difference?"

"That would remain to be seen, but in any case it would be absurd for you to be there. But it has given me a new idea, sweet child. They would be glad of my services; and, as they are protestants, they would be only too pleased to look after you in return."

"But I want to come with you."

He looked at her sadly; "It is out of the question," he said.

"Oh, but please let me."

"No, birdeen, you might be killed."

"Well, that would not matter. I have no friends or relatives in the world to care for me; it might be the simplest solution of our difficulties, if I died trying to help a good cause."

"You must not talk like that, Aline; I cannot bear to think of it."

"But I have made up my mind. I am coming. You might be wounded and I might be just the one to help you and prevent your dying." She drew herself up as she spoke and Ian knew that further argument was useless.

"In that case we can wait and rest here, in any wise for to-day, the which we both need. I can then go and see the Earl to-morrow and probably we can continue to rest for some days while he is recruiting his forces."

They retired early. Aline had a little room with a glorious outlook. Oh, how beautiful everything was and how good God had been to her. When she was half undressed she sat down and gazed out of the window.335 So this was dear Scotland again, the land of her birth. For the moment the recollection of "Moll o' the graves" clouded the prospect, but it passed away. The sombre hills looked kindly in the gloaming. She felt hardly able to contain herself for joy.

It was true that she was about to face new dangers; but that did not trouble her in the least. She would be definitely doing her duty, as she conceived it, fighting for a good cause along with many others; she would no longer be a hunted fugitive merely trying to preserve her own life.

She knelt down and prayed and felt happier than she had done since her father died, happier even than during the best days in the secret room.

So happy was she that she proceeded to cut off her wonderful hair, just below the level of the shoulders, without the slightest twinge of regret. "I wish I had Audry's long mirror here," was the only thought that troubled her.

Even this was unexpectedly gratified, for in the morning she was down first and discovered a long mirror in a black oak frame, one of the treasures of the hostel.

As she was looking at herself Ian appeared. The sight cost him a pang. "Oh, child," he exclaimed, "what have you done?"

"I've only made myself into a real boy," she answered.

Ian bit his lips; he would not have thought that he could have minded so much.

As they were standing there the door suddenly opened and a boy came in.

"Hullo, Wilfred! is that you?"

"Yes, master, I have brought a letter from Walter Margrove."

Ian took the letter and went over to the window seat on the far side of the room to read it.

"Wilfred," thought Aline; "Wilfred"; it had a familiar sound before, when Ian used the name on the road:—and he came from Kirkoswald,—there was too a tale to be told as Ian had said,—and Ian himself had been using an assumed name. Could it by any chance be the boy of little Joan's sad story?

He held out his hand bashfully, and bent his head. As Aline took it he said;—"I humbly crave your pardon, but I believe now I know who you are."

Aline blushed and then she said quietly, "You have probably guessed rightly. Whom do you think I am?"

He looked at her for a moment. How could there possibly be any doubt; there could not be two such beautiful people in the world; and he had heard Walter and Andrew, besides Ian, allude to her unparalleled loveliness. "You are Mistress Gillespie," he said, and bowed awkwardly.

Aline smiled sadly. "Yes," she said, "I am and I believe I have just discovered who you are. Your name is not really Ackroyd, is it?"

"Yes, Mistress, it is," he answered.

Aline looked baffled, but he continued,—"However, I have never been known as Ackroyd, as I lived with an Aunt whose name was Johnstone."

"I thought so," she replied softly. "Come sit over here, for I have a sorrowful tale for you."

She took his hand and the boy followed, lost in wonder and admiration.

"I used to know poor little Joan," she said very gently.

"Yes, Mistress, I had guessed as much; we heard in Kirkoswald what had happened," and the boy's eyes filled with tears. "I know that you did everything for her that could be done and that she loved you."

Aline felt relieved, as she was spared the worst part of her task. "She often used to speak of you, Wilfred, and before she went away, she gave me her greatest treasures which you had given her long before; and I was to try and return them to you. But, alas, I had to flee from armed men at a moment's notice in peril of my life and I have them not. But they are safe and one day I will fulfil my charge."

She held out her hand. "Oh, I am so sorry for you," she said, "but my words are too feeble to say what I feel."

The tears were now running freely down the boy's face, he took her hand in both his and smothered it with kisses. "Oh, Joan, Joan, my little Joan, how can I bear it? How can you really be dead and I alive? Why is the world so cruel? Oh, Joan, if only I could have died for you."

Aline bent over and kissed him on the forehead. "She told me to give you that," she said; then, after a pause, she went on;—"I am only a little girl and I do not pretend to understand things, Wilfred. But think, if you had died as you have been wishing, poor little Joan would have been as unhappy as you are now. These things are a mystery and yet somehow I feel that the spirit of light in its own way and its own time must triumph over the spirit of darkness. I have always felt338 that; and now that I have my new faith, I am more sure of it than ever."

"I do not see how that can be," said Wilfred, "and yet as you speak I seem to feel better."

"I do not understand it myself," said Aline, "but I have been right before."

Wilfred looked at her. Had this wonderful child with the strange deep dark blue eyes some power that other mortals had not?

"Angus," said Ian's voice from the other side of the room, "Walter has sent us some money; he also offers to help us in every way he can, and there are some other items that will interest you about the rumours he heard in Carlisle. They seem to think we rode through Carlisle and went to Penrith or Keswick. I have written a short note to Walter, which Wilfred can take back. Did you come in the night, Will?"

"Yes, I got a lift on an empty wagon going back to Longtown. There was straw in the bottom and I slept all the way."

"I am afraid I could not sleep in a wagon," said Ian. "Come and join us at our meal, Wilfred."

They had their meal and afterwards sat and talked until it was time for Wilfred to return.

After he had gone, Aline and Ian set off to the camp where the Earl of Hawick lay. When they arrived Ian asked if he might see the Earl, as he wished to offer his services.

The sentry looked at him very dubiously and then at Aline, after which he seemed a little more satisfied, as she was better dressed. Finally he called the officers of the guard, who subjected them to a similar scrutiny.

"I think I can see to your business, my man," he said.

"Thank you, I have a special message for my lord of Hawick," said Ian.

Aline started at the tone and looked at Ian: there was a quiet hauteur about it that she had never heard before.

The man seemed to notice it too. "Who is it that wishes to see the Earl?" he said.

"Say, Ian Menstrie, son of Alexander Menstrie; that will do."

Aline felt a little nervous; as she had never met a real Earl and had something of the child's imagination about the grandeur of such personages.

The officer returned very quickly, but the change in his manner seemed almost to make him a different man.

"Your Grace," he said, bowing very low, "the Earl of Hawick is coming at once."

"I said Ian Menstrie, not Alexander Menstrie," answered Ian, looking a little annoyed.

"Yes, your Grace," said the Messenger, "I made it quite clear; the Earl of Hawick understands."

Aline was very puzzled, they seemed to have strange customs of address in the army, but before she had time to think the Earl appeared. She was a little disappointed. Was that an Earl? He was a fair figure of a man, but was neither as handsome as Ian nor had he, she suddenly thought, as she looked at the two men, the dignity of Ian's carriage.

"I am so glad to see you again, your Grace," he said, doffing his bonnet and bowing as the officer had done. "You are the very man we want. I shall never forget how well you managed on that miserable day at Pinkie Cleugh; and Scotland can never repay you for the rout of Lord Wharton on the Western Marches on that cold February day. It was a sorry remnant that he and Grey took back with them, and it marked the turning of the tide. Our country was indeed at a low ebb then.

"Of course you will share the command with me. I would willingly serve under you, but these are my fellows and they know me; so I shall just follow your advice. On my honour, you shall have all the glory, when it is over; not that you used to care much for that kind of thing, and you were really only a lad then."

Aline's eyes grew rounder and rounder. Hawick continued,—"I heard the news of the old man's death about a week ago. It was somewhat of a shock following so soon after your brother's; but I said, that will bring Ian Menstrie back to us if anything will. I am sure he will throw in his lot with us."

Aline gasped. Who was Ian then, this carpenter-man, as she had thought him? Even in the earlier days she had never supposed that he could be more than a younger son of one of the lesser lairds.

Ian seemed overcome and very sad. "Well, my Lord, if you must know," he said in as calm a voice as he could muster, "I am here by accident. I have just had a run for my life, with my young page here, Angus Gillespie. I am looking rather a sorry object, but let that pass. I had not heard of my father's death, or even of my brother's. It is a terrible shock."

"Poor fellow," said Hawick, "I am sorry to be the bearer of bad news and you are looking a sad wreck. You must take as many days' rest as we can manage."

341

"Before I forget, I want to know if you can let us have a couple of horses; these are not mine and I want to return them to the owner. I also wish to know if you can spare a couple of troopers to take them back to Kirkoswald. They can arrange the matter at Carlisle."

"Are they English horses?"

"Yes."

"Ha! ha! ha! Fancy returning English horses across the border, when once you have got them here. Well, you always were a strange fellow. Yes, you can have as many troopers as you please, and horses and anything you want."

Aline was very impatient to have Ian by himself and was glad when he turned to go, after giving a brief account of his imprisonment and the outline of his main adventures, avoiding all details.

The Earl accompanied them to the inn and then took his leave, promising to send Ian an outfit such as more became his station and, at Ian's special request, everything that under the circumstances could be procured befitting a page of gentle birth.

Aline was pleased to find no one in the hostel. Ian was tired and his wounds hurt him, although Aline had attended to them regularly. He sat down by the fire and sighed.

It was a cold day and Aline crouched at the hearth-stone by his feet. She put her hand on his knee and looked up. Ian's eyes were full of tears. Aline had never seen anything like this; she stood up, stroking his head with her delicate hand and kissed him on the forehead.

He did not speak, but drew her gently to him. The child threw both her arms about his neck and seated herself on his knee. "Oh, I wish I could comfort you," she said.

It was too much for Ian and two great tears actually rolled down his cheek. "My Father," was all that he said. Then making an effort, he controlled himself and looked at Aline's beautiful sympathetic little face. A curious feeling passed through him. He had lost his father; and his father had never been kind to him, and he had gained this child, who was devoted to him. Was this God's recompense?

He passed his fingers through her short locks. "What have you done with all the glory you cut off?" he said.

"It is upstairs. I plaited it in four plaits."

"May I have some?" he asked.

"You may have it all if you like."

"It was a big sacrifice, child-heart," he said softly, and kissed her.

"May I ask you something," she said, "even though it does make you sad: but I would rather learn from your own lips? You know you have not told me who you are. Who are you?"

He paused a moment, while he continued gently stroking her hair. "I am now the Duke of Ochil, little one."

Aline rose from his knee and crouched down on the hearth again. She gazed up at him wonderingly. In after years as she looked back she understood her feelings; but at the time they were a perplexity even to herself. So far from being pleased that he was a duke, she resented it. It seemed to put a barrier between them;—his Grace, the Duke of Ochil, could not be the same as her dear friend Ian.

Ian saw the expression on her face and half-guessed its meaning. "It does not please you, heartsease," he said.

She looked up quickly and then said simply,—"I do not know. It is strange."

CHAPTER XXVI
THE BATTLE OF LIDDISDALE

THE days slipped by and when Hawick had mustered two thousand foot and some 300 horse he decided to move northward up Liddisdale. The Duke of Ochil nominally commanded the cavalry, but was really the guiding spirit of the whole.

Angus, that is Aline, acted as Ochil's page or squire and was soon very highly in favour with all the officers. She was, however, very uncommunicative and kept herself to herself, the which she found much easier, in that there was a reserved hauteur about Ian when dealing with those that were at all his equals, which he never displayed when dealing with inferiors. At the same time every one's respect for him was very marked and his power over the men was immense. This new aspect of his character interested Aline not a little.

There had been rumours for some time of a gathering for an English raid upon Scotland and early on the morning of the third day after leaving Canonbie, their scouts brought word of the presence of an English force, three thousand strong, that had moved up the Tyne from Bellingham.

Before setting forth, the Duke of Ochil spoke a few words of encouragement to the men. "It may seem," he said, "that neither on their side nor on ours are345 there enough to make our encounter of great moment, yet is there more in the balance than that of which ye may be in any wise aware. Our country is in the hour of her trial and a little thing may decide the final outcome. On the one hand there is France and on the other hand there is England, both eager to swallow her up. Yet are there greater issues than this,—not only is the freedom of our bodies at stake, but the freedom of our souls and not only of our souls but of those of mankind.

"Our host is small and our deeds may be obscure; yet though fame is not likely to be ours, that which we do this day may well be the foundation of greater things and by our blood we may purchase liberty of conscience throughout the whole world. No deed is ever so small as to be of no account and if we play the coward it may be the small beginning that shall bring upon the nations an avalanche of woe.

"It is for the higher that we strive,—for all that is noblest in man against all that is low. Yea, I know that many of you here, yourselves forget the glory of our destiny, zealous though ye be within your lights. Yet it is the fight of enlightenment against darkness. It is truth and development, love and beauty against all that is narrow and stagnant, false and ugly. And if victory be with us, see how great is the charge upon us that we ourselves do not fall short of our high endeavour.

"I have said that our host is small and our deeds must be small likewise, and yet it is not a little thing that I ask of each individual man. I ask all that ye have, I ask your lives. Nor do I presume to say that346 the Lord is on our side, but I do say that if each do act according to his conscience, while putting aside all prejudice and all bitterness of heart that might narrow that conscience, it is not for us to fear the issue. Yea, as far as our minds may discern, we fight for God and our country."

So he spoke, and there went up a great shouting, "For God and for our country."

It was a still cold day and the very air seemed tense with the issues involved. Aline's heart beat with excitement, yet she was surprised how calm she felt. "Surely I am afeared," she said, "and yet I am full of gladness and am ready to give my life, as Ian has asked." She rode upon a grey charger carrying the banner of Ochil which she had hastily made at Canonbie with her own hands;—azure, a fesse between three crescents argent.[28] Ian lacked Aline's happy disposition, and looked troubled, but his resolution to do or die was no whit less determined.

28 A blue field divided horizontally by a broad silver band; two silver crescents above and one below.

The English cavalry were, as usual, immensely superior in numbers, and while the Scots forces were forming their line, they hoped to press the advantage by a charge, which at the same time should cover the advance of their own infantry deploying out of the valley.

The Scots were in two ranks, with the reserves below the crest of the hill, every front man, the butt of his pike against his right foot and the point breast high, the while those behind crossed their pike points with those forward. Ian held his horsemen back on the right flank, while the bowmen were on the left.

The enemy charged swiftly over the haugh, their gay pennons a-flutter on their lances, a brave sight to see. And as they came they shouted;—"Down with the heretics; come on, ye coward loons."

"For God and our country," the Scots replied, as the wave of Southrons hurled itself upon the bristling pikes, only to break and scatter as many a man of that goodly host met his doom.

Ian taking them at a disadvantage led the Scots' horse in a counter-charge and menacingly they thundered over the plain, so that despite his smaller force he drove them behind their own lines and numbers more of the English bit the dust and among them the Lord of Almouth, their leader, a noble and brave youth who received a lance thrust in his side and fell to earth gripping the soil with both his hands in the agony of death. And many a gay Scots gallant lay on the ground between the hosts and the corbies gathered in the air watching for their time to come.

Then for a while the battle fell to those on foot and furiously they fought and many doughty deeds were done on either side that day. But terrible was the slaughter, as neither party would yield the advantage to the other; and the shouting of the fighters mingled with cries of the wounded, and ever and anon there boomed the roar of the artillery in the which the English had the better of the Scots.

The fight was stubborn and Aline's mood, at first all eager, now gave place to one of dread, the light began to fail and a voice within the air seemed to whisper, "Whensoever the day goes down, the spirits of darkness will gather for your destruction and then it will be too late." She even thought she saw "Old Moll" stalking through the battle-field and gloating over the slain.

The battle wavered from side to side and at length it seemed for the Scots as though all were lost. They had sadly given way and at the direst moment of their need the Earl of Sanquhar, a man of great valour and a tower of strength, was shot by an English archer and the arrow went in at his throat and pierced right through his neck and he fell forward speechless and the dark mist clouded his eyes. Then the Scots wavered and fell back still more and the end seemed come and had it not been for the Earl of Hawick himself, they would have been utterly worsted. He rushed into the fray and heartened the wavering host and they made a great onset and the battle stayed not.

Yet did the cannon of the English work sore havoc in the Scottish ranks, whensoever they were not in close combat, and the Duke of Ochil came to the Earl and said; "My Lord of Hawick, I will endeavour to capture them and we may even turn them on our foes."

He spoke and Aline followed hard after, and he led his men behind the hill to the other flank and then made as he would charge the footmen on the English right. But, as he came near to them, he swerved and, passing round, he advanced to the mouths of the guns, and left and right his men fell on either hand and their souls fled from them; but Aline rode safely at his side.

And they came right over against the gunners and one of them did shout lustily and swing his rod over[349] the Duke and would have felled him to the earth had not Aline driven the point of her long sword through his mouth even as he shouted, and he fell backward and was trampled under foot, while the rod fell harmlessly upon the saddle bow, and the rest turned to flee but were cut down and not a man of them escaped.

"Thou art indeed the good angel of my destiny," said Ian; but he spake not more at that time, as the fight was heavy upon him.

Then were the English guns turned upon the English host and fear got hold of them, brave men though they were, for that they were taken behind and before; and as they shook and hesitated the Duke with the two hundred that were left to him charged toward them from the rear. And Aline went ever at his side.

But the English horse made haste to come at him from far on their own right, and take him in flank, or ever he closed with those on foot. And as the English foot turned, some this way toward the Scottish horse, and some that way toward the Scottish foot, a mighty shout arose in the Scottish ranks as they closed with the English; "Now are they delivered into our hands," and they waxed ever more terrible till confusion fell upon the men of England and the half of them broke and fled and thus hindered the more part of their own horsemen from coming at the Duke.

So he fell upon the other half and victory came on a sudden into his hands; for all the English were now in flight and the left wing of their horse that would have taken the Duke in flank fled also.

And as he thanked God for his triumph he looked[350] back and his heart failed him, and he shuddered and his breath stood still, for Aline was no longer to be seen, in that the grey horse had gone down at the last.

As he gazed his head swam and darkness came over him. Victory was his, but Aline was lost. He calmed himself and held his spirit in check and even as the wind races over the hills, his thoughts passed through him. "The enemy is scattering on every side. My work for my country is done and therefore may I now turn to that which concerneth my own life."

There was not a moment to be let slip, the remnant of the right wing of the foemen's horse was still unbroken, and although too late now to effect their purpose, yet, if so be that Aline were still alive, they would pass over the very ground where she must be lying or ever a man might run thither, however swiftly he sped.

He swung round and galloped apace, and there, dead upon the earth, was the grey horse, and by it, on the side next the foe, lay stretched the fair slim page still clutching the banner with the silver fesse.

"Surely it will be my own death," he said, as the horsemen bore down upon him. For an instant the thought unnerved him, but natheless he was at her side. "What matter," he cried, "the day is won, my work is done, and, Aline dead, of what avail is life to me?"

He leaped from his horse. It was too late; even now they were upon him; he might not lift her to the saddle and bear her away.

"Can I not break the tide with a barrier of slain steeds?" he said. Then swift as the lightning flashes in the heavens, with his right arm he swung her over her own dead horse, while with his left he raised a fallen351 pike. He leaped back and kneeled before the horse, gripping the pike full firmly, whose butt rested on the ground, while with his right hand he drew forth a pistol from his holster.

On they came, they towered into the sky, the air was filled with their shouting and the thunder of their hoofs. A single man! They heeded him not.

He fired, and the horse that would have trampled him fell low. Neck and croup over it rolled upon the ground and the horse behind, that strove to leap above it, received the pike in its heart, while Ian narrowly avoided destruction under the falling mass.

Then as a stream meets a boulder in its course and straightway divides on either hand, so passed the warriors on the left and right.

The rider of the first fallen horse lay in the throes of death, but the second rushed upon him with his sword so that the Duke had but scant time to draw and defend himself, and the sword cleft the Duke's helm and the wound was deep.

Yet it was no long time they fought, for with swift skill the Duke drove his sword throughout his body and he fell with a loud cry to the ground, stretching his arms to heaven, and Ian drew out the steel and with the blood the life rushed forth and black night covered his eyes.

But Ian, even as he did so, turned to where Aline lay, her face all white amid the ruddy gold. He leaned above her. She was not dead, nor even sorely hurt, but stunned and dazed and cut about and bruised.

He raised her with great tenderness and bore her from the scene of carnage just as the evening fell. A352 cold breath blew upon his face and he fancied he heard a voice that hissed—"Woe's me, we are foiled; it is on us the blow has fallen, even ere the darkness came. Too late, too late." At that moment the sun sank and the light vanished behind the hills. The rout was now complete. Here and there a few individuals made stand against their pursuers, while little groups of wounded men were crying for succour. The haugh was littered with so many corpses of those who had gone forth that morning in the healthful beauty of their youth, that it was a sight most grievous to behold. Ian stumbled with his burden. He himself had been twice sadly wounded again. Whither should he go? There were no houses in sight.

He remembered, however, that the house of the Laird of Dalwhinnie was only about two miles away. There was nowhere else to go, but both the new wounds and the old were exceeding sore and it was with great difficulty that he carried her.

He bore her to the foot of the hill and summoned four troopers, and with their assistance mounted a horse. He would not let any one else touch the child and, accompanied by the troopers, he rode to the house.

The laird was not a protestant, but Ian was graciously received and offer was made to accommodate as many of the wounded as possible.

"You had liever pay special attention to those poor English varlets," said Ian. "There will be few to give them heed."

The Lady smiled a sad smile and led the way to a beautifully appointed room. "Your Grace has a wondrous353 fair child with you," she said. "I marvel not at your care for him. Is he sore hurt?"

"I trust not," said Ian, as he laid Aline gently down. He dared not let any one help him, lest Aline's secret should be discovered; so he dressed her wounds himself and put her to bed.

354
CHAPTER XXVII
THE BIRTHDAY PARTY

AFTER the battle the Earl of Hawick disbanded the greater part of his forces, retaining but a small nucleus in case it should be necessary to bring military aid to the party of Argyle and Glencairn in support of their covenant against the regent. With this small force he moved northward. The Duke was far too sore hurt to travel and neither he nor Aline were able to move for some time.

As soon, however, as they could sit a horse they set out for the Castle of Menstrie, where they arrived in due course and were most warmly welcomed by the Duchess of Ochil and her daughter Shiona, who had been anxiously awaiting Ian's return after they first received news of his arrival in Scotland.

His mother was overjoyed to see him and he briefly told her the story of the child. When he had finished she kissed Aline and said, "You poor sweet thing, now at last you have reached a haven of rest and you must count me as your mother as far as I can be one."

Aline had not before felt shy of her boy's clothes, but the gentle courteous lady made her long for her own things and she blushingly began to apologise.

"You need not distress yourself, dear child," said the Duchess; "we can soon remedy that. Indeed you look very pretty and you make so graceful a page that355 you need not regret your present garb," she added kindly and stooped and kissed her again. "We shall just make you one of ourselves and you have only to tell us what you want. For the present we can send over to Stirling and get everything that you absolutely need this very day."

In the evening, as they were all sitting by the fire, the Lady of Ochil leaned over and, taking Ian's hand, said: "I have some sad news for you, my boy. You know that the estate was very sadly impoverished when your father succeeded. But he has been extravagant and your eldest brother was the same, and always borrowing from him. Worst of all, your brothers induced your father to make over to them during his lifetime, all the estates that he could. The regent, too, has already shown her hostility on your succession. It is a very long story; but you will have little but the title and the small original estates round the Castle. Even those are so burdened that I doubt whether we can continue to live here."

"Do not mind, Mother, about me. I never expected anything, and so I shall not miss it; it is for you that I am sorry. You will feel the change so much."

"No, my son. I am so glad to get you back that I mind nothing."

Aline rose from where she was and sat down again on the floor at Ian's feet. "I am so sorry for you," she said, and once more she had that curious kind of feeling that she had noticed before. She was very sorry for Ian; but was she altogether sorry for the fact in itself? Did it not in some way bring them closer together?

356

Ian's sister, Shiona, had always worshipped her second brother; he was unto her as a god, and as she watched Aline it rather amused her to see, as it were, herself, over again, in the way that the child continually hovered round him. She was the youngest of the family, and now a tall slim girl of seventeen. She felt curiously shy of Ian, as she had not seen him for several years. He still looked very young; but he was now the head of the house in her father's place.

She soon fell under Aline's spell and the two girls became fast friends. Except in appearance and physique Aline was much in advance of her age; and her recent experiences had matured her view of life. The girls occupied the same room and were continually together when they could not be with Ian. Ian sometimes felt even a little touch of envy; he had come to regard Aline almost as though she specially belonged to him.

It was a time of considerable trouble and anxiety, both in public and private affairs, yet it was a very happy household in spite of all their troubles and difficulties. Ian was very slow in recovering his strength. Excitement had carried him through, but the collapse was all the more severe when it came. For two months he could move but little; however, he gradually began to be able to take short strolls out of doors.

Even before this he had set his mind to see what could be done to save the remnant of the estates. Rigid economy had to be practised, for he was determined that property that had been in the family for hundreds of years should not go if possible. Unfortunately only a small portion, even of the fragment, happened to be357 protected by entail. Consequently he found it necessary to reduce the fragment still further by selling two estates that had been acquired by his grandfather. They were so heavily burdened that the margin was very small, but it enabled him to prevent the foreclosure of his most pressing creditors. All the retainers and servants were dismissed except one serving man and a maid, the horses were sold and the castle was all shut up except the hall, the library and a few bedrooms. The arras, the plate and everything of value except the heirlooms were sold. The only thing Ian retained was a famous sword, given to him by the Regent Arran for his services against the Lords Wharton and Grey. It was of immense value, magnificently jewelled. He took it out and looked at it. No, he could not part with that. It was too full of association and interest.

The household arrangements were simplified to the barest necessities. The girls did the housework and Ian himself, when necessary, assisted the serving man. He wore the simplest homespun and his sister dressed as plainly as possible. Ian refused to allow his mother to wear the things that the rest of them did, because, he said, they all had the future before them in a way that she had not.

She smiled and kissed him, and assured him that she would be quite happy whatever she wore, as she had her dear son back again, and she chaffingly impressed upon him that it was still long before she would be an old lady.

Aline absolutely insisted on wearing things that even Mistress Mowbray would not have provided, both gowns358 and body linen. But they were beautifully made by Shiona and herself, and although the material was coarse, the general effect was always charming. She succeeded in getting some frieze in excellent shades of green and brown, that made most pleasing colour combinations with the brownish white of the full sleeves and skirt of her coarse dowlas chemise, and the rich red of her glorious hair.

The result of the new Duke's efforts was that he gained the respect of every one; and two of his largest creditors came to him one day and not only said that they would not press for payment, but offered to lend him more at a much lower rate of interest. This offer he accepted and paid off a number of smaller creditors, who lived at a distance and did not know what was going on.

After a few months he brought things into such a condition that, though he saw no prospect of being anything but poor all his life, he hoped to leave the property in a fairly sound condition when he died.

There was one little extravagance that he had determined to allow himself. Aline's thirteenth birthday took place in April and he resolved that she should have the happiest day of her life, if human means could accomplish it. He pondered for a long time how it was to be done; because he regarded the property rather as a trust than in any way his own. At last he bethought him of the sword. That at least was his own. It was, it was true, his most cherished possession; but he would part with it. He took it out one evening and fingered it fondly. Truly it was beautiful and the only relic of his early youth. Other things might be replaced, but that could not. Moreover it would be a joy forever, whereas a day's pleasure was soon gone by. "'Sdeath. How could he think such things?" He hated himself. So he resolutely shut the case and turned the key. "What was a sword compared with Aline's happiness?"

He had to take his sister into his confidence, as he wanted Aline to have a complete outfit for the occasion, and this Shiona was to arrange unknown to her. Ian took the sword to a goldsmith in Stirling, but the man did not like to take it, the sword was so well known and considered as one of the local marvels. At last he persuaded Ian to let him lend him the value of the sword, allowing a year in which it could be redeemed. Ian gave the man a few commissions to execute for the great occasion and departed.

Everything was planned with all secrecy and Aline was not told about it till two days before, when a number of persons arrived to put the old place into order. The old rooms were thrown open and cleaned, the arras, that had been sold, was temporarily replaced by other fine specimens. Sconces with hundreds of candles were brought and the floor and the furniture and the metalwork was polished till all shone like a mirror. The old heirlooms, including the magnificent nef[29] and other gold and silver plate, which Ian could not sell, but which had been put away, were brought out.

29 A gold or silver centre piece for the table made in the shape of a ship.

The beautiful old castle had never looked finer. Serving men and maids, pleasantly attired, were everywhere at hand. There was a new costume for every one. Ian's was of very simple material, but he looked wonderfully handsome when he met Aline on the morning of the great day.

"I have a very nice present for your birthday, princess," he said, stroking her hair, "but it will be rather a shock at the same time, so you must prepare yourself for it. I have been thinking that you need a lady's maid," he went on, laughing, "and I have succeeded in finding you one."

"Marry, I need no lady's maid," she replied, somewhat puzzled at the twinkle in his eye, "and you must not think of such a thing. I prefer to look after myself. I am not a grand lady and, even if I were, I would rather not have one. I am sure I should not like her."

"I am sure you would," said Ian, "and in any wise you must try and like her, because I insist."

"You must not tease me, your Grace, I really do not want one."

"I will not be called 'your Grace,' pussie," he said, gently pulling her hair.

"Well, if you get me a lady's maid, I shall call you 'your Grace' and then we shall all be grand together."

"But I have gotten her already. I heard of her in a curious way in a letter from Walter Margrove, but I kept it as a surprise until I could get hold of her."

"Oh, but really, Ian, I do not want her," Aline protested. "I should hate her. Yes, by my troth, I should," and she looked genuinely distressed.

"You would not hate this one," he replied a little sadly; "it is some one that you know. But I must not tease you."

"Do you mean Audry?" she asked doubtfully.

"That would not be a shock, sweet child. No,—here361 she is." He then beckoned to some one out of sight through the open door; and a slim girl of nearly twelve came shyly forward and stood hesitatingly on the threshold.

Aline gave a little startled glance and then looked at Ian, who smiled reassuringly. "O Joan," she cried, "they told me you were dead."

"I was very ill," said the child, louting low, "but I was not dead, Mistress Aline; it was the little girl that came from Barnard Castle, who died, whom Mistress Ellen Allen had sent to Durham from Teesdale too, much in the same manner that you sent me."

"But how did the mistake happen, Joan, and why did you not let me know?"

"The woman that was looking after me died, and I was taken to Newcastle. I was ill, oh, so ill for a long time and I knew nothing about it, and when I heard, I could not for long enough get any one to write for me and then, at last, I was told that you had disappeared. When Walter Margrove heard about it he looked me up in Newcastle and then, some time after, he told me that I was to go into service with the Right Honourable Sir Ian Menstrie, Knight of the Most Noble Order of St. Michael, Lord Duke of Ochil and Earl of Strath Allan, and I was so frightened."

Ian could not control himself and the child had to pause while he laughed. "Whoever put all that into your head? Never mind, you can forget it,—just go on."

"It was Walter Margrove, your Grace, and he told me not to be afeared, as I should find some one that I knew. But it was not till I came here last night that I knew who it was and, oh, Mistress Aline, I heard what you362 were saying just now and you will not hate me really, will you?"

"No, Joan, no, I will never hate you and indeed I am so glad to see you looking so much better"; and Aline flung her arms round the child's neck and kissed her, while tears of joy stood in her eyes.

For a time the children forgot everything but themselves and Ian stood and watched them in their perfect happiness. Aline was very much taller than Joan and in contrast with the frail delicate child looked like a goddess of strength. Joan clung to her in ecstatic abandon and gazed into those wonderful ultramarine blue eyes as though they were the windows of heaven. "I never knew before what it was," she said, "to be perfectly happy. Mistress Aline, I think the old folk at Holwick were right. You cannot be a child of ordinary flesh and blood like the rest of us."

"Hush, Joan, you must not talk like that, and I told you long ago that you must not call me Mistress Aline. But, oh, I am so glad to get you back; you cannot tell how glad."

Ian was just going to steal away and leave them to their joy, it was so pure, so unalloyed, when Aline suddenly bethought herself of him and leaving little Joan she rushed forward, seized his hand with both her own and pressed it to her lips. "It was you who thought out all this; oh, you are good to me."

She lifted up her face and he printed a kiss on her forehead. "No, princess; you remember my quotation from Homer. It is you that are good to me. I owe you everything—I do not mean mere physical life—that is nothing—nothing."

363

The guests were to arrive at what a later age would have deemed the very early hour of eleven o'clock, so after breakfast Ian suggested that Aline should go upstairs and get ready.

"But I am ready," she said.

"You cannot appear like that," said Ian. "You must get Shiona to tidy you up," he said with assumed severity.

"But I have nothing better than this," she answered, just a little wistfully.

"Oh, yes, Shiona has some kind of a thing that will look better for to-day. Run along with her and take Joan; it can be an apprentice lesson for her."

When Aline reached her room she was lost in amazement at the things that had been prepared for her and was charmed with them all. Shiona helped her to dress and Joan folded up the things she took off and put them away.

The linen was of the very finest quality that French looms could produce, smoother to the touch than anything she had ever worn, and adorned with bands of tela tirata. There was a pair of the fine silk hose that had recently been introduced into Britain, of a beautiful blue, somewhat lighter than those she had lost, and with white clocks. The broad toed shoes were of white kid, with blue satin showing through the slashes, and a large real sapphire set in silver on each shoe.

The camise was of soft white silk rather full, smocked at the throat and reaching below the knees, with two bands of lace insertion of the finest Italian punto a reticella near the hem. Above this Shiona put on the armless surcoat, which was low at the neck and short,364 showing the white camise both above and below as well as the arms, which were full at the shoulder but tighter toward the wrist. This was decorated round the open sides with orphreys or borders of cloth-of-silver embroidered with white heather, the badge of the Menstries, in which the little white blooms were real pearls.

The cloak was of rich blue velvet with two exquisitely designed diamond clasps and tasselled cords of white silk, the whole lined with white satin and adorned with a short cape and border of miniver. In the two lower corners and again near the clasps, it was delicately embroidered with coloured silk and gold and silver thread, after the fashion of old Scandinavian work. A belt of large rectangular silver plates, each with its own sculptured design, and a chatelaine of gold completed the costume. It was a little old-fashioned in style, but Ian preferred the lines of the earlier date to those that were coming into vogue.

Aline was so overwhelmed with delight that she did not at first pause to reflect; but after a time she suddenly exclaimed horror-struck; "Shiona, what are you doing; you know that I have not the right to wear any of these things, except perhaps the chemise? My father was a gentleman so I may wear white silk, and I might have had black velvet, but not blue. No one below a Knight of the Garter or the highest orders may wear blue velvet. I do not know even whether I may wear the chatelaine. I doubt if father had two hundred merks of land and of course I cannot wear cloth of silver or gold, no one less than barons can wear that; and as for miniver, I do not even know if barons may wear it: I believe I should have to be a countess, and365 I know for certain that diamonds and pearls are reserved for dukes and duchesses. So I shall have to take everything off and just wear my old things and the silk chemise"; and she gave a little sigh.

"It is all right, dear; we thought of that. Ian says that you are his ward now and that therefore they could not object to you wearing anything that I may wear, and I may wear anything I like except purple, which is reserved for the blood royal."

To reach such a height of unimagined grandeur almost took Aline's breath away. "By my troth this is a wonderful birthday," she said, and little Joan looked on in sympathetic wonder, secretly pleased at being associated with any one so exalted. But her cup was filled to overflowing when she found that Ian had provided her with a costume of silk and fine red camlet trimmed with black velvet, besides a small gold chain, which things he said she was entitled to wear as a lady in waiting in his household.

Shiona was giving a few last attentions to Aline's hair and adding the finishing touch, a blue velvet fillet decorated with five large crystals and three pearls;—"What wonderful hair you have, dear!" she said.

Aline had always refrained from any allusion to her hair and even turned the subject aside; but it had grown so phenomenally that she was feeling happier about it and she cried gaily;—"Oh, that's nothing," and darted away to Ian's room, where she happened to find him.

Aline's beauty was proverbial, but she looked more dazzling than ever. Ian caught her in his arms and kissed her. "You are the loveliest thing on earth," he said.

366

"Nonsense," answered Aline, "but I want to show Shiona the hair that was cut off."

Ian took it from its hiding place, handling it lovingly and gave it her. "Come back," he said, "I have something else for you."

She took the hair and with innocent joy showed it to Shiona, who was lost in astonishment. She then returned with it to Ian.

He carefully put it away and then said; "Shiona has dressed you, but I want to do the very last bit myself." He then opened his hand and in it lay a light chain with a subtly designed pendant of which the dominant feature was a brilliant mass of red, one gigantic ruby, which Ian had taken from the pommel of his sword.

He clasped it round her neck and it just fell on the white silk. "One touch of red in the blue and white," he said, "but after all, it's not as fine a red as your lips, heartsease," and he kissed them.

The stone was obviously of immense value and Aline tiptoed hesitatingly backward till she came to the wall. There on tiptoe she stood, with the palms of her hands flat against the wall and her chin slightly lifted till the back of her head also touched.

She was a little dazed. At first the beautiful things had been a sheer joy. Even the momentary cloud of the "sumptuary laws" had been swiftly dispelled; but now the thought suddenly overcame her;—"How could Ian afford it?" She noticed the plain simplicity of his own attire and her quick intuition told her the truth.

"Ian, Ian," she cried, "you should not give me all367 these things. What have you done?—How did you do it?—You have parted with something you should not."

She did not move and looked very tall in the becoming costume, standing with her heels raised high from the ground.

Suddenly Ian realised that she would soon be a child no longer, and then he would lose her. It came like a knife. He had not admitted even to himself how much she was to him; but his love for her had gradually absorbed his whole being. It was the greatest shock he had ever experienced in his life. He stepped forward and picked her up in his strong arms and kissed her passionately. "It was my sword, heart of mine," he said, "but there is nothing in the world that I would not wish you to have."

Aline endeavoured to protest, but he laughingly put his hand over her mouth and led her down-stairs.

There was a large concourse of guests and the dinner was quite a sumptuous ceremony, with a great boar's head brought in with much solemnity. Ian and his mother sat in the middle of the high table and Aline had the seat of honour on his right.

When dinner was over they strolled in the pleasaunce and afterwards came in and played games such as hot cockles, and hunt the slipper, in which every one, both old and young, took part. Then followed the dancing. If the guests had been charmed before by

Aline's beauty, now they were enthralled. Aline and the Duke led off with a stately pavan and all watched with rapt interest the slow dreamy movements, that displayed to perfection the exquisite loveliness of the child's form. Ian[368] had learned dancing in Italy and France and was a consummate exponent of the art, so that the two made a picture the like of which had never been seen in broad Scotland. After the pavan they danced the cinque paces, a new dance not long introduced from Italy, which in turn was succeeded by the lively coranto, that gave a new opportunity for Aline to reveal her light and agile grace, vying in its airy swiftness with the beauty of the more studied movements of the slower dance. Ian's costume was of a blue somewhat deeper in tone than Aline's, with white hose and other touches of white as in hers; and the result made a pleasing colour effect as they whirled together in the dance.

But it was not only by her appearance, but by her subtle charm of manner that the child fascinated every one present. They had heard the main facts of her sad story and each and all did their utmost to give her pleasure. At the close of the evening they held a mock coronation ceremony, in which Aline was crowned with a plain gold circlet and then, while seated on the throne, every guest was presented to the Queen of the evening and they all kneeled and kissed her hand,—barons, earls, countesses and every one present.

Aline could not help a smile when the Earl of Hawick, who was present, kneeled before her. This was the man that only a few months ago she had been nervous to see and now he was humbly kneeling and kissing her hand.

It had been a supremely happy day for Aline, and her only regret was that Audry had not been able to share it. Even this was modified by a curious coincidence, after the guests had gone. They had all left[369] early, as most of them had ridden from long distances and even those who were putting up in Stirling had some way to go.

After the last guest had departed, and while the family were seated round the hearth, the castle bell rang and they heard the drawbridge being lowered. Their own serving man appeared shortly afterward. "My lord, a man named Walter Margrove, who hath a boy with him, hath arrived and saith that he wisheth to see you on a matter of private concern."

"Shew him up," said Ian.

Walter Margrove came in somewhat hesitatingly, accompanied by a still more nervous lad. Aline in her white and blue costume rushed forward to greet them; whereat Walter was quite taken aback and Wilfred, for it was he, nearly turned tail and fled.

Ian advanced and shook their hands and presented them to the Duchess and the Lady Shiona. "If you had arrived a few minutes ago," he said, "you should have been presented to the Queen's Grace. Get on your throne again, Your Highness," he said to Aline, and then with much laughter they made Walter and Wilfred kneel and kiss her hand.

Walter had recently been in Holwick and had decided that he might vary his programme by a tour in Scotland, and make it an opportunity of seeing Ian and Aline and little Joan, and of taking them the news from Upper Teesdale, together with a letter from Audry. The venture had proved a great success and Walter was in an unusually contented frame of mind, even for him.

"Sit down, man," said Ian, "and tell us everything370 about Holwick. We should much like to know all that befell after we escaped."

"Oh, but tarry a little, Ian," said Aline; "there is something that must be done first. You tell Walter what we have been doing, while I talk awhile with Wilfred. Wilfred, come hither," she continued, leading the way to one of the double seated windows.

"I am so glad to see you again, Wilfred," she said, when they had sat down, "and you are looking well."

"Yes, Mistress Aline, and I am glad to see you, and, oh, Mistress, you are looking bonnie in those brave things," he added in a burst of boyish admiration, and then subsided overcome by shyness for having said too much.

"Wilfred," she said, "you recall the last time that we met and what we spake about?"

"I do, indeed, and I shall not forget your sympathy."

"Do you remember my saying that I thought the spirit of light must in its own time triumph over the spirit of darkness? I did not know at the time what moved me to say it. I only meant it in a general way, and yet I had a strange presentiment that it had some special meaning for you."

"What do you mean?" he asked.

"Wilfred, what was the sad news that you heard at Kirkoswald? Tell me."

"They told us that little Joan had gone to Durham and died there."

"Yes, but did you hear it from any one who really knew Joan?"

"No, Mistress, it was from a man who had been over to Holwick."

371

"Then how do you know it was true?"

"Oh, Mistress Aline, Mistress Aline," said the boy, "do you think it might be untrue?"

"I know it was untrue," she said gently.

For the moment the boy was too overcome to speak. His heart beat violently, his eyes grew round and large. "Oh, tell me, tell me," he besought.

206

"I promised that I would bring you back the things you gave to Joan. I cannot do that yet; so I am going to bring you Joan herself. She is here in this place."

"Here in this place!" he repeated as Aline rose and went to fetch the little girl.

She was back in a minute or two and the boy was still seated in the same attitude, dumbfounded.

"Here she is, Wilfred," she said, leading Joan forward by the hand.

The boy looked from one to the other too bewildered to know what to do. Oh, how lovely Joan looked in her red costume guarded with black velvet and the white linen chemise showing below her throat and beneath the velvet hem. But he was too bashful to advance.

Joan, however, was equal to the occasion. "Well, Wilfred, are you not going to speak to me?" and she stepped forward and threw her arms round his neck.

Aline withdrew and left the two children in the window seat, whence they emerged a few minutes afterwards and timidly drew near the group round the fire.

"Now tell us all about Holwick, Walter," said Aline, making a place for the two children.

"Yes," said Ian, "why were they so slow in pursuit?"

"Mistress Mowbray would not let them have the372 horses from the Hall and the folk broke the girths and bridles of their own horses, and finally they had to get fresh horses in Middleton. The excitement was tremendous; but the strangest thing to the most part of us was the behaviour of Mistress Mowbray. She seemed to be greatly concerned and wrung her hands and said, 'By my Lady, I trust the child hath escaped,' and, later in the day, Elspeth told me that she met Thomas in the lower quadrangle and he, knowing the hatred that Mistress Mowbray had toward you, must needs cry unto her. 'Methinks those fresh horses from Middleton will soon bring the jade back,' and she grew purple in the face and said to him that, if they did, she would see whether it were too late to lodge him in gaol because of the corn he had taken along with Andrew. I saw Thomas when I was there last. He is an ill creature, and he much misliked it when it was clear that Mistress Aline was safely away. Yet is he but a white livered knave. Father Ambrose rouseth my ire more than he."

"But you spake of Mistress Mowbray," said Ian.

"Yes, the first thing that she did was to send over to Appleby that very night for Mistress Audry, who came the next morning. Elspeth said that the proud woman wept on her neck, so that it were pity to see. I would not have been in the place of Father Martin or Father Austin if they had fallen into her power. For days she made the household tremble under the weight of her authority."

"The next day Master Richard came back looking like a broken man. He said he had tried everything but could do nothing. As the time passed on, and it373 gradually became clear that the pursuit had failed, he recovered himself.

"Luckily for Mistress Audry no one thought of questioning her as she had been away so long; but every one was marvelling who it could possibly have been that had dropped on a sudden from heaven.

"Then news began to leak through. First they heard that two of the pursuers had been buried at Haltwhistle. Then came the news of the night that you spent at Brampton. Wilfred Ackroyd was found and stuck to his tale that you had gone to Carlisle, but they found nothing there."

"Oh, Wilfred!" said Aline.

"I cannot help it," he said, "I did laugh when I saw them galloping off the wrong way."

"Timothy held his peace," continued Walter, "and no one seemed to connect the drowned prisoner in the Eden with Mistress Aline. Indeed I doubt if the tale of your drowning ever reached Holwick, your Grace. The priests went south and Master Mowbray failed to track them, at any rate at first. I believe he did eventually get into communication, but they refused to say anything.

"It seemed pretty clear that Mistress Aline had escaped but who was her saviour has remained to this day an insoluble mystery."

"Then they guessed nothing from your letter, Ian?" said Aline.

"No," said Walter. "When I was there your note, that you sent in a round about way through Master Eustace Cleveland, had just arrived. They were overjoyed to hear of the child's safety and after much discussion374 came to the conclusion that Cleveland himself had something to do with it in spite of his denial. 'Marry,' said Mistress Mowbray, 'I saw the way he was taken with the child.' 'So was every one except yourself, woman,' said Master Richard, 'that proves nothing.' Mistress Mowbray mumbled something about not taking up with every new face, like some people, and Master Richard did not press the point."

"Who told you that?" asked Aline.

"Mistress Audry, and she says that since the first few days, when her anger had passed, her mother has been much gentler than was her wont to every one. She has had your little garden carefully wrought over. 'Mistress Aline might come back,' she says. She is much changed.

"Master Richard believes that Mistress Aline is somewhere in hiding in Teesdale, but he has forbidden enquiry to be made, as he thinks, under the circumstances, it is safer, in the event of any attempt on the part of the authorities to find her, that they can all honestly say they know nothing. I believe that he personally thinks Master Gower knows more than Master Cleveland."

"Now let me read Audry's letter," said Aline. This was a matter of some difficulty, as Audry was barely able to write; but the evident trouble, that the letter had been, made it a dearer token of affection. Aline made it out as follows:

"To my dearest and most beloved cousin Aline Gillespie,

"Thou canst not think how fain I was to get thy dear letter. Walter will tell thee the most part of the news, but I must with mine own hand tell thee how overjoyed I was to know of a surety of thy safety. When Mother sent for me and I came home I was heartbroken. I used to sleep in thy bed and kiss375 the things that thou hadst worn and cry myself to sleep. But gradually it seemed clear that thou hadst escaped and I offered up many prayers of thankfulness as shall I again and again this night.

"I have one item of good news. Dost remember the linen that Mother found in our room. It was then lying with the wrappings and cord with which it came. She took them all down and must herself have put the wrappings on that little dark shelf near her linen chest. I recognised them one day by the colour of the cord, and I took them down, and lo, within, there was the little book. I have put it in its own secret place in the lock in the library. I am sure this will glad thine heart. Someday I trust thou wilt be able to read the rest to me. Thou wilt indeed be the grand lady now;—to think of thee living in a great castle with a real Duke! May God be with thee.

"From Audry Mowbray."

After Aline had read the letter they told Walter the true state of affairs and how he had happened to come on the only festal day that they had had.

It was arranged that Walter and Wilfred should put up for the night. There certainly was ample room for the horses in the empty stables. The Duchess was tired and went to bed early and was soon followed by Shiona, so that Ian and Aline were left by themselves.

They sat quietly for a long time, Ian gazing silently at Aline, idly sketching her shifting poses on the easel that happened to be standing near; but he was not conscious of what he was doing; his thoughts were far away as they wandered over the strange circumstances of his career. Aline was more like her mother than ever, although still more surpassingly beautiful. He was quite sure about it now. It was undoubtedly Aline's mother that he had loved with that wild boy-love when he was but thirteen, and now Aline would soon be a woman herself! "Who was there," he wondered, "who376 would be worthy of such a treasure? In any case it could not be very long now before some one claimed her. His own mother was married at fifteen, so was the Lady Jane Grey, whom Aline in some ways resembled." He sighed sadly.

"Are you not happy, Ian? I am so happy to-night," said Aline, and came across and kissed him and then nestled at his feet after her favourite manner.

"Not altogether," he said.

"Tell me what it is."

"Not to-night, heartsease," he answered, bending down and kissing the fragrant hair. "Some day, perhaps, I will."

For a time the room was very still. Suddenly a thought occurred to Ian. "I have just remembered something," he said; "I will get it."

The rush of events had crowded the little pouch and its contents out of his mind, but his present mood reminded him of it.

He brought the amulet from its hiding place. Aline was still seated on the floor. He sat down on the floor also, a little behind her, and lifted one of the lovely hands. "I have something else that I meant to give you before," he said, holding up the bracelet.

The strange blue stones shone in the firelight as if they themselves were on fire. "'Weal where I come as a gift of love,'" he read. "Pray God it may be so, heart of mine."

Aline leaned back and lay with her head on his lap, looking up at him as he told the story.

"There are no scars on the beautiful hands now," he said softly.

She half drew the hand away and then stopped and it lay passively in his hold as he lovingly fastened the bracelet round the perfect wrist.

She did not thank him; she did not speak; she only lay there quietly looking into his eyes.

A log slipped from the fire; it did not make much noise, but the sound echoed through the deserted rooms. How absolutely alone together they were!

Somehow the bracelet seemed to have a special significance: perhaps she might be held after all. A feeling of peace, almost of happiness, stole over him.

"You are good to me," she said at last. "Yes, I am happy."

CHAPTER XXVIII
THE LAST ADVENTURE

IN order that Aline should not discover her presence, little Joan had been put to sleep the first night in an upper chamber, in a wing of the great castle remote from that occupied by the family. To avoid extra trouble on the day of the birthday, she returned there the second night, although in future she was to have a small ante-room connecting with the girls' chamber. In the rooms below her were the servants who had been hired for the occasion. She half undressed and, as she sat combing her hair, she looked out at the dark night. Below, she heard the rushing of the burn, and, dimly, under the starry sky she could see the great hills to the north. There was a close feeling in the air, as though there might be thunder or heavy rain. It was a little oppressive but her heart was so full of gladness that she refused to allow it to influence her.

How strangely things had come about. She remembered the horrible prophecy of "Moll o' the graves" about her going away that seemed to mean death. It was curious how it had been fulfilled and yet not fulfilled. Could the old hag really in some way see into the future, and what did the prophecy mean about her beautiful little mistress,—"she shall follow not long after; marry, I see the fire about her"? They had indeed come near to burning her, but she had escaped the flames. "Well, all has turned out for the best so far. Mistress Aline said that the light would overcome the dark. I believe she is stronger than old Moll, after all," she thought.

She had finished combing her hair, and after kneeling before her little crucifix was soon in bed and asleep.

Aline meanwhile, however, lay awake; the heavy storm-feeling in the air would not allow her to rest. She was excited also from the events of the day. After an hour or two she got up and looked out. The stars had all gone and the thick clouds made the night impenetrably black. Shiona was sound asleep. She crept back again to bed and tossed and tossed, but it was of no avail. Another hour passed. She thought she would get up and feel for the tinder box and light the lamp. Where was it? Could she find it in the dark?

As she lay there wondering, it seemed to get a little lighter. Yes, it was certainly getting lighter, surely it could not be morning yet. She lay for a few minutes, things in the room were rapidly becoming visible, but that was surely not daylight; no, it was not daylight. She jumped up and looked out. "Gramercy, the castle is on fire." She looked again; it was the wing where Joan slept. She crossed the room and woke Shiona. "Quick," she said, "the castle is on fire. Wake them all—tell Ian—Joan will be burnt—I must go."

She dashed down the stairs, as she was, without staying to put anything on, and ran across the court yard. There she met the terrified servants rushing from the building.

"Where is Joan, have you seen her?" she asked.

"No, Mistress," they said, "she must still be in her room."

Aline ran to the foot of the stairs.

"You must not go up," they screamed, "you must not go up, the stairs will fall."

It was an unfortunate fact that at some time, when alterations were being made, a wooden stairway had been substituted for the original stone one, which now existed only in a ruinous condition.

But Aline ran on without heeding the warnings and started to climb the stairs. The fire had broken out on the second floor and the flames were raging through to the staircase. Could she get past? She caught up her nightrobe in a tight bundle on her breast to try to keep it from the fire and made a rush. The flames scorched her skin and she burned her bare feet on the blazing boards. But she managed to get past. One sleeve even caught alight, but she was able after she had passed through to crush it out with her other hand.

"Joan, Joan," she shouted, as she made her way into Joan's room. Joan was still asleep, partly stupified by the smoke. Aline roused her and they rushed back to the stairs, but in the interval the whole stairway had become a bellowing furnace and the flames roared up it, so that they could not look down.

Joan gave a little pitiful cry. "We are lost, oh, Mistress Aline, we are lost."

"No, not yet, Joan, keep up a stout heart; let us try if there be not another way."

They ran through two rooms in the opposite direction to the stair and came to a door. But it was locked. They tried in vain to open it. They beat upon it, but381 it was beyond their strength to break, so they went back to Joan's room.

"Can you climb, Joan?" asked Aline.

"No."

"Then I must try and let you down." She seized the bedclothes as she spoke and knotted them together. Alas, they could not possibly reach. She remembered how Ian had saved Wilfred by the rope under the bed and feverishly threw off the mattrass. The bed had wooden laths!

She looked out of the window and saw that a crowd had gathered below. How far down would the bedclothes extend? She made trial and shouted to the crowd that some one should try and find a tall ladder, while others, in case of failure, should bring a blanket and make a soft pile of hay. The crowd scattered and in a few moments there was a great heap of hay and some ten persons holding a blanket stretched above it. Yet, look as they would, no ladder was to be found except a little short thing that was no use. Possibly the other ladder was in the burning building, possibly it had been mislaid in the festal preparations.

Aline's lips were parched and her tongue clave to the roof of her mouth; for the moment she nearly succumbed to her fear. So it was Joan's life or hers? "Why cannot Joan climb?" she thought. Surely she could manage to get down as far as that? She looked at the child; but she was stiff with terror and absolutely helpless.

Somehow Aline felt it was not the same thing as when she had swum the river, then she had a chance of her life; indeed, if she had had no chance there was not382 the slightest use in trying to swim, as it could not have helped Ian. Here there was no chance; could she think of no other way?

212

The flames roared nearer, she began to find it hard to breathe. "Perhaps there is a way," she said, "but who can think in a case like this?"

Joan had now become unconscious. Aline thought no more; the sacrifice was made; she tied one end round Joan and put a pillow on the sill to prevent chafing. She dragged the bed to the window and took a turn with the extemporised rope round one of the knobs to prevent it going too fast. She lifted the child and gently lowered her toward the ground. For a moment she hesitated again. "Could she climb down and untie Joan?" No, the whole thing might break.

The drop below Joan was about fifteen feet. "Hold tight," she shouted, and those below braced themselves together and gripped the blanket firmly and the child fell into it. She was so light that the hay below was not necessary.

The fire had now reached half across the room itself and was breaking through the floor boards in little tongues of flame, when the choking smoke curled upward.

The end had come then; there was no hope. She turned to go and see if by any chance the locked door could be made to yield. It was vain, as indeed she knew, and the flame and smoke in that room was worse than her own. She ran back and looked out of the window. She thought she saw Ian with a white drawn face looking upward, but he disappeared.

Once again in the frenzy of despair she rushed to the 383 other room and flung herself against the door; but had to stagger back to Joan's room before she was completely overcome. The flames again caught her night robe and she tore it from her as she struggled to the window where she might still breathe. The heat was awful; oh, the pain of it! "But I must die bravely," she said, "as father would have me do."

All that she had ever done seemed to rise before her. She saw her mother as in the portrait. She saw her father and Audry, and last she saw Ian. He seemed to be weeping over her! Was she already dead? No, and she prayed;—"Lord Jesus, Thou hast taught me to come unto Thee and I beg of Thee to forgive me all that I have done wrong in my life. Take me in Thy arms and if it please Thee, end this terrible pain. Be with Ian and comfort him, Lord, when I am gone. Watch over little Joan and make her happier than I have been. Oh, Lord, the pain, the pain!" The smoke thickened, she gave one little gasp and spoke no more.

Aline was right; it was Ian that she had seen below. Shiona had first roused her mother and then Ian. He had gone to the stairway just in time to see it give way and come down with a crash. He had then endeavoured to get round the other way, but the smoke and flame was impossible. Once more he had come down and obtained some wet cloths to wrap over his face and make one more attempt. It was on this occasion that he had glanced up and seen Aline at the window.

She looked just as he had seen her in his visions with the flame and smoke rushing round her. It was this then that he had foreseen. It was this that the old woman had foretold. A sword went through his heart, 384 followed by a dull crushing pain that seemed to paralyse his will. He ran as in a dream. Again he reached the range of upper rooms. The flames belched forth at him and the smoke took weird fantastic shapes. It stretched out long skinny arms as though to hold him back and there all round him were evil mocking faces spitting out at him with tongues of flame.

Voices surged through the air. "This is the end, you shall not reach her, she shall die, but you shall live—live." The voices ended in a peal of laughter. What was life to him without Aline. He was going mad. He knew it. Mad! Mad! That was the fiendish scheme of the powers of darkness. He would live and yet never see anything all his life but the dead child. Horrible!

He had come to the worst part; he wrapped one of the wet cloths about his mouth and nose and over his hair and plunged into the smoke and flame. It roared, it stung, it blinded him, he nearly screamed, but he staggered through and came to the great oak door. He tried, like Aline, to open it, but it would not yield. He hurled his weight against it; it was of no avail. Again and again he tried and then stood back to look for some weapon. A heavy oak table all ablaze stood on one side of the room; he dashed at it, and heaved it over, seizing one of the legs and wrenching at it with all his might. He strove and pulled and then kicked it with his foot. It came away with a loud crash.

It was partly burned and the red hot surface bit into his flesh. He did not care but raised it above his head and turned to the door. Tortured by the agony of heat as he was, there, to his excited imagination, appeared the horrible form of "Moll o' the graves," leering at him[385] and barring the way. She seemed to push him back with her bony claw-like hand. He swung the heavy oak leg through the air like a maniac and shrieked,—"All the devils in Hell shall not hold me back." He frothed at the mouth and battered in her skull. She grinned at him as the blood trickled through her teeth and pointed to the monstrous shapes that seemed to gather out of the smoke. He thrust her aside with his foot, his heart ceased to beat, but he thundered on the door. Once. Twice. Thrice. And the fourth time it gave way, while the door flew open and he fell heavily forward.

He scrambled to his feet and hurried on. There, by the window, lay the beautiful little body. As his brain reeled he saw the martyr, George Wishart, standing over it in the fire, holding the evil spirits at bay. Ian's eyes seemed to start from his head. He pressed his hands over them as he advanced and looked again. The flames were actually touching her. Ah, she was dead, but how unutterably beautiful! Why for the second time in his life must death snatch out of it the one supreme treasure? Legions of thoughts swirled through his mind. He would paint her like that. Why was he not a sculptor? He would immortalise her form in marble. What transcendent loveliness!

As he stooped quickly, suddenly his brain cleared, and, gathering up her hair, he wrapped it in one of the wet cloths and drew it in a single thickness over her face. With another he covered what he could of the exquisite white form and picked it up and ran.

This time the fiends seemed unable to reach him, but before he arrived at the third room there was a reverberating[386] roar, part of the floor had given way and a great blank ten or twelve feet wide yawned before him.

Once more the voices shouted;—"You are ours—ours—and she is dead." Yet he heeded them not, but turned back a little way, then ran with all his might and leaped and cleared the chasm.

On he went, down the stairs, the madness was on him again. "Keep back, keep back," he shouted as he tore through the crowd. He looked so terrible, his face distorted with pain, as he ran past that they scattered in all directions. Shiona, at first, alone dared to follow him. He took Aline to one of the lower rooms in the other part of the castle. "Oil," he cried, "send some one for oil and linen."

Little Joan was coming timidly behind and ran for the things. Ian bent over Aline; she did not breathe. He filled his lungs with fresh air and putting his face down to hers breathed into her and drew the air forth. It was the intuition of affection and it saved her life. After a few moments she began to breathe again. Joan had then returned with the oil.

It was the smoke and gases of the fire that had suffocated her, and except on the soles of the little feet there were nowhere any serious burns. But there were great red patches here and there all over her, and the arm where the night dress had first caught fire was slightly blistered. He wrapped her entirely in oiled linen, and laid her gently on a mattrass that had been brought down.

All the time he never spoke a word and Shiona was frightened at his strange manner. Immediately he had finished he fell senseless to the ground. They picked387 him up and laid him on the mattrass. He was badly burned in several places, particularly the palms of his hands; he had also, as they afterwards discovered, strained himself severely in the leap with the child in his arms. For a time he lay still and then began to rave in wild delirium.

They did what they could for him, while Walter took his best horse and galloped to Stirling for a physician. Meanwhile the neighbours from far and near were fighting the fire. There were three well-shafts, carried up to the roof in the walls of the castle; and chains of men and women passed the buckets from hand to hand. The same was done from the burn down below. They did not attempt to do more than keep the fire from spreading beyond the blazing wing. But a new ally came to their aid that helped them not a little. The long threatened storm burst upon them with thunder and lightning, but accompanied by a torrential deluge of rain; and before morning the fire was completely under control.

388
CHAPTER XXIX
A TALE OF A TUB

IT was a beautiful late autumn day and the sun was shining on the moat and the old walls of Holwick. Some few weeks previously news had arrived in that remote corner of the death of Queen Mary and the accession of Elizabeth, and Audry was sitting as she often did, in the bay window of Mistress Mowbray's bower, looking down toward Middleton, when four riders and a pack horse were seen approaching the gates.

Audry had noticed their coming and, as they drew nearer, she recognised two of them and ran eagerly out to meet them. "Oh, how I have hoped for you to come," she said, "and somehow I knew it would not be long before you were here."

Ian dismounted and helped his sister and Aline to alight, while the serving man took the horses. Aline was in perfect health, but Ian was still worn and thin. She had not been long in recovering; but he had hovered between life and death for some time.

"This is the Lady Shiona, Ian's sister," said Aline. Audry came forward a little shyly, but Shiona said, "Oh, I have heard so much about you," and kissed her warmly.

Audry then flung her arms round Aline as though she would never let her go.

"You must not leave Ian in the cold," said Aline.

"No, indeed, I should think not," exclaimed Audry;[389] "why, if it were not for him you would not be here at all," and she held up her face to be kissed.

"She is getting too big to be kissed, is she not?" said Ian.

"Not at all," said Aline, "you kiss me."

"That is a different matter," said Ian, laughing, as he kissed Audry, "you are my ward, you see."

Although Master Richard and his wife were by no means pleased at the political change, they were delighted that it had brought their young visitor, and Mistress Eleanor greeted her with an unusual show of affection. She had been long enough falling under Aline's spell, but the conquest was complete and resulted in the re-development of a side of her nature that had practically lain dormant since, a charming girl of sixteen, Master Richard had met her in York and against all the wishes of his parents had insisted on marrying her. She became more human and more anxious to please, and gradually won the esteem and even love of her servitors and the people of Holwick.

Aline introduced her escort, and while they were being shown to their rooms, she went and found Elspeth.

Elspeth wept tears of joy over her and said; "Now, hinnie, I shall be able to die happy. I thought the sunlight had gone out of my life forever."

They had a long talk and in the afternoon she went down with Elspeth to the Arnsides. Janet seized a stool and dusted it for the young mistress; and John, who was just outside the house, came in.

"O John," Aline said, "I can never repay you or thank you enough, it is no use my trying to put my thanks into words."

[390]

"What I did was nothing," he said.

"But if you had not done it, the Duke of Ochil would never have come and I should have been lost."

"No one who knew you, Mistress Aline, could have done less."

The time seemed all too short to the Arnsides, when Aline turned to go. "I shall ask Cousin Richard to let us stay here for at least a month," she said, "even if I do not come back here to live. I am going to teach you to read, John, and I have brought you this," and she produced a beautifully bound copy of the Scriptures, which she had bought for him with all the money she had left.

John was confused with gratitude, and Aline fled, leaving him an opportunity to recover by himself.

She had had a long talk with Ian in which they had decided that it was right that Master Mowbray should hear the whole story and be told about the secret room, as after all it belonged to him.

So that night she secured the little book and took it up to her old room with Audry.

As they were undressing, Aline took off the ruby pendant, which she was wearing concealed beneath her simple costume.

"Oh, how lovely!" exclaimed Audry, "diamonds and pearls and—what a marvellous ruby! But Aline, you have no right to wear this."

"I feel a little doubtful, but Ian says it is all right, as at present I am in the position of his ward and in any case I am Scots and not English."

"But if you are father's ward then you will count as English."

391

"Anyway, I shall not wear it in public; so it does not matter."

"Your luck has come at last, Aline; just fancy your wearing diamonds and pearls like a duke's daughter. But you deserve to be lucky after all you have been through. I would not go through what you have been through, for all the luck in the world, you beautiful lovely thing."

Audry had by this time begun combing Aline's hair. "Why, Aline," she said, "your hair is not quite so long as it was!"

"Oh, I forgot to tell you," said Aline, and she told her all about the cutting off. "But it has very nearly grown again, it has been extraordinarily quick."

"Yes, you are beautiful," Audry went on, "look at that hair, look at that neck, look at those perfect ears."

"Do not be silly, Audry!"

"Yes," said Audry, not heeding, "and the luck is not over yet. You will be married very soon."

Aline blushed. "Be quiet, Audry."

"But you are far too beautiful and charming and good to be left long unmarried," and Audry embraced her impulsively.

"Come, let us get into bed and sit and study the book."

So Aline read to the end and discovered that it explained how to open the great iron chest.

The next day they managed to leave Shiona with Mistress Mowbray, and Aline, Audry and Ian took Master Mowbray into the library.

They sat in the great window seat and Aline read out of the little book and told the story of their adventures,392 which was frequently supplemented by Audry and Ian. Richard Mowbray was again entranced and he thought Aline's new tale even more wonderful than Malory.

When she had finished they all went down to the secret room and Master Richard asked hundreds of questions about all their experiences. They examined everything and explored the secret passage to the cave and back.

"But there is still one thing that we have to do," said Aline, "and that is to open the great iron chest and see what is inside. I have only just discovered how it is done and there is a good deal that requires doing first. But listen to this: Exactly under the middle of the great oriel window of the library, the book says,—that a foot and a half below the water in the moat is a chain made of links of greenheart wood, so as to withstand the wet; and at the end of that is a large round ball also of greenheart, and embedded in it with pitch is the great key of the iron chest. I have been thinking how to get it and, if the chain has not rotted and we do not have to dredge for the ball, I think I might go a-sailing for it in a tub, which would be fun. We might see to that this afternoon and then open the chest to-morrow."

"You will probably upset," said Audry, "but, as you can swim like a fish, that will not matter; but I shall laugh to see you tumble in."

"You bad girl," said Aline, and chased her round the room. "Well, I am going to try anyway."

After dinner Master Richard went and ordered two of the men to bring a great tub from the laundry, while Aline went upstairs and changed her things, putting on393 a pair of boy's trunks. She then threw a cloak about her and came down.

The tub was rolled round till it was opposite the window and then Aline insisted that the serving men should go away. A board, hastily thinned down at one end, made a sort of rude paddle and, with shrieks of derision from Audry, the others held the tub and Aline cautiously got in and squatted tailorwise on the bottom. They all laughed so much that they nearly upset the tub at the outset.

Aline then started on her perilous voyage, but, the tub being circular, every time she took a stroke with the paddle, it simply spun round and round.

Those on the bank held their sides with laughter, but the more they laughed the more confused Aline became. She tried taking a stroke first one way and then the other. This was not quite so bad, but the tub revolved backwards and forwards like a balance wheel.

"Try little short strokes pulling the paddle towards you," shouted Ian, when the laughter had a little subsided. This answered somewhat better and the tub slowly made its way across, but with many vagaries and strange gyrations.

At last she reached the wall right under the great projecting corbel of the window, and, very cautiously putting down her arm, she felt the chain.

"Hurrah!" she shouted, "I have it"; but she spoke too soon. As she pulled the chain, the tub over-balanced and Aline tumbled head first into the moat. Audry collapsed altogether at this and rolled over on to the grass.

Ian, however, for the moment took it seriously and394 was going to jump in, but Audry seized one of his ankles to stop him and laughed still more till the tears ran down her cheeks. "You'll kill me, you two," she said, as Aline's head appeared above the water with long green weeds hanging in her hair.

Aline swam to the chain and found that the ball was very heavy. She then righted the tub.

"Get in, get in quickly," shouted Audry mischievously, and Aline, without thinking, made the attempt with the result that the tub lifted and turned over on her like an extinguisher. Audry was convulsed.

"You little mischief," said Ian, and picked her up and held her out over the water at arm's length; but she only laughed the more.

Aline meanwhile again righted the tub and then shouted to the others to bring an axe. Audry refused to go. She said she must wait for the end of the performance. So Master Richard ran and called one of the men, who brought the things required.

While he was gone Aline, with difficulty, got the ball into the tub. She then swam across for the axe and, taking it over, she cut the chain, threw the axe in with the ball and, pushing the tub before her, swam back to the other side.

"You will be getting to know this moat," said Audry, as Ian pulled Aline, all dripping, up the bank. "This is your third adventure in the moat since you came."

She then went up and changed her clothes and joined the others in the solar. There she found that Father Laurence had just arrived. He was looking worn and worried, but a smile lit up his face as Aline came in.

395

The old man's hand trembled as he laid it on her head. "You are growing tall, my child; we shall soon see you a woman. I have just arrived with some strange and horrible news, which I have been telling my Lord of Ochil. You remember old 'Moll o' the graves,' Aline."

"Yes, Father."

"She's dead, my child; I saw her a few minutes ago on my way up. She was lying at the foot of the Crags."

Aline shuddered.

"We cannot leave the poor creature there," he continued; "can you let me have a couple of men, Master Richard, and would you mind her lying here for the night? I will arrange for the funeral to-morrow."

"Certainly," said Master Mowbray, and he arose and accompanied Father Laurence.

Twenty minutes later Aline and Ian were crossing the courtyard and saw the bearers carrying the body on a hurdle into the room below the granary. Ian at once drew Aline away in another direction, that she should not see the horrible sight. He had caught one glimpse of the face, and it was enough. It was the same as he had seen in his awful vision in the fire,—the terrible grin,—the blood trickling through the teeth. "Come away, little one, let us go elsewhere," he said.

After all was quiet again, Thomas Carluke walked stealthily across the quadrangle and entered the room where the body lay. A sheet had been placed over it, but he drew it aside. The grin on the face seemed to mock him. "Aha!" he said, "you fooled me twice, you old wretch, but you will never do it again. You need not laugh at me like that. I have cleared my score 396 with you now. Did you not tell me that you would get rid of the child?—and they got her out of the moat. Did you not tell me she would be burnt?—and now Queen Mary is dead and there are no more burnings. You miserable worm, what was the good of your hate? You were no better than Andrew, no better than Father Ambrose. Pah! You defied me just now on the Crags, did you? Well, here you are; and I would do it again. Oh, it was so easy,—one little push. Ha, you still mock; no, you cannot hurt me,—

no, no," he repeated apprehensively. "You are dead, you cannot come back. I will not believe it. The devil has your soul. But I must go, must go."

He drew the sheet over the body again and went out. "Fool," he said to himself, "what am I afraid of? Fool, I say."

Meanwhile Aline was walking with Audry through the garden.

"I am glad the horrible old thing is gone," said Audry. "Are not you?"

"It seems too dreadful to say so," Aline answered, "but I cannot pretend that I am sorry. She always seemed to me a sort of evil influence, a spirit of discord and hate."

"Yes," said Audry, slipping her arm round Aline's waist, "just as you are the spirit of love."

"Don't be foolish, Audry; besides I do not believe that any one could love everybody."

"No, but need you hate them? Come now, did you hate old Moll?"

"I do not know; somehow she seemed too mean, too petty and spiteful to hate. You could not fight her exactly. She was not worth fighting, so to speak."

"But I always felt," said Audry, "that behind the old woman, not in the old woman herself, was a power of evil and hate, a great power that could be fought."

"Oh, yes, quite so. I think there are things to hate. I do not believe in sickly sentiment; but that poor wretched old woman in herself was rather a thing to be pitied than hated, and, now that I come to think of it, I never did meet any one really to hate."

"What about Thomas?"

"That is just a case in point," said Aline. "I despise him, pity him, but one would lose one's own dignity in hating such a poor thing. Now if one could find some one really strong, really great and wicked, one could hate them. But no one of that sort has ever come my way."

"Have you thought of Father Martin?"

"I did not hate him. I was afraid of him and I did not think him altogether a good man; but in the main he seemed to act up to his lights. Father Austin, I might have hated, perhaps; but I do not know enough about him. There is some one over there that I love," she said suddenly, as Father Laurence appeared at the other end of the garden. "I think he is the best man I have ever seen."

"Better than Ian?" asked Audry.

"I do not know, and it is impossible for me to say. Dear Ian. I used to feel that there was something weak about him, but I think I was wrong. The wonderful thing about him is that he is developed on every side. It is true that we have mainly seen the softer398 side and also for a great part of the time he has been ill. But I keep discovering new things in his character. In any case he has a far more difficult position than Father Laurence. I should think that really it would be a much easier thing to retire from the world like a priest, than to try and make oneself a more complete and fully developed being and remain in the world. And after all, the world would cease to exist if we were all priests and nuns. To live the worldly life is certainly the lowest, and to come out of the world is higher than that; yet I am not sure that there is not something harder and higher still; and I believe Ian has done it; but here comes Father Laurence."

The children ran to him, and the three walked round the garden together. It was a rare picture, the fine tall figure, slightly bent, with the wonderful spiritual face, an epitome of the glory of age, and the two exquisite children, just approaching the threshold, on the other side of which they would soon reach the mysteries of adult life.

After they had talked for some time Audry asked, "How do you suppose, Father, that Moll met her death?"

"I cannot say, my children; she may have fallen over by accident, but Master Richard thinks that she threw herself over. You know, little girl, how she hated you," he said, turning to Aline, "and she must have been bitterly chagrined that everything has gone so well with you. Perhaps he is right, but let us speak of other things."

He stopped, and for a time no one said anything at all. Then, moved by some motive that he could not explain,399 he went on,—"Children, I shall soon have to bid you farewell."

"Oh, why?" they both said in a breath.

"I do not know what prompts me to tell you, Mistress Aline," he said.

Aline started; it was the first time he had ever addressed her like that; and the old man continued,—"I have not yet said anything to any one else, even of the old faith; and I know, child," he went on, dropping into the more familiar manner, "that you are not of us; so why I should tell you, a mere child, and a heretic,"—he lingered on the word regretfully,—"I am unable to say. The Queen's Grace is minded that there shall be an act of Uniformity for this realm and that the prayer book of 1552 shall be re-affirmed. It liketh me not and I shall not subscribe and therefore shall lose my benefice. I had hoped to end my days in Middleton, but it cannot be, and I must, if he be willing, take up my abode with my nephew. It will be a sore grief to me after all these years.

"But my work is done and I must not repine. One thing, Aline, child, I would say, and that is this,—thou mindest how I have ever told thee that the light must overcome the dark, and so has it been with the machinations of that poor evil woman. So hath it been with you; not that it will be ever so with things temporal, but it will be so in the world of the unseen and eternal. But farewell, my children, and I must go. Benedicat vos omnipotens Deus, in nomine Patris et Filii et Spiritus Sancti. Amen."[30]

[30] May almighty God bless you, in the name of the Father, the Son, and the Holy Spirit. Amen.

400

When he had gone Audry said, "How unjust it is that Father Ambrose will remain and that Father Laurence should go."

"How so?" said Aline.

"Have you not heard; Father Ambrose hath said that he will subscribe to anything that will keep his place, and he is the very man who persecuted you in the name of the Church?"

"What a scoundrel!" said Aline. "I had liever see Father Laurence, the Catholic, than Father Ambrose, the protestant, hold his own, protestant though I be. I must see if the Duke may not be able to do something, though he be not of this realm. Now that Queen Elizabeth's Grace hath come to the throne he hath many friends who are right powerful in this land. Father Laurence is an old man, and will not be long in this life in anywise; methinks it will not be a hard matter."

"I hope you will succeed," said Audry, "and I shall do my best with Master Richard that Father Ambrose be moved, whatever dishonest shifts he may practice."

They had reached the door that led into the garden. "Come, Audry, the afternoon is spent and it is time for supper."

401
CHAPTER XXX
THE GREAT IRON CHEST

THE next morning Master Mowbray went over to Newbiggin to look at the cottage that had been occupied by "Moll o' the graves," as it was his property, on the old Middleton estate which was much larger and more important than Holwick. The cottage was in poor condition and he decided that it should be rebuilt. It was dinner time before he came back, so they were not able to go down to the secret room till the afternoon.

"Now," said Aline, as they entered, "first the chest has to be laid on its back."

This they tried to do, but it was too heavy. They pushed and pulled, but they could not stir it.

"Let us use some of those stout poles there, standing in the corner," said Ian; "then we can lever it over."

This they did and with some difficulty the chest was turned over.

"I expect that is the very thing for which the poles were used," Audry suggested.

"Probably," said Aline, as she put her finger on the top right hand rivet head and slid it an inch to the left.

"Oh, that is how it works," exclaimed Master Richard, greatly interested.

"Now you have to turn it back again."

"Oh, dear," they all cried; but set to work, and again the chest stood upright. Aline then moved the second rivet in the same way.

"Now turn it over again," she said.

"This is too much, we are not galley slaves," expostulated Ian. "You are a tyrant, Your Highness."

"Well, anyway I help, my Lord," answered Aline, with mock gravity.

"'Help,' you wee kitten!" said Master Richard; "I think I do most of this; and it is my belief," he added, "that it is not to my interest that the chest should be opened at all."

"Why not?" they all exclaimed.

"Never mind. Come. I want to see what's inside i' faith."

Once again they heaved and tugged and turned it over. Aline then moved the rivet. "Now turn it back again."

"Look here, we cannot go on that way," said Master Richard. "There must be thirty rivets. We shall rebel, my liege."

"No, you must do your duty."

So once more they struggled and turned it back.

"There, you have done your part," said Aline, and they all stood round and laughed at each other, when they saw how hot they looked. Every one watched Aline with great curiosity as she now slid aside the whole of one of the iron plates of the chest and disclosed a small lock. Into this she fitted a key and turned it with some difficulty. It was the key on the bunch in the library, whose use Master Richard had not known. This enabled all the central part of the front to hinge down and disclose the large lock to which belonged the key from the moat.

The lid was very heavy and it took two of them to open it. The contents were covered by a black velvet cloth, and above it lay a parchment upon which was inscribed in large letters:

ALINE GILLESPIE
IN ACCORDANCE WITH MY WILL, WHICH
LIETH BEHIND THE LOCK OPPOSITE THAT
WHICH CONCEALETH THE BOOK.
James Mowbray.

Aline gazed in blank astonishment when she saw her own name.

"That is your great-grandmother's name," said Master Richard, "but it is all right, the chest is yours all the same, as you are the sole heiress of that line. But if you do not mind I should like to see the will, even before you lift the velvet cloth."

Aline ran upstairs, her heart beating with wild excitement, and was followed by Audry. The lock moved exactly as the other one had done and there lay the lost will.

"How stupid of us not to find it before," said Audry, "but, oh, I am so glad that something really good has come to you at last."

They ran down again.

"Here it is," said Audry, who was holding the will.

"Let his Grace read it," said Master Richard, "as he is a disinterested party."

It was a long will, but the tenour of it was,—that the old Mowbray estates at Middleton went to James Mowbray's404 son, but the little Holwick property, with half the contents of the library, was left to his daughter, Aline, and to her heirs after her forever.

The will concluded,—"And that the said Aline Gillespie and my son-in-law Angus Gillespie may be able to keep up the Holwick estate in a manner that is befitting, I also bequeath for the use of the said Aline and Angus and their heirs after them the great iron chest and its contents, the which chest, with the name of Aline Gillespie inside, is now within the secret room; and the means for the discovery of all these things are in the little book in the library, concealed in the lock opposite to this. The parchment with holes, that is hidden in the cover of the aforesaid book, is to be placed over each page in turn and the letters that appear through the holes may then be read as words."

"Well, little one, I always suspected that the Holwick property might be yours; but James Mowbray died suddenly and the will was never found," said Master Richard.

He saw clouds of anxiety gathering on the child's face, so he went on,—"You must not think about it now; let us look at the chest."

Aline lifted the velvet and on the top was a tray. It was filled with orphreys and other embroideries of the celebrated opus anglicum and was of immense value. So perfectly had the chest fitted that the colours were all as marvellous as the day they were done.

Below this was another tray, which contained exquisitely carved ivories and wonderful enamel work, several beautifully bound illuminated manuscripts of the highest possible excellence, many of the covers being elaborately garnished with precious stones, and two jewelled swords, one of Spanish make and one from Ferrara that almost equalled Ian's own.

Beneath this tray again was a layer of soft leather bags in ten rows of five each, every one of which contained five hundred gold pieces.

This brought them about one-third of the way down the chest. The remainder was in three portions. In the middle was a large oak box, that exactly fitted from front to back, and left about a fifth of the chest on each side. These fifths were filled with solid gold and silver bars, packed like bricks to fill every crevice. Their total value was four or five times that of the gold pieces in the bags.

Richard Mowbray and Ian lifted out the oak box and it was found to contain a collection composed of the choicest examples of art in metal work that any of them had ever seen in their lives. There were large mazers and other cups, a wonderful nef, and skilfully wrought platters. There were daggers and hunting horns and belts. There were chatelaines and embracelets and diadems. Then in a smaller receptacle were lesser things, such as rings, pendants, necklaces, chains, clasps and buckles. But finely jewelled as many of them were, it was the supreme art of the designs and the craftsmanship of their execution that was their main attraction.

Little Aline was too overcome to speak. At last she recovered herself sufficiently to say;—"And are all of these things mine?"

"Of course they are," said Master Richard, "and I do not know any one more worthy of them."

She was silent for some time and then said,—"Well, we cannot leave them all lying round. I must put everything back."

The others helped and, although every one kept commenting on the lovely things and the strange experience, Aline never said a word all the time. It was clear that she was thinking hard and that the putting back of the things was only to give her an opportunity to settle her thoughts.

When they had finished they all stood up.

"Now we can save the Ochil estates," said Aline triumphantly. "Ian, I give you half the gold and silver and one of the swords, and you are to have the other half, Audry darling, and Cousin Richard is to have Holwick Hall as long as he lives and the other sword. Then everybody is to have some nice presents from the trays and the box, Audry and Cousin Richard, and Joan and Mistress Mowbray and all the others, and Ian is to have the rest."

"Impossible," said Ian.

"Nonsense," said Master Richard.

"Absurd," said Audry.

"I absolutely mean what I say," said Aline.

"But you have left nothing for yourself," objected Audry.

"Yes, I shall have Holwick when I am old and no longer able to do anything; and if you are not married we can live together."

"My little maiden must not be foolish," said Ian. "I think you are quite right to let Audry have half, unless you let Cousin Richard have the use of it first, for it would go to Audry, and I am sure you are right about Holwick; but my estates have nothing to do with you,407 sweet child. Besides how are you going to live until you are too old to do anything? You cannot go a begging, princess, and some one would have to take care of you."

"O dear, I had not thought about that. Yes, I suppose I should need some one to look after me."

"I will look after you, little heart, if Cousin Richard will let me," said Ian softly.

Richard Mowbray laid his hand on the young man's shoulder. "I agree," he said.

Aline put up her hands and drew down Ian's face till their lips met. A look of happy content shone in her eyes. "Then I shall be well protected," she said.

My dear Children:

The time has now come to say good-bye, both to you and Aline; but it might interest you to know that I read the story to a little girl before it was quite finished and asked her if there was anything she would like to suggest. "Yes," she said, "a birthday party."

Now a sixteenth century birthday party was rather a difficulty as I never saw one described; but then there were so many difficulties of that sort. People in those days, for instance, thought that shaking hands was a much warmer sign of affection than kissing. You probably know that in France men still kiss each other at the railway station. But that would not do for my story. So, as in the case of language, I have modernized to suit my purpose. When, therefore, your learned uncle tells you that the story is all wrong and that they did not fence with helmets and that the curtsey was not invented till much later and that the library is far too big and so on; you just tell him to write you a sixteenth century story and then you send it to me, and we will see how he gets along.

If any of you would write to me and tell me what you would like altered or what else you would like put in, I should be delighted. The story is only written to please you and I wish I could see you and tell it to you myself. Also you might let me know what you think ought to happen to Aline and then, if you like408 the story, I will write you a sequel. But you must tell me how old you are, that is a very important point.

With best wishes from Avis and myself;—now do not tell me that you do not know who Avis is,—look at the dedication and the first chapter and guess.

Yours aff'ly,
Ian B. Stoughton Holborn.

Made in the USA
Columbia, SC
14 July 2022